She Who Fights Monsters

Book Two of *The Black Parade* series

By: Kyoko M.

To all the kick ass women in my life. This book wouldn't be here without you.

BOOK FOUR: AERIA GLORIAM

"He who fights monsters should see to it that he himself does not become a monster. And if you gaze for long into an abyss, the abyss gazes also into you."
-**Friedrich Nietzsche,** *Beyond Good and Evil*

PROLOGUE

There was a stranger in my house.

I knew it wasn't Trent and Marie. They had taken a father-daughter trip to the beach. My duties as a kindergarten teacher didn't allow me the luxury of a three-day vacation, nor did the ridiculous cold I'd caught, and so I had stayed home by myself.

Normally, I would just shake it off as house-settling noise, but there was one slat in the kitchen's hardwood floor near the stove that made an unmistakable creak if you stepped on it. No way in hell I could shake that off, not when I was home alone.

I slipped from beneath the comforter and knelt beside the bed, my fingers finding the cool metal of my trusty baseball bat. My daughter was only seven years old and I wouldn't let Trent bring a gun into our home, so we had agreed to this as our form of protection. Ears straining, I opened the bedroom door, praying the hinges remained silent, and tiptoed to the stairs. Silence. A normal person would go back to their room and sleep, but there was a cold feeling in my chest that whispered something was wrong.

The carpet was soft under my bare feet as I crept down the steps one by one. The staircase spilled into the foyer and from where I could see, the front door was still locked. No broken glass or muddy footprints. I turned to the left and peeked around the corner to see into the living room. Every shadow looked like an intruder. I knew it was just my paranoid brain going into overdrive so I ignored it and carefully maneuvered past the den to the dining room. Nothing here either. That left the kitchen.

I pressed my back against the wall, closing my eyes and saying a quick prayer that I was just a hyper-vigilant crazy lady before darting around the corner.

The kitchen was empty.

I licked my dry lips and snuck over to the double doors that spilled out onto the patio and the backyard. I pushed the curtain aside. Darkness greeted me. Nothing more. False alarm. I was indeed a hyper-vigilant crazy lady.

I started to lower the bat and turn around, but then I felt something cold and wet on the bottom of my foot, between my bare toes. Confused, I knelt to touch it with my fingertips. As soon as I was close, the smell hit me even through my stuffy nose.

Gasoline.

Then the floorboard creaked again.

I whirled around. A man stood there swathed in shadows and black clothing, but that wasn't what caught my attention.

He was holding a gigantic scythe.

I screamed as he swung it at me and threw myself into a forward roll. The enormous blade crashed through the window in the back door, sending glittering shards all over the floor. I scrambled backwards on my hands and knees until my back hit the legs of the table and then got up.

I brandished the bat at the intruder. "Who are you? What are you doing in my house?"

His voice was so soft I almost didn't hear it. "I am sorry, but your death is necessary for the safety of mankind. Please forgive me."

"I'll forgive you when you get the hell out of my house!" I yelled, swinging at his head. He blocked the blow with the staff—a smooth, effortless move—and I stumbled backwards, my eyes darting around to look for the closest route of escape. He had already knocked the back door partially open but he stood a few inches to the left of it, barring any chances of me reaching outside. I could make a break for the front door, but it would leave my back vulnerable. *Shit!*

I kept swinging, hoping to corral him away from the door, but he merely blocked the blows and stood his ground, never turning into the light so I could see his face. All I could see was a fedora, a black leather jacket, and gloves. Desperation began to set in and with it came the blind hope that I could talk him out of his homicidal intentions.

"Why do you want to kill me? What did I ever do to you?"

"Nothing," the man said, adjusting his hold on the weapon. "It is what you may do to the world someday. Human beings have such a poor perception of time and fate. Your death is for the greater good—to prevent the Apocalypse itself."

I shook my head, hating the hot tears pouring down my cheeks. "You're crazy."

"No. I am prepared."

"Get away from me!" I kicked the table over and shoved it towards him, making him jump back. I raced for the front door, my feet pounding against the hardwood floor as I ran, and grabbed the doorknob. I yanked on it as hard as I could, but it wouldn't budge. He had somehow jammed it from the other side, trapping me in like a mouse in a snake pit. No more options. I would have to face him and look my death straight in the eye.

Only he didn't give me the chance.

The blade tore through my spinal column as if it had been made of paper. The tip burst out of my rib cage. My world dissolved into pain for a few seconds, but then a blessed numbness cascaded over me. My brain faintly realized the shock blocked out what should have been an excruciating death.

He stepped backward and I slid off his blade, collapsing on my back. Blood bubbled out of me in crimson rivulets, tainting my husband's t-shirt. How unfair. He'd have to see my corpse wearing it when he came home.

The stranger reached into his pocket and withdrew a lighter, flicking his thumb to awaken a single orange flame. I watched him light the gasoline that had been poured at the base of every wall in my beautiful home, watched the paintings and furniture become engulfed in fire, watched the fire slowly creep closer to my dying body. The stranger pressed one cold, gloved finger to my forehead and made a cross, his voice constantly murmuring the same words over and over again. The cadence of his voice made the chanting stay with me until the last spark of life snuffed out and everything dissolved into darkness.

CHAPTER ONE

JORDAN

"I have to go to work."

"Mm-hmm."

"The bus leaves in fifteen minutes."

"Mm-hmm."

"…I can't leave if you don't stop kissing me," I said in a mildly amused voice from around the lips of my husband who had managed to trap me against the kitchen counter. He towered over my humble five-foot-six body with his six-foot-one frame, his long sinewy arms content to rest on either side of the counter by my waist so that I couldn't wriggle away. It was a nuisance yet somehow pleasant. A conundrum, if you will.

I thought my words had finally got through to him when he pulled away for a moment, but his head dipped down and his lips found the edge of my jaw, my neck, making my poor knees wobble. I could feel the roughness of the stubble that had grown on his chin since he hadn't shaved yet. His absurdly dark brown hair tickled over my collarbone, sending involuntary shudders down my spine. Normally, when he cooked breakfast he pulled his hair back into a short ponytail, but I suspected he'd taken it down with the intent of seducing me. Crafty bastard.

"I'm not stopping you," Michael drawled against my throat. His baritone voice made the hairs on my arms stand up at attention. There was maybe a centimeter of space between our upper bodies. He'd done it on purpose to tease me. He bit down softly at the point between my neck and shoulder. I jumped, my fingers gripping the counter for strength.

"You're blocking my exit," I said.

He finally rose to full height, smirking at me with those plush lips, arrogance beaming down from his sea-green eyes. "And you're stalling."

He stared at me. I stared at him. I sighed and grabbed two handfuls of his shirt, jerking him down to my mouth.

"I'm gonna get fired."

Half an hour later, my best friend Lauren Yi was shaking her head when I scampered into the restaurant and clocked in as quickly as possible. Mercifully, Colton was nowhere to be found, but he'd still know I was forty minutes late anyhow since he was the owner. I'd be in for it later and I knew it. The restaurant had been hit with the usual lunch rush so I had to get ready as soon as humanly possible.

"This is the third time in a week you've been late," she reminded me as I walked towards the lockers in the break room. I popped mine open and checked my reflection in the mirror, piling my mussed black hair into a loose bun.

"I know, sorry. The bus was late."

Lauren rolled her eyes. "Are you really pulling that one on me?"

I glanced at her, keeping my face blank and innocent. "What?"

"Your skirt's on backwards and you've got pancake mix on your sleeve." She arched an eyebrow and then crossed her arms.

"He caught you in the kitchen again, didn't he?"

A flush of heat rushed up my neck and over my cheeks, thankfully hidden by my brown skin. I tied my apron on and cleared my throat, keeping my voice level and guilt-free. "I have no idea what you're talking about."

The Korean girl lifted the apron and turned my skirt the right way, brushing off the remainder of said pancake mix. "It's a sad day when Jordan Amador has more of a life than I do."

"Should I be flattered or insulted by that?"

"Both. Now get out there and wait tables, you shameless harlot."

I batted my eyelashes at her. "Love you too."

She stuck her tongue out at me as we walked back onto the floor and started greeting customers and taking orders. It never ceased to amaze me how quickly I could switch into Waitress Mode. Without thinking, I became amiable, even a little charming on my better days — a direct contrast to my actual personality. Lauren had once dubbed me a "cranky, antisocial hermit crab" and it disturbed me how accurate that description had been at the time. Michael had done a remarkable job of reversing the worst aspects of my behavior over the past year.

After I took care of a couple of teenagers and a large group of people who had just gotten out of church, I greeted a redheaded man in a hunter green suit and black tie sitting by himself at a window booth. "Hi, what can I get you?"

His brown eyes scanned the menu, his voice a little shy. "What would you suggest?"

I lowered my pen and pad. "Well, what kind of things do you like?"

He shrugged. "No preference, really."

"I recommend the fish and grits. The fish is fried whiting and the grits are cheesy and thick, just like down South."

"South?"

"Alabama, Mississippi, Georgia, and the like. I've never been that far down, but my boss insists it's much better than up here," I continued with a playful roll of my eyes.

The redhead folded up his menu and handed it to me, smiling. "That sounds good. Thank you, Jordan."

I scribbled down his order and smiled back. "No problem."

I gave the slip to the kitchen and grabbed some cleaning supplies to clear off a table in my section. Lauren came to help, taking the salt, pepper, Tabasco sauce, and napkins off of the table before I wiped it down.

"Who's the redhead?" she asked.

"No idea. Never seen him before."

"He's not part of the usual Sunday crowd. He seems...very out-of-town-ish, especially with that suit. By the looks of things, it costs more than half of my closet."

I flashed her a grin. "Well, you do have a bad habit of buying knock-off Gucci."

She scowled. "Those who shop at thrift shops shall not throw stones."

"It's economical, dammit!"

She rolled her eyes at me, handing me the spray bottle of Clorox.

"You're married to the lead singer of a rock band. You should be able to afford decent clothing by now."

I pursed my lips, squirting the liquid on the table. "We have better uses for the money than clothing, thank you very much."

"Condoms?"

I whirled, aiming the spray bottle at her face. "I'll do it and say it was an accident."

She giggled, pushing my arm down. "Relax, Dirty Harry. Or would that be Clean Harry since you've got Clorox?"

"Ha-ha. A comedic genius you are not." I finished cleaning off the table and replaced the condiments and napkin container. One of our chefs called me since an order was ready and I brought them to the customers. I took the fish and grits to the redheaded gentleman, who was staring out the window as if distracted.

"Here you go. Enjoy!"

"Thank you."

The lunch rush came and went like the tide—seemingly overwhelming at first, but manageable to the trained eye. I didn't notice anything out of order until midway through my shift when I returned to the seat that the redhead had been in to find I had a rather substantial tip waiting for me.

"He left you *a hundred dollars*?" Lauren screeched from behind me and grabbed my shoulder to look over it. I held the bill between my hands, my mouth hanging open and getting dustier by the minute.

"I...he...maybe he didn't have change?" I sputtered. I searched the sidewalk outside the restaurant to see if he was out there, but he had disappeared.

My best friend threw up her hands. "I don't get it. You come in late and yet you're the one standing there with a fresh hundred bucks. Do you have a leprechaun stuck to the bottom of your shoe or something?"

Sheepishly, I glanced underneath my foot. "...No?"

"Ugh, I'd hate you if I didn't love you so much." Lauren sighed, scooping up the empty plate the mysterious redhead left behind. I tucked the tip in the front of my apron, staring blankly out of the window. I started to hand her a glass only to drop it as something caught my eye across the street.

A plump woman in her early forties stared back at me. Her hair was black and curly around her round face, and her brown eyes were full of worry. I knew her—not from Albany, but from the pages of a manila folder I had poured over rigorously for the past month. Erica Davalos.

A murdered Seer.

"Jordan, what's wrong?" Lauren asked, flustered at the shocked expression on my face.

I hid my distress, stepping over the bits of broken glass. "Nothing, sorry. Just a bit clumsy today. I'll go get the broom."

I hurried to the break room and grabbed a broom, but I didn't head back out there. Instead, I snuck out the rear entrance that led into an alleyway and stuck my head around the corner, signaling for the ghost to come towards me.

"Hi," the ghost woman said when she was within earshot, her voice light and apprehensive. "My name is Erica."

"Yeah, I know."

She frowned, tilting her head. "Excuse me?"

"My name is Jordan Amador. I'm a Seer."

"A Seer?"

"Yes. It's someone who can see and hear ghosts, angels, and demons. Long story short, they're the descendants of the original twelve disciples. I've been trying to solve your murder for the past month-and-a-half."

Her eyes widened. "Oh my goodness, I had no idea. I've just been wandering around for the longest time looking for someone to help me."

I offered her a small smile. "Well, you've come to the right girl. I get off work in a few hours so I want you to stay in this area and meet me out front at six o'clock, okay? We'll get everything sorted out, I promise."

"Yes. Thank you so much."

She headed back towards the street as I went inside to clean up the mess I'd made. Lauren was still looking at me funny, but I convinced her it was a mere case of the butterfingers. After all, Lauren knew nothing of my other life and I had to keep it that way for her own safety. Rules were rules. Even if I didn't like them one bit.

After I dumped the glass in a trashcan, I sent a text to my other best friend, Gabriel, explaining that he needed to meet me at my apartment after work if he was in town. The last time I spoke to him, about a week ago, he and Raphael were in Haiti doing volunteer work. I didn't know if they were still there, but I figured they would have to pull some strings to get to me in a reasonable amount of time from their current location. It helped that Gabriel had his own private jet.

I tried not to show my impatience for the remainder of my shift, but at the end of it I scurried out of the door and met Erica outside, reaching into my grey duster for a pen and my trusty little notepad. I also got out my Bluetooth, which I hardly ever used for real. It was just my cover to avoid drawing attention to myself. Normal people wouldn't be able to see or hear her. I didn't want to come off as a crazy lady talking to thin air.

"Alright, give me everything you remember from the top and don't spare any details, even if you think they're minor," I told her as we walked towards the bus stop.

"I remember my last name, Davalos, and that I'm from Raleigh." she said.

"I can't believe you walked all the way here from North Carolina. You're definitely a trooper." I scribbled the information down along with a brief description of her facial features and clothes. She wore a lavender button up shirt and grey slacks beneath a black sweater, no jewelry. Her feet were of course missing. She was a ghost and all of them were like that because they were no longer tied to Earth but suspended between the living world and the spiritual world. The clothing was a result of her internal self-image, which all souls inherently had.

"And I remember that I was a kindergarten teacher and I loved my kids. I have a daughter. She's seven."

"Okay. Is there anything you can tell me about your death? Anything at all?"

"Yes. I couldn't see his face, but I heard his voice. It was saying something in Latin. I studied it back in college so I actually remember what he said quite clearly."

I winced. "My Latin's a bit rusty, but Gabriel should be able to translate for us. Go ahead."

She took a deep breath and closed her eyes, her brow furrowing. "It went like this: *Is quisnam suscipio lux lucis superne, ex fontis of lux lucis; haud alius doctrina postulo, sentential tribuo verus.*"

It took me a moment to get all the spelling correct—I could read and write in both English and Castilian Spanish but Latin was tricky—and by the time I finished, the bus arrived. We climbed aboard and sat in the back to stay out of earshot of other riders. Usually, I'd wait until we were home to ask all these questions, but an entire month with no new leads made me overeager.

"He was repeating it like some sort of chant while he stood over me, lighting the place on fire as if he were...I don't know, trying to purify it," she said, frowning.

I wanted to reach out and touch her hand in comfort, but it wouldn't do her any good. It would pass right through her and send chills through me. Only poltergeists were solid and they were rare. I had only met two of them in my entire life.

"Well, that says a couple things to me," I told her. "The killer is well-read, perhaps a linguist, if he was pronouncing all of that well enough that you remembered it. Two, we're looking for someone with a religious background. You're not the first dead Seer that I've been investigating."

"Really?"

"Sadly, yes. Over the past five months, there have been five others murdered in different parts of the world. Four of them were stabbed in the chest, laid on the floor, and then their homes were burned to the ground. One was strangled and his car was set on fire. It always happens on the eve of their Awakening, just like I'm assuming yours did."

"Awakening?"

"That's when your powers mature. It happens at a different time for every Seer. Mine didn't hit until I was eighteen. Yours came a bit late, it seems."

"How is it possible that he knew when it would happen for me?"

I shook my head. "We don't know. Gabriel is supposed to appear whenever someone's powers awaken, but this serial killer somehow knows exactly when and where these Seers surface and always beats him there. However, you are the first Seer soul to stay behind. The others passed over into Heaven and they gave the same report as you each time."

"So what's going to happen to me?"

"We're going to find out what your final wish is and that will set your soul free so you can cross over for your final judgment."

"We?"

I smiled. "My friends and I. They're archangels."

A mixed look of astonishment and skepticism crossed her face, making my smile widen.

"Really?"

"Yes, really. Don't worry—you're not the first person to say that. I have a, um, complicated sort of life. You'll meet them when we get home."

A few minutes later, we arrived at my bus stop and I led Erica to my humble abode. The apartment was nothing close to nice. It was smack dab in the middle of a crowded, shady neighborhood, squished between a liquor store and a barbershop. That was why it was so affordable.

We walked down the street and up a short flight of stairs to my apartment on the first floor, second room over. When I opened the door, there were two men at the kitchen table eating banana bread. The first was a blond man who was almost seven feet tall with sky blue eyes dressed in an impeccable Armani suit. The second was a significantly shorter curly-haired Hispanic man with brown eyes dressed in a tan sweater vest over black slacks and a black button up shirt. I didn't panic. They had keys, after all.

"Jordan," Gabriel said as he unfolded his enormous frame from the chair after I shut the door.

"Hey, Gabe." He pulled me into a hug and kissed my forehead in the same spot as always—over my right eyebrow. "Good to see you."

I hugged Raphael. "Hey, Raph."

"Evening, Jordan."

I grinned as I noticed half of my homemade banana bread had vanished. "I see you've helped yourselves to my sweets."

Gabriel blushed. "I...did not eat lunch today. Forgive me."

The urge to laugh was immense, but I pushed it aside. "Just this once. I'm charging you for the next one."

I gestured to Erica, who seemed politely bewildered by the two men before her. "This is Erica Davalos. I met her outside of the restaurant a few hours ago."

The blond archangel bowed his head to her. "My name is Gabriel. I am God's Messenger here on Earth."

Raphael did the same. "Raphael. I am God's Healing Missionary. We are terribly sorry for the loss of your life, Mrs. Davalos."

"Why? It's not your fault some jerk-off killed me."

"I am responsible for facilitating instructions to new Seers. If I had arrived sooner, I could have prevented your death. For that, I am truly sorry." Gabriel's voice was low with shame. I could feel his sadness like a cold weight in my stomach and started to say something, but Erica did it for me.

"I don't blame you. No one's perfect, not even angels. I just want to make sure that my family is taken care of now that I'm...gone."

Raphael offered her an encouraging look. "Your husband and daughter are safe, Mrs. Davalos. They have found somewhere to stay and they are being watched over. Nothing will happen to them. I swear it on my honor as an angel."

"Thank you," she murmured, finally smiling again.

I withdrew the notepad from my pocket and flipped to the page with her name on it, then addressed Gabriel. "She remembered something that the other victims didn't when I spoke to her earlier this afternoon. You told me that they heard the killer chanting something, right?"

Gabriel nodded. "Yes, but we were never able to get a transcription."

"Now we've got one. It's Latin. Can you translate it?"

He took the notepad from me, his lips just barely moving as he read. "I know these words. It's an excerpt from *Paradise Regained*."

"What does it translate to?"

He took a second or two, as if trying to remember his English. "He who receives light from above, from the fountain of light; no other doctrine needs, though granted true."

"You've got a damn good memory, Gabe."

"Well, I did help dictate most of it for Milton in my earlier years. Still, this is a strange thing to chant while murdering someone."

"Why is that?"

"It suggests that this killer thinks that he is following orders from on high, perhaps that he has a superior knowledge or truth. The fountain of light implies Christ or God the Father rather than heaven itself. In my opinion, it sounds like he thinks that this 'truth' he has discovered is his only mission and that he will follow it without question."

"Great. There's nothing worse than a man on a mission. And it still brings us back to the same question..." I sat in the chair by the kitchen table, suppressing a long sigh. "Why hasn't he come for me yet?"

Erica spoke up then. "I don't understand. If you all work for God, can't He just tell you who is doing this?"

Raphael shook his head. "God will not interfere on Earth until the Rapture. He charges the angels with solving any problems between heaven and the world below it. He believes that this will bring us closer together if we work as one without His help."

"Oh." She paused. "That sucks."

I grinned in spite of myself. "I know. I said the same thing when I found out."

"Regardless," Raphael continued, though he was smirking. "I will escort Erica back to her home and help her find her final wish."

"Thanks. Be careful." He nodded to Gabriel and I before gesturing to the door. Erica waved to me before walking through the closed door while Raphael left the traditional way.

I ran my fingers through my hair, trying to absorb the new information I'd learned. My skull felt fit to burst.

Gabriel sat down across from my chair, watching me. "What's going on in that head of yours, Jordan?"

"I don't get it, Gabriel. I'm not an exceptionally powerful Seer. Why is it that I've been spared and six other people lost their lives just for being born of a certain bloodline?"

"It's possible that whomever is doing this knows that your soul is bound to Michael's and it would be nearly impossible to kill you without risking his own life. The other Seers led normal lives. You're living with a dyed-in-the-wool warrior."

I frowned harder. "But that's not right. I shouldn't get a pass just because I happen to be married to an archangel."

A soft chuckle escaped him. "Jordan, are you telling me that you're feeling guilty because someone has *not* tried to kill you? It's a far cry from your usual behavior."

I snorted. "Point taken. No one's tried to kill me in over a year. I'm starting to miss the adrenaline."

"Perhaps I could make an attempt on your life if that would make you happy."

I had to smile. "Thanks, that's sweet of you, but I've got a reminder right here to tide me over for a while."

I touched the spot over my heart where an ugly brown scar lay beneath my button-up shirt where the Spear of Longinus had once pierced over a year ago. I couldn't believe it had been that long since my life changed forever. "Dying once is enough, trust me."

"Indeed." He went silent and a thought occurred to me.

"Tell me something. Why would this killer recite that passage in Latin? Wasn't *Paradise Regained* originally written in English?"

His brow wrinkled. "Yes, you're right. That is curious. Perhaps he knows that Latin was one of the languages most used by the angels in earlier times?"

"But what does that imply? Clearly, he knows about Seers and angels or else he wouldn't be able to always disappear before you arrive. What's the connection?"

"Maybe he sees himself as the angel of death for these Seers? But, again, that leads to another question: why is he killing them in the first place?"

I massaged my left temple. "I'm starting to think I should start wearing an expressionless mask and a blue fedora."

"Pardon?"

"Nothing." I glanced at the clock on the microwave and groaned.

"Shoot, Michael's concert starts in half an hour. I'd better get dressed. You coming?"

"Unfortunately, I can't. I have other obligations for the night. Please give him my support."

"No worries. You're overdressed anyway."

He grinned as he stood. "I thought you had finally come to terms with my preferred attire after I bought you that Dolce and Gabbana dress for Christmas."

"It was lovely, but it's so nice that I'm afraid to wear it," I admitted. It was an evening gown the color of dark chocolate that was made of pure silk. Gabriel often invited me to his high class social events, but half the time I couldn't go because I could never afford the right clothes. He decided from then on to upgrade my wardrobe whenever he got the chance. It was beyond thoughtful of him.

He chuckled again before bending to kiss me on the forehead. "Good night, Jordan. I'll see you soon, hopefully with good news about the case."

"Night, Gabe."

CHAPTER TWO

JORDAN

"I take it from this supposedly mandatory back rub that things didn't go well with the talent agent?"

My husband sighed and the smooth skin on his shoulders shifted with each exhale. My fingertips worked small, slow circles in the middle of his spinal column where I could feel knots of tension. An archangel with back problems. Who knew?

"She said that we had the talent and the look, but we're not 'marketable enough'," Michael said with no small amount of bitterness in his tone. It hurt to hear. He worked at Guitar Center to pay the bills and took the odd gig on the side. He wanted to work on his music full-time, but with two apartments and all the traveling working on cases, he had to compromise.

"That's the third agent to tell me so. I'm beginning to think this profession isn't as enjoyable as I once hoped."

"C'mon, don't say that. You love music. You'd better not even think about giving it up," I scolded, but in my most supportive voice.

"Besides, getting a record deal is like getting published. All it takes is one yes, so you're going to have to wade through a hundred no's before you get there."

He took a deep breath and let it out slow, folding his arms to prop up his head. "Yeah, I know. But it still sucks."

I leaned down and kissed the top of his head, resting my hands on his shoulders.

"Welcome to showbiz, stud."

A soft sound escaped him, one similar to a laugh. "How'd you get to be so savvy about this?"

"Life. Alright, let's get to work." I reached over and grabbed the manila folder lying next to us and handed it to him. Gabriel had left it for me on the kitchen counter and I hadn't seen it yet since I'd headed straight to the concert. He pushed up on his elbows and opened it, reading the files out loud while I resumed my careful massage of his lower back.

"Victim Number One: Danny Bowen. Thirty-four. Mechanical engineer. Kentucky resident. Found murdered in his home five months ago. Deep puncture wound in the chest. Traces of steel found in the rib cage indicate a large blade. Entry and exit wounds suggests it's shaped like a sickle."

He flipped to the next page. "Victim Number Two: Todd Lovett. Twenty-one. Biochemistry major at Oxford. Found murdered in his car four months ago. Strangled to death in the front seat at roughly three o'clock in the morning. First to remember the killer chanting something in Latin as he died."

Next page. "Victim Number Three: Imani Ibekwe. Thirty-one. Missionary. Found murdered in her home in Nigeria four months ago. Wounds consistent with the first victim. Confirms that if it is the same killer, he's using the same weapon. Angle of the wounds suggests the killer is less than six feet tall."

Page four. "Victim Number Four: Faye Cunningham. Forty-two. Nurse at a hospital in Poland. Found murdered in her home like Victims One and Three with the same wounds three months ago."

Page five. "Victim Number Five: Yusef Nolan. Twenty-five. Television producer. Found murdered in his studio apartment in Brisbane two months ago. Defensive wounds on his forearms suggest the killer knows an extensive amount of martial arts as Yusef was a brown belt in judo and still ended up dead."

Page six. "Victim Number Six: Erica Davalos. Forty-three. Kindergarten teacher. Found murdered in her home a month and a half ago. First victim not to immediately cross over. Like the other spirits, she remembers seeing a man chanting in Latin."

I rested my chin on the top of his head, folding my arms across the back of his broad shoulders. "Aside from being Seers, what do we have on similarities?"

He flipped to the last page. "Based on the records I had some of the angels compile, Todd and Faye are of the same bloodline. They're descendants of Matthew. Danny is a descendant of Luke, Imani is a descendant of John the Baptist, and Erica is a descendant of Thomas."

I shook my head. "That doesn't really have any relevance. So far, their Awakenings tie them together, not their bloodlines. What else?"

"Their homes and possessions were all burned to the ground. That suggests that the killer believes in some sort of purification ritual. However, he doesn't leave markings on the ground afterward or any memorabilia. If it's a cultural thing, it's not one we've seen before."

"Which means it's newly formed by Captain Psychopath. Great. And you're sure this isn't a demon's doing?"

"No. Demons can only sense the Awakening of a Seer sometime after the angels, not exactly when it happens. Only archangels and experienced Seers can sense when someone's powers are developing. It gives us a bit of a head start. Besides, we've been tracking Belial's movements for the past year and they aren't consistent with the murders."

A little shudder went down my spine at the mention of the demon's name. I had been fortunate enough not to see him for over a year and that still wasn't long enough. Every time I left the apartment, I felt a tiny shadow of fear rest between the back of my shoulders—fear that he was watching me, waiting for the opportunity to strike and get back at me for foiling his plans three times in a row.

"Good to know," I said, though a little softer than I intended.

Michael noticed and pushed up on his hands, forcing me to slide off his back. He turned to me and cupped the side of my cheek in his large hand.

"Hey, don't get so tense on me. He's out of our lives. You know that."

I tried to return the smile but it didn't quite stick. "Yeah, but he's always been a wild card. I can't shake the feeling that he won't try to come after us again."

"Well, you've gotten pretty good at kicking his ass so I think we're safe," the archangel said, pressing a light kiss to my lips. I allowed myself to be lost in his touch and then a couple minutes later I was lying on my back and my shirt was on the floor and I knew exactly what would happen if I didn't stop it.

It took a massive amount of will power to quit kissing him but I finally did, suppressing a wistful sigh. "It's late. We probably shouldn't, uh…you know."

He grinned. "I'm so happy you're the voice of reason in this relationship."

I flicked him in the forehead. "Someone has to be, otherwise I'd be a paraplegic in the span of a month. Are you staying here tonight or heading home?"

The grin faded at the edges. "You know, it'd be a lot easier if I didn't have to keep making the decision."

I took a deep breath, raking fallen strands of hair out of my eyes. "Can we not have that discussion tonight?"

A frown bunched between his eyebrows, but he swallowed the argument and crawled off the bed, grabbing his t-shirt from where it dangled on the headboard. "I'd better head to my place. We have an early rehearsal and I have more talent agents to find and disappoint."

I watched him pull the shirt on with a certain amount of regret. I had learned enough in my six months of marriage to be able to tell when he was unhappy, and he was because he wouldn't maintain eye contact. Michael's eyes always gave him away. In some ways, they were his best feature and thus they were his deadliest.

"Would it help if I showed up in a cheerleading costume for your next performance?"

He chuckled. "I thought we tried that one already. Or was it the Naughty Nurse?"

He ducked when I threw my sock at his head, swooping in for a goodnight kiss. I cradled his face between my hands for a long moment before letting go. My bed was always colder — literally and figuratively — when he didn't spend the night.

"*Buenas noches, amor,*" I murmured.

He kissed my forehead. "*Igualmente.*"

Warm fingers mapped my spine, tracing the long curve of naked skin down to the small of my back, slowly, soothingly, purposefully. The sheets beneath me were clean and fresh like a summer morning — nothing a laundry detergent could pull off, either. This scent was as if someone had bottled the air at sunrise and sprayed it over cotton. I never felt more at peace, more relaxed. I'd found a small corner of heaven to lie upon.

The hands at my back had long fingers that hinted at strength and masculinity as they slid upward towards my scars. The rough fingertips followed the jagged lines zigzagging over my spinal column where my aunt's switches and belts and extension cords had cut the skin too badly to heal. The scars had turned to brown worms and melted into the rest of me. A long time ago, I had been upset over them, afraid to wear certain shirts and dresses, but over time they became as much a part of me as my black hair or morena skin or knobby knees.

I sighed as his thumbs pressed against the blade of my shoulders, massaging in a circle, smoothing away the tension. Seconds later, soft lips touched the spot and silky hair brushed along my spine. My eyes opened and focused on his hand, palm flat, lying to my left. The skin was as pale as alabaster instead of the natural tan I was used to. Wait. Something was wrong.

My pulse sped up as I gathered the white sheets beneath me to cover my bare breasts and rolled over only to find the archdemon Belial on his knees above me.

I opened my mouth to scream, but he clapped one of his large hands over it, drowning my shout of alarm.

"Don't. This may be a dream, but your screams are still quite irritating, my pet."

I tore his hand away from my lips, glaring at him to hide my fear. He still looked the same — a narrow nose, perfect slender cheekbones, and wickedly sensual lips. He looked vaguely European to me, but he didn't have an accent. His voice was deep, cold, and empty most of the time unless he was mocking me. He appeared somewhere in his late twenties to early-twenties, but I knew he was damn near as old as time itself. He wore an unbuttoned navy dress shirt that flapped loosely around his chest, granting me an eyeful of his perfectly carved abs.

"What the hell are you doing here?"

"I need to speak with you."

"What? You don't own a phone, jackass?"

He cocked his head to the left, one dark eyebrow rising. "Would you have listened if I called you? No. You'd hang up and we both know it. I was forced to find an alternate method of communication."

"Yes, and the bed was entirely necessary as part of the communication," I growled with the utmost sarcasm. He smirked.

"I would be remissed if I didn't try to make a pass at you. In the real world, I am no longer able to..." He paused, licking his bottom lip. " — taste you, but in the dream world, I am free to do as I please."

I glared. "Do you have a point?"

"Ah, yes, that." The humor and flirtatiousness abated, leaving his nearly white eyes to focus on me with a serious look in them. It never failed to creep me out that his pupils weren't round but slits like a snake's. It was the mark of all archdemons, a sign of royalty.

"You are no doubt aware of the murdered Seers, yes?"

"Of course. Don't tell me you're gonna confess to them?"

He snorted again, seeming offended. "Nonsense. I would have left a signature if it were my doing, but that is why I have chosen to contact you. I wish to report that these killings are not being committed by one of the Fallen."

"Why the hell should I believe that, Belial? Lying is like air to you."

"Because you know as well as I do that our side would not kill Seers indiscriminately. They are of as much use to us as they are to you and we are at a disadvantage when there is only one of them hanging around. One who just happens to be married to an archangel," he added with another insufferable smirk.

I ignored the comment. "So let's pretend you're telling the truth. If it's not a demon, then who is it?"

"I would advise you to reexamine your so-called saviors."

"The angels?"

He nodded. I shook my head. "You think we haven't considered that? Of course we have. But there's also the fact that not a single angel has ever gone rogue since the Fall. Why would one start now?"

Belial shrugged. "Perhaps he knows something we do not? The roster in Heaven is infinite. It is possible one of these angels slipped through the cracks. Ask Michael if there have been any unusual absences in Heaven, perhaps someone who left for Earth without a specific order."

"Why are you so eager to find this killer?"

"As I said before, my pet. Seers are just as valuable to my side as they are to yours. It is necessary to find him and stop him if we ever want to get anywhere."

I shifted underneath him, becoming even more nervous now that our little chat was coming to an end. "Great. Thanks for the tip. Now get out of my damn head."

"So soon?" the demon purred, leaning down enough to make my heart rate spike again.

"Is there nothing about this situation that interests you, Seer?"

"Nothing at all," I said through gritted teeth.

A rather smug grin crossed his lips. "Mentirosa."

I tried to punch him but faster than I could see, he grabbed both my wrists and pinned them to the mattress. Squirming, I tried to knee him in the groin. He crawled upward and straddled my waist, rendering my legs useless under his weight. An arrogant laugh trickled out of his throat as he watched me struggle in vain.

"I adore that you still resist me even in a place where no one can see us. A less stubborn woman would at least be honest with herself."

"Honest about what?" I spat. "How much I despise you? How much you disgust me?"

"And how much I turn you on?" he offered. Despite my anger, a creeping heat found its way on my cheeks and I hated it.

"You don't-"

"I'm inside your head, Jordan. I can feel everything." He lowered his face to my neck, not touching me but just barely letting his hot breath flow over my skin and his jet-black hair glide across my collarbone.

"I can feel it like the blood rushing through your veins. Your angel may be handsome and valiant, but he does not excite you the way that I do. You crave danger like a creature of the night. Like a demon. Like me. Sooner or later, you will accept that about yourself."

"You've been out of my life for a year and a half. I don't miss anything. Can you feel that?" I shot back.

"No, I cannot. Perhaps if I try a little harder..." He pursed his lips and blew at the sheets just barely clinging to my chest. They slipped downward a couple of inches, revealing the scar over my heart, and Belial's hot tongue laved the length of it, making me gasp. I squeezed my eyes shut, ashamed and angry as my body started to tremble with a horrible combination of fear and excitement.

A buzzing sound woke me. I jolted upward in bed, my hands flying to my chest as I felt the ghost of Belial's touch fading away with the nightmare. Light touched the edges of the bedroom through the blinds of my window. I glanced about to detect the odd noise only to discover my phone had received a text message. I sighed, swiping sweaty tendrils of hair off my forehead, and grabbed my cell phone.

I'll be over for lunch around 1:00. Te amo.

-Michael

"Saved by the bell," I muttered, dropping the phone in my lap. A shudder went down my spine at the thought of what might have happened if he hadn't woken me up. With Michael beside me, my dreams were protected because he emitted a subconscious protective aura. Without him, I was vulnerable. Open. Prey.

A knot began to twist in my stomach, sagging there like a boulder. I knew that ache. Michael and Gabriel had taken turns rehabilitating me from my alcohol dependence, but I still got cravings during high stress situations. This sure as hell was one of them.

So I did what any person would do.

I cooked.

MICHAEL

"The evidence is stacking up."

"I know," my brother sighed, his voice sounding absurdly tired through the cell phone. The bustling citizens of Albany on either side of me made it somewhat difficult to hear, but I'd sacrifice my hearing ability as long as it didn't require me to ride public transportation. Technology continued to evolve leaps and bounds every few years and yet we still had to clamor onto mechanical death traps that dragged through the streets like anchors at the bottom of the ocean.

"Any luck finding anomalies?"

"None so far. I am afraid the system was not designed for such a broad search."

I snorted as I stopped at a crosswalk, checking the streets. Cars flew past at ridiculous speeds. Gusts of wind tore at my face, my shirt, my jeans. Maybe I should have taken the bus after all. "Is it just me or is that completely unacceptable?"

At last, a touch of humor crept into Gabriel's tone. "It's not like you can just Google every angel that has ever existed. Being human has made you lazy, Michael."

"We should invent that after this mess is over. Heaven Google. We can call it Hoogle."

He chuckled. "Indeed. But I do have some good news — we are coming up on the last third of the names."

"Great." I paused. "This is going to suck, isn't it?"

Gabriel sighed. "Whole-heartedly. Betrayal of the Father is a death sentence on Earth and banishment from Heaven in the spiritual world. I sincerely hope the murderer has a good reason for this."

The humor bled out of me all at once. "There is no good reason to kill the innocent. You and I both know that."

"I agree, but I also have lived here longer than you have. Sometimes there are reasons for these things, even if they aren't apparent at first. He must think he's helping us out, somehow, in his twisted mind. It is not like the angels to be without sanity."

He paused, adding, "Well, except for that one who married a human. What was his name again?"

I rolled my eyes. "I'm gonna tell Jordan you said that."

"You'll do nothing of the sort. You love me too much."

I stifled a groan. "Call me back when you have something useful to say."

"Will do. Goodbye." I hung up and opened the door to the candy shop, darting inside to save myself from the humid streets. Air conditioning and the hanging scent of caramel greeted me. I took a deep breath, savoring the aroma. My stomach growled in response. The last thing I ate was spinach dip at Stan's place. Sweets were a welcome reprieve.

To my delight, Doris was the cashier today—a plump woman in her late fifties with a pageboy haircut and irreversible crush on me. Shameless as it was, I used it to my advantage, if only because this place made the best caramel apples in the Northeast.

"Doris, my love," I purred when it was my turn to step up to the counter.

She grinned, revealing dimples in her doughy cheeks. "Ah, there's my handsome man. Still married?"

I lifted my left hand to show the silver wedding ring. "Sadly, yes. Sorry to disappoint."

"Nonsense. I know I'll win you over one day," she said, reaching inside the glass display for the two caramel apples she knew I was going to order. I was a creature of habit, after all.

"I believe it. How are the kids?"

"Ha!" she said, placing the apples on the scale. "Bobby's got himself a new main squeeze. This one drives a Harley and smokes like a film noir detective. I suspect she'll last about a month. Maggie's wrapped up studying for her LSATs. We're praying she passes this time."

"Well, I'd be happy to find her a tutor if you need it. I know people," I offered, withdrawing my wallet to find my Visa card.

"I'm convinced there's no one you don't know. You sure do get around," she replied with a mischievous glint in her brown eyes. A couple clicks and the price dropped another dollar as she applied her associate discount for me.

I winked. She chuckled before swiping my card and handing me the treats. "Stay gorgeous, gorgeous."

"You too, Michael, dear." I ventured back out into the heat, digging one caramel apple out of the little plastic bag she gave me and tossing the wrapper into a nearby trash can. The fruit made a satisfying crunch when I bit down, spilling tart juice and sticky caramel across my tongue. Ah. The simple marvels of humanity. You couldn't get stuff like this in Heaven.

I probably should have missed my home above more, but close to two years on Earth had changed my perspective more than I could have imagined. Centuries of observing mankind from on high had made me a hard man and an unflinching soldier. Back then, they seemed like chess pieces — pawns mostly, but a few knights, rooks, and queens here and there. It wasn't until my mission to retrieve the Spear of Longinus from an auction in Albany in 2008 that I began to realize my perception was skewed. Enter Jordan Amador, my greatest challenge, and eventually, my wife.

It was probably fitting that I fell in love with my complete opposite. Jordan used to be asocial, defensive, and cynical. It took me months to peel back even the first layer to her personality. She had built up walls around her to keep everyone out because she was afraid of getting hurt, thanks to her rough childhood. She had every excuse to be a terrible person, but somehow, she became someone who was brave, self-sacrificing, and hopeful.

Still, as much as I loved her, we had our share of problems — particularly the apartment situation and the fact that she still hadn't planned the wedding ceremony. Jordan was a low maintenance girl and so we had a small courthouse marriage with the agreement to eventually hold a wedding for our friends and family, who had been pestering me non-stop about it lately. That was six months ago and every time anyone brought it up, she changed the subject or said she'd get to it eventually. Same with the fact that we still had separate places. Not an easy thing to juggle in Albany, New York between a waitress and a guitar salesman-slash-musician. In the grand scheme of things, it wasn't that big of a deal, but I'd be lying if I said it didn't concern me. I didn't need a wedding, but the fact that she still kept part of herself separate from me didn't inspire much confidence.

The blast of a car horn shook me out of my thoughts. I'd walked an entire block without realizing it. Half of the caramel apple was gone too. Damn. Needed to pay attention unless I wanted to end up street pizza.

Then again, my personal life was small potatoes compared to the still unsolved murdered Seers mystery. I hated the thought of it being an archangel gone rogue, but it was becoming more likely with every day that passed. Angels were not like police officers or guardians, as some humans seemed to believe. We were more like free agents with the same mission: to protect humanity and vanquish evil. Some chose to follow the orders that I issued as needed, but for the most part, they came and went as they pleased. We'd never had a need to keep track of each other because everyone did what they were supposed to and had since the beginning of time with the exception of the fallen angels. Either way, things were going to be different from now on. Very different.

Just as I jogged through the crosswalk to the other side of the street, I felt a sharp tugging in my gut that raised the hairs on my arms and along my nape. Immediately, I reached inside and spread my metaphysical senses to detect what had set the alarm bells off in my soul. There, leaning against the building across from the street lamp, was someone I knew from the olden days. He was just over six feet tall with pale skin, greasy blonde hair, sharp cheekbones, and long, bony fingers. He lit a cigarette and then cut his dark green eyes up at me as soon as I spotted him.

"How's it hanging, Mikey?" Shylock the peddler demon asked.

I adopted a nonchalant expression, though I was sure he'd appeared here on purpose. I hadn't seen him in over a year, not since before Jordan and I were a couple.

"I'm surviving. What's the occasion?"

Shylock blew out a stream of smoke, grinning enough to reveal his slightly sharp, tobacco-stained teeth. "You don't have to sound so suspicious. I'm not here to cause trouble."

I finally scowled. "The last time we met, I stopped you from killing someone and claiming a soul for your collection. Forgive me if I suspect you're holding a grudge."

He straightened his leather jacket, pulling the cig from his thin lips. "You know me better than that. I'm the forgiving sort."

I snorted. Our paths crossed back when I was sent to investigate a string of murders overseas a few decades ago. Turns out he was working as an assassin-for-hire in exchange for souls. We fought. I bested him, but he was so impressed with me that we agreed to a ceasefire. Of all the demons I'd met, he was the closest to not being a total dickwaffle. That being said, he was still a dangerous bastard.

"Whatever, man. If you've got something to say, say it. I'm in a hurry."

His shark-like grin spread wider. "Heading home to the wifey?"

I glared. "So what if I am?"

~ 28 ~

"Can't blame you. She's pretty plain for my tastes, but she's got killer legs."

I stepped forward threateningly and he held up his hands. "Whoa, calm down, mate. It was a compliment, not a threat. I'm just here to confirm the rumor."

"What rumor?"

"Seers are dropping like flies. Our archdemon lord hasn't made any orders, and neither has anyone down below. Word on the street is that you've got yourself a traitor."

A nerve in my jaw twitched. I didn't care to confirm it because I truly did not want to believe one of my brothers had fallen. We lost enough of them in the Battle in Heaven all those centuries ago. I couldn't stand the thought of a repeat of history. I lost a lot of good friends that day. "I'm not the kind to gossip, Shy. You want that, go elsewhere."

I turned my back on him, starting towards the next street. He trailed behind me, his voice borderline whiny. "Ah, c'mon, Mike. If he's whacked as many Seers as I've heard, then you're gonna need help. A gun for hire."

I laughed mockingly. "Oh, so that's what you're up to? You want me to hire you to kill this guy?"

"We'd make a good team and you know it."

"Yeah, there's just that little matter of you being evil and also a dick."

Shylock caught up to me and pouted. "Well, you don't have to be mean about it."

That almost made me laugh. Damn. "Sorry, Shy. Not going to happen. We'll find this guy on our own dime, not yours."

"I'll give you a discount."

"Forget it."

He sighed, grumbling, "Fine, but I won't be the only one asking."

I stopped dead. I whirled around, intent on demanding what that meant, but by then, he'd disappeared. I searched the crowd along the sidewalk. Gone. Not surprising. Demons could move fast enough to break the sound barrier if they felt like it. He'd been cryptic on purpose, the asshole. Nothing I could do about it now.

I checked my watch. Ten minutes 'til one. Three blocks to my wife.

At least the day was looking up.

JORDAN

The shrimp slithered against my fingertips as I peeled off the tails, tossing their little grey striped corpses into a strainer in the sink. The music of the Stranglers poured over the room and I plucked the lyrics out of the air every few seconds, trying to get my mind off of Belial and the dream. Behind me, a pot of water, saffron, and chicken broth simmered, waiting eagerly for my attention. Once the shrimp were shell-and-tail free, I'd move on to the chicken thighs. One step at a time. Cook. Breathe. Calm down. In that order.

I was halfway through sliding the raw chicken into a hot pan when I heard a knock at the door. I glanced at the clock on the microwave. Ten minutes to one. Michael was early, and had clearly forgotten his key again. He had the worst habit of leaving things at my apartment.

I finished shoveling the chicken into the pan, washed my hands, and answered the door with a sigh on my lips.

"We've got to work on your memory, Mi—"

The man standing on my welcome mat was not my husband.

He was black, in every sense of the definition. His skin was far darker than mine, nearly reaching Wesley Snipes' infamous hue. His hair was black, but the edges near his hairline were peppered with grey, as was the hair on his stylish goatee. He wore a dark blue suit and white tie, his dress shoes polished to a high sheen, and a leather jacket was tossed over his right arm. It was too hot for these clothes. I figured he was a Jehovah's Witness because he looked like he'd just stepped out of a church, or out of a Tyler Perry movie, for that matter.

I cleared my throat, trying to mask my confusion. "Can I help you?"

"Yeah," he said in a deep voice. "Jordan Amador?"

"Yes?"

He smiled. "Figures. You look just like her."

My brow furrowed into a frown. "Like who?"

"Your mother."

My blood ran cold. I gripped the door to keep myself from swaying at the sudden sensation of panic. No one knew my mother except me, my aunt, the angels…and the demons. But I couldn't sense any power coming off him.

"Who are you?" I demanded.

His smile didn't waver.

"Lewis Jackson. I'm your father."

CHAPTER THREE

JORDAN

"Mind if I come in?"

I nodded, too numb to speak, and he stepped inside. I shut the door, slumping against it, still trying to wrap my head around the words he'd just said.

"That's not...that's not possible. My Dad ran out on me when I was born," I mumbled, raising my eyes to look at him again.

He tossed his jacket across the kitchen chair, facing me again. "I wouldn't put it that way, but I guess you're right."

"How did you find me? How did you even know my name?"

He reached into his pocket and withdrew a box of Marlboro menthols, lighting one before he spoke. "Your mother decided on a name long before she had you. Catalina's a woman of faith, wanted your name to have...what did she call it...symbolic resonance?"

Lewis chuckled then. "Always had a way with words, she did. Anyway, I ran your name in a Google search and saw you were hanging out with some guy in a band. Flew out here, asked around until I came to this Southern diner called the Sweet Spot and they told me you lived near here. Ran into the mailman and he said you live in this apartment."

He shrugged. "So here I am."

I took a deep breath, trying to flatten out all the thoughts racing through my mind. "Flew in from where?"

"Detroit."

"Long way to fly for your *long-lost daughter*," I said, drawing the last three words out slowly as I crossed my arms beneath my chest. His explanation kicked me out of my stunned state. Some things were just not adding up with his story.

"What exactly prompted this reunion?"

Lewis grinned again. "Damn, you talk just like her, girl."

I narrowed my eyes at him. "Answer the question."

He inhaled deeply, staring at me with eyes that were the same color as mine—like Hershey's milk chocolate melting on a sidewalk during a hot day. After blowing smoke at the ceiling, he walked towards me and stopped a few inches away. I didn't back up because I knew at least four different ways to knock him out if he dared touch me.

"Got some people that ain't exactly happy with me right now. Business partners. Ain't the friendly type either. Thought you might be able to help me out."

The vagueness of his words weren't lost on me. Hell, he was already dressed like a pimp so finding out he was one certainly wouldn't shock me. "Business partners?"

"Yep. Investments. That sort of thing."

I shook my head, smiling. "You flew that long a way and still can't be honest with me? That's pretty rotten, Daddy-o."

He flinched at the name, and I savored the expression.

"What?" he asked. "You want me to be honest now, is that it?"

I shrugged. "Might as well. Can't hurt your chances any."

"Business is business, little girl. I don't need to get into no details. All you need to know is that I got a lotta people bangin' down my door and I need some help."

"How much do you owe?"

He sucked in another mouthful of smoke. "Fifty-thousand."

I laughed. He blinked at me, surprised by my reaction. I clapped my hands once, wagging a finger at him as I walked towards the kitchen where my chicken was in danger of burning in the pan.

"You're good. Very good. Best scam artist I've seen so far."

Lewis' face melted into an offended look. "You think I'm lyin'?"

"No shit, Sherlock," I scoffed, flipping over the sizzling meat. "First of all, you haven't asked about taking a paternity test to even prove you're my so-called father; second of all, the way you found me sounds like pure bullshit; third of all, only a fool would think I had or could get a hold of that kind of money. So yeah, I think you're lying."

He stalked towards me in quick, angry strides, and reached into his pocket. I tensed, ready to lay him out if he tried to hit me, but he came away with a photograph, thrusting it into my face.

"Is this good enough for you?"

I stared. It was a photo of my mother and my supposed father at the altar of a church. Some of the bitter amusement drained away. It looked pretty real. A cold spot formed in my stomach but I ignored it, hardening my expression.

"Any fool can Photoshop."

"Mm-hmm," he said dryly, and then reached into his pocket once more. This time, it wasn't a picture that appeared. Black beads dangled from his fingers, tapering down into an old cross so worn at the edges that the paint faded away to reveal the brown wood beneath it. My mouth went dry. I remembered the way the beads felt against my cheek when I fell asleep with my head nestled in my mother's chest. Once, when I was an infant, I chewed on the end, forever marking the bottom of the cross with tiny teeth marks. She told me she got the rosary from her mother the day before she died. Her mother was a devout Catholic. My mother hadn't really been, but she kept them anyway.

I took them from him, my fingers trembling. "Where did you get this?"

Before he could say anything, I heard the lock on the door turn and then Michael walked in.

He froze with a hand on the knob, green eyes dashing from my lifeless expression to the tall black man standing only inches away. I saw many things flicker in his face—shock, anger, suspicion, worry— before his expression settled into a neutral look. He shut the door, shoving his keys back into his pocket and dropping a plastic bag with what appeared to be a caramel apple in it on the table.

"Hi. And you are…?"

"Lewis, this is Michael. Michael, this is Lewis. My…" I couldn't say the word. It choked me with cold, dry fingers.

" —her father," Lewis finished, frowning at my hesitation.

Michael's eyes widened to epic proportions and then darted to meet mine. He stepped forward, as if he wanted to touch me, but restrained himself. Lewis' face darkened with anger as he glanced between the two of us.

"Who's he?"

I licked my lips, mumbling, "My husband."

"You gotta be shittin' me, girl," he snapped, stepping back to give us both disapproving glares. "You married a white boy? What the hell your mother been teachin' you?"

All the horror and sadness that had been bottled up inside me suddenly burst outward like a crack in a dam, the water erasing every shred of decency I once possessed.

"She's dead."

Lewis' eyes also went wide, his jaw slack. "She's—"

"Dead," I spat. "She died when I was five years old. The only thing she had the time to teach me was to be strong in the face of evil, but I guess you wouldn't know about that, would you?"

The annoyance came rushing back into his features then. "You ain't gonna talk to me like that. I'm still your father."

"Calling yourself that doesn't make it true. You can say it all you want. Father, father, father. You're still just some asshole sperm donor."

He stepped close, pointing a finger at me. "Better watch your mouth. I didn't leave you and your mother because I was scared. I thought you'd have a better life without me. We wanted different things. It woulda happened eventually if I didn't split when I did. Thought I'd be making things easier for you."

A bitter laugh escaped me. "*Easier?* You thought our lives would be easier without you? Let me show you how my life has been without you."

I grabbed the hem of my shirt and began to lift it up. Michael caught my wrist and his expression was strained as if he were distraught by the fury blazing inside me, spilling out of every corner of my skin. "Jordan, you don't have to do this."

"No, let him see. Let him see his so-called easier." I yanked off the shirt and Lewis' gaze fell upon the scar on my chest, and he couldn't hide the look of abject horror. I turned around, exposing the network of scars down my back.

"Does this look easier to you? After my mother was taken, they sent me to live with Carmensita."

"Christ," he croaked. "What did she do to you?"

"What *didn't* she do to me," I said in a low voice before turning around to face him.

"Clearly leaving us was the best decision you ever made. I suggest you do so again, since it worked out so well last time."

"Jordan—" He tried to touch my arm, but I jerked it away.

"Get out."

"Wait—"

"Get the *fuck* out of my home."

Lewis stared at me until I screamed, "GET OUT!"

Slowly, he gathered up his jacket and left. Michael said nothing. I threw my shirt on the floor and pressed my hands against the counter, forcing myself to breathe, but the air had evacuated the room, leaving nothing but poison to fill my lungs. My shoulders started to shake. I pressed my forehead into the cool surface, stifling the sob building in my chest. I felt Michael's arms wrap around me, and his soft lips against the nape of my neck. Somehow, this simple touch made everything unravel. He slid his palm over my bare stomach to my arm and turned me around, folding me into his chest. I cried while he held me, still silent, still kind, still mine.

A headache woke me up. The ache settled behind my left eye and throbbed, as if a tiny man with a jackhammer was going at it with my skull. I groaned and rolled onto my stomach, pressing my face into the pillow. Several slow breaths helped some of the pain subside. I stood up, slowly, experimentally, and then shuffled into the bathroom. Two Advil, a glass of room temperature water. Easy fix. Wish I could say the same for the rest of my life.

Michael sat at the kitchen table, hunched over his laptop, one hand folded over his mouth. He glanced up when I walked in and concern rushed over his face, replacing the concentration.

"Hey," he murmured.

I offered him a small smile. "Hey."

I noticed an enormous black pot on the stove and lifted the lid, surprised to find yellow rice dotted with shrimp, chicken, sausage, and diced peppers inside.

"You finished the paella."

He shrugged one shoulder. "Figured you'd be hungry when you got up."

I replaced the lid, walked over, and kissed him. He slid his hands around my waist, fingertips gliding over my bare skin. I sighed and pressed my forehead to his.

"Thank you."

"*De nada*," he whispered back.

I sat sideways in his lap with my feet dangling a couple of inches above the floor, and rested my face in the side of his neck. "Am I a horrible person for reacting the way I did?"

He shook his head. "I'm still amazed that you didn't punch him in the face. I was definitely thinking about it, to be honest. What did he even want from you?"

"Fifty-thousand dollars."

Michael gaped at me. "You're serious."

I nodded. "Apparently, he's in trouble with some 'business partners' and ran out of options so he tracked me down."

"Did he have proof that he was your father?"

I nodded towards the counter where the necklace still sat. "He had my mother's rosary. The one she got from her mom. I remember it from when I was little. I don't know how he got it, especially since he didn't know my mother died."

"Didn't the psychiatric hospital forward all your mother's stuff to your aunt?"

I nodded.

"Maybe he went to see her first. She must have been holding out on you last year when you went to visit. Not sure why she would have given him the rosary."

I snorted. "Because it's twice as cruel to let him have that and not tell him she died than to tell him the truth. What a bitch."

"That's the understatement of the century."

Silence fell. I sighed. "Baby, what should I do?"

He met my eyes. "What does your heart tell you to do?"

"My heart doesn't speak English."

He chuckled then, kissing the corner of my lips. "Then I'll just have to translate. But we don't have to do that now. One problem at a time, hmm?"

"Yeah. Murdered Seers come before deadbeat dads who may or may not be pimps."

My husband made a noise between a laugh and a sound of horror. "That's not funny."

I shrugged. "It might as well be. What are you looking at?"

"Police reports filed on the last murder. I was hoping we could find any evidence of the getaway, but there doesn't seem to be any. The guy just…vanished. Besides, it happened in the middle of the night, so there weren't any witnesses."

"Sounds supernatural to me. Speaking of which…" I bit my bottom lip and cleared my throat in anticipation of the difficult oncoming sentence.

"Belial contacted me."

Michael went still, staring at me with a mixture of anger and worry etched into his face. "When? How?"

"Last night, in a…dream." I fought to keep a straight face. The memory of the demon's mouth on my skin made guilt rise up inside me, even though I hadn't done anything wrong.

The archangel closed his eyes. "What did he want?"

"He said he wanted to report that the murderer is not a demon. None of them are under orders to harm Seers."

"He expects us to believe that? We have no reason to trust what he says."

"True, but he does have a point. It's got to be an angel gone rogue. Nothing else adds up. How's the search in Heaven going?"

"Not well. We've had a league of angels pouring through the roster for months and it's still not finished. We can't exactly call them all in, either. Many of them are deployed in dangerous areas or are on important missions. We're going to have to find another way to locate this guy."

I stood up, scooping my shirt off the chair where it dangled. "Maybe that's it. Maybe we're not looking in the right place."

"What do you mean?"

I pulled on my shirt, gathering my thoughts as I did. "How do angels and demons enter the human world?"

"The Doors. There are two of them — one for angels and one for demons. They have to pass through in spirit form and into bodies engineered by what we call Puppeteers. Without a body, the spirit will fade back into the void between Heaven and Earth or Hell and Earth. Since we don't know who the angel is, it would be useless to ask our Puppeteer if they gave him a body."

"Wait a second. What if he used the Demons' Door?"

"What?"

"Think about it. If he didn't want us to figure out what he looked like, then he would enter through the Demons' Door so we couldn't trace it back to our side."

"But that would mean that the demons would know who he is. Why would Belial contact you if he already knew what the rogue angel looks like? And why wouldn't he tell you that?"

"Maybe he was trying to drop a hint. Maybe he needs our help to stop him. He told me that demons wouldn't kill a Seer because they're too valuable. He might have the information, but that doesn't mean he has the means to catch the rogue angel. We should be able to get a picture or something."

"We'd have to ask him to get in contact with their Puppeteer."

"Why can't we do it ourselves?"

He frowned at me. "We can't see the Puppeteer without an archdemon present. She won't talk to us alone. We've tried it before."

I massaged the bridge of my nose. "Let me guess — the only archdemon on Earth right now is Belial?"

"Naturally."

"*That's* why he contacted me. He probably knew that we'd come to this conclusion sooner or later. Bastard."

Michael stood and then touched my shoulders. "You don't have to do this if you don't want to. There might be another way."

"We're already running out of time. We're gonna have to find him and ask him to take us to the Puppeteer."

"It won't come cheap."

"Nothing ever does."

My husband exhaled and then reached for his cell phone. "I'll contact Gabriel. He should be able to get us a location soon."

"Great." I grabbed the caramel apple on the table and unwrapped it. Truthfully, I wasn't hungry—I just needed a sweet distraction. That cold knot from before burrowed into my guts and stuck there like a chewed up wad of gum on the bottom of a desk. Everything in me did not want a reunion with Belial, but I knew it would have to happen. If I wanted to save the future Seers of the world, I would have to make a sacrifice. Somewhere, Belial was whetting a knife for me and preparing for the feast.

Eat well, you son of a bitch.

CHAPTER FOUR

JORDAN

"You're not stupid enough to not call for back up if you get in over your head, are you?" Michael asked, staring into my eyes as if he could tell what I was thinking.

I kept my voice playful to disguise my growing anxiety. "Do you think I am?"

"You really don't want me to answer that."

I rolled my eyes. "Then don't ask rhetorical questions. I'll be fine, I promise."

He leaned down and pressed a short but sweet kiss to my lips that made me feel just a tiny bit calmer. "You'd better be."

I nodded to Gabriel before stepping out of the car, instantly swallowed by the cool darkness of night. I waited for traffic to pass and jogged across the street, muttering sarcastic comments to myself as I went.

"It's no biggie. You're just strolling into a club full of demons with no backup. Big deal. People do it all the time."

The Morsel was a nightclub in Queensbury. Gabriel had done some digging to find Belial's most recent public appearances in the New York area and they were primarily at this place. It was a nest for demons, a safe haven, if you don't mind the irony. They let some humans in "for fun" but it was mostly the Fallen that populated its insides. Lucky me.

The doors to the club were blood red, a color not lost on me considering my background with the fallen angels, and there was a sinewy black man wearing a frown standing outside with a clipboard. The line wrapped around the side of the street like a snake, bristling with new activity as the demons spotted me walking towards the entrance. When I was close, the black guy arched one thick eyebrow at me.

"Can I help you?"

"I need to get in," I said without any malice or fear. It took quite a lot of effort, to be honest.

An arrogant smirk tugged at the edge of his lips. "First of all, there's a line, and second of all, I doubt you really want in. They'd eat you alive."

My smile widened. Ah, yes, that familiar feeling of annoyance. Right up my alley. "I can clearly see the line but thanks for pointing it out. The reason you're going to let me in is that I'm relatively sure your boss wouldn't be thrilled if you turned me away."

He snorted. "And who's my boss?"

"Belial."

When I spoke the demon's name, the bouncer's smirk withered, replaced with a serious but contemplative look. "Name?"

"Jordan Amador."

His brown eyes grew large. Well, well. He did know who I was. "Prove it."

I stared. "What do you mean prove it?"

"Word on the street is that you've managed to send Belial and Mulciber home with their tails tucked between their legs on two separate occasions. It's hard to think a little thing like you can do that kind of damage, if you don't mind me saying."

I sighed. He had a point, but it was still an incredible nuisance. "Fine. What kind of proof do you want? I don't have a driver's license, but I have ID."

The bouncer shook his head. "Papers can be forged. I want to see the scar."

I went still. "The scar?"

"The scar the Spear made. Then you can go in." His gaze didn't waver on mine. Several feelings boiled in my gut: anger, humiliation, and defiance, but none of them would help me get into this joint so I stuffed them all down. I yanked the neckline of my shirt downward to expose the mound of scar tissue over my heart. He let out a low whistle and stepped aside, opening the door amongst the groans of jealousy from the people in line.

"Don't say I didn't warn you, Seer."

Pulsing music surrounded me in an instant as I walked up the stairs — also tastefully done in crimson — that led to the main part of the building. It served as both a bar and a dance club. There were black lacquered tables everywhere with people seated at them and a huge hardwood dance floor in the middle. Behind it stood a stage where there were four men in tuxedos: two at microphones, one on the drums, and one on a white guitar. I stopped when I reached the top of the steps, glancing around at my harrowing surroundings. The bar was along the left wall, crowded with demons clamoring for drinks, but there was another staircase leading to a basement to the far right. I tried to ignore the pounding chorus of the Kills song the band played telling me that I was a fever.

I let my energy flow out of me and fill the club, distantly aware the demons were whispering to each other about my presence but ignoring it. Finally, I felt a fiery energy coming from the basement. It had to be him.

I maneuvered my way past the tables near the basement staircase. I felt the gaze of every single demon as I walked, locked on my solitary form like lions watching a lamb. The key was not so much acting like they didn't scare me but rather acting like they wouldn't bother me. They were naturally suspicious of my presence because of the rumors and because I wouldn't have just wandered in here for no reason. They were cautious predators.

To my utter shock, there wasn't a huge, intimidating man at the next set of double doors but a little girl no more than twelve or thirteen years old with chestnut hair and lifeless green eyes. She was at least seven inches shorter than me and held a clear clipboard in her pale hands.

I cleared my throat, trying to disguise my surprise as I spoke. "Hi. I'm looking for Belial."

"He's busy," she answered without batting an eyelash. Creepy.

"I'm sure he is, but I get the feeling he might be interested in seeing me if you let him know I'm here."

She gave me a very bored once-over. "I'm not so sure about that."

That stung. I brushed past it anyway. "Could you check? Please?"

The girl continued staring at me before touching her earpiece. "I've got a Seer here that wants to see the Master. Should I let her in?"

A muffled voice on the end replied. She lowered her hand to the door and pushed it open, nodding for me to go in. "Knock twice when you want out…if you make it that far."

"Thanks, Sunshine," I deadpanned, brushing past her. This hallway was long and dimly lit with concrete steps and bare walls, but the noise was entirely different. I heard the distant rumble of chanting as I walked, squinting as I tried to see what lay at the end of the hall.

When I reached the archway, I could see stadium seating all centered around a raised arena with a rusted metal cage over the top like a wrestling match. There were two men locked in a vicious fistfight, hurtling each other from one end to the other. I wondered what the hell was going on when one man slammed into the side of the cage nearest to me, and then I saw it—a long curtain of jet-black hair. Belial.

Just as I recognized him, he raised his head and looked over his shoulder right into my eyes, slowly smirking as he realized it was me. Seeing that smirk in person after so many months made the skin on my arms crawl.

He straightened up just as the other man ran at him, his fist cocked. With inhuman speed, he whirled around and shoved his palm into the man's nose, breaking it. The man hit the floor howling in pain and clutching his face. The spectators went wild, their voices eventually melding into one terrifying chant of, "BEL! BEL! BEL! BEL!"

The demon strolled over to one end of the cage and one of his associates unlocked the door, letting him out. He hopped off the stage and crooked a finger at me without turning around. I took a deep breath and followed him up the steps of the stadium to an office.

The chanting stopped as soon as I closed the door, meaning these walls were sound proof. Of course they were. Shit. I couldn't dwell on this fact for long because Belial spoke, catching my attention.

"Well, well, well. Jordan Amador. I never expected to see you darkening my doorstep."

I squared my shoulders and turned, intent on being firm and cold with him, but then my eyes fell across his bare chest and words died in my throat.

I hadn't seen the result of the angel feather I'd once plunged into Belial's chest until now. It was ghastly. The skin over his heart rippled with brown burn marks and nearly bisected his abs, starting at the shoulder and dripping down to his bellybutton. It looked almost shiny in the dim light, meaning that his human body had tried its best to heal the damage but probably never would.

Belial caught my gaze, flashing me a brief smirk. "Admiring your handiwork, I see?"

"That's not—"

"You don't have to make excuses. You should be proud. No one's ever managed to mark up one of my human bodies to quite this extent." He walked over to his desk where a fresh towel had been laid. He began drying off the sweat and blood from his upper body, which was mildly distracting for reasons I didn't want to admit to myself and probably never would.

~ 43 ~

I crossed my arms beneath my chest, making sure to keep my voice level so that Gabriel and Michael could hear our conversation. "Why don't you just get another one?"

"For the same reason you still have your scar. A memento, as it were."

I frowned. "It's not the same thing. I keep this to remind myself how dangerous and evil your kind is. You keep yours because you're vain."

He chuckled—a dry sound that made the skin along my spine prickle. "Perhaps."

Now blood-free, he tossed the towel aside and walked towards me. I dropped my arms as adrenaline pumped through my veins in an instant, preparing me for a fight. He couldn't touch me because my soul was bound to Michael's, making me too pure for any demon to withstand bare contact, but it didn't mean he wasn't going to try to make a pass at me anyway.

I made a small sound of alarm when my back hit the door, not noticing that I'd retreated so far. Belial stopped mere inches in front of me, placing one hand on the door to trap me against it. I wished very badly for my gun because I had almost forgotten his annoying habit of invading my personal space.

"To what do I owe the tremendous honor of your presence?" Belial asked, rooting me in the spot with his reptilian gaze. "Did you miss me? Is your sex life with the angel less than satisfactory?"

I glared up at him. "Even if it was, I doubt I'd be coming to you."

He let out a short bark of laughter, startling me again. "So you say. But here it is, a year later, and you're once again in my presence. Admit it, Seer. You need me."

"Go to hell," I spat.

He flashed me that poisonous smile again. "A little late for that. Now why don't you tell me what brings you and your little angel brigade to my doorstep?"

"How did you—"

Belial snorted, looking as if he were insulted. "Like they'd really send you in alone to see me. I'm not an idiot."

He yanked my duster aside to reveal the tiny microphone clipped to the inside of the lapel. Damn. "You're losing your touch, Prince of Heaven's Army. Though I must admit I appreciate the gift of seeing my dear sweet Jordan again. Perhaps we'll make this an overnight stay —"

I jerked the cloth out of his hands. "That's enough."

He rose to full height, shrugging one shoulder. "Very well. What do you want with me, Seer? Other than my charming smile and rapier wit, of course."

I rolled my eyes. "We're here about the rogue angel. We think he had a human body engineered to keep us from tracking him. We suspect he didn't use one of ours and so that means he had to have used one of yours. You're the only one privy to that information and that's why I'm here."

The arrogance and amusement slid aside to reveal a pensive expression. "So you want to know if my Puppeteer made him a body?"

"Yes."

He scrutinized me for a long moment and then walked back to his desk. "What will I get in return if I surrender this information?"

I took a deep breath, forcing the words out of my mouth. "What do you want?"

He tilted his head, making his long hair cascade towards the left side of his face. The movement seemed perfect, almost like he practiced it in front of a mirror. He probably had, the vain bastard.

"A favor."

"What kind of favor?"

Belial leaned his backside against the desk and propped his hands on its surface. The small movement drew more attention to his chest. I ignored it now that I was sure he was doing it on purpose.

"I don't know yet. But one day, I will call on you and you will answer."

I shook my head. "No way. That's too vague. I'm not going into this agreement blind."

He nodded. "Very well. Let me ask you this first: what do you intend to do if I am able to help you locate this rogue angel?"

"We're going to find him and stop him before he can kill anyone else."

"Stop him, you say?"

I nodded. A devious look flickered across his eyes. "Will you kill him?"

That stopped me in my tracks. I paused, brushing the hair out of my face in a nervous gesture. Truthfully, I hadn't thought about it.

"I...don't know. If it comes to that, maybe."

"Then may I suggest I throw my hat in the ring? Let me come with you to kill the angel."

I went still, shocked by the request. "What?"

He crossed his arms. "You cannot imagine the amount of satisfaction I will gain from killing one of God's personal soldiers. I'll accept that as my payment."

"No," I said, shaking my head. "Out of the question."

Belial shrugged again. "Fine. Then be on your way, Seer, because there are no other terms I will accept."

My phone buzzed inside my pocket. I reached for it, holding up a finger to the demon and turning my back on him as I answered.

"Hello?"

"Tell me you're not considering his offer," Michael said, his voice hard with anger.

"What other choices do we have?"

"I'm not sure," Gabriel chimed in. "We can continue the investigation regardless of Belial's assistance, but we still do not have a description of the angel and it will be that much harder to find him."

"How do the odds look that we'll find him without the demon's help?"

"Slim."

I sighed. "I figured as much. What if I negotiate the terms?"

"That may help. See if you can get him to reach a ceasefire. If he gives his word, he's bound by demonic law to uphold it."

I arched an eyebrow. "Isn't demonic law an oxymoron?"

"Somewhat. The conditions that allow the demons to walk the Earth are contingent upon their cooperation with a certain set of rules. I'll explain it to you later. The natives are getting restless downstairs so you'd better get moving."

"Alright. I'm sorry, Michael. I don't like this any more than you do."

"I doubt that," he said with a bitter tone. "But do the best you can."

"I will. See you outside in a minute." I hung up, turning around only to yelp in surprise when I noticed Belial standing less than a foot away. He was buttoning a hunter-green shirt, a black tie looped around his neck. Weird. I'd figured he would want to take a shower after a vicious cage match, but maybe he liked the grunge.

"What is the verdict, my pet?"

I brushed past the nickname. "Give me your word that you won't try to harm anyone other than the rogue angel and that you won't interfere with the investigation in any way, and we have a deal."

He clucked his tongue. "Take all the fun out of life, why don't you."

"Take it or leave it, demon."

Belial bowed his head. "I give my word as one of the Fallen Princes of Hell that I agree to these terms."

"Whoopee. Now when can we meet the Puppeteer?"

"I will contact you when we've arranged a time and place."

"Contact how?"

His smile widened and yet another shudder crawled up my spine. "That has yet to be determined."

"Could you be more suspicious?"

"For you, perhaps. Now if you'll excuse me, I have to make an appearance downstairs…"

He reached out. I flinched, but he only touched the doorknob, amused by my behavior. "…and you have to get back to your little angel brigade, sweet Jordan."

"Stop calling me that."

He chuckled, pulling the door open. "As you wish, my pet."

I suppressed an annoyed groan and followed him out of the office. Gabriel had been right. I could feel the heavy gazes of the other demons as we walked through the stadium and back through the club area. Some of them licked their lips and made catcalls, inviting me to let them have a taste.

A leggy blonde intercepted the two of us before we got to the front door, placing one hand on her hip and making her bright green dress inch even higher up her white thighs.

"Who's your friend?" she purred at the archdemon, though her brown eyes were fixed on me.

"She is my guest," Belial replied, watching her with a cool but wary look.

"Guest, huh? Are you telling me you're not going to share? I'm sure there's plenty to go around. We're generous people, Beli," the woman simpered, but the hunger in her eyes didn't match her innocent tone. I knew she'd kill me and eat me if given even the slightest chance. After all, demons drew power from sin and death.

She reached out to touch my hair, but Belial caught her wrist with inhuman speed. He kept his voice level, though I could tell he was running out of patience. "But I am not. Stand down or I will make you."

Annoyance crossed the heavy makeup on her face, but she snatched her arm back and stepped aside, harrumphing like a six-year-old who had been told she couldn't have another cookie.

I wondered if I should thank him, as silly as it sounded, but then he lifted my arm by the sleeve and kissed the cuff right above my hand, smiling that poisonous smile once more.

"Until the next time."

I tugged my hand loose and walked down the stairs, breathing a sigh of relief once I had reached outside. I'd been right in comparing myself to a lamb in the lion's den. Either way, I was sure as hell not about to dirty my fluffy little tail by going in there ever again.

No pun intended.

Okay, maybe a little.

"Auntie Jordan?"

"Yeah, squirt?"

"How come you haven't had a wedding yet?"

I stopped in mid-lick of my ice cream cone and looked at the seven-year-old perched on a stool next to me. Lily's black hair had been pulled up into two pigtails on the top of her head with bright green barrettes—the way she liked it. Her mother liked it better without them. She thought it made her look like a bunny rabbit. I gave the kid a break when I could. After all, it was her hair.

"Why d'you ask?" I countered, arching an eyebrow.

Lily licked her mint-pistachio ice cream, her brown eyes staring up at me with an earnest light in them. "'Cause I wanna be a flower girl. My friends say it's fun."

"Hmm, you have a point there."

"Well, I guess I'm just not ready yet."

"How come?"

I squirmed in my seat. "I forgot how many questions you ask."

"'M sorry. Mama says that too."

I pinched one of her cheeks. "I didn't mean it in a bad way. You should always ask questions. It's what makes you smart."

"Do smart people answer questions?"

That made me roll my eyes. "Anything to wear a little pink dress, huh, kid?"

Lily beamed at me then. "So…when?"

"Soon. You have my word."

"Yes! It's gonna be so much fun!"

"Mm-hmm. Now finish your ice cream. Your Mom gets off work soon."

Fortunately, Lily's elementary school was only a few blocks from the restaurant. Almost every Tuesday and Thursday, I'd pick her up and get her a snack while her mom worked. Things were still rough with her father—Drake Gibson, CPA and douchebag extraordinaire— who took her on weekends, but the girl was too young to really let it upset her just yet. I prayed it stayed that way for as long as it could.

The wind kicked up as I opened the door, automatically reaching down for the child's hand. She took it willingly. The afternoon rush of Albany had already begun so the air was cluttered with the sound of honking horns, tennis shoes and high heels on concrete, and music seeping out from cracked car windows. Chaotic. Noisy. Home.

Still, even with the comfortable feel of the city around me, I didn't let my guard down. Without turning, I knew how many people were walking behind me and how tall they were. I knew how many cameras were pointed into the streets at the corners. I knew the height and weight of the cop standing beside the hot dog vendor across the street. I knew how many of the shuffling masses were demons. The information simply faded into my consciousness—there when necessary, but not prominent. It wasn't just for Lily's sake. The last two years had taught me caution. Constance vigilance. It wasn't paranoia. Or so I hoped.

We crossed two streets, closing in on the restaurant, when I noticed that someone was following us. Instantly, my heart rate spiked and I tugged Lily a little closer to my side. I let my eyes slide to the windows alongside us so I could see him. Five-foot-eight, blonde hair, five o'clock shadow. No demonic energy. Maybe a pick-pocket?

He started to catch up to us. The restaurant was still a block away. How could I fend him off while keeping Lily safe?

"Hey, squirt, you mind if we stop to use the bathroom in here?" We stopped in front of a comic book shop, one where I knew the owner and he'd let me go in without asking questions. She nodded and I opened the door, ushering her towards the back of the store. There were a few teenagers perusing the shelves. None of them looked particularly scary. I'd have to fight the guy on my own instead of playing the helpless victim card.

I reached for the doorknob only to find it locked. Shit. He was almost on me. I pushed Lily behind me and whirled, grabbing him by the thumb and twisting it just as he laid a hand on my shoulder.

"Ow! What the hell are you doing?"

"Why are you following us?" I demanded, my glare ice cold.

He stuck his other hand out, waving something under my nose.

"You left your wallet in the ice cream shop."

I immediately let go of him and felt a cold wash of relief spill over me. "Oh. Jesus, I'm so sorry."

He stumbled backwards, rubbing his finger after handing it to me. "Forget it."

The man turned his back on me, muttering, "Freak" before he exited. I took a deep breath and let it out slowly. I deserved that. I'd gotten paranoid.

"Auntie Jordan? What's wrong?" Lily asked, tugging at my duster.

I shook my head, tucking my wallet in my pocket. "Nothing, squirt. C'mon."

"I thought you had to go to the bathroom."

"I can hold it. Let's go."

We reached the restaurant in no time at all, though I had to stop to take the barrettes out of her hair before we went inside—our little secret, I told her—and she raced towards her mother as soon as she spotted her. Lauren dropped her waitress apron and scooped the girl up, grinning like a Cheshire cat. I smiled at the scene. They were a perfect pair. Mother and daughter. No one could take that away from them. Not while I still drew breath.

Lauren pulled her purse over her left shoulder, settling Lily against her hip as she walked towards me. "Where'd you two go this time?"

I shrugged one shoulder. "Nowhere special. We just—"

"Auntie Jordan kicked some guy's butt!" Lily exclaimed.

I froze. Lauren glanced at her daughter, her smile fading somewhat.

"She did what?"

"This blond guy at the comic shop. It was so cool!"

Lauren turned towards me with a question in her eyes. I kept wearing the smile to hide the panic starting to grip me.

"It wasn't like that. She misunderstood what happened."

~ 50 ~

"Oh. I see." No, she didn't. She gave me a 'We'll talk about this later' look and led the way out of the restaurant, asking Lily about school as we went. I tried not to drag my feet. Lauren was going to give me the third degree and I knew it.

A couple of hours later, Lily was taking her afternoon nap and I sat across from her mother on her balcony overlooking the street. Lemonade sweated in a glass on the table. Lauren sipped hers, then put it on a coaster. Folded her arms. Stared.

"So what happened?"

I sighed. "It's not what you think."

"You don't know what I think."

"We came out of the ice cream shop and there was a guy following us. I thought he was a pickpocket. Turns out I left my wallet at the shop and he was giving it back to me."

"So you kicked his ass?"

"I didn't kick his ass!" I protested, knowing how childish it sounded and not caring.

"I just…disabled him."

She lifted an eyebrow. "That's politically correct."

"Twisted his thumb. Paralyzes the arm for a few seconds. No biggie."

Lauren shook her head. "You know, you once joked that you were Spider-Man. These days, I'm starting to believe it."

"Oh, come on. Clearly I'm Batman."

She glared at me. "Not funny. You're not telling me something."

"What do I have to hide, Lauren? Seriously?"

"I don't know. I can just feel it. Ever since Michael, things have been different and I feel like there's this wall between us that you won't let me climb."

Her heavy gaze made me want to wince. Lauren was laid-back, but there was a fierce intelligence under the charm. Of everyone I knew, she was the hardest to lie to—not only because she was my best friend, but because she was just too damn smart.

"There's no wall. You know me. I wouldn't do that to you."

She took another sip of her drink, continuing as if I hadn't said anything. "I was serving a couple of regulars the other day and overheard them talking about you. They said something about a rumor. They see you around town asking questions about missing people. Some of them think you're nuts."

I licked my lips, trying to buy time. She had me there. "I've been working at a few homeless shelters with Gabriel. A lot of people from there go missing all the time. I check up on them when I can."

"That makes sense, but you're still lying."

I opened my mouth to protest, but she cut me off. "You don't have to tell me now, but if we're gonna continue being friends, I'd like you to be honest with me. I'm not a child. You don't have to protect me like you protect Lily. Remember that."

Before I could answer, Lauren stood up and pointed to the den. "Now come on. The new *Castle*'s on the DVR."

CHAPTER FIVE

JORDAN

"The Master will see you now."

A Japanese girl in a blood-red kimono smiled as she pulled open a huge ivory door. I walked inside and she closed it, leaving me in a white room with a few steps that led up to a black bed. At first, I thought the only things in the room were me and the bed, but then something stirred.

Belial lay on his back, propped up by his elbows, nearly blending in with the color scheme on account of his attire: an open black button-up shirt and matching slacks. He wore the most maddening smirk as I walked up the short steps to where he lounged.

I crossed my arms beneath my chest. "An Asian chick in a kimono? Really? That's stereotypical even for you."

Belial made a scornful noise in the back of his throat. "You have no sense of style, Seer."

"Sue me. Would it have killed you to pick up a phone?"

"I never did like those things. They're too impersonal. I like to add my own touch to messages when I have the opportunity."

I suppressed a deep sigh, knowing that he would keep up this routine for the entirety of the dream sequence despite my lack of interest. "Fine. What's the message?"

"The Puppeteer has agreed to see you. I will meet you at the Door in three days."

"You realize that I'm not going by myself, right?"

"Naturally. It will be just like old times."

"Peachy. Now, if you don't mind, answer something for me."

"Anything."

"Why can you contact me through my dreams? I thought that Michael's energy protected me from nightmares."

Belial slid off of the bed in one smooth motion, stepping towards me until his shadow fell across my upper body. I tensed, praying he didn't notice. "It is true that I have a few tricks up my sleeve, but the most accurate reason is that you do not find my presence all that..."

He paused, searching for the right word. "...unpleasant. Thus, I am allowed access to your mind."

He took hold of my wrist and lifted it to his mouth. A fluttering sensation skittered through my stomach when Belial pressed his lips against the palm of my left hand, those alien eyes locked on my distressed expression.

"Stop that," I said, though it came out as an unsteady mumble rather than a command.

He let out a small chuckle, dragging my fingertips across his lips. "Why? Your lover knows nothing of this dream. Will you resist me even here, where there are no consequences for your actions?"

I shook my head, taking a deep breath to ground myself. "I've been in this life long enough to know that there are consequences for everything, especially things done in the dark."

He licked a quick line over my wrist. "How noble of you."

Before I could say anything else, he yanked on my arm and spun me around towards the bed. I toppled over onto the impossibly soft mattress and silken sheets, my chest heaving with panic as he leaned across my helpless form with a combination of lust and hunger in his eyes. I shoved my hands against his shoulders, trying to keep him away, but he drifted closer, his hot breath curling along my mouth as I chanted hoarsely, "Wake up, wake up, wake up!"

His lips closed over mine – searing hot and enticingly soft, his tongue brushing my own, his teeth tugging at my lower lip enough to make me gasp. His large hand drifted below my shirt and began to stroke my stomach as if trying to coax me to let him in. His hair swept on either side of my face, making me feel even more trapped than I already was. My strength meant nothing here. He had me drawn and quartered, ready to be eaten, and the demon would have his fill.

"Jordan?"

The dream vanished. I found myself staring up at my husband, safe and sound in my own bedroom. Thank God.

He sat beside me, his brow wrinkling with concern at the way I frowned. "Hey, are you okay?"

I didn't answer him. Not with words, anyway. I gripped the collar of his shirt and pulled him to me. I kissed him, lips parted, tongue slipping inside his mouth, pressing as much of my upper body against him as I could. His scent—AXE cologne and his own natural smell—filled my nostrils and erased the cold feeling that Belial's touch had instilled. He seemed shocked at first, but eventually he wrapped his arms around my back and let me inside. I rubbed the side of his jaw, clean-shaven since it was morning, and let my fingers slip to the nape of his neck, playing with the tiny hairs there. Finally, I broke away.

Michael stared at me, breathing heavily, a question on his lips but a need in his eyes. "Not that I'm complaining, but what was that for?"

"We meet the Puppeteer in three days."

Then I slid out of bed, walked into the bathroom, and took a shower.

Gabriel's long fingers were careful as they reached inside the box of Triscuits — selecting the perfect square to be sacrificed to a glob of olive dip and his mouth. He sat beside me at the kitchen table, calm and appropriate as always. Michael hovered nearby with his arms crossed over his chest sending suspicious looks between the two of us. Cold water dripped from the ends of my hair onto the towel around my shoulders, making me shiver every few seconds as the cloth dampened.

"I take it from this awkward silence that you two have something to tell me," Michael said after a while.

Gabriel chewed and swallowed his snack, nodding. I glanced at him. He tilted his head towards his brother, wordlessly giving me the go-ahead.

"I think that Gabriel should accompany me to the Demons' Door."

Michael's green eyes narrowed. "What?"

I held up my hands in supplication. "Don't get all bent out of shape. It's for a good reason."

"What reason is that? Do you know what you're asking me? You're asking me to stay here while you go into what is essentially the entrance to Hell led by a demon who has tried to murder and rape you on multiple occasions. Is that about the size of it?"

I paused. "Well, yes. But it sounds really negative when you say it that way."

He pushed away from the counter, balling his hands into fists. "Is this a joke to you, Jordan? Because I'm having a hard time finding the humor in it."

"Of course not —"

"Great, because there is no way in hell I'm letting you do this. Belial won't show restraint once you make it to the Door. What then?"

"Michael —"

"What if it's a trap? What if he's got another scheme going and you walk right into it?"

"Michael," Gabriel spoke up, turning his icy eyes on his brother.

"At the risk of sounding rude...shut up."

Michael went silent. I had to physically stop myself from gaping at Gabriel. I'd never heard him say a cross word to anyone other than demons. It was unnerving.

"Jordan is perfectly capable of taking care of herself. If I remember correctly, she has saved your life on three separate occasions, and mine on one. Furthermore, I know that you are the Commander of Heaven's Army but I have been alive for as many millennia as you and I am perfectly capable of protecting her from harm. Therefore, your concern is appreciated and duly noted, but this is the way it needs to be."

"Why?"

Gabriel sighed. "You know why, brother. Belial will undoubtedly make sexual remarks about Jordan and you will lose your temper. He is not even in the room and you're already furious. We can't get their cooperation if you start a fight. I am more qualified for this mission because I won't get angry on her account."

I lifted an eyebrow and he flashed me a small smile. "No offense, my dear, but I'm not in love with you."

"None taken."

"So what am I supposed to do while you're gone?"

"We'll contact you as soon as we know the identity of the murderer. If possible, we'll send you a photo and you can contact the angels in the police department to get an APB on him."

Michael's jaw shifted as he swallowed another argument. "Fine."

He stalked off to the bedroom. I let out a long breath. "*That went well.*"

"Indeed. Thank you for calling me. I get the feeling you couldn't have convinced him on your own, at least not in ways I will permit myself to think about."

I bit my lip to stop a smile. "Why, Gabriel, are you uncomfortable thinking about me seducing your brother?"

The archangel coughed in mid-swallow of a Triscuit and turned an interesting shade of pink. I giggled, unable to help myself.

He regained composure and then sent me a frosty glare. "That was unnecessary."

"I know, but it was still funny."

I stood, dropping some of the humor in my tone. "So I'm guessing the Demons' Door is in a nicely ironic location. New Jersey? Baghdad? The Vatican?"

"Nice guesses, but no, none of the above."

He stood. I stared at his neutral expression. "You're just gonna leave me in the dark, aren't you?"

He kissed my forehead. "Consider it payback for the seduction comment. I'll come to collect you in three days, early morning. Michael will know what to pack for the journey. Be good to him. I know this won't be easy."

"Life seldom is. See you, Gabe." He waved and left the apartment. I took a deep breath and walked into the bedroom.

Michael had already pulled out my suitcase and was currently filling it with my underwear. He didn't look at me when I walked in.

I leaned against the doorjamb, trying to figure out how to handle the situation. "That bra doesn't go with those panties."

"Ha-ha-freaking-ha," he grumbled, yanking open another drawer to find socks.

I closed the bedroom door and continued drying my hair. "I'm liking the fold-and-pack service. It's very Alfred."

"Jordan, this is not a good time."

"Seriously, if you can just slip into that maid costume in the back of my closet, that would be the cherry on top."

He slammed the drawer shut, turning around. "Why is everything a joke to you?"

"Why *isn't* everything a joke to you?" I countered. "You've spent enough time on Earth to know that not everything is life or death. It might as well just be funny."

"Well, I'm sorry. I don't have your Chandler-Bing-like tendencies. I can't joke about you walking into the lion's den with a T-bone around your neck."

"Michael, you knew this would happen eventually. We can't be on every single mission together. You need to have more faith in me."

"Maybe I would if I didn't know you were having fantasies about Belial when I'm not here."

I stopped breathing for a handful of seconds. "You knew about that?"

He snorted, seeming insulted. "Of course I did. It was in your voice when you told me. I'm not an idiot."

"Did you also know how bad it shook me up? I wasn't consenting in those dreams. I didn't enjoy them."

"How do I know that, Jordan? I wasn't there. I don't know how he's been twisting your mind. That's what he's good at—changing your thoughts so that things appear the way he wants them to."

"It doesn't matter what he wants me to see. I know what's there. The man who did this—" I jerked aside the hem of my shirt to show the scar.

"—is the same man no matter what dreams he manipulates. Why can't you believe that?"

"Because I've been around too long. You heard what he did to Uriel's lover. Who's to say he won't try to do the same thing to you?"

"Me."

He fell silent, staring at me. For the first time in the entire argument, I could tell he really heard what I'd said.

Michael took a deep breath and then let it out slowly. He sat next to me on the bed, lowering his voice. "I trust you, Jor. More than anyone else on this Earth. But that doesn't mean I'm strong enough not to get jealous or worried. I'm not perfect."

"No one ever said you had to be," I whispered, wrapping my hand around his.

"We'll get a face and a name and we'll hunt this son of a bitch down and save the world because that's what we do. Then I'll come home and bake cookies and make out with you on the couch."

He finally smiled. "You make it sound so easy."

"I'm just a girl who can't say no."

He chuckled, leaning in to kiss me. "Got that right."

I pinched his thigh. "Ow!"

"I resent that."

"You resemble that."

"Shut up and finish packing my underwear, Alfred."

MICHAEL

The scrolling white text on my laptop mocked me with the same line every thirty seconds: *You should be writing.* I stared at it with the utmost loathing. My ratty green notebook lay beside it at the kitchen table and exacerbated my irritable mood. There were songs that needed to be written and lyrics to be edited, but I couldn't focus. Every so often, I glanced at the clock on the microwave to check the time. Jordan wouldn't land for another hour.

"You are so whipped," I groaned, dragging my fingers down my face. My five o'clock shadow was starting to peek through and I hadn't showered yet. I'd spent most of the day on the couch watching Emeril Lagasse and trying not to think about the murdered Seers. Truly pathetic. It seemed like my life before domestic bliss had been a dream—a thick fog that clung to the edges of my mind. Time didn't exactly exist in Heaven, so it was all the more startling when I realized I hadn't been there for nearly two years. The angelic part of my soul mourned the loss of its home, but the man didn't really miss it. Mankind thrived on conflict. Naturally, Heaven was fresh out of that.

I spun the silver wedding band on my finger, feeling the smoothness of the metal soothe my nerves somewhat. The rings were Gabriel's idea. He suggested that I smelt part of my holy armor to make them. Symbolic gesture. It reminded me of my duty as Commander but also of my duty as a husband. Too bad I wasn't fulfilling those duties at the moment.

At the very least, I didn't have to worry about Jordan and Gabriel when they were together. He'd known her long before I did and watching them interact always amused me. She brought out a sly part of his personality that I hadn't seen much of in the recent centuries. Gabriel was the Messenger for a reason. He was always kind, calm, and collected—never lost his temper, never sinned, never failed to complete a mission. I'd always admired that about him.

The home telephone—Jordan's idea, in case our shenanigans caused us to lose one of our cell phones—blasted through my thoughts. I fumbled for it, answering in a breathless voice, "Amador residence?"

"I'm looking for Jordan Amador."

An unknown male voice. I suppressed a sigh. "She's out. Who's calling?"

"This is the Albany Police Department. A man claiming to be her father has been arrested on gambling charges. He said she'd be willing to post bail."

I froze. "I'm sorry, what?"

"Lewis Jackson has asked that you post his bail. He used his phone call to contact Mrs. Amador, but there was no answer. Are you going to post bail?"

The words, "Hell no" were climbing up my throat and bouncing off the back of my teeth, but I swallowed them. Did he deserve to rot in prison? Yes. Definitely. Was it my right to make that decision? Maybe. Probably.

In the end, I rubbed my forehead and decided to be merciful. "Yes, sir."

"Alright. Have a good day, sir."

"You too, officer."

I slammed the phone down on the receiver. Son of a bitch. I'd never seen one man cause so much trouble in such a short amount of time. Righteous fury filled my lungs and I could already hear a speech constructing itself in the back of my mind, but I knew it was just on Jordan's behalf. He hadn't wronged me. He'd wronged her. Getting angry wouldn't solve anything.

Time for a field trip.

Before he saw me around the corner, Lewis Jackson looked nervous and twitchy, as if he'd spent most of his night looking over his shoulder. He probably hadn't slept. They had only put him in holding, not lockdown. I suspected he hadn't been in prison for extended periods of time if he was this shaken up by the common crooks in an Albany PD. Maybe I could drag him into a federal pen someday, show him the real monsters, ones that the demons looked up to. Really give him something to twitch about.

His face hardened to stone when he spotted me standing near the counter, having just finished signing the last of the papers. I'd shaved, slicked my hair back, and thrown on a suit jacket, button-up shirt, and jeans. I looked clean and wealthy, and he knew it.

He sneered at me. "What you doin' here?"

I tucked the pen in the pocket of my suit jacket, keeping my voice neutral. "Bailing you out, apparently."

"Don't need no handouts, boy. I can take care of myself," Lewis said.

I lifted an eyebrow. "Clearly."

He sucked his teeth at me and started walking towards the door. I fell in step beside him, slipping both hands in my pockets to appear casual.

"Where's Jordan?"

"Why's that any concern of yours?"

He shoved the double doors to the police department open and walked out before giving me a filthy look. "I'm her father, ain't I? I got a right to know why she didn't come down here to get me out."

"Why should she? Blood is nothing but blood. It dries up under the sun just like anything else. You've done nothing for her so why do you expect something in return?"

"See, that's something you white boys don't understand. We take care of our folks where I come from."

I let a dry chuckle spill out of my mouth. He stared at me, surprised through the mask of anger. "Y'know, I've met a lot of men like you in my time."

"Is that so?" he asked with a derisive snort.

"Yeah. We call you Soul Men. You're straight outta the '70's, slicked back pimp-walking old-fashioned guys. Don't tolerate back talk, expect everyone to respect you because of your age and skin color. You think just because I'm white that I'm given everything on a silver platter. While that may be true for some men, it's not for me."

I stepped forward, meeting his dark eyes. "I work for a living. So I know the difference between a man who's down on his luck looking to reconnect with a daughter he wronged and a lowlife punk who wants the easy way out tugging on his long-lost daughter's heart strings."

"You better watch your damn mouth, boy," Lewis growled.

"Or what?" I shot back. "You'll kick my ass? Give the cops another excuse to throw you back in the hole? Believe me, it's a tempting idea, but I'm trying to make a point here. I bailed you out because I love my wife and even though she's hurt and angry, I think she'd want me to do this for her. I may be wrong. Don't know. But don't think for a second that I'm going to let you shit all over her life and leave me to clean up the mess. If you really want Jordan's forgiveness, I won't stand in your way. But if you're just here for you,

you can kindly take your ass back to Detroit on the first thing smoking."

He said nothing, seeming to stew in his own anger, but I could see in his eyes that he had heard me. The racism bullshit evaporated and we were left two men glaring holes in each other's souls.

I straightened my jacket and nodded to him. "Be seeing you, Mr. Jackson."

With that, I walked down the steps and disappeared into the crowd.

CHAPTER SIX

JORDAN

"Rush Limbaugh?"

"No."

"Julia Roberts?"

"Of course not, why would you even ask that?"

"Her face is creepy. Charles Manson?"

"Yes."

"Lee Harvey Oswald?"

"Surprisingly, no."

"Phil Specter?"

"No."

"Dr. Phil?"

"Yes, actually."

I gaped. "I was just kidding that time. Really?"

Gabriel nodded, pausing to sip his ginger ale. The flight attendant had poured it into a wine glass just because it looked nicer than the little plastic cups the people on commercial flights would normally get. How delightfully pointless. Then again, private jets were known for their luxury.

"Really. His good intentions are enough to throw you off his scent. All the dirt he does is behind the scenes. Little things. Mainly psychological manipulation."

I shook my head. "I always knew there was something demonic about that guy. Never could put my finger on it. Someone should have warned Oprah."

The archangel smiled. "I suppose all the 'good' he's done cancels things out. We keep a close eye on him anyway. Anyone else?"

"No, I've had my fun for now." I stretched my back, glancing out the window at the blue horizon drifting past us. Up here, it looked like we were crawling across the globe as slow and steady as a turtle when in actuality we were burning through miles like a flame climbing up a match. My first plane ride, and it was on a private jet. How lucky was that?

"I still can't believe the Demons' Door is in Canada. I was right about the ironic location thing," I said, crunching on a pretzel. The jet had much nicer things to eat—the attendant even offered me steak—

but I was told regular passengers got a soda and pretzels and I wanted my first plane ride to be authentic.

"Canadians aren't as innocent as you think," Gabriel said with a secretive look in his eyes. He loved to tease me with tidbits of information about the nature of the world. I wasn't allowed to ask many questions about Heaven or Hell, but things on Earth were pretty much up for grabs. No one knew more dirt than Gabriel when it came to angels and demons.

"Besides, it turned out to be convenient once the United States was founded. The younger demons are very attached to America because it's rather easy to make a living corrupting people here. The older demons favor developing countries. It's easier to get followers there."

"Makes sense." I exhaled, letting the humor slide out of me. "What should I expect when we get down there?"

"Well, Belial will be up to his usual tricks—mainly, trying to get a rise out of you—but the Door itself is different. I only know of it. No angel, save our rogue, has ever visited it. I must advise you to be on your guard because this meeting is most likely some sort of trap."

"Do you know about any plans in the works?"

The archangel shook his head and then brushed his blond hair out of his eyes. He usually kept it short and neat, but he was overdue for a haircut so his bangs dipped down over his eyebrows.

"Nothing yet. It is possible that the demons are working with the rogue angel in secret and that they want us to do something for them, but I've heard nothing to confirm that yet. I'm hoping this trip will enlighten us."

"Enlighten." I snorted. "That's a pretty word for it. The last time we met with the demons in person, it was a war. Should we be expecting the same thing?"

"So far, I haven't heard of any holy items surfacing, but being prepared for war isn't a bad idea. We're already in one anyway—it's just more subtle. The stakes are still the same."

I squirmed in my seat. "You sure know how to instill confidence, Gabe."

He leaned forward, patting the side of my knee. "We'll be alright, Jordan. We always are."

Just then, the intercom beeped and I heard the Captain's voice. "We're beginning our descent into Edmonton. Your attendant will come by to pick up trash momentarily. Make sure you have all your items and have a pleasant stay."

"He wouldn't be saying that if he were coming with us," I muttered. Nine hours on a private jet, even a nice one like this, had made me antsy and restless knowing that Hell was literally waiting for us down there. I refused to sleep during the flight for fear of Belial contacting me through my dreams again.

There was a limousine waiting for us when we landed — Gabriel didn't believe in public transportation, amusingly enough — that took us through the city to its outskirts. Belial had left a number for us to use when we arrived as well as the address to the Door. He had offered to pick us up, but we both firmly declined, which amused him. He knew it sounded like a trap, but that didn't stop him from asking anyway. The only way to get out of this situation was to stay smart and getting our own reliable transportation was the first step in the right direction.

To my surprise, the limo stopped in front of an abandoned paper mill about ten miles outside of downtown Edmonton. Snow had fallen that morning, leaving several inches for us to crunch through in our boots. I was used to cold weather having lived in both New Jersey and Albany all my life, but Canada cold was a completely different animal. I had about three layers of clothing on yet the bitter wind still nipped my cheeks and forehead.

Gabriel leaned down and tapped on the car window. The driver was an angel, and according to Gabriel, a rather effective bodyguard so I felt a bit safer.

"We should be out in less than thirty minutes," Gabriel told him. "If you see anything suspicious, or if we take longer than that, send for back up. I've got a team on standby for extraction."

The bodyguard nodded and rolled his window back up. Not a moment later, a second limousine glided up over the black ice and stopped. I tensed, sliding my gloved fingers into the pocket of my parka to touch the rosary I always carried. *Calm down, Amador. It's just a car.*

The door opened and Belial unfolded his tall frame from inside the car. He wore sunglasses and had braided his long hair to keep it out of his face. The rest of him was covered in black, as usual, but I felt a little better knowing that even he couldn't pull off alluring in this kind of weather. Too much clothing.

"I trust you had a pleasant flight," the demon said when he was within earshot of us.

Gabriel smiled, ever polite and civil, but it was as frigid as the ice beneath our shoes. "Of course. That's what private jets are for."

"All these years and you're still as posh as ever, Gabriel. I find it charming. You really should try to impart some of that on your brother."

He angled his face towards me, his smile widening to a grin. "Jordan. You look positively fetching. Like a female Michelin man."

I rolled my eyes. "No one looks sexy when they're cold."

"Not for lack of trying."

"Can we go inside now or are you going to continue flirting out here in the freezing cold?"

"How rude of me. I can certainly do that inside. This way, if you please."

He started across the empty parking lot towards the side door of the old building. The outside walls were such a dark grey that they looked almost black and they were caked with ice and snow. Surrounding the building were several acres that eventually stretched into the forest. The street ran past it for miles, but there were no houses or businesses in this particular area. No witnesses. Sounded like the perfect place for the entrance to Hell.

Gabriel went in after Belial for safety reasons and I followed, shutting the door behind me. The inside looked no better — old, rusty machines populated the floor dimly lit by the holes in the roof. I expected demons to pop out from the corners with weapons, but nothing happened. Just an empty, suspicious factory.

"Nice place," I said. "How much did Leatherface make you pay for it?"

Belial took off his sunglasses and clucked his tongue as he walked over to the nearest machine. "So cynical. You should know by now that things aren't always what they seem."

He peeled off his gloves and yanked a large black-handled lever. The panel slid out of sight and revealed a shiny metallic one beneath with a keypad and palm-recognition pad. Belial punched in a six-digit number and placed his hand on the pad. It beeped twice and the ground vibrated beneath us. We stepped back as the paper machine slid aside to reveal a set of stairs down a narrow passageway. There was one bare bulb to light the way.

"*That's* not suspicious," I said, unable to help myself.

Gabriel sighed, shaking his head at me. "Ever observant, aren't we?"

"Why, Jordan, are you saying you don't trust me?" Belial asked, widening his blue eyes to look innocent. It almost made me laugh. Dammit.

"I'd trust Hannibal Lecter before I'd trust you."

He flashed me a toothy grin, altering his voice to sound like the cannibal himself as portrayed by Sir Anthony Hopkins. "I hate rude people."

Gabriel and I shared a look. He shrugged. "Well, you walked right into that one."

"I did, didn't I?" I turned to Belial. "I'll go down your Death Stairs, but you go first."

Belial bowed his head. "With pleasure."

The demon began his descent. I glanced at Gabriel and couldn't disguise my reluctance.

He squeezed my hand, dropping his voice to a murmur. "If anything happens, run. Do not wait for me, do not hesitate, do not be a hero, just get out of here. Understand?"

I nodded. He turned and went down the stairs. I took a deep breath and forced myself to follow him, placing both palms against the cool stone walls as I went. The rough solidity helped me stay calm despite my limited line of sight. Our footsteps echoed in the constricted space, seeming to punctuate the sound of my heartbeat in my ears. The bulb served as my vantage point. I had counted about fifteen steps when I passed it and figured we were about halfway down. All at once, the vibrations from earlier rumbled down the walls and then I heard a heavy, slithering sound.

"What's that?"

I whipped around to see the panel sliding back over the entrance to the stairwell, eliminating the last bit of light other than the bulb. My breathing hitched up. I fought to stay calm as I turned back around to continue down the steps.

Belial spoke and the narrow stairwell made it sound like he was all around me. "Is there a problem?"

"No," I said, attempting to sound unaffected. "How much farther is it?"

"Not far," the demon replied in a dreamy voice. He was playing with me. Bastard.

We kept walking and everything disappeared in the inky depths, so dark I couldn't even see my hand in front of my face. I waited for something to grab me or for a knife to be jammed into my side, but then I stepped onto a landing and bumped into one of the guys.

"Forgive me, there is another door here. I always have trouble finding the key," Belial said, and I could hear him moving around.

"The key? How can you *possibly* see the lock right now?"

"I have excellent night vision. You'd be surprised at what I can see."

I felt hot breath next to my face and jerked backwards, colliding with Gabriel in the dark.

The archangel steadied me, hardening his voice. "Enough games, demon. Let us in or I will make you."

"Killjoy."

I heard the click of locks sliding back. Light spilled onto the landing. I squinted, putting my hand up as my eyes adjusted, and walked through. The room wasn't much of a room at all, but rather like a hallway leading to yet another door. There were two hulking men standing with their backs to the adjacent walls decked out in armor as if they were on some sort of SWAT team. The energy bubbling around them told me they were demons, and powerful ones at that. The automatic weapons in their gloved hands also spoke volumes about their purpose.

"Gentlemen, we need to see the Puppeteer," Belial said.

The two men glanced at each other through their goggles and nodded. "You'll need to be searched," one of them said.

I glared at the back of Belial's head. "You didn't say anything about that."

He turned enough to give me his profile. "It must have slipped my mind."

I stepped forward and Gabriel caught my arm. "Relax. It's nothing we can't handle, right?"

"Right," I muttered, unzipping my parka.

The man on the left took it, hanging the garment on a hook nearby. He searched all the pockets, finding my rosary and three vials of holy water, while I unzipped my second coat. He took that one as well, discovering my .38 Chief Special Smith & Wesson, and glared at me. I shrugged and took off my jacket last. He went through it, finding

~ 68 ~

nothing but peppermints, my cell phone, and my wallet. He motioned for me to put my arms against the wall.

I pressed my palms to the concrete, reminding myself not to panic as the tall guard came up behind me and started patting me down.

"I don't suppose there's any way I can take over for you?" Belial asked the guard.

"Shut up," Gabriel and I both chorused. The demon merely chuckled in response.

Once he was sure I was weaponless, the guard went back to his spot by the door and the second guy searched Gabriel. When he finished, he regarded us both with a heavy expression. "Don't make us have to come get you."

When he opened the door, I expected to see another huge door with flames belting from around it and maybe some sort of mystic chanting. Wrong.

The first thing I noticed was that there was music playing— some sort of Bollywood 1960's swing tune—and we were no longer on the lower most level of the place. Metal clanked underfoot leading up to a huge computer console with six monitors. The acrid stench of sulfur permeated the air. Several feet behind the computer was the Demons' Door.

The Door stood at about nine feet tall and was hidden behind thick glass panels on three sides. There were three chambers on either side of the panels with intercoms built into the glass and a metal tube coming from the top of each one. The Door itself looked like a portal from a sci-fi film. It didn't appear solid but rather like something between a liquid and a gas. Every few seconds, something would make it ripple and the color would change from dark brown to umber to emerald and then back to brown. I would have stared at it forever had I not noticed something else.

An enormous leather chair had been pulled up in front of the massive keyboard of the console. Propped up on one side were two skinny brown legs with varicose veins mottled over the skin.

Belial cleared his throat when we walked over and the chair turned, revealing an old black woman with short grey hair and dark freckles spotted on her cheeks. She held a half-eaten Kit Kat bar in one bony hand, regarding the three of us with eyes the color of chimney smoke.

"Well, now. Wot de hell you doin' here, boss?"

My eyebrows rose at the sound of her thick Jamaican accent. Demons never failed to surprise me.

"We are in need of your services, Morgana," Belial said.

She bit into the chocolate, eying him. "Wot fer? Ain't you got it all figured out, boss man?"

"Brilliant as I am, I'm not omniscient. You know this better than most."

Morgana snorted. "Got dat right. Why you bring de angel and de girl fer?"

"A truce. We need to find someone."

"Ah, ah!" She chortled, dropping her feet to the floor. "I know wot you come fer, boss man. Been waiting fer your call."

"Good, then you can make this quick—"

"Not so fast, sweet talker," she interrupted, pointing the candy at his chest.

"You got to have sometin' I want too, y'know."

Belial glowered at her. "I am one of the Princes of Hell. I don't need to bargain with you. You have no choice but to obey me or—"

"Or wot? Ya send me back? I been in Hell before. You can't make de experience any worse fer me."

"She has a point," I admitted.

Belial sent me a dirty look. Morgana eyed me, eating the last piece of her Kit Kat before speaking. "A Seer, hmm? You got to be de one giving him all dis trouble."

I hesitated, not sure where she was going with her comment, but then the old woman grinned. "You a hero, y'know. He tink he know better den alla us, but you prove him wrong. Makes you kin."

I bit my lower lip to keep from smiling at Belial's annoyed expression. "Uh, thanks."

"Shall we get back to the task at hand?" Gabriel interjected.

Morgana frowned. "Always business, Gabriel. No time fer fun. Don' miss dat about you."

She faced Belial again. "So wot you gonna give me if I help you?"

"What do you want?"

"I want off dis job. Seven centuries I been here. Cold. No food. No interesting thing to talk about or do. Jes give dese demons bodies and dat it. You give me dat and I tell you where he is."

Belial stared her down for a handful of seconds. She didn't flinch. Brave woman.

Finally, he extended one hand. "Deal."

She shook it once and wheeled around, going to work on the console. She had to swipe at least ten empty Kit Kat wrappers out of the way before she could get to work. A demon with a sweet tooth. Who knew?

"Mebbe six months ago, we get an angel here askin' fer a human body. In all my years, I never hear of sometin' like dis. I tell him to go back but he plead wit me, promise he give me sometin' in return. Again, I tell him to go back. He say he know sometin' about de Apocalypse. I thought dat might be worth de trouble comin' so I make him a body."

"Apocalypse? Perhaps you'd like to clarify?" Gabriel asked.

She tossed an annoyed look over her shoulder. "Bright lights. Trumpets. Four horsemen. How much Bible you done read, boy?"

Gabriel sighed. "Did he mention what would facilitate this so-called Apocalypse?"

"No. When I ask him dat, he say I will know when I see it. But he had sometin' wit him, sometin' important dat came through wit his spirit."

"What did it look like?"

She paused. "Mebbe a page of sometin? Like from a book?"

Gabriel nodded, his face settling into a frown. "Unusual. I'll look into it. What kind of body did he ask for?"

"Nuttin' special. Wanted sometin' plain, sometin' dat would make him blend in wit de rest of de humans. I got it right here. Hold on."

Her bony fingers went to work typing and clicking with her wireless mouse. Eventually, she pulled up a photo. My entire body went cold.

It was the redheaded man from the restaurant.

I stumbled, catching myself on one side of the console after my knees went weak.

Gabriel immediately came over to me. "Jordan, what's wrong? Do you know this man?"

"He was...he was at the restaurant a few days ago," I whispered, hating how my voice trembled when I spoke. "He could have killed me, Gabriel. I wouldn't have even seen it coming."

He rubbed my shoulders, trying to calm me down. "It's alright. You're safe now. That is what counts."

"But why didn't he try to kill me?"

Gabriel opened his mouth to answer, but Belial did it for him. "I'm sure he knows that you're married to Michael. Killing you would constitute a betrayal and so he left you alive out of respect."

"Why would he care about respect? He's butchered six innocent people."

Belial shrugged. "Even murderers have a code of honor."

I glared at him. "You would know."

The first sign of anger flickered across his face. Gabriel squeezed my arm in warning. He was right. I was scared and so I wanted to hide it by picking a fight. Stupid and childish of me.

I took a deep breath and cleared my mind. "Morgana, is there any way to track him?"

She sucked her teeth. "Course der is. We can't let dem all run amok. Dey got a tracking chip implanted in each body."

The demon went to work again and activated the man's tracker. The computer screen brought up a globe and started to search for the signal. Seconds later, we heard a beeping sound and red letters appeared at the top of the screen: SIGNAL LOST.

Morgana's jaw dropped. "Dat can't be right."

"Check it again," Belial ordered.

She typed in the code again, but received the same message. "Dis can't be."

"Why?" I asked.

Morgana pointed to her breastbone. "De trackers come implanted right next to de heart. If dey try to get it out, it causes cardiac arrest. Don' know how de hell he managed to remove it."

"That means he had to have seen a very talented heart surgeon," Gabriel said. "At least we have somewhere to go from here. Pull up his last known whereabouts."

She retrieved a list of coordinates. The globe spun around until it landed on Cleveland, Ohio.

"Print off this and a photograph," the archangel continued. "We need to get moving immediately. There's no telling when the next Seer is going to Awaken and we have to find him before that happens."

She obeyed and gave the papers to Gabriel and another copy to Belial. "If dat is all, I got bags to pack. Seven hundred years of de world to catch up on."

I smiled in spite of myself. "Good luck with that."

Morgana grinned. "Same to you."

We went back up to the surface and got in the limo.

"Let's return to the airport," Gabriel said. "Call your husband. He'll want to know what's going on."

I nodded and dialed Michael's number. He answered on the second ring.

"Hey, gorgeous. How's it going?"

"Oh, just dandy," I answered with an exhausted sigh, leaning my head back on the leather seat. "We found out who the rogue angel is. It turns out he's the guy who left that hundred dollar bill for me at the restaurant a few days ago."

"What?"

A weak smile crossed my lips. "Yeah, I know. But the good news is that now we have a photo and a clue to follow. He deactivated the tracking chip inside his human body and his last known whereabouts is Cleveland. Since you're the combat expert, you can join us if we pick up on his trail."

He sighed. "Alright. I'm just glad you're okay. Well, okay-ish."

I snorted. "Don't jinx it. I'll call you when we land in Cleveland. *Te amo.*"

"*Igualmente.*"

He hung up. I stuffed the phone back in my pocket and pressed my forehead against the cold glass of the window, watching as we pulled off into the street to head back to the airport.

Gabriel was studying the papers Morgana had given him with the places that the rogue angel visited before he took out the tracker.

"So what kind of paper do you think he had with him?"

"I'm not sure," Gabriel said, scanning the pages. "But I have a hunch that this rogue angel may have been a Scribe."

"Scribe?"

He glanced up. "Yes. It's an angel assigned to keep track of the written records in Heaven."

"There are records in Heaven? Of what?"

"Everything in existence. Only God is all-knowing. We only know what gets translated from *Et Symphoniae Temporis*, or the Symphony of Time."

I held up a hand. "Okay, wow, you're gonna have to explain that one for the slow people in the audience."

The archangel chuckled before continuing. "In Heaven, the events of the universe unfold within an infinite stream of music. We have Scribes that record every strain of music and then translate it into words. This way, the people who missed out on life when they were alive may have the chance to read about it if they so desire when they enter into Heaven. The translated version is called *Et Liber Tempor*, or the Book of Time."

"Why are the names Latin?"

"It's a dead language, and so it's the best method of communication in emergencies. If we need to speak about something that men need not know about, we use Latin. In Heaven, there is a universal language. I can't really explain it to you, but you'll understand when you get there someday."

I paused, absorbing this information. "Is it possible that this rogue angel stole a page from the Book of Time?"

"It's unlikely, but I suppose it is possible. I'll have my resources check to see if anything is missing. It would at least explain how he is able to kill the Seers before their Awakenings."

He paused. "We really should invent Hoogle."

"What?"

"Nothing."

CHAPTER SEVEN

JORDAN

"We shouldn't be doing this, y'know."

"Why's that?"

Michael shook his head, hiding a smile that I could still see out of the corner of my eye. Craig Ferguson, lovely talk show host though he was, couldn't keep my attention whenever Michael spoke to me in the dark. My senses were always somehow sharper at two o'clock in the morning, even with the TV on.

"You have work tomorrow. You should be sleeping."

I tried my best not to scowl, but it didn't work. "Well, we both know why I'm not. If you wanted me to sleep, you could always go down the street and get me a shot of bourbon."

Michael sighed. "I knew going cold turkey would make you cranky, but this is kinda ridiculous, Jordan."

"Deal with it," I grumbled, sliding downward so that the base of my skull rested against the arm of the couch. The suede rubbed my shoulders, unhidden by the tank top, and felt comforting, though not enough to lull me to sleep. I'd found this couch five blocks from this apartment and paid to get it steam cleaned three times before I hauled it into my place for permanent residence. The faded maroon still looked good against the hardwood floor in the den, even after a year.

Something about the late hour erased a few of the lines I had tried to keep drawn between Michael and myself, particularly the physical ones. My apartment was humid tonight so I was wearing boxer shorts and a tank top while Michael sported a plain white t-shirt and cargo pants. He lounged in the middle of the couch with his bare feet propped up on the coffee table while my legs were carelessly stretched out over him, bent slightly so that only my calves touched his thighs. Insomnia had consumed me in the midst of my rehabilitation from alcohol dependence. I hated it.

"You can go home, you know. You don't have to keep staying up late with me," I offered in a less hostile voice after the Late Late Show went to yet another commercial.

The archangel shrugged. "It wouldn't be very angelic of me."

I rolled my eyes. "Right. My fault. But you're still wasting your time. It'll be about four o'clock before I conk out and you really shouldn't put yourself through that."

"Well, that won't do." He shifted over a bit and, to my complete surprise, took hold of one of my feet, and started to massage it.

~ 75 ~

I stared. "What the hell are you doing?"

"What? You've never gotten a foot massage?"

I licked my lips, trying to figure out how to explain my predicament to him. "Yes, I've had them before, but never from someone who wasn't trying to have sex with me."

He laughed, clearly startled by the bluntness of my comment. But he also didn't stop massaging my foot. Hmm. "Oh. I didn't know foot massages had that connotation to them."

"That would be because you still haven't seen Pulp Fiction. But back to my original question…what the hell are you doing?"

"It's supposed to relax you."

His thumbs moved in circles over the arch of my foot. I had to bite my bottom lip to keep from sighing. Damn him. Did he have to be perfect at everything?

Eventually, the will to argue drained out of me. I flopped backwards on the couch, tossing one arm over my eyes.

"Fine, but I'm telling Gabriel that you're trying to seduce me."

"Are you seducible?"

"You'll find out if you keep that up."

He chuckled again, a low sound, and everything seemed to click – the atmosphere, the low Scottish voice and canned laughter in the background, Michael's long rough fingers against the thin cotton of my socks. I drifted off. I had always thought sleeping in front of the TV wasn't really sleeping because while most of my senses shut down I could still hear and feel things on some level.

By the time the show went off, Michael had figured I'd gone to sleep and turned off the TV. Gently, he deposited my legs on the couch and stood up. My left arm dangled off the side of the couch cushion while the right was curled up by my face. I had twisted half my body in mid-slumber so it probably looked odd to him. Faintly, I heard the rustling sound of cloth and then a heavenly weight over me, almost feather-light. He'd draped the blanket over me.

I was still conscious enough to feel his hand brush the hair away from my forehead and the quick press of his lips at the spot between my brows. Footsteps echoed across the room and the front door closed. I cuddled a throw pillow in the warm darkness and slept on.

From then on, Michael and I fell into an unspoken routine. It didn't matter what time either of us got home – he had a key, after all – we would collapse in front of the couch watching TV and he would give me a foot massage until I fell asleep. Every night, I told him he didn't have to wait up with me and every night he ignored me. I never told him, but his devotion meant as much to me as his protection from demons.

After a while, I realized that sleeping on the couch hurt my back so we migrated to my bedroom. I didn't realize it then, but those couple of weeks were a way for us to skirt the rules we knew all too well. Intimacy without sex. Closeness without wrecking the system. A kiss on the forehead, the soft touch of his fingers on my skin, were substitutes for what we really wanted, but could not have.

Eventually, my insomnia faded and the other withdrawal symptoms began to dissipate and so our nightly ritual ended, but something else filled the hole. Michael kept showing up and I kept letting him in. Unconsciously, we made the decision to walk that dangerous path step by treacherous step.

"Jordan?"

I stirred as I felt a warm hand on my shoulder. Gabriel stood over me.

"We'll be landing soon."

"Mmkay," I yawned, sitting up in my chair.

He sat and buckled his seatbelt, looking at me with a fond expression. "Sweet dreams, I trust?"

"How'd you guess?"

"You were smiling."

Heat washed over my cheeks. I was blushing. Good Lord. "Really?"

He chuckled. "Really. Why do you look so bashful about it?"

"It just sounds cheesy that I was smiling because I was dreaming about my husband." I fiddled with my wedding band. Michael smelted it himself. The craftsmanship was lovely, to the point where people at the restaurant asked me where I'd gotten it and I had to fumble for a reply. Couldn't tell them he made it out of his battle armor. I imagined they would send me to the funny farm.

"You're supposed to enjoy domestic bliss, you know," Gabriel said, arching an eyebrow.

"I know, but…" I hesitated, shrugging and glancing down at my hands. "…when you've had a lot of bad stuff happen to you in rapid succession, you get a little cautious about enjoying things. I keep waiting for the other shoe to drop. Wondering what the next horrible thing will be and if I'll be able to handle it."

Gabriel's expression softened. "You will. You underestimate yourself, Jordan. Your resilience is something that I admire more than any of your other traits."

His energy — a soothing aura — filled the air around me. I let it in. My nerves slowly relaxed until the anxiety was gone. He had always been good at keeping my paranoia at bay.

"And your gift for flattery is what I admire most about you."

"It comes with the territory of being God's Messenger. Make sure you call Michael when we land. I'll take care of contacting the demon."

"Thank you. Belial is unsettling enough in person. I don't want to hear that voice of his coming out of my cell phone," I said, making a face. "Besides, I doubt he'll flirt with you."

Gabriel arched an eyebrow. "You really don't know him, do you?"

My mouth dropped open. Before I could get a question out, the pilot came on the intercom again and instructed us to prepare for our descent into Ohio. We had two destinations on our list: the Cleveland Clinic, then the Cleveland Police Department. We needed the medical records of whatever the rogue angel had done to remove the tracker implant and the police department would allow us to fax all the information we had about him to the authorities as well as our own sources. If we got a name to go along with his face, even if it was a fake one or an alias, we'd have a much better chance of catching him. The angels had eyes everywhere and even though he seemed like a ghost, someone would spot him sooner or later.

I called Michael when we landed and told him to head to his place so we could send him the information via fax machine. Gabriel called Belial and told him to meet us at the clinic on Euclid Avenue, where the Health Data Services were. Gabriel had a friend in the department who could get us what we needed without too much of a fuss. Luckily, it was only ten minutes away from the police department so we wouldn't have to go too far. It was a little past four o'clock and we were going to have to get a hotel for the night before heading back to Albany in the morning — a four and a half hour flight. Too bad I didn't fly commercial. I could get some killer flyer miles on this trip.

We took a cab to the hospital, a modest thirty-minute ride, and arrived to find the demon waiting outside with a cigarette clutched between his lips. He had shed his enormous parka and instead wore a tasteful grey trench coat over a black suit with a red tie. The ensemble brought attention to his white skin and dark hair, still braided, and I suspected he had taken great care in picking out the outfit. I had met many demons in my time, but he was by far the most preoccupied with his appearance.

He smiled when we walked up, exhaling a long stream of smoke from one corner of his mouth. "Shall we?"

"Why do you look so happy?"

Belial tossed his cigarette onto the concrete and stomped it out. "I'm a hunter by instinct, my dear. We've got ourselves a trail. There's nothing I find more thrilling than pursuit."

I shook my head. "Figures."

He arched one thin eyebrow. "And what does that mean?"

I cleared my throat, my cheeks filling with hot blood. That hadn't come out right. It sounded like I was implying that he enjoyed chasing me. "Nothing. Let's go."

Belial followed us inside the clinic. The glass doors parted and frigid air smacked me in the face, brushing my hair back for a second. Hospitals were always bone-chillingly cold. I could feel my pulse racing. I tried to breathe slowly. This place wasn't a psychiatric hospital like the one I'd been dragged into when they took my mother, but all hospitals made me feel uneasy. Something about the shiny floors, non-descript paint on the walls, and the unnervingly calm medical staff bugged me. It probably always would.

Gabriel stepped up to the front desk and began talking with one of the nurses. I stood out of earshot with my eyes closed so I could concentrate on breathing normally. Naturally, the demon next to me spoke up.

"Something wrong, my pet?"

I opened my eyes and glared at him. "You know damn well what's wrong."

"So the mighty Jordan Amador has a weakness," he mused. "Though I suppose you do have a good reason for not liking hospitals. The irony is quite amusing. Hospitals are places of healing and birth yet for you, they have always meant harm and death."

"You're really not helping."

He shrugged one shoulder. "Wasn't trying to."

I quelled the anger building in my gut and focused on keeping my heart rate normal. Out of the corner of my eye, I saw Belial looking around with a contemplative expression. It instantly made me suspicious. Gabriel and I had been looking for a trap ever since we got here and it would be so very like Belial to spring one in a hospital. After all, he'd done it before.

There was a pretty brunette nurse talking to a patient seated behind us and I could tell he was checking her out. She finished speaking with an older man and caught Belial's gaze as she straightened. He smiled, and I recognized that smile. It was pure seduction. Nothing overt—just a smile that promised a good time.

She walked over, clearing her throat, and I could tell she was trying not to seem eager. "Can I help you with something?"

"No," I answered, hoping I'd be able to break the spell he'd cast on her. "We're good. The nurse at the desk is calling someone for us."

"Oh." She faltered a bit. I prayed for her to run as fast as she could in the opposite direction before the demon could get his hooks in.

As if reading my mind, Belial spoke. "Thank you for offering, Nurse Ramsey. It was very kind of you."

She smiled, exposing twin dimples. "No problem. It's my job."

"Well, if you don't mind me asking, do you get a coffee break sometime in the next half-hour?"

"Yes. Why?"

"I've been doing some research about hospital personnel and I'd be grateful if you would give me a little insight into your job," he asked with picture perfect politeness.

"That'd be fine. I know a nice place around the corner—"

"Oh, damn," I interrupted, throwing up my hands. "I just remembered we have an appointment at another hospital in ten minutes. Maybe a rain check, Nurse Ramsey?"

She seemed a little crestfallen, but she nodded anyway. To my dismay, she handed him her card and hurried off down the hallway. I sighed, hoping the interaction would put her off of him, but I knew better.

Belial watched her go, stuffed the card in his pocket, and then gave me a nasty glare. "I cannot believe you just cockblocked me."

"That doesn't count," I hissed. "For all I know, you'll take her back to your hotel and eat her throat out. I'm not gonna let some innocent woman die because of you."

He stepped closer, a smirk sliding across his lips. "I rarely kill my prey. You should know that better than most. I draw power from corrupting the innocent. She was not in mortal danger."

"Like hell."

The demon let out an amused snort. "You seem quite protective of people you don't know, Jordan. How do you know I wasn't merely going to invite her back to my place for sex? Or is that why you stopped me? Because you're—"

I held up my hand. "If you say 'jealous,' I swear I'll jam my rosary so far down your throat that you'll shit a cross."

"Very well. Envious, then."

I moved towards him, but Gabriel stepped between us. "Our contact has asked us to come to the records lab. Can you two stop bickering enough to join me?"

Belial swept a hand in the direction of the hallway. "Ladies first."

"Bite me," I muttered, walking past him.

"Is that a request or a command?"

I glanced at Gabriel. "Can I shoot him? Please?"

The blond archangel shook his head at me. "I swear, you are almost as bad as your husband sometimes."

"I take that as a compliment in this case." We continued down the hallway to the lab where the records were held. When we walked in, I spied a gentleman in his late fifties with curly white hair and a mustache.

He smiled when he spotted us, rising from his seat in front of a computer. "Gabriel. It's been a while."

Gabriel shook his fellow angel's hand. "Too long. Jordan, this is Dr. Robert Stanton, an old friend of mine."

"Nice to meet you, Doc."

Dr. Stanton nodded to me and then frowned when he noticed Belial standing behind us. "And what's he doing here?"

Belial smirked. "A pleasure to meet you too."

"An unavoidable complication," Gabriel answered, ignoring the demon. "Belial was kind enough to take us to the Demon's Door and has been assisting us on our hunt for the rogue angel."

Dr. Stanton's frown deepened. "It's still hard to believe that one of us could do something like this. Him—" He jerked his thumb in Belial's direction.

"—I could understand."

"Perhaps we're not so different after all," the demon said, earning a glare from all three of us.

Gabriel shook his head and gestured to the computer. "Why don't we get started? Now, we don't have a name but we do have height, weight, a picture, and a window of time when he would have been through here."

"Sure." Dr. Stanton took the paper and typed in the date and other information we had on the rogue angel.

"What kind of procedure would he have gotten?"

"Heart surgery," Gabriel said. "The demons have tracker implants that will cause cardiac arrest if they are removed. He would have needed a very talented surgeon to get it out without killing him."

Stanton continued typing and we held our breath for a second as the computer did a search. After a moment, it came up "No Matching Results."

"There's no one matching that description who had a scheduled operation like that," the doctor said, rubbing his chin.

Gabriel shook his head. "That can't be right. This is one of the best cardiology clinics in the world. He had to have come here for that reason."

"Doctor?" I asked. "What if he came in as an ER patient?"

He glanced at me, confused. "Can you clarify that a bit?"

"Well, what if he did something that would cause him to need to be defibrillated? Maybe that shock would deactivate the tracker. Plus, if he ended up needing emergency surgery I'm sure the ER docs would have removed it."

Stanton paused. "I suppose that's an option. He could do something like overdose on potassium. They would have to get it out of his system and then defibrillate him. I'll check for that."

He entered the new information in and did another search. This time, a file popped up. We leaned in and I read it out loud.

"Male patient, mid-twenties to early thirties, five-foot-six, 160 lbs., brought in off the street from potassium overdose. Resuscitated at 11:03pm. Patient placed in facility overnight. Doctors went to check on him and he disappeared. Police report filed with the Cleveland Police Department the next day."

"Who was the attending physician?"

"Dr. Lee Creswell. He gave a statement to the police. I can help you with the records, but if you go poking around without the proper authority, you could get in trouble."

Gabriel nodded. "Alright. Then we go to the police station and see what we can find. I know someone in their department. If he skipped out on the bill, they'll have a file on him that should help us. Do you have a fax machine I can use?"

"Certainly." Stanton pointed to the one across the room and Gabriel scooped up the papers.

Belial stepped forward, addressing the doctor. "If they had removed the tracker, what would have been done with it?"

"Not sure. It would have been up to the doctor. My guess is it would have been thrown out as trash or given it to the police when they filed the report. They probably would've thought it was some kind of shrapnel."

I glanced at Belial. "Why does that matter anyway?"

He shrugged. "I am merely being careful. If the authorities did get the tracker, that may present a problem if they have any detectives who dig their noses into the case. Our entire operation would be under fire if the human government became involved. We have always found ways to circumvent detection, but slip-ups like this are dangerous. The government may not be very smart, but it's persistent."

Gabriel returned a moment later, shoving his phone in his pocket. "We've got the files sent to Michael and he'll get them to the proper authorities. Let's get going. Thank you again, Dr. Stanton."

"Always a pleasure, Gabriel. Good luck."

With that, we left.

"Alright. Let's review what we know. Just the facts. No speculation."

"Okay. We know that he had the demons engineer him a body because we'd be able to trace him if he were in an angelic body. We also know he deactivated the tracker implant. We know he has extensive martial arts and weapons training. We know he is aware of my existence but has chosen to avoid attacking me so far. Security cameras at the airport have him boarding a plane six months ago heading for Kentucky where we found our first murdered Seer, Danny Bowen. He booked the flight under the name Edmond Saraf. His last known whereabouts is Raleigh, after he murdered Erica Davalos."

Gabriel pressed one hand to his mouth as he paced back and forth at the foot of my bed. The hotel room was stunning—not by my efforts, of course, but Gabriel's. He insisted that I stay with him in his luxury suite, which was so nice that I had been afraid to touch anything when we walked in. The room was done in burgundy and gold. It could have easily allowed for another king size bed in addition to the two already in it. The bathtub had Jacuzzi jets and the room service was unbelievable. The archangel had ordered blackened salmon with bleu cheese sauce, asparagus, and white wine. At his urging, I'd gotten a twelve ounce steak, mashed potatoes, and sautéed spinach. No alcohol, naturally. Being Gabriel, he had asked if it was okay for him to have some in my presence. What a sweetheart.

"What do we have on theories?" he asked.

I dropped my gaze to the pages scattered on the bed before me. "Whatever he saw in the Book of Time spooked him and made him think that the Seers of the world would bring about the Apocalypse. What did Raphael say about the missing page?"

"He told me that he checked with the Scribes and they were able to confirm that there was a page missing for the time span that includes this year. They will have to go back through the Symphony of Time and retranslate it. It will take a while, unfortunately."

"So does that mean we can't find future Seers until they finish the translation?" He nodded with a grim expression on his face.

I sighed, raking my hair back. "We can't be reactive, we need to be proactive. We need a tip of some sort or he's going to keep killing innocent people."

"And we need to find out why he came to see you," he added, continuing to pace.

"Could you go before the Father or the Son and request information?"

Gabriel shook his head. "We're not allowed to ask about the future."

"But you do know when the actual Rapture is going to occur, right?"

He glanced at me in surprise, then nodded. I considered this. "So you know it's not the Rapture that he's talking about?"

"No. That's a different matter entirely."

"Then I guess we'll have to start by researching the different types of Apocalypses that are predicted in human history. Maybe one of them is the one he thinks will come to pass. Otherwise, we just have to hope that one of the angels spots him and we take him down."

"Indeed."

I hesitated before asking my next question. "Do you remember when Belial asked if we were going to kill the rogue angel? What's your answer to that?"

Gabriel sighed, pushing his blond locks out of his eyes. "I don't know. It would destroy some part of my soul to have to kill one of my brothers, but if nothing can be done to stop him otherwise…I suppose we would have to."

A hush fell over us. "This sucks."

"Yes, it does."

The archangel took a deep breath and let it out slowly. "I'm restless. I'm going to do a few laps in the pool downstairs. Will you be alright without me?"

I brandished the remote control to the flat screen TV. "I've got cable. We're good."

He kissed my forehead and went into the bathroom with his suitcase to change. I waved when he left and opened my laptop to start researching theories of different Apocalypses. I turned on the TV at a low volume for background noise as I worked, completely consumed by my search until my cell phone rang roughly an hour later. I answered without looking.

"Hello?"

"So…what are you wearing right now?"

I rolled my eyes, sighing. "What do you want, Belial?"

He chuckled before answering. "I trust you and the archangel have some sort of plan for the rest of the week. Would you care to enlighten me?"

"Not really, but fine. We're flying back to Albany in the morning because I've got work but in the meantime, we're compiling different Apocalypse conspiracies to see if we can find one that matches whatever the rogue angel believes in. Feel free to do your own research. Being a demon, I'm sure you've got a lot of plans about ending the world."

"Of course. I'll do my best."

"I'm sure you will," I answered with the utmost sarcasm. Just then, there was a knock at the door. I lowered the phone, calling, "Who is it?"

A male voice answered. "Room service."

Gabriel's two slices of six-layer chocolate cake had arrived. Huzzah. I adored his weakness for sweets. I got up and walked towards the door.

"Well, it's been fun chatting with you, but I've got to go."

"What for? A loving phone call to your husband?"

"No. Something more important than you—cake."

I reached the door and checked the peep hole. It was not room service. The man standing there was my height with red hair and brown eyes.

Edmond Saraf.

The rogue angel.

"Shit."

CHAPTER EIGHT

JORDAN

The door smashed in half as the rogue angel kicked it. I stumbled backwards and yelled into the phone, "Call Gabriel, now!" before Edmond knocked it out of my hand and it crashed into pieces against the wall.

He came at me. His blows were viciously fast and I could barely block them, driven backwards by the pure force of his fists. He aimed at my face and torso, ignoring my legs for the first minute of the attack. I landed a solid punch to his solar plexus, winding him, then kicked him in the same place, trying to put some space between us. He caught my ankle and threw me against the oak desk on the far wall. It hit me hard in the small of my back. I cried out as it sent a damn near crippling spiral of pain through me. The lamp crashed onto the floor, scattering glass.

I grabbed a piece of the broken ceramic and blocked the high kick he aimed at my face, stabbing him in the thigh. He growled and stumbled back, ripping the piece out. Blood oozed down his black slacks.

I scrambled for another impromptu weapon as he darted forward again. Using all my strength, I ripped the flat screen out of the wall and aimed it as his head. He blocked it with both forearms, cracking the screen. I used the couple of seconds' grace to kick him in the kneecap, hoping to dislocate it. He twisted to the side just as I did so the blow glanced off his shin instead. He tore the TV out of my grip and tossed it aside, reaching for me again.

"In the name of the Father, I reject!" I shouted. My shield solidified in front of me and his hands stopped only inches from my throat, giving me a fleeting moment to think. His strength and speed were far too great—I needed to buy time for Gabriel to get upstairs and make this a fair fight.

The rogue angel made a quick sign in the air with his hands, muttering something in Latin. My shield crumbled around me like invisible sand—something I could feel but not see.

"Strike!" I thrust out one hand, and four energy shards launched towards him. He threw himself to the side. They flew past him, though one clipped his right arm, spilling blood.

I used the extra second to rip the cabinet door off its hinges, then swung it with all my might. He blocked it with his forearms, but the force knocked him over. I brought the door down. He stopped it in mid-swing with one foot, using the other to kick my right arm at the elbow. I cried out and dropped the door, stumbling backward as he leapt back up in a blur of motion.

I opened my mouth to use another energy attack, but he chopped me in the throat and kicked my legs out from under me. I fell to the carpet and writhed, unable to scream as he climbed on top of me and wrapped his gloved hands around my throat. I kneed him in the side as hard as I could over and over again, but he wouldn't budge. I clawed at his arms, his face, thrashing like a fish that had been dragged onto dry land. My lungs burned with the need for air, but I managed to squeeze out something as he slowly choked me to death.

"Please...don't...do this."

All at once, his face changed. Throughout the attack, his brows had been set in a hard line and he showed no emotion as he ruthlessly beat me. After I spoke, guilt slid across his plain features and made him seem almost human. What the hell was going on inside his head?

"I am sorry," he whispered. "I must do this. Forgive me. Forgive me, Jordan."

I tried again, though I could feel the creeping sensation of unconsciousness crawling through my body. "Think about...your brother...Michael. Not me. Michael."

He squeezed his eyes shut, but I felt his fingers losing some of their vise-like grip around my neck. "Don't say that. This is for the good of mankind. He will understand."

"Please, let us help you," I croaked. My eyelids began fluttering. If he didn't let go in the next minute, I'd be dead. *Keep talking, Amador. You've got to talk him out of it.*

The rogue angel shook his head, tightening his hold again. "I cannot. This is my burden. He who receives light from above, from the fountain of light; no other doctrine needs, though granted true."

"You're...smart enough...to quote *Paradise Regained*," I rasped through my last bit of air. "You should be smart enough...to know this is wrong."

"The needs of the many outweigh the needs of the few. Someone must be sacrificed in order for others to live. Please forgive me, Jordan."

His fingers dug into my skin so hard that I felt my body go numb. Black began to eat at the edges of my vision, but I could still see the mournful look on his face just before everything went dark.

I woke up in a bed. The massive pain attacking my throat, my arms, and my back was the first indication that I had survived the rogue angel's assault. My eyes felt like they weighed several tons when I tried to open them and the only sound I could make was a reedy groan.

There was something wet and cold on my neck—maybe an ice pack. I lifted a shaky hand to move it. Someone caught my wrist before I could. The sudden touch made me panic, but I still couldn't open my eyes because I felt so drained. I squirmed, trying to free my hand, but the person wouldn't let go, instead pressing it down on the bed by my side.

"Leave it," a soft voice said. "Your throat is badly damaged."

At last, I managed to open my eyes and everything sharpened into focus. Another hotel room. Not as nice as Gabriel's, but still exceptional as far as hotel rooms go. Blue walls instead of burgundy. Flat screen TV. Mini-fridge. Swell.

When I tilted my head to the side, I realized the man sitting next to me was not Gabriel, but Belial.

"Y-You…" I managed to stammer. My mouth was drier than a bone so I couldn't get out a whole sentence.

The demon pressed one gloved finger to my lips. "Don't talk. I need to heal you before you can do that. Here, drink this."

He handed me a glass of water. I stared at him. He rolled his eyes upward in exasperation. "I just saved your life. I have no reason to poison you, Jordan. Drink."

Belial removed the ice pack. I lifted my head far enough to sniff the glass—just to be sure—then drank the water, wincing as it burned all the way down my severely damaged throat. If the rogue angel had tried any harder, he would have crushed my windpipe. I was extremely lucky to be alive.

Belial set the glass on the nightstand, leaning over me on the bed. "Hold still."

I panicked as his face drifted closer to mine and pushed my hands against his shoulders, but he grabbed them and held them down with an annoyed expression.

"Be still, woman. I'm not going to hurt you."

He stopped just short of touching me and blew air over the column of my throat. A cool, tingling sensation rushed down my neck all the way to my collarbone. The raw, aching pain subsided, replaced with a comforting numbness. His hands let go of my arms and he straightened up.

"There. Better?"

I nodded, licking my dry lips. "W-What happened?"

"I called Gabriel right after your phone went dead. We both got up to the room just as you passed out. The rogue angel did a Hans Gruber out the window and Gabriel ordered me to take you back to my room while he gave chase. That was about twenty minutes ago. I have not heard from him since so I assume he is still chasing the rogue angel."

I tried to sit up, but the bruises the rogue angel's fists had left made it hard to balance on my arms. A sharp pain slithered up my back every time I moved.

"N-Need to tell Michael. Let him know—"

"He already knows. I called him."

"What did you say?"

"That the angel had attacked and Gabriel went after him, and that you were safe."

"Did you tell him where we were?"

He arched an eyebrow. "Maybe."

"Asshole. You knew it would upset him that Gabriel left me with you."

"Life is not without its little pleasures," he said with an insufferable smirk.

I shook my head, pulling off the thick comforter covering my body. "I'm fine. Take me back to the hotel."

My back stung yet again and I whimpered, squeezing my eyes shut momentarily. Belial caught my arms and lowered me to the mattress. "You're not going anywhere until your wounds heal. It won't take long. Just be patient."

"Don't have time for patience," I said through shallow breaths. "People will die. Gabriel needs my help."

"You'll do these people no good by getting yourself killed," Belial answered with a harsh glare, his fingers tightening on my upper arms.

"Rest. I may be a murderer among other things, but I will protect you until your archangel returns."

"And how do I know this isn't some kind of trap?"

He let a secretive smile slip across his lips. "I guess you'll just have to trust me. Now be a good girl and rest. I'll wake you when Gabriel returns."

"You tell me to trust you and then you tell me to fall asleep in your presence. How stupid do you think I am?"

"On a scale of one to ten?"

I gritted my teeth to stop myself from yelling at him. "Swear on your demonic law that you will not harm me and I'll sleep."

"You have my word as an archdemon that I will not harm you," he replied with a straight face.

I met his gaze for a long moment and then relaxed. I closed my eyes just before I spoke. "Did I thank you?"

"No, you didn't."

"I will."

His chuckles followed me into the deep warmth of sleep.

Once more, I felt strong fingers on my back, stroking up and down, soothing the ache that had settled in my muscles. Little by little, the pain dissipated until I knew the bruise had vanished. The healing hands traced my sides, tickling my ribs, gliding down to my hips. I groaned as they massaged my waist, relaxing me further, and shivered when warm lips came in contact with the spot between my shoulder blades. A hot, muscular chest melted into my spine and the hands dipped lower, unbuttoning my jeans and sliding inside. A muffled sound escaped me as pleasure unfurled from the intimate touch, spreading from my lower body outward until my breath came in shallow pants.

I awoke with a startled noise building in my throat. I was face down on the bed with someone kneeling above me, his hands on my back. My t-shirt was bunched beneath my arms, nearly exposing my bra, and the pain on my forearms and spine had vanished. I tried to roll over but the strong hands were upon me again, holding my arms down so I couldn't move.

"What the hell, Belial?" I snapped, struggling to get free.

He held me still, replying in a mild voice. "I thought you were a heavier sleeper. Clearly, I was mistaken."

"What are you doing? Why is my shirt halfway off and why are you on top of me?" I demanded, giving up my struggle when I realized I couldn't get loose.

He sighed, sounding exasperated. "I told you to rest because I knew you would not allow me to heal your back while you were conscious. You woke up just as I finished."

"Finished what? What else were you doing to me while I was asleep?" I said, glaring at him from over my shoulder.

He smirked. "Aren't we presumptuous?"

"Presumptuous, huh? Why are my pants unbuckled then?"

"The clothing was getting in the way," the demon sniffed. "I did nothing salacious to you."

"You swear?"

Belial let out a dry chuckle, lowering his face until it was only inches away from mine. "Now that's where I draw the line. I don't have to answer that question because it wasn't part of our deal."

"You can't harm anyone—"

"—and I didn't. If I did something to you, and I'm not saying I did, you can be sure that it wouldn't have been unpleasant. I've had centuries of practice, after all."

I closed my eyes for a second to restrain myself from spewing obscenities at him. "Will you let me up now?"

"Do you promise not to punch me?"

"No."

"Then I guess you'll just have to stay here until you calm down, won't you?"

"I hate you."

"I know."

I lay there breathing deeply until the anger subsided and I could think straight. He was probably telling the truth. I definitely wouldn't have let him touch me like this while I was awake. Furthermore, the pain from the fight was all gone so he must have kept his word about healing me. It also occurred to me that Belial got his powers from violence, death, and sex, so doing something intimate may have increased his energy supply. But that didn't mean the dream was all a dream. He couldn't have kissed me because it would have burned him, but he could've easily done other things wearing those gloves of his.

"You can let go now."

~ 92 ~

His fingers unwrapped themselves from around my wrists. He slid backwards on the bed, giving me some much-needed space. I sat up, tugging my shirt down and re-buttoning my jeans without saying anything.

The demon watched me with a cautious expression. "I didn't know you kept the scars."

I froze and then glanced at him in surprise. The arrogance had left his features and was replaced with a rather genuine expression I rarely ever saw on his face.

"I saw them in the dream and in your ex-boyfriend's memories, but I wasn't sure if you still had them. They're old scars, too. 'Gifts' from your aunt, are they not?"

I winced and looked away. "Why should you care?"

"Who says I do? I merely thought it was interesting that you didn't heal them."

"You of all people should know that you can't erase the past."

He opened his mouth to reply, but then there was a knock at the door. Instantly, my pulse skyrocketed and I had to remind myself to calm down as Belial went to check.

Gabriel walked in, looking incredibly tired, bruised, and disheveled, and I wasted no time throwing myself in his arms. He hugged me, lifting my body a few inches off the floor as he did. The urge to cry branched out inside me and I had to take a deep breath to control it.

"I'm so glad you're safe," he murmured into my hair.

"Ditto," I mumbled back.

He placed me safely on the floor and glanced at the demon standing beside us.

"Know that I will never forgive you for what you have done in the past and when the time comes, I will not hesitate to strike you down. But also know that I am grateful that you kept your word about protecting Jordan."

The demon nodded in acknowledgment. "Fair enough, archangel. Now, what happened?"

Gabriel set his jaw and sat on the bed, running both hands through his hair to smooth it down. I ran some tap water into one of the glasses and handed it to him. He drank the entire thing and cleared his throat to start his story.

After we rushed down the hall to the hotel room, I was granted the sight of two people on the floor. I recognized the skinny legs clad in jeans that could only be one person – Jordan. On top of her sat a man with shoulders hardly bigger than hers, but the way they were strained meant only one thing. He was choking her.

The man's head whipped around to face us. A cold shock flooded through me. The rogue angel, alias Edmond Saraf. I watched fear crawl through his features and he leapt off of Jordan in an instant as Belial and I ran towards him. I shouted, "Stop!" just as he picked up and threw the broken flat screen through the window behind him. He jumped out as I ran to the windowsill, watching in horror as he plummeted several floors before disappearing into the thick branches of a tree below. Damn him. He'd known that would be his exit strategy. I only had seconds to give chase.

"Tend to Jordan!" I ordered, struggling out of my suit jacket.

Belial glared at me. "What? I'm a better hunter than you, archangel. You know that."

"I don't have time to argue, just do it!" I snapped, slapping my cell phone into his hand. "Get her somewhere safe and call Michael. I will find you when this is over."

With that, I jumped out the window. Cold air blasted my face, my hair, my body as I fell. A branch smashed into my chest and I wrapped my arms around it, stopping my descent. Once I was steady, I let go and hit the grass, rolling. The rogue angel was several feet ahead of me, running like a well-oiled machine down the hotel driveway and onto the sidewalk. I broke into a sprint, calling for him to stop. I knew he wouldn't but if the people around me suspected him to be a criminal, they may have assisted me.

The rogue angel raced into the busy street, dodging cars as they honked and screeched on their brakes. He made a sharp right turn and I followed closely, staying on the left-hand side of the road so that I would be parallel with him without running into pedestrians. He darted into an alley on his left and I did so as well, apologizing over my shoulder to a man I knocked down. The sound of our footsteps bounced off the brick walls on either side. I knew he had too good of a lead on me to keep this up. I took a deep breath and shouted, "Strike!"

Three shards of energy sliced through the air and he turned on his heel, holding his forearms up. "I reject!"

The shards bounced off of his shield, but it gave me just enough time to take a running kick at him. He kept his forearms up, but my feet connected, sending him tumbling backwards head over foot. He got up on one knee and I threw my leg up high, bringing the heel down as hard as I could. He blocked, rolling to the side and jumping to his feet in a blur of motion.

I aimed quick punches at his chest and he parried them one by one. He was amazingly fast, and his thin frame did nothing to show the immense strength he possessed. I tried several martial arts styles, flowing from one to the next, but he always had a defense prepared, and soon my limbs went numb from all the contact.

Finally, I managed to catch one arm in a lock and shouted "Strike!" again. He cried out as a shard went deep into his shoulder, spilling blood down the side of his button up shirt. We both stopped, panting in breaths ragged from exhaustion, and I managed enough strength to speak.

"Why are you doing this, brother? We are not your enemy. She is not your enemy!"

"It was never about that," he answered in a pained voice. "I never considered the Seers my enemies. Never."

"Then why?" I demanded, jerking his arm further forward at the elbow.

He groaned, crumpling onto one knee. "They have to be sacrificed or the world will end."

"No, no more of this vagueness. You will tell me what you're talking about or I'll break off this arm like a twig," I spat.

He gritted his teeth, forcing out the next sentence. "Et Liber Tempor states that in this year, a Seer will help the demons unleash a force of evil so great that it will cause the deaths of one thousand people and plunge the world into darkness. That is why I have hunted them down and killed them so that I can change the future and spare innocent lives. You have to believe me!"

"How could you be so arrogant to think that this was the only way? Six dead Seers, brother. These people deserved to live, but you took that away from them. You will never reenter the gates of Heaven. You will never be forgiven."

He bowed his head. "And that is my sacrifice to protect these people. I thought you would understand most of all, Gabriel. We are servants. Nothing more."

"Yes, we are. And it is my duty as a servant to bring you in for the murder of six Seers and the attempt of a seventh."

"I am sorry," he whispered, "but I cannot allow you to bring me to justice yet. My task is not complete. Not while she still lives."

With a roar, he dislocated his own shoulder and slid out of the arm lock. He whirled around and brought his fist down on the base of my skull as hard as he could. Stars exploded in my vision and I fell to my knees, dazed. He stood there, clutching his bloody arm as I tried to regain my strength, but the world had gone dark around the edges and my body trembled like a leaf in a hurricane.

"Forgive me, brother."

He kicked me in the forehead and everything went black.

Gabriel sighed, rubbing his eyelids with the palms of his hands. "I woke up half an hour later. Someone had called 911. The paramedics found me in the alley and patched me up. After that, I felt for Belial's energy signature and found you here."

"This is insane," I said, wrapping my arms around my sides. "How can he believe what he saw in the book? That one of the Seers will betray the angels and bring about the Apocalypse?"

"I corrupted a Seer once," Belial said. "It is not an impossible feat. Even though you have managed to resist me all this time, another Seer might not be as strong as you. He did not say that he thought it would be you who betrayed the angels. He's not taking any chances so he's killing all of them."

"Then why didn't he kill me in the restaurant?"

"Too many witnesses. Too many variables that he couldn't control."

"What about earlier? Why didn't he use his scythe on me in the hotel and burn the place to purify it?"

"Practicality," Gabriel answered instead in a hushed tone. "The other Seers were cornered when they were all alone, but you have stayed mostly in public places or with one of us. He took a gamble coming here, apparently hoping that he could kill you before I returned. You are the most difficult Seer to kill, having escaped death twice, so he has grown desperate. I don't know what this means for us now. You'll have to stay close to one of us at all times until the page of *Et Liber Tempor* is re-translated and we know when the next Seer will Awaken."

"How specific is the Symphony of Time, then? It says when and where these Seers Awaken, but does it have their names?"

"I'm not sure. The Book and the Symphony only record that which they consider to be relevant in the context of the universe. We cannot control what they say. We can only interpret them as best as we can."

"That's a load of help," I said with a sigh. "I don't know, Gabriel, you can't just be my bodyguards until the end of the year. We still have lives to lead. Maybe there's some way to talk him out of it."

He shot me an incredulous look. "Are you insane? The man broke into our hotel room and nearly strangled you to death."

"I know, but when he did it…I talked to him. I told him we could help him. The way he looked at me, I just…" I shook my head.

"He doesn't want to do this. Yes, he nearly killed me, but if you could have seen his face before I fell unconscious, you'd wonder if we could talk him out of it too."

"No," Gabriel said. "It's too late for that. He made his decision tonight. We have no choice but to eliminate him, for your safety and for the safety of the future Seers of the world."

He glanced at Belial, his face firm with resolve. "Kill him on sight if the opportunity presents itself."

Belial nodded. "Very well. What are we going to do for now?"

"I injured him too badly for him to come for her again tonight. However, just to be safe, we'll gather up our belongings from the other hotel and stay here. The two of us should be enough for now. We'll return to Albany in the morning. Michael is a far better warrior than I am and I think Jordan will be safest with him."

Gabriel touched my hand. "Are you feeling well enough to come with me or would you rather stay here?"

I bit my bottom lip. To be honest, I wanted to stick close to Gabriel, but the thought of being in any open spaces where Edmond could get to me scared me more. I squeezed his fingers, keeping my voice level.

"I'll stay here. Call the room phone when you get back and I'll come to you."

"Okay." He kissed my forehead, slowly. His energy, cool and light like a breeze, settled on my skin.

"Be safe."

"You too." He stood and walked out the door.

Once more, I was left alone with the demon. I rubbed my arms, trying to think of what to say. "Can I use your shower?"

Belial arched an eyebrow and I corrected myself. "Alone?"

He smirked. "Of course."

I stood, crossing my arms beneath my chest. "Are you sure it's not too much of a strain to ask you not to sneak a peek while I'm in there?"

The demon chuckled. "My, my, you are high on yourself these days. There's nothing you've got that I haven't seen before, Seer. Be my guest."

That stung my ego more than it should have. It irritated me that I even cared. I had gotten so used to him making passes at me that his nonchalance got under my skin. I wondered if he was doing that on purpose. Probably.

"Fine. Then we're at a ceasefire, right?"

"Right."

"Excellent." I pulled off my shirt and dropped it on the floor right in front of him. His face betrayed nothing, but I could hear him take a deep breath and I instantly felt better. I smiled and sauntered past him into the bathroom, shutting the door. It wasn't until the shower was on full blast that I collapsed onto the bottom of the tub and cried.

CHAPTER NINE

MICHAEL

The doorbell rang. I stood up from the couch and walked across the carpeted floors to open the door. My wife was on the other side, alone, with a sheepish smile on her lips.

"Forgot my key."

The smile was real, but her eyes were already wet. She threw herself into my arms and I lifted her up, ashamed of how glad I was to see her. I had been a hardened warrior for the majority of my existence. I had been trained to let nothing slip beneath my armor, to do whatever was needed to secure the safety of mankind and destroy all evil no matter what the cost. But something about this woman made the warrior in me soften somewhat.

After a moment or two, I had enough presence of mind to shut the door with my foot. Jordan didn't let go, instead wrapping her long legs around my waist and sliding her face upward from where it had been buried in my neck. She kissed me and it tasted salty because she was crying, quietly, just like her voice when she spoke.

"*Lo siento,*" my wife whispered against my lips. "*Lo siento, mi amor.*"

"You're safe," I murmured back. "That's all that matters."

"*Te amo. Te amo, amor.*"

"*Yo sé.*" I knew what she needed, what we both needed, so I carried her to the bedroom and no other words were spoken. I had lost track of how many times she and I made love in the past, but this was the only time it reminded me of our first night together. Everything felt different because we both knew how close she had come to dying. Jordan had cheated death twice in her life and both times, it broke some part of me deep down—knowing that I couldn't always be there to protect my wife, the other half of my soul, the only woman I had ever met who truly understood who and what I was and loved me still.

How could I call myself a real husband when only a day ago some brute had his hands wrapped around her neck? How could I ever let her out of my sight again knowing that he wanted her dead in order to protect the rest of the world? How could I trust myself not to tear through every city in every country looking for him, hunting him, waiting for my chance to rip his throat out for hurting the woman I loved?

When it was over, we were both shaking but somehow I knew we would be okay in spite of everything that had happened. I slid onto my side, pulled her lithe body against me, and wrapped my arms around her. She pressed her ear against my chest and went still, listening to my heartbeat and my breathing. She loved the sound. She told me it made her feel safe more so than anything else I did. I loved that something so simple made her feel at home with me, as stupid as that may sound. Maybe that was why we were perfect for each other. We were both weirdos.

She fell asleep first, as she usually did, and I rested for a while before getting up. I took a brief shower and then leaned against the doorjamb for a bit, watching her. She had always been a heavy sleeper and that worked just fine for me because I often liked to sneak out into the den to practice my guitar or watch TV late at night. It wasn't until this moment that I realized how small and delicate she could be. Jordan always wore a thick metaphorical armor when she was awake. Growing up with an abusive aunt gave her the ability to take a lot of punishment, both physical and emotional, without breaking. She didn't open up to people easily and she always expected them to hurt her, but over time she had learned that there were some people she could trust.

Jordan shifted and the comforter inched downward, exposing one corner of the scar on her chest. A wave of anger flowed through me, tightening the muscles along my shoulders. To her, the scar was a reminder of how dangerous the demons could be, but to me, it was a territorial mark. Belial had staked his claim on her and he would stop at nothing to take her away. Our brief phone conversation had not gone well, which was why I hadn't slept for most of the night.

I had been at my apartment, using my laptop to research theories of the supposed Apocalypse, when my cell phone rang. I checked it, not wanting to be bothered unless it was important, only to find that it was Gabriel. Probably with news. Hopefully good news.

"Hello?"

"Michael."

I froze. The voice on the other end was not gentle and friendly like my brother's. It was cold, dry, and sinister. Only one person could embody those things so perfectly. No, not a person. A demon.

"Belial. Why do you have my brother's phone?"

"There's been an…incident."

Ice water filled my veins, chilling me to the core. His words confirmed the rotten feeling in my gut. I had hoped it was just anxiety or a stomachache, but deep down, I had known something was wrong.

"What incident?"

"The rogue angel broke into Gabriel's room and attacked Jordan."

I closed my eyes, trying to quell the sickening wave of panic that arose inside me upon hearing his words. "How is she?"

"She survived, but she's very weak. Gabriel went off in pursuit of the angel and left her with me. She should be coming around momentarily."

I opened my eyes. A different feeling flowed through my veins now. Very different. "What do you mean he left her with you?"

"I assume Gabriel did this because he does not trust me and wants to hear a firsthand account of the rogue angel's plight rather than one from me. He gave me his phone and told me to call you with Jordan's status. There is no need for concern."

"No need for concern?" I snapped. "The last time you were alone with my wife, you tried to rape her and turn her into your servant. Why the hell should I even believe you?"

Belial sighed, sounding tired. "How else would I have gotten this phone? There is no reason for me to lie to you now, Michael. We are working together, temporarily, and that should afford me some sort of leeway with your trust. I swear to you that Jordan is safe."

"Good," I replied in a low, tight voice. "Because I want to make one thing clear – if you harm one hair on her head, I won't care about the pact we made. I will fly to Cleveland and I will rip you in half, you sniveling metrosexual bastard."

He laughed and it was drier than sandpaper. "Colorful. But I assure you, my intentions are nothing but pure. I want to find this angel just as much as you do and I will not cross you until this ordeal is over. Maybe then we can settle our affairs like men."

"What affairs? You have no chance with her, demon. Get that through your head."

"So you say. But I'm not the one who is hundreds of miles away from the woman I love when she needs me. Farewell."

He hung up. It took nearly all of my strength not to smash the phone to bits and order a ticket on the first thing smoking to Cleveland. Belial was right. He would gain nothing by breaking his word and hurting Jordan. He'd bide his time. But that didn't mean I would.

I was drawn out of my thoughts when Jordan stirred again. Her eyelids fluttered and those dark chocolate eyes of hers wandered around the room, settling on me. She pushed a cloud of black hair out of her face and sleepily mumbled, "*Amor?*"

The Spanish had been my idea. Before we were married, Jordan rarely ever spoke it even though she was bilingual. She had told me the language reminded her too much of her aunt and her mother, but I encouraged her to come to terms with her violent past and accept it as a part of her. Thus, gradually, she began speaking it more. At first she only used it in the bedroom, which I didn't mind, then eventually it became like a habit between us. I also couldn't help thinking about how her mother and Andrew Bethsaida had done something similar. He called her Cat and she called him "*mi amor.*" Years later and we had somehow managed to echo them.

"Hey," I said, giving her a short kiss on the lips after I walked to her side of the bed.

She patted the mattress. "Come back to bed."

"Can't. You have to be at work in an hour."

Jordan groaned, pressing her face into one of the pillows. "Ugh, don't remind me. Why are you such a killjoy?"

"I'm not a killjoy. I'm just being responsible."

She lifted her head, poking me in the shoulder as she sang, "Every party needs a pooper, that's why we invited you, party pooper! Party poo-per!"

I shook my head, trying not to laugh, and kissed her again. "Get up, lazy bum. You need to take a shower or Lauren will tease you about smelling like me again."

"No," she said, sliding her legs to the edge of the bed. "She'll tease me about smelling like sex. Don't ask me how she knows that but she does."

Jordan stood up, stark naked, and stretched, which distracted me for a full six seconds before I caught myself. She found her robe hanging off one edge of the bed frame and put it on, hiding all her lovely skin and curves, much to my disappointment.

I watched her sift through a drawer in the dresser for some clothes before venturing to ask a question. "Can I ask you something?"

"Sure, stud."

"Does this whole situation make you think any differently about the wedding or moving in with me?"

Her shoulders tensed. I was taking a big risk. The wedding ceremony and the apartment situation were hot-button issues I usually tried to avoid, but I had honestly gotten tired of waiting for an answer.

I needed to know why she was avoiding both topics—for the sake of my own sanity, at the very least.

"Michael," she started with a sigh. "Is this really the best time to talk about that?"

"Yes, it is," I said, pushing off of the bed to face her. She wore a guarded expression as she stared up at me.

"Jordan, you could have died yesterday. Life is short. Shorter than you know. Why can't you just commit to doing this with me?"

"It's not that simple—"

"Then make it simple," I interrupted. "Explain it to me. Why don't you want the wedding?"

"I do want a wedding, I just…" She looked away, crossing her arms beneath her chest.

I took a deep breath to calm my temper. "Just what?"

"It's so…official."

"Official?"

She brushed her hair away from her face again, a nervous habit. "Yes. It's like the whole world will know and be able to judge us—to judge whether we have what it takes to make this work or not. It's a statement. I can't take it back once it's done. I mean, I can't do that anyway and I don't want to, but I feel like it's the last thing that'll be gone from my old life."

I let out a snort. "Yes, because we both know *that* was glorious."

She glared at me. "Yeah, but it was still *my* life. Now it's *our* life. And I know I should be used to that by now, but I'm not. I'm still scared of being yours completely."

"Why the hell would you be scared of that?"

"Because…I…" She threw up her hands, starting to walk away. "I can't do this right now."

I put my arm out in front of her so she couldn't brush past me into the bathroom.

"Finish the sentence, Jordan."

"Michael—"

"Finish it."

"Because I'm scared you'll come to your senses!" she shouted finally.

I went silent momentarily, shocked. "What?"

"Michael, you are so sweet and funny and handsome and perfect that I'm scared that once we've made everything official, you'll realize what a complete nut job I am and you'll run screaming for your life," she said, refusing to look at me.

"And I'm scared of living with you because then I'll have nothing left to hide in. No more secrets, nothing. You'll find out everything about me and I'm scared you won't like it. There. Happy now?"

She wouldn't meet my gaze so I touched her chin, lifting her face. "Jor."

"Yeah?"

"That's the stupidest thing I've ever heard."

Her jaw dropped. "What?"

I smiled to soften the blow of my blunt words. "I've fought in more battles than I care to count. I've seen men and angels die in the most horrifying ways. I've seen people butcher each other just for the hell of it. There isn't anything depraved or terrible on this Earth that I haven't seen. I'm pretty sure I can handle *your* crazy ass."

She gave me a look that was a cross between a scowl and a smirk. "I cannot believe you just mocked my psychological trauma."

I let the smile stretch into a grin, then kissed her. "You're damn right I did. You're being silly. I want to know every awful insecure thing about you. That's why I married you. I wouldn't be here if I wanted a perfect woman. There isn't one."

She rolled her eyes. "Flattery will get you nowhere, Mr. O'Brien."

"I beg to differ, Mrs. O'Brien."

"Jordan O'Brien. It still sounds weird as hell to me. Now can I go take my shower?"

"You can...after you tell me what's really bothering you."

Her brows bunched into another frown. "What d'you mean? I just told you."

"And you weren't lying. I know that much. But there's something else you're not telling me. You wouldn't hold back just because you're scared of losing me. What is it?"

She brushed past me and sat on the bed, staring at the floor. Ice filled the pit of my stomach. I leaned against the dresser, expecting the worst.

"This mission we're on...I think it means more to me than it does to you."

"Why's that?" I asked.

"You've been in this fight since the beginning of time. I'm twenty-three. I've only been a Seer for five years. Because of that, I've always felt like it's my responsibility to be someone worthy of being married to the Commander of Heaven's Army."

I opened my mouth to interrupt, but she held up her hand. "Let me finish. I need to become stronger. I need to prove that I can handle the pressure that comes along with living this life. I have to earn it for myself. That's why I've pushed myself so hard. That's also why I've been keeping you at a distance. I wanted you to see that I can make the same hard decisions and sacrifices that are expected of you every day."

She met my gaze and there was firm resolve in her brown eyes. "Does that make any sense to you?"

I nodded, walking over to her. "Yeah, it does. But don't forget how far you've come. You've already made some of the hardest choices anyone in this life will ever have to face. And you're not in this alone. Promise me you'll remember that."

"I promise."

"Good. Now go take your shower." I pressed one final kiss to her lips and then she got up. The bathroom door shut and I knew that my gamble had been worth it.

After grabbing a shirt out of the drawer, I went into the kitchen and put on a pot of coffee because I knew she'd want some when she came out of the shower. She had gotten here shortly after ten o'clock and we had been in bed for a couple of hours. Her shift started at one o'clock and Colton, her boss, would be irritated if she came in late again. I had to admit her recent tardiness was partially my fault. Well, mostly my fault. Entirely. Whatever.

I didn't have to work today, but I had to meet with my band for rehearsal. The sessions usually lasted anywhere from two to four hours—it was only four hours if Casey brought alcohol with her, which she did about sixty percent of the time—so I would be occupied for most of the day. They were expecting me in the next hour, which meant I had time to eat lunch and make one important stop before I got there.

Jordan's fridge was always stocked with great food, but I was a low maintenance kind of guy. I survived mainly on pizza, Chinese takeout, the occasional sub sandwich, and asparagus.

Yes, I know, one of those things is not like the other, but for some reason, I was completely addicted to it. Raphael had brought me some once and from then on I always had a heaping pile stuffed inside a clear grocery bag in the refrigerator drawer. Jordan hated them, told me they tasted like wet sticks, but she even kept a stash for me at her place for when I spent the night.

I scooped four stalks out of the drawer and stood there, chewing on them, feeling remarkably like an off-brand version of Bugs Bunny, as I leafed through the bills. Money wasn't a big deal for the archangels on earth. We all knew each other and if anyone fell on hard times, he or she had someone to back them up. If things got too bad, Gabriel would step in, as he was an extremely wealthy man, and help out. If I'd wanted the life of the upper class, I could probably have it, but I liked where I was at the moment. Except for the not-getting-signed-by-a-label thing. There were angels in the music biz, but I refused to let my status interfere. For once, I'd do things the human way.

I ate a couple of cold slices of pizza, downed a soda, and packed up my guitar, my sheet music, my ratty lyric notebook, and stuffed my keys and wallet in my pocket. Jordan reappeared with one of my shirts on. For a moment, I wondered if she really had to be at work and then mentally slapped myself. She was already in enough trouble with her boss.

"I'll meet you at the restaurant when your shift ends," I told her, tugging her forward by the shirttail.

She lifted up on her tiptoes and kissed me. "It's a date. Be safe."

I leaned my forehead against hers, my voice serious. "You too."

With that, I headed for the bus.

Gabriel's office had a lot of windows. An unnervingly large number. Maybe I had watched too many movies, but it always made me think something would come flying through one of them and attack whomever was inside. He owned several different businesses and charities in many states so he always set up an office for himself to make things easier when he had to stay in one region for an extended period of time. His job was mercurial: some days, he was an entrepreneur, a handsome face in an impeccable business suit; other days, he would roll up the expensive sleeves of his shirt and help deliver babies in third world countries. Of all the angels, I had always considered him to be the "face of the company." Safe, sincere, marketable, and representative of the whole. Granted, not all angels were as jovial as he or Raphael, but he was a good spokesperson.

His secretary was a dainty Czech woman in her late fifties or early sixties who looked remarkably like an owl with her thick-framed glasses. Despite her age, she could type faster than I could blink and answered the phone with a professional yet kind tone. Best of all, she always had a pack of Ice Breakers on her desk when she knew I was coming in with asparagus breath.

Most of the time, Gabriel and I tried to meet somewhere private because in public settings we tended to get interrupted by girls. Gabriel was a hot commodity to say the least, and when they couldn't get his attention, they'd switch to me. I always flashed them my wedding band to scare them off. We were both good-looking guys, but Gabriel's expensive attire got more of the girls' attention.

The door to his office opened and a portly Hispanic fellow walked out, beaming as he shook Gabriel's hand and told him in Spanish that he was very grateful. Gabriel patted his shoulder and told the gentleman to speak with his secretary before he left. He noticed me as I stood up from the comfy leather coach against the far wall and waved me in, closing the door.

He cleared his throat and then sighed as he turned toward me. "Not in the face."

I punched him in the gut, a little below the ribs. He wheezed, wincing and clutching the spot but he didn't buckle. It was much harder to be intimidating when he was a good five inches taller than me, but I knew he got the point.

"What the hell were you thinking?" I demanded.

Gabriel exhaled and leaned against the large table behind him. "I already told you I was sorry."

"You didn't answer my question. What the hell were you thinking leaving Jordan with Belial in a hotel?"

He closed his eyes momentarily, regaining composure. "I could not risk letting the demon catch up with Edmond before I did. We would never have gotten an accurate statement from the rogue angel about why he's doing this. I knew that Belial would not violate his word at such an inopportune time. It was the logical thing to do."

"Of course it was," I replied with heavy sarcasm. "Only one Seer on Earth right now and you left her with the man who has tried to kill her on two separate occasions, and succeeded on one of them. This is exactly why I wanted to go instead of you, Gabriel. When the chips are down, you're going to protect the world instead of protecting her."

"Don't you dare accuse me of not caring about Jordan!" he snapped, stepping forward. "I knew her long before you did and I care for her now as much as I did at the beginning. You cannot fault me for doing the right thing when the stakes are so high. You cannot expect me to sacrifice the world for your wife."

"I would never ask you to, brother," I said, fighting to keep my voice level. "You know that. But you and I both know how bad it could have gotten if Belial had something planned for her. He's always been good at finding loopholes. I don't want a repeat of history."

"Neither do I. I knew Jordan could handle herself around him. She's done it before. No matter how silver the demon's tongue is, she's immune to it because she loves you."

"That didn't stop Zora."

Gabriel shook his head once, his brow darkening. "Don't bring Uriel's lover into this. She is not Jordan. Why can't you see that, Michael?"

"Because I'd be a fool not to. It's been centuries, but history is starting to repeat itself. Don't you remember how few Seers were on the earth back then? How chaotic everything was? What do you think is going to happen if the rogue angel keeps up his game? We'll be right back where we were when Zora was banished."

"It won't come to that," Gabriel said in his most patient voice. "We've got every angel available looking for him. We're going to catch him and this will be over. You've got to stay focused or you'll end up blowing this mission and more innocent people will die."

"Stay focused? I can't just flip it off like a switch. I've watched her bleed to death, Gabriel. I've held her cold and dead in my arms. I will not do it again."

"What would you have me do, then?"

"Make the Call."

He shook his head. "No. Absolutely not."

"Damn it, Gabriel, we don't have time for red tape and politics. You know he has the resources to get this man found."

"And you want me to jeopardize everything I've built for one man?"

"No. Not for him. For Jordan."

Gabriel clenched his jaw. "I will do everything in my power to stop Edmond, but do not ask me to sabotage my own company,

Michael. There are millions of people who depend on my work and my influence."

Anger sizzled through my chest. "No, I understand. The needs of the many outweigh the needs of the few."

I stalked towards the door, wrenching it open and stopping for one last comment. "But you should know…you sound just like Edmond."

I slammed the door shut.

CHAPTER TEN

JORDAN

"I need your help."

Lauren arched one perfectly plucked eyebrow. "With what? Did you kill another customer and you need me to help you shove his body in the sewer?"

"Please. Like I'd put him in the sewer. The oven would get rid of the evidence faster."

My best friend rolled her eyes. "Stop watching so much *Castle*. And I repeat, with what?"

I sighed, not wanting to say the next few words. "...withthewedding."

She gave me a confused look. "Whiffer what?"

I resisted the urge to groan. "With the...wedding."

Her brown eyes lit up and a huge grin spread across her lips. "You're serious? Finally?"

"Yes, I'm serious. I need your help planning it."

She squealed and wrapped her arms around me, crushing the air from my lungs. The other servers sent us bemused glances and a few customers turned their heads to watch.

I pried myself out of her grip, shushing her. "Calm down, I don't need everyone and their mom to know—"

"Are you insane? I'm gonna invite literally everyone in this joint!" she exclaimed, grabbing my arm and pulling me out of sight. We hid in the narrow hallway that led to the break room, whispering back and forth.

"Okay," Lauren said. "What time do you get off? We've got to start checking the basics: the location, places for a cake, a dress, flower arrangements, announcements, food, the works. At least we've got the music taken care of. Michael's band can play, hopefully for no charge."

"Do we have to do that today? When I asked for your help, I didn't mean immediately," I protested, but she waved the comment away.

"There's no time like the present, trust me. It takes months to plan so we have to get started early—"

"Months? Really? Isn't it going to be pretty small?"

She eyed me. "How small were you thinking?"

I shrugged. "Twenty people, tops."

"You've got to be kidding me, woman."

"What? I don't have that many friends. You know that."

"True, but that doesn't mean you need to have such a small wedding. I'd expand that to fifty people. You may not have that many friends, but I'm sure Michael does."

I thought about it. To be honest, I didn't know how many friends he actually had. The people I usually saw him hang around were his band mates and the other archangels, mainly Gabriel and Raphael. Who would be the best man?

"I guess you have a point. But I'm not sure if I can go today, I've got some work to do."

"You always have work to do. We should at least map out where we're gonna go when we shop for real."

It was my turn to lift an eyebrow. "We're gonna shop to plan shopping?"

She grinned. "Now you're getting it. Maybe one day Santa will bring you that vagina for Christmas."

I slapped her in the arm and she cackled, scurrying away as Noah called out our orders. I brought food to several customers and grabbed my notepad as I spotted someone new at one of my tables.

"What can I get…" I walked around to face him and stopped dead in my tracks, the last word falling limply from my lips.

"…you."

Lewis flashed me a small smile. "Hey."

Several emotions crashed against the surface of my mind, but I reminded myself that I was at work and couldn't cause a scene. Instead of yelling, I forced a thin smile across my mouth and spoke through my teeth.

"What are you doing here?"

"I came to see you."

"Do you see a case full of money up my ass? I don't have anything to give you," I said with no small amount of venom.

He held up his hands in surrender. "I ain't here for that. I swear. I just wanna talk. That's it."

"I'm working. I don't have time to talk."

Lewis cocked his head to the side, glancing at Lauren with a smug look. "Uh-huh."

I ground my teeth, raising my pen. "Fine. Order something first."

"I'll take a coffee, black."

"Naturally," I muttered, scribbling the order on my pad and walking back towards the kitchen.

Lauren noticed my expression and followed me. "Whoa, what the hell did that guy say to you?"

"Nothing," I grumbled, grabbing a full pitcher of coffee and a mug.

Lauren glanced in Lewis' direction and then at me. "That didn't look like nothing. Do you know that guy?"

"No. And I don't want to." I stalked back over to his table and set the coffee down, crossing my arms beneath my chest.

"Two minutes."

He sighed. "You are just like your mother. Colder than a polar bear's ass."

"Thanks, that's sweet."

"You're welcome."

Lewis poured the hot drink himself and took a sip before speaking again. "I got caught up the other day. Cops found me gambling and I couldn't shake 'em. Your husband bailed me out."

I went completely still. "He what?"

"I know. I had the same reaction. Didn't think he'd bail me out, but he did. Gave me this whole speech about how I should either get my shit straight or leave town. I still don't like him. He's a punk."

A dark chuckle escaped him. "Kind of like me at his age."

"This is fantastic news, but you're running out of seconds and I'm running out of patience."

He frowned a little, but continued. "My point is that he was right. I came at you wrong. I was in a bad way and you didn't deserve to get thrown in my shit. My situation doesn't matter. You do. So will you give me a second chance?"

It would have been so easy to tell him to piss off. The words were perched on the edge of my lips, so ready to jump out at him. But I didn't say it. As angry as I was with him, there was genuine honesty in those eyes that matched mine. He may have been a criminal and a deadbeat dad, but he was still part of my family. Could I get to sleep at night if I denied him a second chance? Not long ago, I had needed one too.

In the end, I just told him the truth. "I don't know if this is another part of your scam or not, but against my better judgment, I'm gonna give you one chance to make it up to me. Dinner tonight at

Mojo's. Eight o'clock sharp. If you screw that up, we're done. Understand me?"

"Got it. Thanks. I know I ain't exactly been Father of the Year, but maybe I can make it up to you."

"I already have a father."

I turned and walked away without looking back.

"How about this one?"

I followed where Lauren's purple fingernail pointed to the page in the magazine laying open in her lap. I studied the dress, tilting my head.

"Mm, not a big fan of strapless gowns. Mostly because I'm not a fan of strapless bras."

Lauren snorted. "You do know most of these dresses have built-in corsets and bras, right?"

"Oh. Well, then toss that in the Maybe pile."

She tore out the page and placed it on the coffee table where a small stack of magazine pages already lay. We sat on her squishy black leather couch sharing a bag of chips and onion dip. Lily sat on the loveseat, completely enraptured in an episode of *The Fresh Prince of Bel-Air*. Normally, she watched kids' shows on the Disney Channel, but I had a fondness for 90's sitcoms so I bought her the first season to see if she'd like them too. It seems the child was quite taken with Carlton Banks after a couple of episodes, to my great amusement.

"This one?"

Lauren shook her head. "Nah, that'll make you look short. You need something that makes your legs look long and that dress is cut too high."

"Got it." I flipped to another page, scanning it and trying my best to ignore the prices. I hadn't known Lauren before she got married so I knew little to nothing about weddings. I'd managed to talk her out of taking me shopping today and instead convinced her to let me go through the bridal magazines she had kept. I couldn't use her dress for two reasons: one, she was three inches taller than me and a lot more voluptuous; two, she sold her dress the day her divorce was finalized. Got a pretty penny for it too.

"What ideas do you have for the color scheme?"

I shrugged. "I guess I like lavender?"

"That could work. I had my bridesmaids in light blue. Thank God you're not one of those women who insists that the bridesmaids look hideous so she'll look prettier."

I wrinkled my nose in disgust. "Yeah, that stereotype always bothered me. I can accept it if my friends are better-looking than me. I'm the one getting married so who cares?"

"Exactly. The only person who needs to think you look beautiful is Michael. Or, one of your Freebie Fives."

I shook my head. "You're shameless."

"Hey, just sayin'. You have to keep your options open."

"Naturally." I paused, lowering my magazine and nudging her shoulder. She glanced at me as I spoke.

"Are you sure this isn't bothering you? I know things ended badly between you and He-Who-Must-Not-Be-Named."

She adopted a small smirk. "Y'know, Voldemort would have been preferable to my ex. At least he was ambitious."

I gave her a stern look. "I mean it."

Lauren patted my knee. "I'm a big girl, Jordan. I can handle it."

"It's a two way street, y'know. You asked me to be honest with you and I agreed that I would be."

She frowned. "You are, huh? Then what's the real story about that black guy at your table today?"

I winced. I had hoped she would forget about him over the course of the workday, but Lauren had an eye for details. She could tell when something was bothering me even when I tried to hide it. In the end, I just sighed and leaned my head back against the couch.

"He's my...father."

"Your *what?*"

I lifted my head to see her staring at me with her mouth agape. "Are you serious?"

I shrugged. "You wanted to know the truth."

"How can he...I mean, when did he...*what?*" She ended up sputtering again.

I couldn't help but smile a bit. "Yeah, pretty much."

"How did he even find you? And *why* did he find you?"

"Apparently, he Googled me and then found me through my mailman. Showed up at my place a few days ago and told me he needed a loan."

"And you're sure he's not some scam artist or something?"

"He had my mother's rosary. He must have gotten it from my aunt. Who, by the way, neglected to tell him my mother died."

"What a b—" Lauren glanced at her daughter, who of course paid us no mind. "B-I-T-C-H. How much money did he want?"

"More than I've got, trust me."

"So what are you gonna do?"

"He came to the restaurant to talk to me. He claims he wants to make up for his messed up behavior earlier. Wanted a second chance. Against my better judgment, I'm giving it to him. I'm gonna meet him for dinner tonight and see what he has to say."

"Geez." Lauren ran a hand through her hair. "This seriously came out of nowhere. Does Michael know?"

"Yeah. Actually, he bailed Daddy-O out of jail the other day. Neglected to tell me too."

"Hey, don't get that look on your face," she scolded, poking the spot between my eyebrows as I frowned. "He probably thought it was for the best. Michael's a sweetheart and because he doesn't have a family, he knows how important it is for you to have one."

"I know, I know, it's just…" I pulled my legs up on the couch, wrapping my arms around my knees as I tried to put my thoughts into words.

"Lately, I've decided to stop being such a chicken and actually commit to my marriage like I'm supposed to. That's why I agreed to start working on the wedding. But it also opens up a whole new can of worms. We'll have to move in together and spend every waking moment with each other. He seems perfectly fine with it, but to be honest, it scares the S-H-I-T out of me."

"Why? He loves you to death."

"I know he does. That's what I'm worried about. This whole situation with my dad is exactly the kind of stuff I don't want in my life. Michael's probably the best thing that's ever happened to me and I'm already dragging him into my crap. He doesn't deserve that."

"It's not about what he deserves, Jor. The second he put that ring on your finger, he agreed to deal with whatever comes at the two of you. It's not something you have to do by yourself anymore. He's your husband. You're supposed to depend on him."

"I'm trying. It's just hard to do when you've been single as long as I have."

Lauren tugged me into a hug. "God, you are such a friggin' buzzkill."

I hugged her back, unable to keep from giggling. "Every party needs a pooper."

She let go, patting my hand. "You're going to be fine. Your dad will turn out to be as awesome as Liam Neeson in *Taken* and your wedding will be beautiful and nothing bad will ever happen to you again."

"Thanks. I needed that lie right about now."

"I know. Now let's get back to finding dresses. Then we can move on to the fun stuff."

"Fun stuff?"

"Honeymoon night lingerie."

"Oh, God save me."

Mojo's was a small Mexican restaurant tucked between a laundromat and a discount video rental store about fifteen minutes from my apartment. Stan, one of Michael's band mates, had recommended it to us once and we fell in love with it. The service was always fast and friendly, the place was never crowded, and the food was delicious. It quickly became a regular date-night spot for us when our lives were calm enough to go out. Instead of taking the bus, we would walk home so the heavy, delectable food could settle in our stomachs and I could work off some of the extra calories that came with it.

I'd picked it on purpose because not many people knew about it so the atmosphere was always quiet. Plus, if Lewis tried to pull something stupid, I could just get up and leave with little to no trouble.

Michael had met up with me when my shift ended at the restaurant and I let him know about the change of plans. Earlier, we had agreed to meet to discuss Apocalypse conspiracies, but this meeting took precedence over that one for now. I told him I would keep it to just an hour and then meet him at his apartment afterward. Lauren and I hung out until seven thirty rolled around and I left to meet my so-called father.

"Ah, *hola, Señora Amador*! *¿Que pasa?*" River Santiago greeted me with a wide, pretty smile when I walked in. She was in her late forties, but she stayed in shape and looked not a day over thirty.

"*Nada*," I answered. "I'm here meeting someone. He might have a reservation already under Lewis Jackson."

She checked the list and nodded, motioning towards a booth on the right side of the restaurant. "Yes, he's over there. I'll have someone come by with the menus."

"*Gracias.*" I walked towards where she pointed, spotting Lewis under the dim red lights overhead. *Deep breath, Amador. Time to take the plunge.*

"Hey," he said when I sat down, and the tone of his voice sounded like relief.

"Was starting to wonder if you were gonna show."

"I try to be a woman of my word," I replied, unable to keep from sounding cold. The waitress came by and handed us menus. I flipped mine open to avoid having to look at him.

"So what's good here?"

"Everything, really. Michael and I come here all the time. I'd recommend the shrimp tacos for a first time visit. Gives you a good idea of how they season the food."

Out of the corner of my eyes, I could tell he had resisted the urge to frown when I mentioned Michael. An improvement, I supposed. When we went out, Michael told me he sometimes got nasty glares from black guys. I hardly noticed them at all because I didn't care. Lewis didn't seem to share that sentiment.

"Sounds good. I think I'll take that, then," Lewis said, setting his menu aside.

I continued pretending to peruse mine until he spoke again. "So…I'm sorry to hear about your mother."

I lifted my eyes enough to meet his solemn expression. "You really shouldn't lead with that."

"I don't believe in beatin' around the bush, as you can tell. And it's the truth. You may not believe me or care, but I did love your mother. I still love her and I always will."

I lowered my menu and folded my hands. "Alright, fine. Are you sure you want to do this? Lay all your cards on the table, right here? Right now?"

He gestured towards me. "Go for it."

"When I was five years old, Aunt Carmen convinced a psychiatric hospital that my mother needed to be treated because she was a danger to herself and me. They institutionalized her for about a month. She committed suicide towards the end of August of 1993. The day they took her, I was sent to live with Aunt Carmen in New Jersey. I got a part-time job in high school and saved up enough money to run away. An old woman named Selina LeBeau gave me a ride to Albany and let me stay above her candy shop until I had enough money to move out and get my own place. I met Lauren and got a job at the Sweet Spot. I met Michael two years later and we got married last year. That's the abridged version."

His gaze dropped to my chest. My duster was still on, but I knew he was looking for the scar. "Where'd you get that?"

"Mugging that went violent a year ago."

"And the scars on your back?"

"Aunt Carmen."

"Jesus," he whispered. "How did she get away with it? Didn't you try telling people?"

"I could never prove anything. She told the police I got mugged one night and they marked me up. The neighborhood we lived in was thick with gangs so they believed her instead of me."

He shook his head. "Can't believe it. I never liked her in the first place, but I have half a mind to drive back to Jersey and snap her in half."

"It's in the past. I've learned to deal with it and you'll have to do the same thing."

The waitress returned and we ordered our food, waiting until she left to continue the conversation.

"So why are you really here? Do you actually care about me or are you just guilty?"

He stared at me with an unreadable expression. "I finally got a reason to stop being a coward and apologize for what I did. I'm not proud of it. But...what your mother wanted, I couldn't give. I thought it was better if I left before you were born and got attached to me. Figured you could spend your life hating me in peace because I didn't love you and leave you — I just left."

"Where did you go? I know Mom lived in Madrid before she came here and had me."

"Before we...fell out, I ran a consulting business overseas. We met in a study-abroad program the year before we both graduated. She wanted to be a professor to help exchange students learn English so they could move to universities over in the States. My business went under right after she got pregnant. I couldn't handle the pressure so I left. Moved back to Detroit and tried to keep my head above water."

His words were frank and honest. They hurt, but it was better than him trying to win me over with sugarcoated promises. I didn't like being patronized and he seemed to understand that. At least we had that going for us.

"So do I have any other family members?"

"Yeah. I have an older brother and my mother's still alive. Never told them about you, though. If I do it now, I'm pretty sure they'll be pissed."

I almost smiled. "I bet. They'd owe me like twenty-three years' worth of birthday money."

He chuckled. This time, it was a genuine sound and not a bitter one. It felt weird to hear. "I know you were too small to remember a lot about her, but you are almost exactly like your mother. You both have this presence. You're a bit more of a tomboy than her, but it's still the same."

"I think that's the closest you've come to complimenting me yet."

"You're welcome."

A moment later, the waitress returned with our food and we ate in a silence that was far less strained than I expected it to be. When I was younger, I had hated him so much for leaving me in my aunt's clutches, but as time went on, I grew to accept it. If he had come to see me back then, I most certainly would have punched him in the face and told him never to return. Now, while I was still hurt and angry, I didn't feel that same rage. A lot of it had to do with the other things in my life that were more threatening. Compared to murdered Seers and an angelic serial killer, my father wasn't so bad.

We finished our food at a leisurely pace and the waitress put the bill on the table, which left me in an awkward place. He was allegedly fifty thousand dollars in debt, but did that mean he had no money at all or just not enough money? My conscience got the better of me and I paid for it. He muttered his thanks, seeming uncomfortable. Not that I blamed him.

"So what are you going to do about your debt?"

Lewis scratched the back of his neck, avoiding my gaze. "I'll figure something out. I always do."

"So you're not a…"

He glanced at me then. "A what?"

I bit my bottom lip, rephrasing the sentence. "What is it that you do? Or don't I want to know?"

"It's not important. I've got a lead and I'll take care of it. I shouldn't have asked you for help. I was just being an asshole because I heard you were dating some guy in a rock band and I thought you were well-off. Hoped you'd be happy to see me."

I watched him. "You wanted me to get angry, didn't you?"

He shifted in his seat, not answering me. I continued anyway. "You felt like you deserved it so you purposely came at me the wrong way so it could get rid of some of your guilt. I'm right, aren't I?"

Again, he said nothing. I shook my head. "At least now I know where I get my messed up social skills from."

"You're welcome."

I rolled my eyes and then glanced at my watch. "I have to get going."

"Alright, but one more thing."

He took a deep breath, finally looking at me. "Earlier, you said you already had a father. Who were you talking about?"

I winced. "I was angry when I said that, but...it's sort of true. There was a man that my mother knew. He couldn't get custody of me, but he sent me letters that helped me keep my head up. His name was Andrew."

"Was?"

"Yeah. He died a few years ago," I replied in a soft voice, wrapping my fingers around the hem of the grey duster.

"I see. Sorry to hear that."

"Me too."

"For what it's worth, I'm glad you had someone to support you." He stood up and I followed suit. We left the restaurant and stood on the sidewalk.

Lewis reached inside his pocket and withdrew a business card. "Here. You don't have to call me or anything, but if you ever want to, that's where I can be reached."

I accepted it. "Thanks."

He shook his head, looking pained as he did. "Don't...don't thank me. Ever. I'm sorry about everything I've done and haven't done. I know that's not enough, but I thought you should know."

I merely nodded in reply. He stepped back, clearing his throat. "Take care, alright?"

"Yeah. You too."

He turned and walked down the street. I put his card in the pocket of my duster and buttoned it up before going in the opposite direction. I'd have to catch the bus to Michael's place and the bus stop was a few streets away.

As I walked, I felt a prickling sensation along the hairs on the nape of my neck like I was being watched. I kept my same relaxed posture and checked the reflections in the windows I passed to see if anyone looked suspicious. I stretched my energy outward to sense the presence of an angel or demon, but couldn't feel anything.

Just then, someone grabbed me by the arm and yanked me into a nearby alley one street away from the bus stop. I whirled around and punched my attacker in the ribs. He let go in an instant and I raised my fists in a fighting stance.

"It's me, you fool!" the stranger hissed.

I squinted in the dim light to find Belial glaring down at me. I shoved him hard enough that he hit the brick wall behind him.

"What the hell did you do that for?"

"Hush. Come with me." He grabbed my hand in his gloved one and pulled me behind a dumpster, forcing me to squat next to him.

"Belial—"

"Shh," he said, holding up one finger. I opened my mouth to demand what he was trying to pull, but then I heard footfalls in the alley. Heavy, solid, distinctive, as if the person wore dress shoes. A shadow fell across the grimy concrete in front of us. Belial jumped up, grabbing the man from behind. The man thrashed, trying to get the demon off his back, and that was when I saw the gun in his hand.

I leapt up and slammed the heel of my hand into his solar plexus, winding him. His grip loosened on the gun. I grabbed his wrist and twisted it at a painful angle. He cried out and dropped the firearm, but his other fist came around and hit me in the temple. Pain sparked across the side of my face. I went spinning backward, clutching the injured spot. When I recovered, Belial had produced a large knife from somewhere and held it against the man's neck.

"Move again and I'll slit your throat," the demon growled.

The man's face settled into a furious look, but he held up his hands in surrender. He was white, dark-haired, about six-foot-one, easily over 250 lbs., with a muscular frame like an ex-football player: big shoulders, big hands, thick legs, and a heavy stomach. In the dim light of the alley, I spotted a silver class ring glinting on his right hand. Good thing he'd popped me with his left.

Belial shoved the guy against the wall, keeping the knife just below his chin. I stood next to him, still rubbing the sore side of my face.

"Are you alright?" the demon asked.

"I'm fine," I grumbled. "Just tired of getting hit in the face by guys. Whatever happened to chivalry?"

Belial let out an amused snort. "It's a dying art."

He faced the attacker. "Now then, who are you and why are you following my lovely friend here?"

"Bite me."

Belial grinned and it was similar to the way I imagined a lion would at an injured gazelle. "Oh, don't tempt me. Answer the question while you still can."

"I wanted her phone number," the man replied with the utmost sarcasm. He seemed very confident for a guy with a knife at his jugular.

"This is getting us nowhere." I flipped the guy's coat open and found an inner pocket housing his wallet.

I opened the wallet, locating his driver's license. "Marsellus Wallace? Really? That's the best you could do on a fake ID?"

The man shrugged. "What can I say? I'm a Tarantino fan."

"Great. It says here that you're a Detroit resident. So I'm guessing you're here to kidnap me as collateral?"

"Winner, winner, pizza dinner."

Belial glanced at me, arching an eyebrow. "Collateral? I'm assuming this has something to do with the gentleman you had dinner with a few minutes ago."

I shot him a dirty look. "How long have you been following me?"

"That's not important. I'd be more grateful if I were you. Without my help, this fellow would have made off with you and your husband would be none the wiser."

"What? Do you want me to thank you for that?"

He flashed me a smug grin. "You do owe me one."

"Blow it out your ass."

"Jesus Christ, get a room," the man said.

Belial dug the knife a little deeper, forcing the guy to stand on his tiptoes to avoid getting nicked. "Manners, my good man. Manners."

"Alright, Mr. Wallace, who are you working for?" I asked.

"Santa Claus."

I sighed. This guy was the snarkiest henchman in existence. "Look, I know Lewis owes some very bad people money and he hasn't got a lot of time left. If you're here, I'm guessing he has somewhere around forty-eight hours to get the money. If you tell me who you work for, I might be able to get you the damn money. Won't that make everyone happy?"

"Sorry, honey. The man who pays me don't pay me to run my mouth. I just do what I'm told and I was told to pick you up to give Mr. Jackson some incentive."

Belial cleared his throat. "Jordan, may I intervene?"

I eyed him. It was probably a bad idea to let an archdemon interrogate someone, but so far my methods weren't working. Time to take a gamble. "Go for it."

The demon aimed a polite smile at the henchman, one that made my skin crawl. "Mr. Wallace, is it? About how much do you weigh?"

Wallace gave Belial a weird look, unsure of where the conversation was going. "Two sixty and change."

"Ah. So that means you have probably about ten pints of blood in you. Have you ever suffered from massive blood loss before, Mr. Wallace?"

"Can't say I have."

"It's a terrible feeling, really. Especially when caused by a knife. Gunshot wounds are quicker. They may hurt much more, but when you lose blood by a knife, it's a slow process. There's the prick of the blade that causes a sharp pain. However, this depends on where it is on the body. On the arms, it's a very distinct kind of pain. If you cut deep enough, your whole arm goes numb, but the shallow cuts are the worst part of it. My personal favorite is abdominal bleeding. Depending on where the injury is, it can take hours to bleed to death. You can try to staunch the wound, but the internal damage is always what does you in. The pain is deep and your breathing gets labored as you put the pieces together and finally realize that you're going to die. It's amazing how some people react. I've seen some of them cry and beg to be saved, but the ones who are the most interesting are the ones who take the knife and slit their own throat just to make the death a little easier and faster. It's spectacular what one little knife can do."

He started to lower the blade to the man's stomach and I almost grabbed his wrist, but Wallace finally broke.

"Jesus, man, I work for Lamont! Lamont Brooks!"

I stepped forward. "And who is Mr. Lamont Brooks?"

"Jackson wanted to buy a building for his consulting business. Someone came in with a better offer so he had to come up with the money fast. He went to Lamont and took out a loan, promised to pay it back in a month. He bought the place, but Lamont changed his mind, said he wanted it in two weeks. Jackson couldn't come up with it in time and skipped town, so they sent me and one of my partners to follow him."

"How many days does he have left to pay it off?"

"Two."

"Shit," I muttered. "What's he up to?"

"I don't know, but by the looks of things, I think he knows he's a dead man. If you're who I think you are, he came to put his affairs in order before Lamont catches up to him."

"Where's your partner?"

"He's following Jackson. Should be calling in any minute now."

"Here's what you're going to do, Mr. Wallace. You're going to call off your friend and you're going to go back to Detroit and tell Lamont that his little loan shark game is over. If he doesn't listen, you can tell him I can make one phone call and he'll be rotting in jail for the rest of his miserable life."

I fished the phone out of Wallace's pocket. "Do it."

The henchman reached up to take it, but Belial interrupted us. "That won't be necessary."

I glanced at him. "Why?"

"I've already taken care of his associate. You may go on your way now, Mr. Wallace."

He lowered the knife from the man's throat and handed him his cell phone, dropping his voice to a whisper. "But believe me when I say that you had better adhere to your instructions or one day you will wake up in your bed and I will be there in the darkness waiting for you with my knife, and then we will find out just what kind of man you'll be when you die."

Wallace swallowed hard and stumbled out of the alley without looking back. Belial stashed his knife and straightened his clothes.

I faced him. "What do you mean 'took care' of his associate?"

He tilted his head to the side, giving me a contemplative look. "Would you prefer a lie or the truth?"

I balled my hands into fists. "Answer me, you son of a bitch. Did you kill him?"

Belial's face went blank. "He decided not to cooperate. I had no choice."

I closed my eyes as a wave of anger rolled down my body. "You bastard."

"You are the most ungrateful person I have ever met," the demon snapped. "That is twice now that I have saved your life with nothing to show for it."

I opened my eyes and stepped close to him, enough to smell his cologne and feel the heat from his body. "Listen and listen well, Belial. You are not my lover. You do not have the right to protect me and if you ever kill someone in my name again, I will personally send you back to Hell where you belong."

"Since when do you have the backbone to threaten me, human?" His voice came out a deadly murmur. I could feel his anger boiling around him like steam, clashing with mine.

"I could rip you apart before you could blink and send you back to your precious archangel in a pretty cardboard box. And I would enjoy doing it."

"But you won't. Because that violates our agreement and you'd be sent to Hell to report yet another failure to your master," I snarled in his face. His jaw shifted and I could tell he hated the fact that I was right. Good.

"Fair enough. But let me also make one thing clear." He moved even closer, sliding one long-fingered hand into my hair, his warm breath falling across my face, close enough to kiss me if he wanted to.

"When this is over, I will no longer uphold my previous chivalry. I want you for myself and I intend to take you from your archangel. Rest assured that it will be bloody and violent and you will regret refusing me while I was still being a gentleman."

He balled that same hand into a fist, jerking my head upward so that his reptilian eyes filled my gaze. "Do you understand me, Jordan?"

"Knock yourself out."

He threaded his gloved fingers through my hair and waved towards the alley leading to the sidewalk. "Ladies first."

I stalked past him, shoving my hands in my pockets so he couldn't see them shaking.

CHAPTER ELEVEN

MICHAEL

The doorbell rang. I couldn't help but shake my head as I walked towards the door. She always made fun of me for leaving my key, but this was the third time in a month that she had forgotten hers.

"You're late," I said as soon as I opened the door, and then froze.

Jordan and Belial stood on my doorstep. Anger rushed through me so quickly that I almost got dizzy.

"What's he doing here?" My voice came out in an unearthly growl.

Jordan sighed. "Long story."

"Shorten it."

She gave me a tired look. "On the way back from my meeting with Lewis, I found out I was being followed by a Mook who works for the guy he owes money. Belial was kind enough to help me get rid of him. Plus, he has some information for us on the Apocalypse research."

Belial held up the manila folder for emphasis. I narrowed my eyes at him. "Great. Give me the papers and get lost."

The demon's lips stretched into a smirk. "Ah, ah, ah. That's not the deal. The deal is that I help you catch the rogue angel. That includes keeping me in the loop, archangel. Or have you forgotten our agreement?"

I took a threatening step forward and Jordan pressed her hand against my stomach, stopping me. "Michael, you knew this was going to happen eventually. Don't give him the satisfaction."

She brushed past me. Belial remained where he was, smiling like the cat who got the canary.

Jordan glanced at him, confused. "Uh, what's the problem?"

Belial continued staring at me. "You have to invite me in. I cannot enter because he has blessed the apartment."

"What? Like a vampire?" Jordan asked, her voice incredulous.

"In a manner of speaking, yes."

"Figures."

She touched my arm. "You can bless it again after he's gone. Let's just get this over with."

I lifted my hand in front of the door and made a cross, muttering the proper incantation to remove the blessing. Belial walked inside and I shut the door. The angelic part of my soul raged at the very idea that I had let a demon into my home. I agreed with it wholeheartedly, but I knew he served a purpose. Demons were exceptionally good at tracking people down because they could work outside the law. Still, even seeing his face made me want to behead him and play kickball with his skull.

"Feel free to not make yourself at home," Jordan said to the demon, beckoning me towards the bedroom. I followed her and shut the door, rounding on her.

"What the hell is going on?"

She sat on my bed, tugging off her tennis shoes. "Hi, honey, good to see you too."

"Don't get cute. How did he know where you were?"

"I don't know. I think he's been tailing me to see if the rogue angel will make another move, but instead he found someone else tailing me too."

A haggard sigh pushed out from between my lips. "Do you ever have a normal day?"

She spared me a weary smile. "Once. It was a Thursday."

"Not funny. Who was the guy following you?"

"A *Pulp Fiction* fan, apparently. He works for Lamont Brooks—a loan shark in Detroit. It turns out Daddy-O took out a loan and Lamont pulled a fast one on him. Told him to have the money in two weeks instead of four. Lewis couldn't come up with it and skipped town to find me. The guy following me thinks Lewis knows he's out of luck and came to see me before he…"

She struggled to finish the sentence. "…before Lamont catches up with him."

I ran a hand through my hair. "Geez, so he was putting his affairs in order, not trying to guilt you into giving him the money?"

"Yeah, that seems to be the size of it."

"What did you do?"

"Belial did a scary little speech and we sent him packing. Told him to tell Lamont to back off or we'd throw him in jail. I guess that's the best part about marrying into the angel family. We know people." The last part she said with a bit of amusement in her voice.

"Jordan, there's no time to joke about this. I'm sure Lamont sent more than one guy if he was planning to use you to as ransom."

Her smile vanished, replaced with cold anger. "Oh, Belial decided to take care of that for me."

"What?"

"He killed the other guy Lamont sent before he got to the one following me."

I went still. "Were you there when it happened?"

"No. But I believed what he told me. I warned if he ever did that again, I'd send him back to Hell." She shrugged out of her duster, tossing it on the bed.

I settled one hand on her thigh and then touched the side of her face so that she met my eyes. "Are you okay?"

She leaned her forehead against mine. "Not even close. I don't want anyone to die because of me, Michael. Ever. Why does this keep happening?"

"It's not your fault. That man chose to be involved with unscrupulous people and he probably had it coming."

"I don't know about that. Being killed by Belial, it...I can't even allow myself to think about what he did to that man before he let him die. If you heard the way he talked about his knife..." She let the sentence trail off, seeming too disgusted to continue.

I kissed her, rubbing the length of her leg. "We'll get this figured out. I promise."

"I'm sorry."

"For what?"

"Being such a death magnet."

I almost laughed at her word choice. "You're not a death magnet. You're a Seer. Normal was never an option for you."

She gave me a sarcastic look. "Thanks, that's encouraging."

"You're welcome. We'll finish this conversation later. Let's get rid of the bastard sitting on my couch first."

"I wonder if he'd get mad if we had really loud sex in here while he's out there."

I chuckled, tugging her off the bed. "No, he'd probably try to join in. If I'm ever going to be in a *ménage a trois*, it needs to be the cool kind, not a literal devil's threesome."

"Ha. You wish." She gave me one last kiss and opened the bedroom door. I followed her into the den.

Belial had taken off his coat and settled on the couch spreading the papers from his folder out on the glass coffee table. The first two buttons of his forest-green dress shirt were undone, as was his tie, and his sleeves were rolled up to his forearms. He had made himself at home just to antagonize us. Terrific.

"Welcome back, love birds," the demon said as we approached. Jordan sat as far away from him as she could on the couch. I chose the spot on her left to ensure that Belial didn't try to move closer.

"Can the sarcasm. What did you find?"

The demon held up the first sheet of paper. "I compiled a search of Apocalypse theories for the year 2011. The first one to pop up was the one predicted by a radio host by the name of Harold Camping. He claimed that the Rapture would happen on May 21st, and of course, he was wrong. However, interestingly, he later claimed that October 21st would be the end of the world. While I still maintain that this fellow is completely out of his gourd, I took a look at the instance anyhow and found that he believes in a mathematical-based prediction system. I won't bore you with the details, but while he's wrong again, studying predictions for October led me somewhere unexpected."

He selected another piece of paper. "I found an end-of-the-world prediction that also claims that October would be the month of a calamitous change for the earth. It comes from a small cult called Christ's Heel. They believe that the Leviathan would be discovered and awakened to devour the sinful men of earth in order to cleanse it for Christ's return."

"The Leviathan?" I interrupted, shocked.

Belial nodded. "They seem to disagree with the fire and brimstone idea. The cult talks about the Hellmouth being used by a demon and an anointed one. That is where the Seer your rogue angel talks about would come in."

"I read about this during my research too," Jordan said, glancing at me. "But most of the information I got about the Leviathan is pure speculation. What is it exactly?"

"The Leviathan is a sea creature that God made during the first seven days of Creation. However, its power somehow caused it to accumulate the evil that came into existence from the creation of good. It's sort of an equation, really. For every action, there is an equal and opposite reaction. Good needs evil as a balance and the Leviathan became a great source of evil to the point where Satan took notice and used its mouth as a gateway to Hell. Once God banished Satan from the Earth, He sent the Leviathan back to the Waters of Chaos and it was never heard from again."

"So technically, it's still alive?"

"Yes. Its jaws were locked shut by an angel long ago. The only way to awaken it would be to unlock the Hellmouth with a source of purity."

"You mentioned the Waters of Chaos. Where are they?"

"I believe it's an area near the Arctic Circle. The Leviathan was sent there to remain isolated and undiscovered for mankind's own safety. Normally, a creature like that would be killed, but no one has ever been able to do so."

Jordan folded her hands over her mouth, her brows knitting together. "So do either of you think this is a legitimate theory?"

The demon and I shared a look. We had plenty of differences, but I could tell we were thinking the same thing.

"More than likely," I said. "It's too much of a coincidence that this theory is so closely tailored to the rogue angel's actions. Besides, the other Apocalypse theories I researched said nothing about Seers or anointed ones. Most talk about the usual earthquakes and floods and such."

"So what's our next move? Is there any way we can go on the offense or do we have to wait for the translation of *Et Liber Tempor*?"

I started to answer, but Belial cut me off. "That may be where I can help."

He slid a photograph over to us. "One of my men snapped this picture in south Florida. None of them were aboard, unfortunately, but it's still a lead."

In the picture, I could see the side profile of the rogue angel with a duffel bag over his shoulder climbing up the ramp to a large plane. "Any idea where he's heading?" I asked.

"This is a common mode of transportation for criminals and illegal aliens. I was told the particular destination of this plane is São Paulo, Brazil. I suggest you get one of your best archangels down there, and quickly, before he murders someone else."

I stared at the photo. Logically, the best thing to do would be to send a good tracker and a good fighter. There were people I could call to get the job done, but this angel — one of my brothers — had almost murdered the woman I loved. I didn't want to risk losing her again. He would have to be stopped by my hand.

"I'll go," I said, my voice quiet.

Jordan looked at me, apprehensive. "Michael, you don't have to do this yourself."

"He nearly killed you, Jordan. I'm not taking any more risks. I won't let anyone else die."

"Then am I to assume I'll be here acting as her bodyguard?" Belial asked in a mildly annoyed voice.

"No. You're coming with me."

Surprise stole across the demon's face. Jordan stood then, holding up her hands.

"Wait, wait, wait. You're expecting me to believe you're going to fly to Brazil with the person you hate most in this world and work together to stop the rogue angel?"

I frowned. "I don't see how that's any different from what you did in Edmonton and Cleveland."

"It *is* different, Michael. Belial won't kill me yet because he wants to sleep with me."

Belial made a rude noise in his throat. "I'm right here, you know."

She ignored him. "You can't even say his name without turning into the Incredible Hulk. I think you should send someone else."

"I'm the Commander of Heaven's Army. As talented as the rogue angel is, I know he is not a better fighter than I am. Belial is an expert tracker and he can operate outside of the law. He can get me places the angels can't. This is the best way to make sure we stop the rogue angel for good."

She massaged the bridge of her nose. "Have you always been this stubborn?"

Belial and I answered at the same time. "Yes."

"What am I supposed to do while you're gone? Knit a sweater?"

"It'll take a few days at the most, no more. You need to settle things with Lewis. Gabriel should be able to protect you in the meantime. I expect we'll hear from Raphael about the translation soon."

"This is a terrible plan."

"I know. But it's a necessary evil."

Belial sighed. "For once, I agree. This will be a very unpleasant trip, but your logic is somewhat sound. I'll return in the morning. I assume you'll take care of the tickets?"

I nodded. The demon gathered half of his papers together and slid them back in the folder. He held out the rest to Jordan.

"For your records."

She took them and headed to the bedroom to file them away. As soon as she was out of sight, Belial glanced at me.

"Before you fly off the handle, as I suspect you're about to, you should know she wasn't trying to stop you from going to get the rogue angel because she wanted to be with me. If anything, she's been trying this whole time to prove she isn't like me."

I cast a suspicious glare in his direction. "What makes you say that?"

"She hasn't given in once, not even when I kissed her."

My blood ran cold. "When you *what*?"

Just then, Jordan walked back in and I forced myself not to say anything else. We didn't need to fight in front of the demon. He'd enjoy it too much.

Satisfied with his work, Belial went to the door, shooting us both an amused look. "Happy fighting, love birds."

He left. Jordan went into the kitchen, saying nothing. I followed her, watching as she set about washing dishes—her go-to move whenever she was upset. I didn't mind since I had a bad habit of tossing all the dirty stuff in the dishwasher until she came over to turn it on. I sat on the stool in front of the counter, crossing my arms and doing my best to suppress my anger.

"Y'know, this is probably unhealthy behavior."

"What do you expect me to do?" she grumbled, sticking her fingers under the faucet as the water ran. "I can't drink. I can't eat sweets anymore because now I have to fit into a wedding dress. Cleaning is pretty much all I've got left for stress relief."

"That's very Monica of you. Less Chandler than usual."

She gripped the edge of the sink, closing her eyes. "Michael—"

"Hey, you're the one who told me to have a better sense of humor."

She glared at me. "Yeah, but you're being an ass about it. I don't believe for a second that you can cooperate with Belial enough to catch the rogue angel. I saw the look on your face when you opened the door. If I hadn't been here, you would have tried to kill him. Tell me I'm wrong."

"You're acting like that's not justified," I said, dropping the humor from my voice. "Did you forget the 'tried to rape and kill you' bit? I haven't."

"This isn't about me, Michael. It's you. You still haven't learned to control your temper when it comes to Belial. He feeds off your anger and your jealousy. I don't want him getting any more powerful than he already is."

"I think we're way past that at this point."

"What are you talking about?"

"Why didn't you tell me he kissed you?"

Her eyes widened for a second, but she quickly covered it with a frown. "He didn't kiss me."

I didn't remember walking around the counter over to her, just that I was suddenly next to her with one hand around her left wrist. "Jordan. Did Belial kiss you?"

"Michael—"

"Answer the question."

She exhaled. "Yes. It was last year, when we fought in the hospital."

I let her arm drop. Fury wriggled through my guts like a snake and I had to flatten my hands on the counter to keep from punching through the wall.

"That son of a bitch. I knew it. I knew this was what he wanted."

"What?"

"He's following the playbook step by step. He's trying to drive a wedge between us. Make himself look better by saving you. It starts with the dreams. He convinces you that you're like him and that you're attracted to him. Next he'll start trying to show you that I'm wrong, that *I'm* the hypocrite, not him. That's exactly why he agreed to help us. He doesn't care about the rogue angel or the Seers. He wants the one thing he can never have. He wants a replacement for Zora."

Jordan grabbed my arm, making me face her. "Michael, you're insane. Belial can't trick me into wanting him. I know what he is. I know what he's capable of doing. I would never betray you."

"Are you sure?" I murmured. "Because I'm pretty sure you just lied to me about Belial kissing you. That's how it starts. Little lies. They start getting bigger by the second until one day you don't know who you married anymore."

"Oh, I'm the liar? Why didn't you tell me that you bailed Lewis out of jail?"

"Because I thought he deserved a second chance. He may be an asshole, but he does care about you. I wasn't sure you'd be able to see that if you knew he had been in jail."

"Well, thanks for believing in me," she snapped, turning her back on me to go into the bedroom.

I sighed, knowing I had finally gone too far. "Jordan."

She came out with her shoes and duster on, walking towards the door. I stayed where I was, unable to keep the frustration out of my voice.

"Where are you going?"

"Out. And don't wait up."

She slammed the door, leaving me in a vacuum of silence.

She was exactly where I hoped she would be when I arrived. She wore a beautiful red dress that brought out the rich dark sienna of her skin and the black of her long, wavy hair. The red clashed with the endless white surrounding us like a rose petal floating in a pool of cream.

My wings were a heavy but comfortable weight as I walked towards where she sat on a bench at the top of a hill, watching the spirits in the gorge below with an utterly peaceful expression. I took a seat beside her.

A smile touched her lips. "Hello, *mi hijo*."

"Hi, Catalina."

She glanced at me. "You don't seem surprised to see me."

"Very little surprises me these days. Besides, Uriel told me you like to visit sometimes."

"It's peaceful here," Catalina Amador replied, folding her elegant fingers over one knee. "Not that Heaven itself is not peaceful, but I enjoy having some time to myself. This is a tranquil place. Nowhere else in the universe like it."

"That's why I come here to clear my head sometimes."

"Oh? And what clouds your mind right now, Michael?"

"Your daughter."

A flicker of emotion darted through her brown eyes. Concern, mostly, but some regret as well. In many ways, Catalina was as guarded as Jordan, but not about her family. She could be fiercely protective of anyone she cared about and we had that in common. "What about my daughter?"

~ 134 ~

"You don't have to be coy. I'm aware that you've spoken with Gabriel and Raphael and that you know about the rogue angel."

"I do, but the tone in your voice is much more personal. You're worried about your relationship, not just her safety."

I winced and didn't answer. She touched my hand, adopting a gentle tone. "You are safe here, Michael. Please tell me what's wrong. Perhaps I can help."

"We had our first fight. The first big one, anyway. Belial is trying to take her from me and I'm not sure I can stop him," I said, too ashamed to meet her gaze.

"You speak of Jordan like she's an object, not a person. It's her decision to make, not yours. You cannot prevent this on your own."

I opened my mouth to argue, but she held up her hand to silence me. "I'm not saying that all is lost, but you must understand that even if you do everything you can to keep them apart, it is still something Jordan has to overcome. It's your job as her husband to have faith in her and support her even when you are in doubt."

"It's easier said than done," I said, unable to hide my frustration. "We were fine before this all started but the second Belial walks back into our lives, everything goes to hell."

Catalina shook her head. "When will you young ones understand that life is what happens after you've made plans? Did you think that your happiness relied only on when your lives seemed simple?"

"Of course not. But in spite of everything we've been through, our relationship has always been stable. Even when things were at their nastiest, we had each other to lean on. I suppose I've just gotten used to it being that way."

She squeezed my hand so that I'd look at her. "You are a very passionate man, Michael. Before Jordan, you were so strict and hardened. You were the best soldier any of us had ever seen, but you were missing something. Now that you've found that part of yourself, you're scared of losing it and going back to the way you were. That's why you've been so protective of Jordan. You're afraid of going back to that life."

I sighed. "Am I that transparent?"

"You're allowed to have a weakness. Everyone is."

I stood abruptly as anxiety and anger surged within me. "But I'm not supposed to! I'm an archangel. That is who I am. I can't have insecurities or fears or doubts because if I do, people will get hurt."

Catalina stood as well, keeping that perfect calm she always had. "You are not just an archangel. You are a man as well. And you will continue to struggle with these problems until you accept that about yourself. Being human isn't a weakness. You of all people should know that by now."

I stepped closer to her, lowering my voice. "But what if that isn't enough? What if I'm not enough?"

"Shh," she whispered. "*Mi hijo,* you are enough. I promise. If you need proof of that, just look at what you've done. Yours is the sword that cut the side of Satan. You have saved this world and the heavens above it more times than anyone cares to count. Jordan would not have fallen in love with you if you weren't enough."

"Then what should I do?"

"Have faith in yourself and in Jordan. Don't let your fear override your responsibilities to her and to the people you are sworn to protect."

At last, I managed a weak smile. "I'll try."

She kissed my forehead. "You'll succeed. I know my daughter is stubborn, but she'll forgive you."

"She misses you."

"I know."

"Ahem."

We both turned our heads to see a tall, dark-haired man in a grey duster identical to Jordan's, a white dress shirt, and black slacks, his tie loose, hands in his pockets. He arched an eyebrow, the one with a thin white scar through it, and smirked.

"Am I interrupting something?"

"No," I said, resisting the urge to grin out of sheer fondness. "I was just leaving."

"Uh-huh. I always knew you had a thing for Cat," he mused, walking over to Catalina's side.

She rolled her eyes. "You are insufferable, Andrew."

"I know, right? Isn't it sexy?" the Seer teased, giving her a kiss. "They're asking for you upstairs. Something about new recruits not knowing how to be sophisticated and devastatingly beautiful."

Catalina sighed. "Very well. If it gives me an excuse to get away from you, then I'll accept the call."

"Ouch," he said with a mock-offended look.

She gave him a peck on the cheek and then nodded to me. "Take care, *mi hijo*. Give Jordan my love."

"I will." She picked up the hem of her dress and started down the hill.

We watched her go and then Andrew spoke. "I take it by your presence here that you're having a few marital problems."

"That's putting it mildly," I answered. "But Catalina seems to think I'll be able to handle it."

"It's not just her, y'know," the older man said, his tone not unkind. "There's a reason we'd follow you into the gates of Hell and back."

I raised an eyebrow. "No pressure."

Andrew chuckled. "Point taken. Still, I think you should give yourself a break. Jordan doesn't need you to be perfect. She just needs you."

I smiled. "Thanks."

"You're welcome. Be good to her. I'd hate to have to kick your ass." With that and another roguish grin, he turned and headed down the hill as well. I stood there for a moment and then returned the way I came, feeling just a bit taller.

CHAPTER TWELVE

JORDAN

Question One: where do you go to blow off steam when you're recovering from alcohol dependence and pissed off at your husband?

Question Two: where do you go to blow off steam that isn't packed full of drunk guys who want to take you home?

Answer: a lesbian pool hall.

The Lemon Drop was a club that had bought out the basement of an old barbershop. There was no dress code, no long lines, and no Ladies Night, for obvious reasons. Movies and TV always made such places look like obscenely campy joints, but this place had decently priced drinks, nice pool tables, and great music. I knew this only because Lauren had taken me here a few times when her asshole ex-husband worked her nerves and she wanted to hate men for a while.

The temptation to drink hung over my head like an obnoxious, overweight ghost, but I ignored it and played a few rounds of pool with some girls I met. Only one of them tried to get my number, but I flashed my wedding ring and she respectfully gave up. The girls could tell by the look on my face that I didn't want to chat or rant about men. I just wanted to go somewhere and think about something other than my life.

I wasn't any good at pool—just okay. Raphael had taught me to play. Every so often, he came through town and gave me lessons. Somehow, we had stumbled across the subject when he helped heal me after the incident with the Spear of Longinus. He was soft spoken, but whenever I saw him play, he shone with a brilliance that most guys would die to possess. The stereotype of the cool pool player was a staple in American culture for a reason. I enjoyed watching his dark eyes take in the position of the balls on the table, the steadiness of his hands when he aimed, and the small upward tilt of his mouth when he got a shot just right.

"You wanna break this time?"

I climbed out of my thoughts when Carol, the blonde woman I was playing against, spoke. I waved a hand at her. "Nah, you go ahead. I break like a sissy."

She snorted, tucking her cigarette in one corner of her mouth while she aimed. *Clack!* The balls scattered across the table. The solid one clunked into a pocket.

"You're pretty quiet. Sure you don't want to blow off some steam?" she asked, taking aim.

I leaned against the wall behind me. "Not really."

She made the shot, walking around the table to pick another ball. "C'mon, you've got to give me something. It's dull if we don't at least talk shit about each other's game."

"You're welcome to. I know I'm not that good."

"Yet," she corrected, and missed the next shot. "You just gotta practice. It's all about repetition. After a while, it's second nature."

I aimed carefully. "Tch. To be honest, I don't even trust my first nature, let alone a second one."

The blue striped clattered into a corner pocket. Maybe anger was the key to my game. Big surprise there.

Carol watched with an amused look. "Why's that?"

I shrugged one shoulder. "Seems like I'm wrong about a lot of things. It takes me forever to trust someone and then, when they mess up, I always bail. It's like I'm watching myself on TV or something and I pretend like the consequences don't affect me."

I missed the next shot and Carol took over. "That's not uncommon, y'know. I know I distance myself from some decisions I make so I won't feel guilty if things go bad."

"Any idea how to fix it?"

She paused, letting smoke curl up out of her nostrils. "Find something that's worth feeling guilty over. Like that lucky husband of yours."

I lifted an eyebrow and she grinned. "C'mon, I saw you reject that hot brunette. Don't pretend like you're not straight."

I pouted. "Aw, does that mean you're gonna kick me out?"

She rolled her eyes. "Smart ass."

"Regardless of my backside's education, you wouldn't say that if you met my husband. He's this stubborn, overprotective friggin' know-it-all. Sometimes I think he doesn't trust me even though I know he does and that drives me crazy. I doubt myself enough—I don't want to start doubting him."

"Side-pocket."

I glanced down at the table and realized I hadn't been paying attention to her methodically knocking all her balls in until only the eight ball was left. It bothered me enough to send her a frosty look over the table. "Did you start this conversation just so it could distract me and you could win the game?"

"Who, me? Nah." She shot straight and true, winning her second game. We were tied now. Good thing I hadn't put money on it.

"You're a crafty lass, I'll give you that," I said, tipping my cranberry juice to her.

She raised her amaretto sour in respect. "Trust me—if you're this distracted, you don't need to be here talking to me. You should be talking to him."

I sighed. "You're such a buzzkill."

She laughed. I felt my phone vibrate in my pocket and resisted the urge to suck my teeth in annoyance. Michael had called a total of eleven times in the last two hours.

Carol gave me a flat look. "Will you just answer it? The poor guy probably thinks you're cheating on him."

"Buzzkill."

"Answer the damn phone."

I groaned and flipped open my phone, growling, "What?"

At first, I heard nothing so I pressed one hand over my other ear, straining to listen.

"Hello? Michael?"

Then, faintly, I could hear the sound of a guitar and then his deep voice joined it. It was the opening stanza to the acoustic version of "If You Were Here." It was the first song I'd ever heard him sing.

I closed my eyes, trying not to react to the strained emotion in his soulful voice. Damn him. He knew what his singing did to me.

"Michael, this isn't going to work."

He kept singing through the second verse. I made myself hang up, but then I could hear it. The same music, only faint and gentle like an echo. I placed my pool cue on the table and walked towards the entrance to the bar. At the top of the stairwell stood my husband with his guitar and his cell phone propped up on the wall, singing as if it were perfectly normal and not some sort of 1980's version of an apology. I walked up the stairs, wearing my best poker face as he continued through the song, watching me get closer and closer. A small crowd of girls had gathered behind him to see my reaction, which somehow made it both better and worse at the same time.

When I finally reached him, I crossed my arms beneath my chest and spoke loud enough for him to hear over the music.

"If I come home, will you stop playing this damn song?"

He quit singing and smirked at me, his long fingers still strumming the tune.

"Nothing says 'I love you' like pressuring you into forgiving me in the middle of a crowd of random spectators."

I wanted so badly to be angry with him, but I couldn't stop the smile spreading across my lips as I stared up at him in all his ridiculous glory.

"Jackass."

"I love you too, baby."

He played the final note and the girls behind him all clapped, cheered, and made catcalls. Michael slung the guitar around his back and took my hand, tugging me onto the step right below his and kissing me.

"You know this doesn't mean I forgive you," I mumbled against his lips. He smiled.

"I know. Let's go home."

The mattress tipped to the side and woke me up. My hair had shaken loose during the night so I pushed it out of the way to see my husband sitting next to me. A groan crawled out of my throat as I peered around looking for the clock.

"What time is it?"

"You don't want to know," Michael said. "It's a ten-hour flight so I had to book the earliest one I could find. Just wanted to say bye."

"Mmkay. Call me when you land."

"I will."

A short, tense silence fell between us. After he came and got me from the bar, we didn't talk about the fight. We just returned to his place and went to sleep since he had such an early flight. There were things I wanted to say and things I needed to say, but the words stuck to the back of my throat.

In the end, I sighed and placed my hands on his shoulders, pulling him close. I kissed him, as gently as possible, my voice low. "Come back to me in one piece, okay?"

"I will. I promise. Be careful."

"I will. *Te amo.*"

He leaned in again, his lips soft and warm on mine. He cupped the side of my face, his thumb rubbing along the curve of my jaw. After what seemed like a blissful eternity, Michael pulled away and murmured, "*Te amo.*"

He stood and walked out the door, closing it behind him. Darkness surrounded me. I tugged the covers over my shoulders, praying that God would keep my dreams safe and my husband safer.

CHAPTER THIRTEEN

MICHAEL

Most of the time, I had no problem flying coach, but for a ten-hour flight, I decided to try Gabriel's first class approach. I had to admit my other reason for flying first-class was to keep Belial from working his dark magic on the other passengers. It would be a snap for him to convince some poor girl to join the Mile High Club and feed both his demonic energy and his ego. Not on my watch.

It didn't quite hit me that I'd be trapped on a plane with my mortal enemy for several hours until I woke up from my initial nap. Jordan and I had spent hours in bed, but I hadn't slept for most of them. Offhand, it seemed unwise to fall asleep in front of someone who wanted to kill me, but Belial had no feasible escape plan even if he did try to murder me. Besides, it violated the terms of the agreement so I was safe enough. It was still disconcerting to wake up and see him sitting across from me leafing through a book.

I yawned, checking my watch. "How long was I out?"

"Roughly seven hours," the demon replied in a nonchalant voice.

I eyed him before sitting up in my seat and reaching for the bottled water the flight attendant had been nice enough to leave me. "Been reading this whole time?"

"Well, the first in-flight movie was *The Last Airbender*, so yes."

I choked on the water in mid-swallow, laughing at the utter scorn in his voice. "Good call. After she saw that movie, Jordan asked me if Shyamalan was one of you."

Belial smirked. "Come now. Not even demons are that evil."

I chuckled and screwed the cap on my water. Belial was definitely a prick, but he could be pretty damn funny when he wanted to be. "Fair enough. What are you reading?"

"Doing some research on the Leviathan. It's a rather popular figure in mythology. I've never seen it myself, so I figure I should be prepared in case the situation presents itself."

His explanation made perfect sense. Thus, I became suspicious. Belial could easily facilitate the betrayal that the cult prophesized. He had always been known for his cunning even in the earlier days of history. I only hoped that the translation we got from the Symphony of Time would be more specific about who would betray whom.

~ 143 ~

"Mm. Expect the unexpected and all that," I said, grabbing my backpack from underneath the seat. I had shoved a bunch of books in it because I hadn't gotten the time to read in a long while. Truthfully, I just wanted an excuse not to pick a fight with Belial until we were at ground level and could properly rip each other a new one.

"I can finish this later," the demon answered, setting his book aside. He linked his fingers together and set his pale eyes on me, his face unnervingly blank. "I thought we could take a moment to get reacquainted."

I let out a dry chuckle. "Are you serious?"

Belial shrugged. "We're both men. Perhaps we can find some sort of common ground."

"We lost the last common ground we had when you fell from Heaven. I think it's best if we focus on the mission and not on each other."

"And we will be unable to do so until this tension is addressed."

I stared at him and then lifted an eyebrow. "Are you coming on to me?"

Belial rolled his eyes. "Vanity does not befit an archangel."

"Your crappy phrasing isn't my fault."

"I am interested in your wife."

I went very still. Anger crept up my stomach, spilled through my arms and my spine until it consumed my entire person. But this wasn't the time or the place for it, so I merely sat back in the chair and crossed my arms.

Belial continued now that he had gotten my undivided attention. "I have made it clear to her and so I will do the same for you."

"I'd consider that a chivalric gesture if you actually had a chance with her," I replied with a sneer. "So what's your point? Do you want to have a duel? I'd be happy to whip out a glove and smack you with it."

He ignored my sarcasm. "I am telling you this because up until this point, I have played by the rules. Once this case has been resolved, I will not stop until she is mine. I felt it necessary to inform you because I don't want you to cry foul once I've made my move."

"So this is your version of being fair?"

"Yes."

"That's damn civil of you, Belial. I wish you all the luck in the world."

He narrowed his eyes at me. "You're not taking me seriously."

"Oh, trust me, I'm taking you seriously," I said, permitting some of the fury to slip through into my voice. "But I already know how this story ends so if you want to play mind games, try it with somebody more insecure. I know what you're doing. I've known for a while. You're trying to play Jordan and me against each other because you think that I'll break her heart and she'll come looking for you. If you're waiting for that to happen, better grab a book 'cause you're gonna be waiting for eternity."

"That is one thing you archangels never learned. Your victories are always handed to you, and so you no longer appreciate patience. You're always concerned with the battles, never the war. I see the big picture. Sooner or later, she will give in to me. It's just a matter of time."

"Are you sure you're not mistaking your arrogance for patience?"

The cold smile on his lips stretched. "Quite sure. Do we understand each other, archangel?"

"Perfectly."

"Excellent." Then he picked up his book and opened it as if we hadn't just been talking about him planning to steal my wife. Wonders never ceased.

I took a deep breath to settle my rattled nerves and fished the laptop out of my backpack. After a minute or so, the demon spoke again.

"And for the record, I *was* coming on to you."

"Shut up and read, Belial."

The plane arrived at Guarulhos International Airport at half-past five in the afternoon. As soon as we landed, I tried to call Jordan and let her know we were on the ground, but her phone went straight to voicemail. It worried me, but I pushed past my paranoia and focused on the task at hand.

Belial arranged for his people to wait for the rogue angel's arrival. He left the States hours ahead of us so we would be playing catch up, but hopefully not by too much. The demon's henchmen spotted him hitching a ride into a small city outside of downtown São

Paulo. They would report back when they knew where he got off. For now, Belial and I were headed for a hotel to wait for their call.

We split a taxi to the Hilton at Morumbi—a wealthy district of São Paulo that was several miles from downtown. I had taken care of paying for the flight so Belial booked two rooms right next door to each other. I knew it would be fruitless to insist that we stay in a less opulent place. Belial was oddly like Gabriel in that he believed in taking advantage of luxury whenever there was an opportunity. He had amassed a fortune over the centuries in business ventures and economic advisement. He used different names and different bodies, but the money always stayed close at hand.

I slipped the doorman a generous tip as he left, then went to the window to look out at the city below. We were on the tenth floor of the shimmering silver hotel and so I could see for miles. I'd never been in this part of the city before. The São Paulo I knew was not the decadent part, but rather the seedy underbelly where honest people struggled to get by. Crime was thick in this town, both the blue and white-collar sort. The city had made progress over the years, but some things would never change no matter how pretty you dressed it up.

Belial remained in the doorway, calling over to me. "Don't get too comfy. I expect my men will be calling soon."

"Got it."

"Heard from the wife yet?"

I turned my head and frowned at him. He chuckled. "Forget I asked. *Até logo*, archangel."

With that, he shut the door behind him. I shook my head and shrugged out of my jacket, tossing it on the bed. It was a shame I had to be here under such unpleasant circumstances. I had thought about taking Jordan to Brazil someday. Going to Edmonton was the first time she had ever left America. She still hadn't been to Madrid, her mother's birthplace, and I wanted to take her there for our official honeymoon after the wedding. Jordan thought it was silly to make a Bucket List, but I secretly kept one in my head for her. Our lives were hectic, but that didn't mean we couldn't have a few dreams left in us.

I unpacked the notebook containing the lyrics to my songs and started editing. I became completely consumed in the work until I glanced at my watch. I had been sitting here an hour with no word from Belial. Suspicious.

I closed my eyes and let my energy flood out of me. He hadn't left his room. I could feel his presence there, which meant the rogue angel was still en route to wherever he was going. Or maybe Belial's henchmen had run into trouble. I hoped it was the former rather than the latter. We couldn't find the rogue angel's energy ourselves because he had learned to mask it, making him blend in with everyone else. Most experienced angels and demons knew how to do that, but the Seers unfortunately could not mask their energy without being taught how. I had taught Jordan how to do it a while back, but she wasn't an expert just yet. It took a certain amount of control that she was still working on.

A few minutes later, there was a knock at my door. I opened it to find Belial in casual clothing, which was rare for him because he mostly wore suits. I suspected it was to prevent drawing too much attention to himself. He wore a white button-up shirt and black jeans. It bears mentioning that the ensemble probably cost just under five hundred dollars.

"Looks like this is taking longer than I thought," he said. "I propose we find ourselves some food and get acquainted with the local culture."

I eyed him. It sounded like the reasonable thing to do, which made me even more wary than usual of him. "Right."

I went back into the hotel room and grabbed my jacket as well as the card for the room. I closed the door behind me and followed the demon to the elevator. It still struck me as surreal that I was traveling with one of my enemies as if we were friends. Then again, long ago, Belial had been one of my brothers. I never told Jordan, but before the Fall I had even liked Belial. Back in Heaven, he was very popular among the other angels because of his eloquence. Being around him again reminded me of those days before everything had literally gone to Hell.

"What sort of food are you feeling?" the demon said once we had reached the lobby of the hotel. "There are some American restaurants around this area, but I know of some good local places if you want that instead."

"I can eat American food whenever I want. Let's go local."

"Very well." We both stood on the sidewalk and flagged down a cab. Belial gave the driver our destination—a Brazilian steakhouse— and we were off. A while later, we stopped in front of a crowded place with a red tower and *Fogo de Chão* in black letters. Belial gave the name James Brennan, one of his known aliases, to the maitre'd, who nearly tripped over himself welcoming us. The demon had definitely worked this area before.

The interior was nearly all wood—from the floors to the chairs—and chandeliers hung from the ceiling above the tables. The areas were open rather than arranged with booths like at other places. I had heard about Brazilian steakhouses before and couldn't pretend like I wasn't interested in trying the food and the infamous All-You-Can-Eat carved meats.

A waiter came up and showed us to our seats. He explained how the restaurant worked, with little cards that had a green side to indicate you wanted more food and a red side to indicate you'd had enough. Belial ordered a glass of wine while I went for a soda. I didn't drink while working. Maybe later, after we'd caught the murderer.

"So what's the game plan after my men find the rogue angel?" Belial asked, crossing his arms and meeting my gaze.

I folded my hands on the table. "Recovering the page from the Book of Time is my first priority. You'll be the one more concentrated on stopping him."

"You don't want to exact revenge yourself?"

"This isn't about revenge. It's about justice."

"Bullshit."

I narrowed my eyes at him. "Excuse me?"

"Don't pretend like this isn't personal. You may have Jordan fooled, but I know you better than you think. You want this man dead for hurting your wife."

"Are you sure you're not projecting your feelings onto me?"

The humor slid out of Belial's face. I could tell I had gotten close to the central issue, at the very least. "I find it cute that you think I still have feelings."

It was my turn to smirk. "I know you too, *James*. You also have Jordan fooled into thinking that this is all about power and possession."

"Fine. What do you think I want?"

"I know you want power, probably more than anyone save your master, but the way you've fixated on Jordan makes me think there's more going on than you want to admit."

"What makes you say that?"

"You forget that I knew Zora."

His posture stiffened, but his expression never changed. "So?"

"They have a lot of the same traits. Maybe you do want Jordan and maybe you remember what it was like having Zora around and you miss her."

"Careful," Belial said, his voice soft but threatening. "To imply that I miss a mere human might inspire me to break the agreement we have in place."

The waiter returned with Belial's selection of wine and poured him a glass. Red wine, of course, to go with the red meat. He continued staring at me as if he wanted to tear my throat out and drink my blood instead. Even in the crowded restaurant, I could feel his hostile energy pouring off of him in waves. I'd definitely struck a nerve. Good. Belial delighted in playing head-games with me, but he often forgot I could do the same thing to him.

"How's the wine?"

"Delicious," he answered after a sip, setting the glass down on the table and waving the waiter away. One of the many gaucho chefs moving about the restaurant came by with the first selection of meat, which he introduced as *picanha*—a type of top sirloin. The intense conversation dropped for a minute or two while we ate the delectable food.

"You should know I intend to use lethal force," Belial said after a while. The anger had disappeared, replaced with that unnerving calm he was a master of, even while saying or doing terrible things. "Are you sure you won't stop me at the last minute? Edmond is one of you, after all."

"He *was* one of us," I corrected. "We now have to consider him to be one of the Fallen. I won't hesitate and I won't try to save him."

A ghost of a smile touched Belial's lips. "That sounds rather cold for an angel. Shouldn't you be offering him a chance to repent? Isn't forgiveness part of your whole heavenly schtick?"

I shook my head. "He lost that chance when he confronted Gabriel. It's too late."

"So you're saying there are some sins one can commit that are unforgivable?" the demon simpered. "How un-angelic of you."

I frowned. He was pushing my buttons and I knew it, but it still annoyed me. "I'm not saying he's unforgivable, but he has to be held accountable for his actions. The rules in place for angels are different from the ones for humans. You're oversimplifying the entire process."

"Perhaps, but you seem to be handling this situation like a demon. Conspiring with the enemy to eliminate a target, use of lethal force, hunting him down like an animal…maybe you and I are more alike than you think."

"Are you really trying that cliché on me?"

Belial shrugged. "Sometimes clichés are based on facts, my friend."

I had to bite my tongue to keep from saying, "I'm not your friend." It should have been easy to shake off his words, but I couldn't manage it. Our current methods were less noble than usual when fighting evil. I had gotten my hands dirty before many times, but never against one of my brothers. Maybe, just maybe, Belial had a point.

The chefs continued bringing us different types of meat and I got pretty full by the time Belial's cell phone finally rang. I watched with trepidation as he answered it, saying "yes" a few times before hanging up.

"Was it your men?"

Belial merely smiled and flagged down our waiter. "Check, please. We've got a murder to commit."

CHAPTER FOURTEEN

JORDAN

I was sitting on the couch watching T.V. when the doorbell rang and nearly scared me out of my seat. It took me a second to calm down. Ever since the rogue angel, whenever I heard a doorbell or someone knocking, I jumped out of my skin. Great. First, an intense fear of cats thanks to Belial, and now doorbells. I really was a nut job.

There wasn't a UPS or FedEx guy outside when I checked the peephole. In fact, there was no one there at all. When I opened the door, I found a small box sitting on the welcome mat. I glanced up and down the hallway, but still didn't see anyone. The box had my name and apartment number on it. No return address. Curious.

I picked it up and shut the door, locking it before taking the box into the kitchen. It wasn't very heavy, but there was something solid inside. Maybe a gift from Michael to cheer me up while I waited for him to come home? He sometimes did sweet little things like this to make me feel better when he had to travel.

I pulled the tape off the sides, opened the box, and found a white card on top of a cluster of tissue paper. The front of the card had my name in capital letters, nothing else. I flipped it open and read.

Since Mr. Wallace was kind enough to lend you a hand, I thought you might like to keep it.

-L.B.

"What the hell?" I muttered, poking through the tissue paper to see what was inside. The thin tissue parted to reveal something pale and almost waxy looking. For a second, I couldn't believe what I was seeing because I didn't want to, but reality tore through my mind and made me realize I was staring at a man's severed hand. The thick fingers and the silver class ring were a dead giveaway.

Wallace's right hand.

Lamont had given me Wallace's hand.

Revulsion, disgust, and sheer panic crept up my stomach. I stumbled over to the sink just in time to vomit. Stomach acid burned my throat as I retched, tears streaming from my eyes, sobs clogging my lungs like poisonous gas. A hand. He sent me a human hand and it was *all my fault*.

I clutched the sink as I began to hyperventilate. My shoulders quaked as I fumbled for my cell phone, hitting speed dial. The phone rang and I could hear myself hoarsely chanting, "Oh God, pick up, please God, pick up the phone..."

"Hello?"

"G-Gabriel, please, I need you...I need someone...it's all my fault," I whispered in between gasping sobs, sinking onto the floor as my knees gave out.

"Jordan, what's happening? Are you hurt?"

"He s-sent me his hand. I did this to him. Oh God, it's all my fault!"

"Where are you?"

"At t-the apartment."

"Stay there. I'll be over as soon as I can." He hung up. I dropped the phone, clutching my ribs as they started to ache from the lack of air in my lungs. I couldn't breathe. I was going to suffocate. *All my fault. All my fault.*

I couldn't tell how much time had passed between the phone call and Gabriel rushing through my front door. My entire body had broken into uncontrollable shudders and I couldn't speak because the lump in my throat had gotten too big.

Gabriel knelt in front of me, gripping my face in his large hands, his voice soft and soothing. "Jordan, look at me. You have to calm down or you'll go into shock."

I shook my head. "Can't. Can't do this anymore. I can't."

He swore under his breath and scooped me up in his arms, carrying me over to the couch. He took off his suit jacket and draped it around my shoulders before pulling me into his arms, rubbing my back in slow circles and murmuring that everything would be okay. I cried into his chest, clutching the front of his shirt and wishing my husband was here.

"Apple cinnamon or lemon?"

"Apple cinnamon," I mumbled. Gabriel placed the tea bag in the mug of hot water sitting on my coffee table. He went to the kitchen and brought me some sugar. I watched the red from the tea stain the clear liquid and shuddered, tugging Gabriel's massive suit jacket tighter around my shoulders. Maybe I should have chosen lemon.

Once the tea settled, I poured in some sugar and blew on the cup before taking a careful sip. My hands only shook a little as I held the mug up to my lips. Gabriel sat down beside me and we drank in silence for a couple minutes. I broke first.

"I'm sorry," I said. "For all of this. I didn't mean to drag you into it."

"Jordan...you do realize you just apologized to me for having a panic attack after some sick criminal sent you a human hand in the mail," Gabriel replied.

I winced. It did sound silly when put into words. "Yeah, but you were probably doing something important before you came here—"

"Jordan, stop it," he snapped. "You are not just some girl to me. You are family. My family. It is my duty to help you in any way I can. You don't need to feel guilty every time you need help dealing with something."

"I can't help it, Gabriel. You're an archangel. There are literally millions of people who need you more than I do."

"The people of the world don't need me and me alone. That's what my brothers and sisters are for. Trust me, we've got them covered to our best ability. Now tell me who did this so I can rip him in half."

"It's Lamont," I said, pushing stray strands of hair out of my eyes. "He's sending a message. I told one of his flunkies to back off my dad and he didn't take it well. I figured there would be ramifications, but this...this is something I've never seen before. I've seen the demons do horrible things, but this is barbaric. I have to do something about it. Lewis won't stand a chance against someone who would butcher a guy just for talking."

"Well, first, we must act logically. I have a friend who can take a look at the hand and give us some clues as to who this man is. We need to stop the problem at the source."

"We?"

"Yes, we. You didn't think you were going to take on a loan shark in Detroit by yourself, did you?"

"Not exactly."

"Good. All we need to do is find out who he really is and end this."

I checked my watch. "Are you sure we can do that in twelve hours? That's how long Lewis has before his time limit is up. They'll come for him and me."

Gabriel flashed me a dangerous smirk. "I'd like to see them try."

He pushed my cell phone towards me. "Call your father. Find out where he is. We need to get him somewhere safe before we make our move."

"Thank you," I said, unable to keep my voice from wavering a bit. "I don't deserve a brother like you."

He lifted my hand and kissed it, smiling. "Think nothing of it, my dear. Make the call."

I picked up the phone and went into the kitchen to find my duster. I'd tucked Lewis' card into one of the pockets for safekeeping. Taking a deep breath, I dialed his number and drummed my fingers on the back of the chair as I listened to it ring. Finally, on the fifth one, someone picked up.

"Hi, my name is Jordan Amador. Is Lewis there?"

"Yes, but he's not available at the moment."

"Okay. Could you have him call me back at this number? It's important."

"Oh, I'm not sure that's going to be possible. He's scheduled to be shot in the head in six hours."

I froze. It took me a couple of seconds to regain composure. "Who is this?"

The male voice on the phone was silky and pleasant, but I could tell it was just a façade. "I take it you got my present, Mrs. Amador."

My fingers clutched the chair. "Yes. What have you done with Lewis?"

"My boys and I picked him up from the airport. We're just now leaving."

"What do you want?"

"My pound of flesh," he sneered. "Your Daddy's gonna pay with cash or blood. You'd better hope he's got the green, little girl."

Anger bubbled up through my chest, chasing away the fear. "If you hurt him, I swear to God, I'll make you pay."

"Is that a threat? Hmm, maybe I'll send you another present. A foot, perhaps?"

"This is not a game," I hissed. "You let him go right now or heaven help me, I'll kill you myself."

"Sorry, but I don't have time to die. I've got money to make. Stay in school, sweetheart."

He hung up. I screamed and kicked the chair over.

Gabriel rushed to my side, apprehensive. "What happened?"

~ 154 ~

"They already have him. Or at least that's what the creep on the phone said," I said in a low voice. "And he's changed the deadline from twelve hours to six. We have to get to Lewis now. It doesn't matter if they get the money or not—they'll still kill him."

Gabriel dialed away on his phone. "I can have my friend here in fifteen minutes. Pack an overnight bag. I'll get the jet ready for a flight to Detroit."

I went into my bedroom and threw some clothes into a duffel bag. I was halfway through stuffing soap into my toiletry bag when I realized there were tears on my cheeks. Shit.

Exactly fifteen minutes later, the doorbell rang. Gabriel answered it, opening the door to reveal a short Hispanic woman in her fifties. She had curly salt-and-pepper hair, wore a crisp blue pants suit, and carried a large brown bag in her left hand.

Gabriel shut the door and waved her towards the kitchen table. "Jordan, this is Molly. Molly, this is Jordan."

She gave me one brief nod. "What am I looking at?"

I pointed to the box and leaned against the counter, averting my gaze as she pulled on a pair of gloves and pushed the tissue aside. Out of the corner of my eye, I watched her use a pair of forceps to pick up the severed hand and hold it up into the bright overhead light.

"Judging by the state of it, I'd say it was done less than twenty-four hours ago," she said in a calm, clinical voice. "Neat, too. One clean chop, didn't saw it off like in the movies. The wound at the wrist makes me think a cleaver."

I swallowed hard and took a deep breath. "How is that helpful?"

"Well, every little detail tells us something. We're working with professional brutes here. Some bad guys are sloppy, but this is precise. The lack of blood in the box means they knew to let the limb bleed out for a while before packaging it. I'll dust for prints in just a moment, but I probably won't find any," she said as Gabriel cleaned off the table so she could set out some of her tools.

She took out a mounted magnifying glass, a small brush, a black light, an unidentified powder, an inkpad, and a sheet of paper. Carefully, she dusted the severed hand for prints, then the tissue paper and the box. She then pressed the fingertips into the ink and made prints on the blank sheet of paper to later run through a criminal database. After that, she used the handheld black light over the hand. Nothing appeared.

"Hmm," she mumbled as she held the box underneath the black light.

I walked over, curious. "What? Is that a good 'hmm'?"

"Maybe," Molly said, peering at the bottom of the cardboard box. I could make out a small spot that the light showed.

"Someone sat this box on top of a bit of cologne. Smells expensive. I'll get a sample and run it in my lab. I'll call you with the results. Detroit's roughly four hours away and I can tell you where to head by the time you've landed."

"So you're saying you can help us narrow down our guy with cologne?" I asked, teetering on the edge of uncertainty.

She glanced at me. "These guys may be professionals, but they're not perfect. If this Lamont guy is a big wig in his town, he'll be rich, bourgeois, and well-dressed. The cologne is probably something imported, something rare. That kind of thing is traceable."

"Good to know. Thank you for your help."

She shrugged. "Any friend of Gabe's is a friend of mine. I'll get this down to the lab ASAP. You guys get in the air as soon as you can."

"Thank you, Molly," Gabriel and I chorused. She packed up her equipment and the hand, then left.

Gabriel turned to me, his eyes searching my face. "Are you ready to do this?"

A weak smile touched my lips. "Would you believe me if I said yes?"

"Probably not," he admitted. "But I had to ask. You're in enough trouble as it is. If you wanted to stay home, I wouldn't blame you."

"No. He's my family. I have to help him."

"Things will probably get nasty."

"Nasty is a nice step up from what we usually deal with."

Gabriel smiled. "Sad, but true. But you have to do one thing for me before we go."

"What?"

He rested his hands on my shoulders. "On the phone, when you called me...you said that this was your fault. It's not."

I shook my head. "If I hadn't sent Wallace back to Detroit—"

"—he still would have met a similar fate. If he worked for someone like Lamont, then his comeuppance would have happened one way or another. Guilt is not going to help you save your father. Guilt breeds doubt. We cannot afford doubt right now. I'm not saying it's going to be easy, but you must let this go and accept that getting your hands dirty is part of being a Seer, and part of doing the right thing."

"I just don't want to be responsible for any more deaths, Gabe," I whispered. "Is that too much to ask?"

He brushed a lock of hair behind my ear. "No, it's not. But you can only control yourself, not others. Remember that."

He kissed my forehead and stepped away, his voice hardening with resolve.

"Let's go save your father."

CHAPTER FIFTEEN

MICHAEL

We took a cab to Jandira, a municipality of São Paulo where Edmond had been spotted. The entire ride was spent in a taut silence. We kept our eyes sharp for anything out of the ordinary. Darkness closed over the sky and made it harder to see so my other senses became increasingly hyperactive.

When I stepped out of the cab, I felt a sense of dread as I observed the street where we had stopped. The road stretched for miles into a heavily populated neighborhood. There were teenagers leaning against the walls of the buildings, laughing, talking, and playing on their cell phones. I even spotted a couple of children playing jump rope under a dim streetlight. After all, it was only around eight o'clock here.

"This is going to be even more difficult than I thought," I said to Belial, who merely shrugged and rifled through his pockets for a moment. He withdrew a pack of cigarettes and a lighter, firing up a coffin nail and exhaling the smoke with a relieved sigh. He couldn't smoke in the cab and I could tell he'd been jonesing for one ever since we left the restaurant.

"We don't have time for discretion, archangel. Let your flunkies clean up the mess once we're done. Now let's get to work."

He tucked one hand in his pocket and started walking. I almost asked him where we were headed, but then he wandered over to a group of teenage girls before I could say anything.

"Excuse me," he said in Portuguese to the nearest girl – a pretty brunette. "But I'm looking for someone's apartment."

Belial held up his cell phone to display the address. "Would you please tell me where this is?"

The girl smiled. "Sure. It's three blocks down on the left, *tio*."

Belial's smile wilted. I had to bite my lip to keep from laughing. In Portuguese, younger girls used "*tio*" as a slang term for an older gentleman. It had definitely landed a blow on the demon's ego.

I stepped closer, jumping in before he could say anything rude. "Do you know who lives there?"

The girl paused. "My friend Maria babysits a little girl there. I can't remember her parents' first names, but I think the girl is Juliana. The name on the mailbox is Freitas."

Belial and I shared a look. We really didn't need an innocent bystander to get mixed up in this mess. We nodded to the girls and headed down the street in a hurry, though not in a full run because it would spook the neighbors.

The Freitas family lived on the second floor near the rear of the building. Thankfully, there weren't people around when we climbed the stairs and found their front door. I took a deep, calming breath and tried the knob. Unlocked. *Damn it.*

Belial reached for the holster under his arm and withdrew his gun, a Smith and Wesson .9mm that held seventeen rounds of blessed bullets. It could certainly get the job done if we got the drop on Edmond. Getting a body from the demons was a mixed bag. We hadn't been able to find him, but it also meant he shared their vulnerabilities. The element of surprise was our most important asset right now.

I opened the door and the pounding thrum of capoeira music spilled out of the apartment. The smell of gasoline permeated the air, confirming the rogue angel's presence. I could see a modest den with a couch, a bookshelf, and an old record player spinning in the corner. Belial went in first, his gun held high, his pale eyes scanning the room. I closed the door behind us and nodded to the doorway towards our left. Belial headed that way, and I heard him utter a curse before I followed him in.

A young girl, no more than sixteen, lay sprawled on the floor face-up. I rushed to her side, checking her pulse and finding nothing. The bulge in her throat and bruised skin were tell-tale signs that he'd broken her neck.

"Son of a bitch," I whispered, resting my hand on her forehead and saying a brief prayer for her soul. I rifled through her pockets and found a small wallet, confirming the girl to be Maria Guerrera, the babysitter. The parents didn't appear to be home. One of them had to be the Seer Edmond was looking for. What had he done with the daughter?

Belial went out of the kitchen and walked through the den with me at his heels. I stretched my energy outward to feel for the rogue angel. Even with his energy masked, close proximity allowed me to sense him. It was faint, but I caught a signature in one of the bedrooms down the hall.

"Last one on the right," I said to the demon. He reached for the doorknob. Locked.

"On three," he mouthed. I took the spot across from him, raising my fingers one by one.

On three, we both kicked in the door. It smashed against the wall, revealing a small bedroom with purple walls and blue curtains that had teddy bear patterns on them. Edmond Saraf stood beside the bed with a girl no more than four years old in his arms. She had short, curly brown hair, dark eyes, and stared at us with confusion and fear on her tearstained face. She appeared unharmed, but Edmond held a knife underneath her chin as he watched us. Judging by the power coming off it, he'd acquired a special weapon, one the demons used to destroy angels' bodies.

"Let her go," I demanded, already filling my body with energy to attack him.

Edmond shook his head, his voice soft. "I'm afraid I can't do that, brother."

Righteous fury billowed inside me. "Don't you call me that. No brother of mine would murder an innocent girl and take a child hostage. Have you forgotten where you're from? Have you forgotten everything we angels are charged with in this life?"

"I have not forgotten. We are charged with protecting mankind. Sometimes to keep everyone safe, certain individuals must be sacrificed."

I shook my head. "That doesn't justify your actions. You should have come to me if you discovered a great calamity. "

"I am but a humble Scribe. You are the Prince of Heaven's Army. Such a task is beneath you and so I took it upon myself to carry out my mission. Besides, you are married to a human. You would not have the will to do as I have done."

I gritted my teeth. "You're right. I would never kill the people I am sworn to protect. Now let the child go or Belial will drop you where you stand."

"I cannot."

I glanced at the demon. "Can you make the shot?"

"Not without hurting the girl," Belial answered, aiming the gun steadily at Edmond's head. "I am bound by demonic law not to harm anyone but him."

"I'm curious as to what your plan is," he continued, addressing Edmond. "Will you kidnap the child to get her Seer parents to willingly give themselves up?"

"Once again, you misunderstand. I'm not after her parents. Juliana is a Seer."

I went still. "What? But she's just a baby. That's impossible."

"If the angels are retranslating the Book of Time as I suspect they are, you'll find that I am right. I must do this, Michael. A thousand lives are at stake. I am sorry."

"No," I said slowly. "Not yet, you're not."

I looked at Belial and he met my eyes for the briefest second before we both yelled, "Strike!"

Two shards of energy flew through the air and hit Edmond in the arms simultaneously. He cried out, dropping the child. She fell on the floor, wailing, and Belial opened fire. I dove for the girl, snatching her out of the rogue angel's reach. Edmond threw up his energy shield and the bullets bounced off it, ricocheting into the walls. He dove for the bedroom door, smashing into the wall in the hallway as Belial gave chase. Now alone, I slid the closet door open and placed Juliana inside.

"*Mamãe! Eu quero mamãe!*" the child sobbed. I cradled her face in my hands, making her look at me.

"Stay here, Juliana," I whispered in Portuguese. "No matter what happens, stay here. I'll get you back to your mom, I promise." I kissed her forehead and pulled the closet door closed, then raced towards the den where I could hear Belial and the rogue angel fighting.

Edmond had Belial on his knees in a chokehold, knocking picture frames down as they struggled against the far wall.

"Where's the gun?" I yelled.

"K-Kitchen," Belial rasped, ramming his elbow into Edmond's side over and over to try to get himself loose. I ran into the kitchen and found that the gun had gotten tossed under the table in the melee. I checked the chambers and found only four rounds left. *Shit!*

I hurried back to the den, aimed the gun at Edmond's head, and pulled the trigger twice. He ducked. The bullets missed by mere inches, biting into the wall behind him. He grabbed Belial by the arm and threw him at me. I tried to dodge, but Belial crashed into me, sending us backwards into the bookcase and knocking the record player over. The music stopped and everything suddenly felt much more real.

Ignoring the pain lancing through my back and shoulders, I shoved myself upward and shot at the rogue angel again, but he recovered the knife he'd had and threw it at me. I ducked, which gave him enough time to kick the gun out of my hands. It landed with a heavy thunk on the carpet several feet away.

I shoved the dazed Belial off my lap and brought up my forearms in a block as Edmond brought his heel down on my head in a powerful kick. I grabbed a broken chunk of the bookshelf and hit him in the left thigh, giving me a couple of seconds to stand as he stumbled backwards, hissing in pain.

I helped Belial up and we both attacked. Edmond went into a defensive stance for the first few seconds of the vicious onslaught, blocking our kicks and punches with amazing speed, but I could see him beginning to tire. I aimed a kick at his left knee and it connected, forcing him to kneel. Belial executed a perfect roundhouse kick to the side of his face, knocking him down for a couple of seconds. The rogue angel spat blood onto the carpet and dove into a forward roll when we both tried to kick him. He pushed to his feet and reached into the pocket of his leather jacket, withdrawing a lighter.

I lunged for him as he threw it in the corner of the room, tackling him off his feet. To my horror, the lighter hit the baseboard and sparked a fire that quickly spread, tracing the line of gasoline the rogue angel had poured through the entire place.

"Belial!"

"On it," the demon answered, tearing off his duster and trying to beat out the flames as they spread.

I wrapped my hands around Edmond's neck and jerked him close, unable to stop the rage coursing through my veins at finally having the elusive bastard in my grip.

"You tried to kill the woman I love," I hissed into his face. "You will not leave this place alive."

"If that is my fate, then so be it."

He moved his left arm and that was when I saw it. I'd tackled him too close to where the gun had flown. He pressed the muzzle against my left shoulder and pulled the trigger.

I screamed as pain ripped through my entire upper body and collapsed onto my back, clutching the bloody wound. It hurt so bad that bile rose in my throat.

Edmond stood over me with the gun as I struggled onto my knees. I tried to push up onto my feet, but my left arm crumpled under my body like a useless twig. He pulled the trigger. It clicked empty, giving me just enough time to grab the knife on the floor and make one last-ditch effort to stop him.

I plunged the knife into his stomach. The gun clunked to the floor. Hot blood poured from the wound onto my skin, painting it a dark red like some sort of sickening sculpture. For a few seconds, we just stood there staring at each other, inches apart. I expected to see fear in his brown eyes, but all I found was acceptance.

The front door burst open and I heard the muffled voices of men in uniforms screaming, "*Polícia!*" through my ringing ears. I didn't even flinch, too absorbed in the moment. Edmond sunk to the floor with the knife in his belly, still staring at me and saying nothing.

Slowly, I lifted my hands in surrender and got on my knees as a numb feeling climbed up my body. Finally, I had stopped him. I had taken revenge on the man who tried to kill my wife. I should have felt something — relief, pride, satisfaction — but instead I felt nothing.

Curious.

JORDAN

Detroit Metro Airport bustled with activity and the hurried pace of the travelers made me even more anxious than I already was. Thankfully, Gabriel was on hand to keep me calm and assure me we would find Lewis in time.

He stood on the sidewalk next to me dialing Molly's number while I tried to flag down a cab driver. We didn't know where we were going, but we would need a ride and it was damned hard to get one right now with all these people around.

After several tries, I managed to get a cab. I tossed our duffel bags in the back, telling the driver to give us a moment to figure out where we were going. Gabriel beckoned me when he got through to Molly, putting the call on speakerphone so I could hear.

"Based on the high quality ingredients of the cologne, I was able to narrow it down to a perfume called *Buena Suerte*. It's imported from Spain and there's only one place that supplies it in the Detroit area. I'll text you the address in just a moment."

"Thank you, Molly. Let us know if anything else comes up."

"I will." Gabriel hung up and took a deep breath.

"Alright, here is how this is going to work," Gabriel said. "We have to get over to that store and find out who orders the cologne, who picks it up, and if there is an address attached. That should lead us to one of his lackeys and if we give him a good shakedown, we should be able to find Lamont's headquarters. That is when I'll call my friend at the precinct and see if we can get some officers down there."

His phone vibrated a moment later with a text from Molly. We got into the cab, heading into the city. Luckily, the place wasn't very far so the ride was short. We got out on the corner, paid the driver to wait again, and paused to come up with a game plan.

"They're probably not going to give up this info easily," I said. "We're either gonna have to bribe or sweet-talk it out of them. And I'm guessing you're better at seducing female sales clerks than I am."

Gabriel offered me a faint smile. "Sadly, that is more up Michael's alley than mine, but I will try my best."

"Good man. Let's go."

Gabriel had of course been too modest. The clerk fell in love with him on sight and he managed to schmooze the location of our henchman out of her. He was aptly named Jules Winnfield, another *Pulp Fiction* alias that proved we were on the right track.

We left the shop and climbed back into the cab, heading for the address the sales associate had given us. We pulled up in front of an apartment complex a few blocks away. The cab driver required a little more convincing to stick around this time. The neighborhood looked decidedly rough.

There were clusters of teenagers hanging out under busted streetlights and rusted cars parked next to broken meters. This was the first time I'd ever felt I'd be better off without Gabriel. His unusual height and exceptionally nice clothing had the potential to draw attention from the wrong kinds of people.

As we ascended the five flights of stairs to Jules' place, I couldn't help asking Gabriel something that had been bothering me since we left the perfume shop.

"So...I've never seen you intimidate someone before," I said, trying my best to sound polite rather than insulting. "How does that work exactly?"

He glanced at me, lifting his eyebrows. "You're serious, aren't you?"

I offered a sheepish smile. "Sorry, but you've been nothing but nice to me ever since I met you. I can't imagine you threatening someone."

He shook his head. "That's because I've made a point to remain pleasant in your company. I didn't want your opinion of me to change if you saw me interrogate someone. I may not care what many people think, but I do care what you think."

"Geez. It's that bad?"

He sighed. "Let's just say it's not a part I enjoy playing."

We reached the fifth floor and walked over to the last door on the right, Apartment 547. I took a deep breath and lifted my hand to knock, but Gabriel caught it, making me look at him.

"No matter what I say in here, remember that it's just a bluff. Okay?"

"Okay." He let go and I knocked on the door. A moment of silence followed before the door opened, revealing a tall, thin white man with tousled hair and a scraggly five o'clock shadow. Guess the nickname was ironic.

He leaned against the doorjamb, lifting his eyebrows at us. "Can I help you?"

"Mr. Jules?"

He eyed Gabriel. "Who's asking?"

"A couple of concerned citizens," the archangel replied in a flat voice.

Jules glanced between the two of us and his expression hardened. "If you two are cops, I got nothin' to say to you. And you can't come in without a warrant, so I suggest you kick rocks."

He tried to slam the door, but Gabriel caught it with one large hand.

"Have you ever loved anyone, Mr. Jules?"

"What the hell are you talking about? Let go!"

"Because that's why we're here. We need answers and you just so happen to be the one who can provide them."

"I'm not kidding, man. Let go of the door or I will fuck you up."

"This is going to go one of two ways, Mr. Jules. One, you let us in, answer our questions and we leave. Or two, you don't answer them, and I make you."

"That's it." Jules let go of the door and reached for the small of his back. I didn't wait to see what he pulled. I drew my gun and pointed it between his eyes. He froze, shocked that I'd done it so fast.

"Back away from the door."

He stepped backward and we walked inside, closing the door behind us.

I motioned towards his midsection with the gun. "Turn around. Slowly."

Jules glowered at me but obliged. I lifted up the hem of his t-shirt and took the rather sizeable handgun tucked into his jeans. I checked to make sure the safety was on and stashed it in the largest pocket of my duster.

Jules faced us again. "You ain't cops. I can tell. They don't dress like you around here. So what d'you want? You here to rob me? 'Cause if you are, you ain't gonna get far."

"We don't have time for your questions, Mr. Jules," Gabriel said. "We're on a deadline, after all. All we need you to do is tell us where Lamont Brooks is and then we'll be on our way."

At the mention of Lamont's name, Jules shook his head.

"Shoot me."

My eyes widened. "What?"

"I'm not answerin' shit. Shoot me, because he'll do worse if I talk."

I glanced at Gabriel. His eyes had the same spark of interest as mine. This guy wasn't being loyal because he liked Lamont—he was flat-out scared of him. Had Wallace been the same way?

"What if he doesn't know you told us?" I asked.

"He's got ears everywhere. There's no way he wouldn't find out, somehow. I'm in too deep, so you can either kill me or torture me or whatever you like because I'm not talking."

Gabriel grabbed two handfuls of Jules' shirt and shoved him against the far wall so fast that I jumped. He held him there, dangling inches off the floor, and addressed him with a cold voice that scared me half to death.

"Are you sure that's what you want?"

Jules swallowed hard. "Y-Yeah."

"Very well. Where would you like to start? If you've got a good strong chair, we could try water boarding."

Sweat beaded on Jules' brow. Gabriel adopted a positively evil smile.

"No, no, that's much too cliché. Perhaps I could drop you out the window. The fall wouldn't kill you—just break your legs. I'm sure Lamont would love to know how you got that limp."

Jules said nothing, but I could see him getting sweatier as the archangel kept going.

"Y'know, there is this new thing I've been wanting to try. You tie someone down, put a bag of ice on his forehead, and leave it there. The shock to your blood vessels causes a pain so intense you'll be begging me to drop you out of the window."

Once again, Jules kept his mouth shut and so Gabriel pressed on. "Then again, I could have my friend here just shoot you and then you'd bleed to death. People watch too many movies these days. They think getting shot means instant death, but actually only a percentage of people die on the spot. Most people bleed out for hours. How long do you think it'll take you, Mr. Jules?"

Gabriel glanced at me with a completely serious face. "Aim for the gut."

He dropped him. Jules stumbled, clutching the wall behind him. Gabriel stepped back and I pointed the gun at Jules' midsection.

"Make sure not to hit the spine. Don't want to end the party early."

Just as my finger slid over the trigger, the thin man broke, waving his hands. "Don't! I'll talk. Just don't shoot me, please."

I met eyes with Gabriel, who nodded, and lowered the gun, though I kept it in my hand just to be safe. "Where would Lamont take someone he's thinking about killing?" I asked.

Jules winced, glancing nervously at Gabriel. "Look, I'll talk, but can you just...let me talk to her? I can't think with you staring at me."

Gabriel glared at him until I touched his arm. He looked at me and I nodded towards the kitchen behind us. He disappeared around the corner.

Jules let out a shaky sigh, sagging against the side of the couch. "Jesus Christ. What was the question again?"

"Lamont's going to kill someone," I said, using a tone less harsh than before since the guy was pretty damn freaked out already. "His name is Lewis Jackson. I need to find out where they are."

Jules rubbed one side of his face and then massaged the bridge of his nose, his tone heavy with regret when he spoke. "There's a place by the river where he likes to take people he's gonna kill. It's under Wayne County Bridge. He ties them down with cinderblocks and tosses them in. He owns half the cops around here so no one ever goes searching for bodies or rats him out if they see him and his boys at it."

"How many guys will he have with him?"

Jules shrugged. "Maybe six or seven? Just in case any of the honest cops are hanging around looking for trouble."

"Got it."

"Look, I don't know who you are, but if you're gonna try and save this guy, you're insane. You can't touch Lamont. He'll bury you. If he doesn't kill you, he'll dig up dirt on you and make you work for him. That's how he got me."

"Don't worry about us," I said with a faint smile as Gabriel came out of the kitchen and opened the door.

Jules followed us, still confused and anxious. "Why? What makes you think you can take this guy by yourselves?"

I paused in the doorway and met his eyes with my best Dan Aykroyd impression.

"He's not gonna catch us. We're on a mission from God."

CHAPTER SIXTEEN

JORDAN

"Come on, Henry, this is important! There's got to be something else you can do."

I watched Gabriel pace back and forth on the sidewalk with dread filling my gut. I couldn't hear the other side of the conversation, but I knew things had taken a turn for the worse.

Gabriel hung up his cell phone, running a hand through his blond hair. "The soonest Detective Henry can get units over to the bridge is in an hour."

I checked my watch. "We only have forty-five minutes left. Lewis'll be dead by the time the backup arrives. What are we gonna do?"

Gabriel sighed, unable to keep his frustration in check. "What can we do? There's a bank robbery with a hostage situation in progress and a riot on the other side of town, so the officers are spread out all over the place. Seems like Lamont picked the perfect time for a murder."

I shook my head. "Then the two of us are gonna have to be enough. I have my .38 and Jules' .45 with me. Plus, Lamont doesn't know we're coming."

"Jordan, do you know what you're talking about? These are Detroit criminals. If we could use our abilities, it would be a fair fight, but you know we're bound by the rules of man not to use them in front of normal people. We're outmatched."

"I don't care, Gabriel. I'm not going to lose another family member. I'm not going to let someone I care about die again!" I shouted, ignoring the tears that had started to well up in my eyes.

The archangel gave me a long, penetrating stare before speaking. "This is different. There won't be any backup. It's just you and me. Do you understand?"

"Yeah. I do."

"Then let's go."

I climbed into the back of the taxi and Gabriel followed, instructing the driver to head towards the Wayne County Bridge. The guy gave us a funny look, but shrugged and shifted his gears, pulling out into the street.

Minutes ticked by, each one making me more and more anxious. Luckily, we reached the bridge with twenty minutes until the deadline. Trees clung to the edge of the river beneath the bridge, illuminated by a few dim lights. The water looked black and daunting as we stepped out of the cab. I sent the cabbie away and turned towards Gabriel to ask him something. To my utter shock, he leaned down and kissed me, cupping my left cheek in his hand.

I froze, completely bewildered. He pulled away from my lips and buried his face in my hair, and then I heard him speak.

"There's a lookout at the edge of the bridge. Bald, six feet tall, past my right shoulder."

He wrapped his arms around my back and shifted a little so I could see a big man in all black standing at the top of the hill near the edge of the bridge. We had gotten out of the cab several feet away so he was out of earshot, but we'd definitely caught his attention. That must have been why Gabriel had decided to play the lovey-dovey couple routine. Though I really wished he'd told me ahead of time.

"What's the plan?" I whispered.

He kissed my cheek, keeping his lips near my ear. "He's going to come over to get rid of us. Pretend like you're drunk until he gets close enough that one of us can knock him out."

"Got it."

He nuzzled my neck and I giggled loudly, running my fingers through his feathery hair. The lookout had started walking towards us, calling out "Oy!" to get our attention. I pretended not to notice, counting down the seconds before he'd be within range.

Gabriel pulled away and held my hand, tugging me towards the edge of the bridge. We both looked over the side, spotting a group of men below by the shore. There were six of them plus Lewis, who was handcuffed on his knees by the water. Thankfully, we were too far up for them to hear or see us.

"Oy! This ain't a party. Piss off," the lookout said through an Irish brogue, glaring at us.

"Aw, c'mon, man, check out this view!" Gabriel slurred, brandishing a hand at the skyline. "It's awesome!"

"I don't care. Get out of here or I'll kick your drunken ass back to wherever the hell you came from."

I smiled, stumbling a little as I shuffled closer to him. "Don't be such a party pooper, baby. We just wanted to sightsee."

The lookout sneered at me, cupping his crotch. "I got somethin' for you to see right here, sweetheart."

"Don't mind if I do." I kicked him in the nuts as hard as I could. He groaned, dropping to his knees, and Gabriel punched him in the right temple. The lookout hit the pavement like a sack of hammers.

We checked for witnesses—it was pretty late so no one seemed to be around at the moment—and I found another .45 like Jules' on the unconscious henchman. Maybe it was a theme thing, just like the *Pulp Fiction* names.

"Nice work," Gabriel said as we hurried towards the end of the bridge.

"I know, right? Although you could've warned me first."

"My apologies," he said, checking the safety on the .45 as we slipped into the woods lining the river's edge. "It was a spur of the moment idea. I hope you weren't traumatized."

"I'll survive. I just hope it wasn't weird for you."

"Nonsense. It was like kissing someone you care about. Like a friend. Or a dog."

My mouth dropped open. I smacked him in the shoulder. "A dog, Gabriel? Really?"

He shot me a look. "Is this really the time to discuss that?"

I scowled at him. "Fine, but you're not getting a Christmas present this year."

The archangel rolled his eyes. "I'll go out first. If Lamont's as arrogant as I think he is, we may be able to end this if we threaten to kill him unless he lets your father go. All we need to do is stall them. The cops will do the rest when they get here. If things turn nasty, do *not* be a hero."

"When have I ever done that?"

"You really don't want me to answer that." He nodded towards the shore. "I've got the men on the outer rim of the group. Ready?"

"Yeah."

"Three...two...one!"

Gabriel leapt out from behind the tree, his Gators sliding against the gravel. Four gunshots bit through the air, echoing into the night. Three of Lamont's men instantly dropped and the rest turned around, whipping out their weapons.

"Don't move!" Gabriel commanded, holding the gun on Lamont.

While the men were distracted, I snuck my way through the tree line until I reached the edge of the bridge. I pressed my back against the wall and peeked around the corner, analyzing the remaining three men. Two of them were black guys, tall and built like Wallace had been, and the third was white, about five-foot-six, and overweight. The dim light overhead shone off his bald spot and the assortment of silver rings on his hands. His trench coat looked expensive and crisp as if he'd just bought it. I'd bet money he was Lamont.

"Who the hell are you?" one of the bodyguards barked.

Gabriel smiled as he kicked the guns away from the injured Mooks. "Just a Good Samaritan."

"Cute. You know what we call them in real life?" Lamont asked, his silky voice filling the clearing with pure sleaze. "Suckers. Plus, I don't recall the Bible being fond of men with guns."

Gabriel's smile widened. "Well, it has strict rules about killing, but fortunately, there aren't any passages about knee-capping folks when the situation calls for it."

Lamont laughed. "Well done. I gotta admit I like your style. Too bad my boys have to kill you."

I darted around the corner and pressed the barrel of the .45 against the nape of Lamont's neck. "Not gonna happen."

He didn't move an inch. I also noticed that his breathing didn't hitch up. Either he was a fool or a lot of people had pointed guns at him in his lifetime. Neither option made me feel any better.

One of the bodyguards trained his gun on me, but I stayed behind Lamont, one hand on his shoulder to keep him from running off, the other holding the gun steady. The others stayed where they had dropped on the ground, nursing their wounds.

Lewis' gaze switched from Gabriel to me and a look of both astonishment and horror crossed his bruised face. A chain connected the cuffs around his wrists to the ones around his ankles, both tethered to a sizeable cinderblock.

"Jordan? What the hell are you doing?" he asked hoarsely.

Lamont spoke up before I could answer. "Well, well. Looks like I underestimated you, little girl."

"A lot of people do that," I replied, letting the anger bleed through. "It keeps my list of enemies short."

Lamont chuckled again, still sounding casual as if we were talking about the weather. "Oh, I don't think that's the case anymore, kid. You just opened up the proverbial Pandora's box on you, your dad, and your handsome friend over there."

"Really? Doesn't look that way to me. I could just shoot you and drop you in the river like you were planning to do to Lewis."

"That's hardly necessary. I'm a businessman. There's always time to negotiate."

I gritted my teeth, stopping myself from telling him to blow it out his ass. He was right. We were in a good old-fashioned Mexican standoff, and I needed to get Lewis out of here. His survival meant more to me than killing this bastard.

"Fantastic. Here's what's gonna happen. Your bodyguard's gonna untie Lewis and let him go. As soon as he's out of sight, I'll back off and so will my friend. Sound like a good deal to you?"

Lamont nodded. "I can see where those terms are fair. But honestly, I prefer deals that are more beneficial to me. If I let you go, my reputation will take a massive hit."

"Too bad. That's your only option."

Lamont tilted his head until I could see one of his eyes. It was dark brown, nearly black in the poor light above us, and something inhuman had crept onto his face. It was a look I had seen in the demons I'd fought just before they did something unforgivable.

"That's where you're wrong."

The bodyguard closest to Lewis kicked him in the chest, sending him flying into the river with a huge splash. I heard someone scream. I realized it had been me seconds before Lamont whirled around and grabbed my wrist. My training kicked in and I blocked the incoming punch with my left arm, kneeing him in the groin. The hit connected and he stumbled backwards for a second, but just as I aimed the gun at his head, he tackled me. I crashed onto the ground, winded. He landed on top of me, pinning my right wrist.

Behind us, Gabriel had taken off to find cover as one of the bodyguards opened fire. He'd shot the one who kicked my father, but that left me alone with Lamont. Lewis would drown in less than two minutes. *Shit!*

I slammed my left fist into Lamont's rib cage again and again, holding onto the gun with a death grip. He punched me in the mouth once and pain exploded across my skull, rattling my teeth, but I didn't let go. He reached for the gun. I shoved the heel of my hand into the soft flesh of his throat. He gagged and loosened his grip for a split second, which was all I needed. I smashed the butt of the gun into his temple. He rolled sideways, nursing the wound. I scrambled to my feet, spitting out blood, and aimed the gun at Lamont.

"Don't move!"

He stayed where he lay, staring at me with those lifeless eyes. "Do it. Shoot me. I fuckin' dare you."

"Shut up!" I spat, checking the shoreline for any sign of Gabriel. I couldn't see very far in the dark and the only sounds around me were the lapping of the water and the pained groans of the barely conscious bodyguards. Less than a minute now.

"It's me or him, little girl," Lamont said, grinning at the panicked look on my face. "What are you gonna do? Shoot me or save your daddy?"

I turned and scoured the black water, searching desperately for any sign of bubbles coming up to the surface. Nothing but waves. Had I failed? Had another person died because of me?

"Tick tock, tick tock," Lamont whispered. A cold sensation filled my chest as I stared at him in all his arrogance, enjoying my pain, enjoying the fact that my father was drowning and I couldn't save him. It would be so easy to put a bullet between his eyes. Watch the lights go out. Watch him bleed all over the ground and never hurt another human being again. Just one squeeze was all it would take.

I walked closer to him, tears burning down my ice-cold cheeks. The wind kicked up, whipping strands of hair into my eyes as I glared at him.

"It's too late, kid. He's already dead and you don't have the guts to pull that trigger."

A weak laugh spilled from my lips. "That's where you're wrong."

I shot him in the right thigh. He screamed. It was the most beautiful sound I ever heard.

I threw the gun into the bushes and walked towards the river. Thirty seconds left. Either I would save my father or die trying. Time to find out what I was made of.

Just as I stepped towards the water, I heard a man's voice—one word, one syllable.

"Oy."

I turned and saw the Irish lookout standing there. He smiled and shot me twice in the chest. Everything faded to black before I even hit the ground.

CHAPTER SEVENTEEN

JORDAN

My chest *hurt*.

I woke up coughing and clutching the two spots on my chest where pain burned like someone had stabbed me with a red-hot poker. It took me a moment to breathe normally and open my eyes to see where I was. I was lying on a fold-out couch with powder blue sheets that were so clean they had to be new. I wasn't in a bedroom, but rather what looked like someone's den. Across from me sat a coffee table, a bookshelf against the far wall, and a flat-screen television. The walls were wood paneling instead of concrete and a ceiling fan twirled above me.

I tried to push myself into a seated position, but then a female voice spoke. "Whoa, take it easy."

I tilted my head to see a black woman in her early thirties walking towards me from the kitchen. She wore a dark green button-up shirt and slacks. I'd never seen her before in my life. Panicked, I stretched out my energy and then relaxed when I realized she was an angel.

"W-Who're you?" I said, clearing my throat.

She held out her hands for me to use to pull myself up. I took them, groaning as I moved. "Filipa Ferguson. Nice to meet you."

"Catchy," I rasped, relieved after my back nestled against a small pile of pillows. "You should be in television with a name like that."

"Yeah, I get that a lot. How're you feeling?"

"Shitty," I said. No reason to lie.

"I'll bet." She pulled up a chair from the corner. On it I spotted the bulletproof vest I'd been wearing when the lookout shot me. I lifted the neckline of my shirt and saw the two gigantic bruises on my chest that matched the divots on the vest.

Filipa tossed me the vest and took a seat. "You were out for more than an hour. I'm surprised you woke up so soon. Most people need more rest after getting shot."

"Yeah, well, I'm definitely not most people," I replied, mentally thanking God I'd survived a gunfight. The vests had been Gabriel's idea. Yet another thing to thank him for.

In a rush, memories of the entire evening came back to me and another surge of panic went through my body. "Where's Gabriel? Where's my dad?"

Filipa held up her hands, trying to calm me. "They're okay. Gabriel's taking a shower. He should be out in a second. Your father's in the guest room recuperating."

A flood of relief went through me. "Thank God. What happened?"

"I think I can answer that." Gabriel walked out of the kitchen in a tank top and loose jeans with a towel around his neck. Water dripped from the mass of blonde curls piled on his head. Normally, it was straight, but it curled a bit when wet. It was the first time I'd ever seen him look so normal, and somehow it made me feel closer to him.

He sat on the edge of the bed and I hugged him, ignoring the way my chest stung when it brushed against his. He held me for almost half a minute, mostly because I didn't want to let go since I had been scared I'd never see him again.

"Are you okay?" I asked when he pulled away.

He let a little humor slip into his voice. "I'm fine. Just had to get my body temperature back up after I took a dip in the river."

"What happened? The last thing I remember is that damn lookout shooting me."

Gabriel continued drying his hair, the smile disappearing. "Most people think getting shot is nothing because of the movies. It depends on the size and weight of the person. You're not even a hundred and fifty pounds so the force took you right off your feet and knocked you out. I came up right before he could make another shot and took care of him, then went for Lewis. He wasn't in great shape, but I managed to resuscitate him and called Filipa. This is a safe house. I didn't want to take you guys to a hospital if Lamont has as many people on his payroll as Detective Henry suspects."

"What happened to Lamont and his men?"

"The cops showed up not long after we left. They're all being held for kidnapping and premeditated murder, among other things."

I shook my head. "That's never gonna stick. You said he owns a lot of cops in this town."

"That would be why I wore a wire."

My mouth dropped open. "You what?"

"I knew it would be hard to convict Lamont so I had some of my friends in the police department give me some equipment to record him in the middle of a crime. It should be enough to lock him up for a while and get him out of our hair."

"But you jumped in the river. Wouldn't that have ruined it?"

"Took my jacket off first. This is not my first time busting a criminal, you know."

"I can't even begin to describe how much I love you right now. I'd kiss you, but then again, I know how you hate that," I added, giving him a sour look.

He rolled his eyes. "You're never going to let that go, huh?"

"Not a chance."

Filipa glanced between us. "Are you two always like this after nearly dying?"

"Yes," we answered simultaneously.

She shook her head and smiled. "Good to know. Your father's still out at the moment, but if you want to go see him the guest room is down the hall to the left. If you're hungry, there's plenty of stuff in the fridge or I can order out. Right now, you need to get some rest before you heal yourselves. I'll be in the master bedroom if you need anything."

I touched her hand. "Thank you."

"You're more than welcome."

She nodded to Gabriel and headed back through the kitchen towards the hallway. When she was out of earshot, Gabriel nudged my shoulder so I would look at him. "What happened back there? When I came back, Lamont had a hole in his leg. A few inches over and the bullet would have hit the femoral artery."

I crossed my arms beneath my chest, leaning against the pillows. I kept my expression blank. "Didn't want him to run away."

Gabriel's eyes narrowed just a bit. "Are you sure that's all?"

I sighed. "What do you want me to say, Gabriel? I thought my father was dead. Did I want revenge? Yes, maybe. I'm not perfect, you know."

"I would never want you to be perfect. But I am worried. We bent the rules quite a bit tonight and I had to pull a lot of strings to keep you out of jail. If I hadn't been cooperating with the police department, things would have gotten nasty."

"I lost control. I'm sorry. Really."

He shook his head. "I don't want an apology. I want to know how far you would've gone to save your father."

"Gabe—"

"Answer the question, Jordan."

"Look, I don't know, okay?" I said, letting the frustration come through. "I'd just gotten punched in the face, I thought Lewis was gonna die, so I just did what I had to do. My life isn't important. I'm supposed to protect people. It's my job."

Gabriel slid closer, dropping his voice to a murmur. "This is what I'm talking about. You're not an archangel. You're a Seer. It's my job to save people, to sacrifice my own safety for them. It isn't yours. Why do you expect so much of yourself?"

"What do you mean?"

"Everything is always all-or-nothing with you. Life or death. If your husband knew how you acted tonight, what would he do?"

For the first time in the conversation, I saw his point. "He'd probably tie me to the bed, and not in the fun way. Are you saying I'm too reckless?"

He brushed some of the damp hair out of his eyes, sighing. "Not exactly. I just wanted you to know that the last few days have made me realize you don't think about your own safety when it comes to other people. That worries me. It worries Michael too."

"Thank you for telling me. And I'd be really happy if you edited out some of what happened whenever you talk to Michael."

He arched an eyebrow. "Are you telling an archangel to lie to his brother?"

"No, just...leave a few details out. Maybe the 'me getting shot' part."

Gabriel pursed his lips in a scowl, but nodded anyway. "Fine. But you owe me."

"I always do. Thanks for saving my bacon. Again." I kissed him on the cheek and stood up, suppressing yet another groan at the stinging pain in my chest. I walked through the kitchen and down the hallway to the guest room, taking a deep breath before I opened the door.

The guest room was large and the walls were painted mint green. Lewis lay sleeping in a queen-sized bed with the hunter-green covers pulled up to his chest. Filipa had cleaned the cuts on his face, but his bottom lip was still swollen and there was a sizeable bruise on his left cheek. He looked so bad I wished I could heal him, but the wounds had been inflicted before he got kicked into the water so he'd notice if they were gone.

I shut the door behind me and pulled up a chair I found nearby. I started to hold his hand, but couldn't bring myself to do it. Too domestic. I'd only known this man for what? Three days?

I leaned my arms on my knees and pressed my hands to my lips. A small cut on the inside of my cheek stung a bit. Lamont was a pompous bastard, but he threw a good punch.

"This is so stupid," I muttered. "I haven't known you a week and I almost died trying to save you. Is this all part of that parental guilt trip I never had as a child? Maybe it's a good thing you weren't there."

A bitter laugh escaped my lips. "Y'know, when I was a kid, Aunt Carmen used to tell people she'd adopted me out of the goodness of her heart. They always believed her because my skin is so much darker than hers and her family's. She told each person something different about where I'd come from. Nigeria, Egypt, South Africa, the works. The worst part was that she'd do it in front of me and if I said anything, she'd beat me when we got home. After a while, I stopped caring. I started focusing on how to get the hell out of there."

I tugged the ponytail holder out of my hair and started running my fingers through it, picking at the tangles that had formed. "I ran away five times. Never got very far. The cops always picked me up and brought me back. They never believed me when I told them how badly she treated me. There were supposed to be social workers who checked on me, but they never showed up. Aunt Carmen didn't tell me about my mother dying until a week after it happened. She didn't even let me go to the funeral. What a bitch, right?"

Once all the knots in my hair were gone, I sat back in the chair, crossing my arms. "I didn't find out until years later where they buried her. Both her parents had died years earlier, but you already knew that, didn't you? Because of that, Aunt Carmen had to pay for the coffin and she picked this plot in the middle of nowhere. Michael and I were thinking about holding a memorial for Mom someday. She deserved better than what she got. It's not all bad, though. I know she's up there with Andrew taking care of business."

I paused, softening my tone. "Part of me wonders what I'd be like if Andrew had raised me. I don't know much about him, really. It took me years to piece together details about his life. He seemed like he'd be a strict kind of dad. He'd tell me to clean my room and take out the trash and walk the dog. Threaten any cute guys who wanted to ask me out. But I always got this feeling that he'd also be really nice too.

Take me to movies on the weekend or let me stay up late watching boxing matches and eating junk food."

I smiled. "I don't know why I'm telling you this. I mean, I quit worrying about having a dad when I turned twelve. It probably wouldn't matter if you decided to be a part of my life now anyway. My expectations are all based on crap I've read in books and seen in movies and TV. You came to tell me you were sorry because you thought you were going to die and in the process, you endangered my life by leading Lamont's guys right to my doorstep. So I guess it sort of makes us even, in a really screwed up way. I guess what I'm trying to say is that I don't know what you're gonna do when you wake up, but whatever you decide won't change how I feel about you. If you stick around, great. If you leave, great. It's still nice to say I have a father."

I stood up and hovered near him, unsure of what to do. Just as my fingertips brushed over his knuckles, the door opened. Gabriel poked his head in the room. His face had a look on it that made my stomach churn.

"What's wrong?" I asked.

"Michael and Belial are in jail."

MICHAEL

I hadn't been incarcerated since the last turn of the century. Not much changed. Jail in Brazil didn't feel all that different from jail in any other country. The stale smell of inmates with bad breath permeated the air along with the metallic scent of rust on the bars. The cots were thin and itchy. The cuffs were cold against my wrists. Yeah. Same old, same old.

I'd been in my cell, alone, for over eight hours while they processed me. I sensed Belial in a nearby cell as well. It was logical to isolate us. The Brazilian police officers thought we were criminals—and had every right to considering what they walked in on—and didn't want us conspiring or corroborating our stories before a member of the American embassy showed up to speak with us.

Before then, though, they'd taken me to the prison medical ward and pried the bullet out of my shoulder. It hurt like hell, but I'd had worse wounds. Unfortunately, I wasn't able to see if Edmond had died on the way to the prison. I couldn't sense him, either. When an angel's body is at death's door, his energy slips away and cannot be tracked again until he pulls through. I'd just have to hope I'd gotten lucky.

Now, I sat in an uncomfortable wooden chair in an interrogation room with my hands cuffed behind my back, still caked with both Edmond's blood and my own. Faded ivory walls. Dirty linoleum floor. It looked nothing like the shiny steel boxes you'd see in one of those police shows. There was a one-way mirror across from me, but it was cracked in a few places and there were handprints all over it.

An armed officer stood by the door. The woman from the embassy finished asking me questions about my arrest and the current charges. Belial had said we should do the job and worry about clean-up later. I went along with it, but truthfully, I hadn't wanted to. In the movies, the good guys slipped off into the night and never had to sit in jail cells that smelled like shit. In real life, saving the day meant paperwork, answering a million questions, paying people off, and generally doing favors to keep your name out of the news. And that was in the States. In Brazil, we were playing an entirely different ball game. Their rules. No cheat codes. Things would get hairy.

I glanced up from the wooden table in front of me when the door opened. I expected to see another officer but instead, someone different walked in. A black woman, mid-thirties, with thick-rimmed glasses, a sharp grey suit, and a hefty brown folder, entered the room. Her hair was long and pulled back in a ponytail, and I caught a faint whiff of perfume as she sat down in front of me.

"I'll take it from here, ma'am," she said to the woman beside me.

Without a word, the American ambassador stood and left. I had to hide my surprise. Not even a question. Who the hell was this woman?

She adjusted her glasses and brushed a bit of lint off the folder, speaking without looking at me just yet. "Mr. O'Brien, my name is Ana Corona. Have you ever heard that name before?"

I stared at her. "It's the name of a beer, I believe."

A thin smile touched her lips. "Yes, I hear that a lot. But that's not what I meant. Do you know who I am?"

"No."

"Would you like to guess?"

I let my eyes travel down all five-feet-three inches of her and decided to answer the question truthfully.

"You have a slight accent that makes me think you're Haitian, or at least partially. You're dressed well in tailored clothing and you've got perfume on, so you're probably wealthy. The fact that my liaison left without a single word makes me think they knew you were coming so you've got ties to America. Plus, there's the way you walk. Shoulders straight, head back, chin parallel to the ground. Military background. I'm thinking…FBI."

The thin smile stretched and she met my eyes. Cold, hard mahogany. Yep. Definitely worked for the U.S. government.

"Impressive. You're a quick study."

I shrugged, leaving my face blank even though the gesture hurt. "I do what I can."

She folded her hands. "Do you know why I'm here, Mr. O'Brien?"

"I'm assuming it has to do with my case."

"Your case?" She snorted, shaking her head. "We're way past this being 'your case.' You broke into a civilian's home with deadly weapons and assaulted a man on Brazilian soil. Normally, someone in your position would be rightfully and completely screwed."

"But I'm not, am I?"

"No, you're not. You knew that when you did it, I'm guessing."

She opened the folder, giving me a glimpse of the paperwork she had on me so far. "After your arrest, we received calls from several different police departments who confirmed that you and Mr. James Brennan have been civilian assistants tracking down serial killer Edmond Saraf. My office has briefed me on his background. Six murders, prior to the one committed last night, and not just on American soil. This guy is bad news and somehow, you and Mr. Brennan managed to track him to Jandira. You saved a little girl's life. Despite the fact that you've broken a half a dozen laws and nearly murdered a man, you've done your country a great favor."

I went very still. "Nearly murdered?"

She adjusted her glasses and flipped a couple of pages. "Edmond Saraf is in the prison hospital undergoing surgery. He hasn't regained consciousness so we're unaware if he'll pull through or not. But he's the least of your problems right now."

"How so?"

Ana glanced at me again. "Mr. O'Brien, how did you learn the location of Edmond Saraf?"

"James knows some of the locals and had them look out for his appearance in the area."

"Why didn't you contact the local police department after you found out where he was?"

"We were worried they wouldn't arrive in time so we went to stop him ourselves."

Ana lifted the corner of one of her papers, her voice flat. "And can you explain how the lead singer of an underground rock band has enough experience to subdue a serial killer?"

"Don't ask rhetorical questions," I said, still trying to figure out what this woman wanted to get out of me. "If you know my background, you know I've had extensive training in martial arts and weaponry."

"Very true, but that still leaves me with one question: why? Why you? What connection do you have to all of this, Mr. O'Brien?"

I gritted my teeth, forcing the next unpleasant words out of my mouth. "James Brennan is an acquaintance. It was a favor."

"An acquaintance, you say? So this has nothing to do with the fact that Mr. Brennan is Juliana Freitas' biological father?"

The blood drained out of my face so fast that I got dizzy. I had to fight to keep the shock from creeping onto my features. She stared at me with that hard gaze of hers, trying to dig her way beneath my mask.

"Did he tell you that?" I asked.

"Yes. They interrogated him first and he talked the officers into letting him do a cheek swab to prove it."

"I don't understand why that's relevant. Juliana has a mother and father already."

Ana's eyes narrowed. "They've gone missing."

"When?"

"Six hours ago. Francesca Freitas never made it back from her tutoring session. Guillermo Freitas was last seen taking a taxi to a local bar. He went into the bathroom and the bartender said he never saw him come back out. But you wouldn't know anything about that, would you?"

I exhaled — a slow, quiet, calm sound. "What do you want, Agent Corona?"

"There are things about this case that don't add up. I represent a taskforce who has been studying you and your relationship with Mr. Gabriel Solberg. He is one of the most powerful, influential people not only in the United States but throughout in the world and he personally vouched for you after you were incarcerated in this facility. Furthermore, if he had not donated millions of dollars to the poverty and educational programs in this country and in the U.S., you would not be cleared of your charges as you are now. There have been several incidents regarding the two of you in the past couple years that are causing us to ask questions. You can believe that I have a lot on my plate but, I intend to get the answers to those questions one way or another."

Cold fury filled me. "Are you threatening me?"

"The U.S. government does not threaten its citizens. I'm just here to keep the peace."

"Your version of peace," I said, unable to keep the anger out of my voice. If she knew how many centuries I had spent building the country she now served, she wouldn't dare use such an arrogant tone with me. The angelic half of my soul raged against the idea of submitting to the rules of Man. How much had I sacrificed to keep them safe? How many of my men had died in their stead? Who held these people accountable for the sins they committed each and every day?

I felt my anger pervading the room, hot, boiling, and invisible. It crept closer to the small woman in front of me and I almost let it touch her, but I retracted at the last minute. We weren't allowed to emotionally manipulate human beings. It constituted a violation of trust. If I wanted this woman to back off, I'd have to do it the old fashioned way.

She closed the folder. "Consider this a courtesy call. You will be released from this facility after you've filled out the appropriate paperwork and it will reflect on your permanent record that you assisted in the capture of a dangerous international criminal. In return, the court has determined that you are banned from entering Brazil for the next five years in lieu of imprisonment. If you cooperate fully with everything they ask of you, you will be allowed to return after that time. However, you're still under investigation with the United States government. You will be deported to the States until we have determined that you are not a threat to national security."

"What's going to happen to Juliana?"

Ana looked at me, and this time, I could see past the cold professional. A tiny crack appeared in her armor. I'd surprised her.

"The police will continue searching for her parents, but in the meantime, she'll be taken to a foster home."

"She doesn't have any other family?"

"My records show her grandparents are both in hospices in São Paulo and she doesn't have any other living relatives."

The gears in my head got to turning. "Would James be able to claim temporary custody of her until her parents are found?"

"I don't see the courts agreeing to let a man who was just arrested for assault claim custody of his estranged daughter."

A small smirk touched my lips. "You've never seen him in a court room before."

Ana's eyes widened a touch, but the look disappeared in under two seconds. "We'll see."

"He's going to need time to pull some strings for an expedited application procedure. I know you want us to get the hell out of here so how much time did the officials give us to leave town?"

"Forty-eight hours."

I winced. Not great, but it was a start. "Am I free to go?"

"You are." She gestured to the officer at the door as she stood. "Take Mr. O'Brien and process him out."

"*Sim, Senhora* Corona."

The officer hauled me to my feet and unlocked my cuffs, to my relief. My shoulders had been sore for hours, and the bullet wound had been throbbing ever since they stitched me up. It took me a moment to move my left arm without severe pain.

Agent Corona sent me one last frigid stare over her glasses. "We will be watching you, Mr. O'Brien."

With that, she turned and stalked out of the room.

CHAPTER EIGHTEEN

MICHAEL

Belial and I were about three steps away from the police department when I grabbed two handfuls of his shirt and shoved him against the nearest wall, my voice a deadly growl.

"Why the *hell* didn't you tell me you were Juliana's biological father?"

The demon stared back at me with a placid expression. "You didn't ask."

"Cut the bullshit, Belial, or I swear I'll tear your throat out."

Again, his expression betrayed nothing, but I could already feel his energy crackling around me like static. "If you unhand me, I'll tell you. Otherwise, you'd better make this worth my while, Mikey."

I winced. I had always hated that nickname. No one dared to call me that since Satan's fall. The arrogant bastard had sought to patronize me in front of his army by calling me that name and it still made me want to rip things apart whenever I heard it.

I dropped my hands. "Answers. Now."

Belial dusted off his shirt, taking his sweet time before replying. "I didn't know she was my daughter until that teenage girl mentioned the name, Freitas. Four years ago, I was traveling through this area for work and I met a woman named Francesca Freitas at a bar. Her husband is an alcoholic and they'd been having problems. Plus, she was quite fetching. Naturally, it sounded right up my alley so I took her back to my hotel and showed her a good time. I left Brazil about a day later and thought nothing of the matter."

I ran a hand through my hair as I followed him down the short flight of steps from the police department to the sidewalk. The sun peeked above the horizon in the distance, chasing away the thick navy from the night before. The air was damp and chilly. There were a few people around, mostly joggers and folks getting ready for work. After all, it was half past five in the morning.

"I don't understand. I've never seen a demon and a human mate and come up with a Seer before."

"Trust me, I was just as shocked as you when I realized the girl was mine. This is unprecedented," he said, tossing up his hand to flag down a taxi. "How much time did *la petite putain* say we had to skip town?"

I couldn't help but smirk. I hated Belial, but he had a knack for giving people appropriate nicknames. "Forty-eight hours."

"Excellent. We need to send in an agent to finish off the rogue angel before he gets sent to prison. I suspect that was his plan all along."

"I figured as much. He had probably hoped we would arrive too late to save the girl and the cops would stall us long enough for him to get into their custody. Even with your friends in low places, it'll be hard to get to him now."

"What do you suggest then?"

A numb tiredness had settled behind my eyes from lack of sleep and an overabundance of stress. It made it a lot harder to think straight. "I'm not sure. I have to talk to Gabriel. We need some kind of game plan. It's not going to be easy with the government breathing down our necks."

"*Our* necks?" he asked in a haughty voice. "I'm not bedfellows with Gabriel. I should take the lead on this particular mission."

I glared at him. "Like hell."

He laughed. "I'll just let that one slide because you're tired. I'm going to have to speak with some lawyer friends of mine and try to nab a court date to get the kid. In the meantime, you can contact your brother and figure out what to do. I'll give you one day. Then we're doing things my way."

"Yes, because that always works out so well," I said, my voice flat.

A cab finally pulled over and Belial opened the door, arching an eyebrow at me over his shoulder.

"When's the last time *you* sired a Seer? Oh, right, never."

"Bite me."

"Is that a request or a command?"

"I'm sorry…*what?*"

I collapsed on the bed in my absurdly expensive hotel room, wrinkling the crisp white comforter all to hell, and released an exhausted sigh into my cell phone. "It's true."

"No, I could've sworn I misheard you," Gabriel continued. "What do you mean the Seer is Belial's daughter? How is that even possible?"

I massaged the bridge of my nose. "You got me. I've never heard of anything like this. But I guess it's possible. Demons only transfer genetic material, not any holy properties like angels used to. If the Freitas bloodline is pure enough, I guess it doesn't matter."

He sighed. "I swear, this has been the most infuriating week of my life."

"Ditto."

"What are we going to do about this, then?"

"I'm not sure. On the one hand, if he gets custody of her, we can make sure she's safe while we're trying to figure out what to do with Edmond."

"I don't understand why we need to do anything. Won't he get the death penalty?"

"It depends on where he'd be tried. He's an international serial killer. That makes things way trickier. Plus, I'm not going to wait around for the system to process him. If he regains consciousness, he's capable of escaping and slipping back into the wind. I don't want to take that chance."

Gabriel went quiet momentarily. "Are you suggesting we send in someone to kill him while he's in prison?"

"Perhaps."

He sighed—a deep, regretful sound. "That…is a very ugly thought, brother."

"I know," I whispered. "We're soldiers. When we kill, it's supposed to be justice. But this…entire mission feels wrong. It felt wrong the day we agreed to let Belial help us."

"I've felt the same way. But think about the alternative. If Edmond gets loose, we'll be on absolute lockdown."

I snorted. "Oh, and there's the silver lining. The United States government is putting me under surveillance for suspicious activity."

Gabriel spewed a string of curses in Latin. "Father in Heaven, what next?"

I let out a bitter laugh. "Don't tempt Him. He has way too good a sense of humor, you know."

"Point taken."

"How did things go on your end?"

"Oh, the usual. Blood was spilled, faces were punched, and lives were saved. I'll tell you the entire story when you get home. When will that be, exactly?"

"We've been given two days to get out of Brazil. I'm banned from the country for five years. Gonna have to apologize to Jordan. I suspect that since she's my wife, they won't let her travel down here either if they're worried I'm a criminal."

"I've got ears inside the FBI. I'll see what I can dig up on these government agents. Who came to see you?"

"Ana Corona."

"Describe her."

"About five-foot-three, mid-thirties, black, possibly Haitian, wears nice suits and perfume. She's like Jordan's less sarcastic evil twin."

"If that's true, then I definitely fear for your safety." At last, a bit of humor crept into my brother's voice and I felt a little better. "I'll see what I can do."

"So I take it you still don't want to make the Call."

"No. I have other resources to try. Call me back when Belial secures a trial for custody of the girl. In the meantime, Jordan wants to speak to you."

Movement, then the soft, apprehensive voice of my wife filled my ears. "Hey, you."

A faint, relieved smile touched my lips. "Hey, baby. How are you?"

"I've been better," she said. "I heard most of that conversation. I think you actually managed to screw up worse than me for once."

"I know. It's weird. Like a role reversal."

"*Cállate,*" she muttered, but I could hear the smile in her voice. "What's this about Belial being someone's baby daddy?"

I choked on a laugh. "That's one way to put it. Juliana is his daughter so he's going to try and get custody while the police search for her parents. I'm not thrilled with the idea of being a babysitter, but at least we'll have two Seers instead of just one."

"Hurray. I'll start making club t-shirts. When are you coming home?"

"Two days at the most. They really want us out of here."

"Okay. Please, for the love of God, be safe. *Te amo.*"

"*Te amo.*"

I hung up and tossed the phone on the pillow next to me. My eyes slid shut and I fell asleep in less than a minute.

CHAPTER NINETEEN

JORDAN

After all of my recent traveling, my apartment looked beautiful when I finally made it home. Gabriel collapsed on the couch while I went to take a shower, grateful to be back under the pathetic water pressure of my own bathroom. Things were still hectic, but I had learned to take solace in the few quiet moments I got—everything from taking a hot shower to napping on the couch with my husband watching old cartoons.

I had just finished getting dressed when the doorbell rang, which made me jump yet again. I pressed a hand to my forehead and told myself to calm down as I stuck my head out the bedroom door to see Gabriel answer it. To my surprise, Raphael walked in with a long, rolled up piece of paper in his hand.

I dried my hair with a towel as I walked out of my room. "Hey, Raph. Why does it feel like I haven't seen you in forever?"

"Going to Heaven tends to have that effect. How are you?"

I hugged him. "Surviving. What've you got for us?"

He brandished the paper, his expression sobering. "The Scribes finally finished translating the missing page of the Book of Time."

"Then let's get cracking." I gestured to the chairs at the kitchen table and we all sat down.

Raphael unfurled the paper. I hadn't known what to expect, but part of me was excited to see something from Heaven with my own eyes. Few humans ever got that privilege. It was about the size of a large poster and instead of a book format, there was a timeline with Latin words written in lovely cursive beneath each of the small dots.

"Alright, my Latin's a bit rusty, so you'll have to help me out here," I said, trying to lighten the mood. A heavy atmosphere of anticipation had settled among the three of us, and with good reason. These were the answers we had been searching for and they would determine our actions from here on out.

"Well, first, you should know that every translation is different," Raphael said, smoothing out the edges of the paper. "The Scribes come from all walks of life and they determine what is the best way to record what they hear from the Symphony of Time. Therefore, we don't have the same translation as the one that the rogue angel has and it's unlikely that we'll be able to recover his version now that he has been apprehended."

"For the current time period, we have a lot of information about significant historic events both on Earth and in other parts of the universe. If we travel back along the timeline, you'll see the notations where the Seers appear. Strangely, the names of these Seers are not given; rather, it speaks of times and exact locations. It predicts when each will Awaken and consequently when they will die."

"Does it say who kills them?"

Raphael shook his head. "No. That isn't exactly the problem anymore. What we need to focus on happens here."

He pointed further down the timeline. "October 31st, 2011. This is the event that the rogue angel is trying to prevent."

I arched an eyebrow. "On Halloween? Seriously?"

The edge of Raphael's lips twitched upward—not quite a smile, but close. He always seemed amused by my cynicism. "It may seem like too much of a coincidence, but there are facts linked to the celebrations of the dead. Nothing as trite as ghosts rising from their graves, but evil does tend to manifest on that night because it is the night before All Hallows Day, one of the holiest days of the year. The Book states that a Seer will betray the angels and awaken the Leviathan. This can only be accomplished by acquiring a source of knowledge and purity. I believe that this coincides with another date on the timeline."

He shifted to another point. "Here, it states that there will be a visit to the Garden of Eden."

My mouth fell open. "The Garden of Eden? You're shittin' me. It still exists?"

Gabriel shook his head. "Only you would include a curse word in the same sentence as such a holy place."

I glanced at him with an indignant look. "Hey, give me a break. I'm not a Bible scholar."

"Clearly."

I smacked him in the arm and he chuckled. "Where is it? I don't understand how no one has found it by now."

"The Garden is hidden deep underground," Gabriel continued. "Human exploration is still only in its earliest stages. Besides, no human can enter—only supernatural beings like us angels or even a Seer like yourself."

~ 192 ~

"So what in the Garden would be powerful enough to wake the Leviathan? And if it's so evil, why does it need something holy?"

"Fruit from the Tree of Knowledge caused man to become self-aware. It would work the same way for the Leviathan. Balance is the key to most things good and evil on Earth. For instance, an archangel would be unable to wake the Leviathan because angels are not born of Earth nor are they capable of being evil. Some can be misled, like the rogue angel, but it is not the same as a Seer or a demon. The Seer represents all three of the worlds: Earth, Heaven, and Hell. That's why only he or she can wake the Leviathan."

I bit my bottom lip as a cold sensation of fear crawled up my chest. "Does it say the name of the Seer anywhere in the timeline?"

"Unfortunately, no. That is why the rogue angel didn't take any chances. He killed all the ones who awakened this year except for you and the child."

I shut my eyes. "Raphael...are there any more Awakenings noted in this year?"

His voice came out soft. "No."

I clasped my hands together and rested my forehead on them. "I was hoping you wouldn't say that. I really was."

Gabriel laid a hand on my shoulder. "Jor—"

"Don't. I'm not a child, Gabriel."

"Jordan, you cannot doubt yourself. You would never betray us. I believe that with all my heart and soul."

I shook my head. "You don't know that."

"Yes, I do. I have known you for many years. You are incapable of doing something like this."

I glared at him. "Then what? A four-year-old girl is going to send the world into chaos? It's one or the other. There aren't any other choices."

Gabriel set his jaw. "This is a translation. For all you know, it could be inaccurate. There could be someone else who will Awaken before the 31st. Don't do this to yourself."

Raphael spoke up, though I could tell he was hesitant. "Brother, we still have to consider it an option. I don't believe Jordan would do this either, but it would be prudent to take the idea into account."

The blond archangel sighed and dropped his hand. "Then what are you suggesting?"

"She stays under the care of the archangels until after the 31st. We cannot allow her anywhere near the battlefield if this comes to pass."

"If this comes to pass? Are you saying this isn't definite?" Gabriel asked.

Raphael winced. "It's hard to say. It appears that the rogue angel believes that he can change the future, even though his efforts are already recorded in the Book. If he believes it, then perhaps it is possible to avoid releasing the Leviathan."

"And I take it that the demon's name isn't listed on the timeline either?" I asked.

He shook his head. I swore under my breath. "Great. So basically I just have to sit around doing nothing and avoiding demons. I'm glad to be so helpful."

"I'm sorry. I know you feel frustrated, but there is nothing more we can do right now. If the rogue angel is killed, he will be sent to judgment and we can get the rest of the answers out of him then."

An idea sprang into my head. "Wait. What if his translation of the Book of Time is different? Maybe more specific than ours?"

Raphael gave me a puzzled look so I kept going. "What I'm saying is why don't we get him to give us the page he translated to see if he caught anything we missed?"

"The page was not recovered when they apprehended him in Jandira," Gabriel said. "It's unlikely that we'll ever find it now. He probably memorized it and burnt the original to prevent it from falling into the wrong hands."

"What if we get him to retranslate this page? Maybe he could give us clues like names or events that the Scribes didn't catch."

"There is no way he'd cooperate. He clearly has mental instability."

I shook my head. "There's still a chance he could help. Is there any way to contact him before the authorities put him on trial for the murders?"

"No. Since the first murder took place in Kentucky, he's going to be transferred stateside when he's out of critical condition. He'll serve the consecutive sentences in each country where the crimes were committed, and that is only if he does not get the death penalty. Besides, he won't speak to any of the archangels because we have orders to kill him on sight."

"But what if he'll talk to me? I'm not under orders."

Gabriel sighed again, sounding tired instead of frustrated this time. "That is too risky. Even Michael had difficulty subduing him. He is too much of a threat to engage directly. We'll just have to try something else."

Anger rolled through me, mixing with the fear—a dangerous combination, but I couldn't help myself. "Fantastic. If anyone needs me, I'll be in my room seeing as I'm grounded and all."

I stormed out of the kitchen and didn't turn when he called after me. I knew he meant well, and so did Raphael, but neither of them understood. There was a good chance that I would cause the deaths of one thousand people. I had tried so hard these past three years to protect the innocent, to save lost souls, to sacrifice life and limb for those who couldn't help themselves, and yet here we were. All of the doubts and fears inside me festered within my chest like bacteria, eating away at what was left of my faith.

I slammed the bedroom door shut and stood there in the middle of the room, my breath shallow, on the borderline of panic. What could I do? There had to be something I could do to stop this. I didn't care what it was as long as it worked.

I thought about calling Michael, but he'd have the same opinion as his brothers. Keep me safe and prepare for war. He wouldn't listen to my plan, either. Who did that leave?

The answer came to me in a quiet voice. No. There was no way I could ask *him*. If I did, it would be the end of everything. No one would ever trust me, and Michael would never want to speak to me again. But then, isn't that what I had been afraid of this whole time? Doing something so horrible that my husband would push me away? Would he forgive me for this? I didn't know. It didn't matter, not really. If the choices were my marriage or innocent lives, I would have to make the sacrifice whether I wanted to or not.

I crawled into bed and pulled the covers over my head to block out the sunlight. It was late afternoon and the chances of my new insane plan succeeding were slim, but I at least had to try. I squeezed my eyes shut and concentrated on falling asleep with his face in mind, praying for God to forgive me as my mind started to drift.

Christopher Nolan had been right about dreams—I never remembered the way they began. I always started in the middle and had to catch up to what was happening. For instance, the clothes I currently wore weren't mine. I wore a blood-red cocktail dress with high pumps on my feet, and I could feel that my hair was pinned and curled in some kind of complicated up-do. Diamonds glittered on my throat and at my wrists, which were outstretched because I was dancing with a man in an old 1940's-style black tuxedo. We were in my kitchen and there was an old radio sitting on the counter, belting out the upbeat lyrics to "Ain't We Got Fun" from an old Tex Avery cartoon.

The man in black twirled me and then caught me in his arms, allowing me to recognize him at last.

"My, my," Belial said with his usual insufferable smirk. "This is quite a surprise."

I examined his fancy suit and then caught a good look at myself in the reflection of the microwave door. "What is it with you and these stupid themed dreams?"

He clucked his tongue, settling his large hands on my waist as we swayed back and forth to the music. "You have no imagination, my pet. It's much more fun to be someone else for a change. You seem to be indulging in it as well."

I scowled. "Don't start. I'm already mad enough without your help."

"True. Speaking of help, what can I do for you? It must be important. You've never contacted me before."

I took a deep breath, stuffing down the frantic voice in my head that told me not to go through with this horrid idea. "I need a favor."

Belial arched a thin eyebrow. "Another one?"

"Shut up. This is not something you can laugh off. This is serious and I'm about to ruin my life by asking you."

The teasing smile faded. "I'm listening."

"Raphael showed me the retranslated page of the Book of Time. It states that on October 31st, a Seer will wake the Leviathan and it's going to kill a lot of people. He also said that no other Seers will Awaken before then so it's going to be either me or your daughter. You can tell where I'm going with this."

His hands tightened on my hips a bit. "You're convinced it's going to be you."

A lump formed in my throat and I swallowed hard to push past it. "Yes. But I wanted to recruit the rogue angel to take a look at the translation himself and see if he knows any more details. Dates, times, places, anything that might stop me from waking the Leviathan. The archangels refused to agree to this so I'm asking you to help me break the rogue angel out and convince him to work with me."

He let out a harsh bark of laughter. "Are you insane? Releasing the Leviathan would suit both my purposes and my master's. What makes you think I would help you?"

"You're still bound by demonic law to hunt the archangel. He's not dead. Your contract with us isn't up until he dies. Besides…"

I took a deep breath, forcing myself to continue. "If I do this, Michael is probably going to leave me. You'll get your shot at turning me into your servant."

Belial said nothing, staring down at me with his cold blue eyes as we continued waltzing. I could almost see the wheels in his head turning as he thought about my proposal. Still, even in my dream state, I was so afraid that there were goosebumps all over my bare arms. Being close to him scared me beyond all reasoning, but there was also a dark part of me that felt intrigued by the danger.

"I have a hard time believing that you would sacrifice your marriage for people you don't even know," he said finally.

"That's because you're a demon. You couldn't understand sacrifice if you tried," I replied, fighting to keep my voice level.

Belial scoffed. "Your arrogance is astounding. You act like you know me, but you don't. You only know what you've read and what your archangels have told you."

"Fine. Then who are you really, Belial? It's just the two of us in here. No one will hear you except for me if you tell the truth."

"The truth? Why would I reveal such a thing to the likes of you?"

I shook my head. "You are such a coward."

In a flash, he spun me so that I faced away from him and then wrapped his arms around my upper torso, trapping my wrists in his iron grip. He crushed me against the front of his body, sending jolts of pain up my spine and my ribs. I couldn't help gasping and trying to wriggle free, but he didn't budge. His hot breath washed over my ear as he leaned down, pressing the side of his face into my hair, his words quiet but terrifying.

"Careful, my pet. My patience isn't endless."

I closed my eyes, ignoring how shaky I sounded. "Do we have a deal or not?"

He let out another one of those sandpaper chuckles. "Always business with you, isn't it? But before I give you my answer, I want to hear you say it."

"Say what?"

"That you're truly willing to give up your sweet Michael and the friendship you share with Gabriel and Raphael to save these so-called innocent people. That you're willing to betray your loved ones even though they have given you everything. If you do this, there is no turning back. You will do things my way and my way alone. Now say it."

Tears gathered in my eyes, but didn't fall. "I am."

A long sigh escaped his chest. He let go of my left hand and slid his fingers around my neck. The fear inside me shifted. I had been afraid he would tear me apart, but now I could feel the heat from his body, every inch of him, even the part I didn't want to think about, and knew I would never forgive myself for what I had done. I deserved to be in his clutches. We both knew that.

"So be it, Seer. We have an accord. I will contact you again when we arrive in the States. Until then, act as if nothing is wrong."

"Fine."

He licked my neck — a slow, sensual movement. "Shall we kiss on it?"

"Don't get it twisted. I may be working with you, but I still hate you and I always will."

"So you say. But who knows what the future might bring?"

His lips slid across my ear and he bit down on the lobe, hard enough that everything went white for a second from a quick rush of pain and pleasure.

I woke up in my bed with tears on my cheeks and an icy cold sensation gliding across my skin. I sat up and wrapped my arms around myself to quell the tremors flooding through me, and couldn't remember the last time I had felt so alone.

CHAPTER TWENTY

MICHAEL

I could tell the desk clerk at the Child Services office had gotten annoyed with me because I couldn't stop tapping my fingers on the counter. If she had any inkling of the things weighing on my mind, she may have understood my fidgety nature. Impatience bubbled around me as I stood there, waiting for Belial to return with Juliana so we could hop on a plane and get the hell back to Albany.

I hadn't spoken to my wife in almost a day. Not by choice, of course. Gabriel called when Raphael returned with the newly translated page of the Book of Time and told me everything. Understandably, neither Jordan nor I had taken the news well. I wanted to talk to her, but Gabriel told me to let her settle down first. He had a point. Jordan needed time to evaluate the situation. Hearing her worried husband wouldn't facilitate that. But I still wanted to call. Every second of the day, I wanted to call and tell her I didn't give a shit what that page said—I didn't believe for a second that she would wake the Leviathan.

I didn't surprise me that Gabriel didn't believe it, either. After all, he had known Jordan longer than I had so we were both in agreement about asking Raphael to return to Heaven to have someone else analyze the page. There had to be something we missed—another Awakening, or some way to avert the Leviathan's uprising. We needed to prevent the deaths of those one thousand people and we needed to make sure nothing from the underworld would be able to make it through to Earth from the Hellmouth. Again, the damn page did not specify the details of the incident so we were basically taking a shot in the dark.

Meanwhile, I'd been stuck with Belial as he secured all the paperwork and worked his magic on the judge to grant him custody of the child for the time being. Any normal person would have gotten a firm and rightful no, but Belial's silver tongue had always been his greatest asset. Plus, he had paid off a shitton of people to get a trial date and a verdict in his favor.

The police were elbow-deep in the case of Juliana's missing parents—interviewing locals, checking the last places they had been seen, and spreading the word. The Freitas family was well known in the area so a lot of people were concerned, which made things a little easier. The more informed the neighbors, the better our chance of finding them.

So far, I theorized that the rogue angel had some sort of accomplice who had been ordered to kidnap the parents if he failed in his mission to kill Juliana. He might have thought they would be bargaining chips for his release, but since he got arrested, things were out of our hands. Still, even with that hypothesis, I had doubts. Kidnapping didn't seem like his kind of deal. Something just felt off about the entire situation and I aimed to get to the bottom of it.

I snapped out of my thoughts when I heard the unmistakable cry of a little girl. Seconds later, Juliana and a very irritated Belial came around the corner. He let go of her hand to sign out at the desk and she continued wailing as if she had nothing else to live for. Sympathy rushed through me in a wave. I knelt in front of the child, thinking fast.

"Hey, shh, it's alright," I said in Portuguese, rubbing the top of her head. She got a good look at me this time and I could tell she recognized me from her traumatic night, though it only made her cry a bit less.

"Do you like candy?"

She sniffled and then nodded. I reached into my pocket and withdrew a lollipop I'd swiped from the front desk. Juliana tore off the wrapper, then popped the sweet into her mouth. I wiped her face clean as she continued watching me with her cautious brown eyes.

"There you go. Do you know my name?"

She shook her head. "It's Michael. I'm going to be helping to take care of you for a while, okay?"

Another slow nod. I paused, thinking. "Do you speak English?"

She rolled the candy around to the side of her mouth and spoke in a hoarse voice, still in Portuguese.

"M-My Mama taught me a little."

"Good. That means when we get to America, you'll be able to read signs and talk to people. Do you like reading?"

She nodded again. "Great. Then that's what we'll do."

I scooped her up in my arms and she didn't fight me — automatically sliding her hands around my neck like she was used to being carried. When I stood up straight, I noticed the rather amused expression on Belial's face.

"I'm sorry, whose kid is this again?" he said in English.

We started walking towards the exit. I replied in English as well to avoid bothering the child. "What? She's upset and you weren't doing anything to help."

"I'm not really the paternal type."

"Big surprise there."

"Suck my—"

"Oy," I said in a sharp voice. "Language."

Belial rolled his eyes. "I'm beginning to regret this decision already. What time is our flight?"

I shifted Juliana in my arms, checking my watch. "We've got about three hours. Let's head straight to the hotel and get packed up. We're probably gonna hit traffic on the way to the airport."

Belial stepped out onto the sidewalk and waved for a cab. I turned my attention back to the girl as she spoke up.

"Where are we going?"

"Back to the hotel so we can get ready to leave for America. Have you ever ridden on a plane before?"

She shook her head. "Is it fun?"

"Yep. We'll be really high in the sky and you'll get to see what Brazil looks like if you're a bird."

"Higher than the clouds?"

"Yeah."

For the first time, a faint smile touched her now cherry-red lips. "Mmkay."

Another wave of affection went through me at her shy acceptance. I almost groaned at myself. Jordan made fun of me for being what she called a "softie" and I always denied it, but I knew she had a point. I was a sucker for cute kids, and Juliana was the cutest, even though her father was literally hellspawn.

At last, Belial managed to flag down a cab and we climbed in, telling the driver to head for the Hilton at Morumbi. I tried to get Juliana to sit between us, but she insisted on sitting in my lap. She didn't seem to feel comfortable around Belial. Not that I blamed her. He usually put on a façade for people he needed to manipulate, but that rarely included children, so he acted like himself around her. His perfectly foul, normal self.

The ride was long and Juliana fell asleep halfway through, her head on my chest and a thumb in her mouth. Bad habit for a kid at four years old, but I knew some kids did that whenever they felt uneasy so I let it slide. I wanted to ask Belial about the assassin he had planned on sending after the rogue angel, but we were still in public so I had to hold off on it. I didn't like leaving things to chance. Even if it felt wrong, I wanted Edmond dead by my hand, not some anonymous demon's. Plus, I wouldn't have confirmation of his death until his soul crossed over.

I forced myself to stop thinking about it and instead focused on what to do about Jordan. She wouldn't like having to sit around. She wanted to help just as bad as the angels did even though it would be dangerous. I had been thinking about training her in the more advanced martial arts. She knew the basics, but nothing as extensive as me. Plus, her energy-shielding needed some work. She took to attacks, like me, but defense was just as important in a fight.

The cab pulled up to the hotel and Belial paid the driver. I opened the door and hefted Juliana in my arms as I stepped out. She stirred a little, but didn't wake up. She probably hadn't slept at all the night before. Poor thing.

When I made it to my hotel room, I laid her down on the bed so she could continue napping while we got our stuff together. Once I was sure she was asleep, I turned to Belial.

"What's the word on your guy on the inside? Can we get to the rogue angel before they transfer him stateside?"

"The last time I spoke to him, he told me defenses were too tight, even for him. There would be no way to get to Edmond without massive casualties, and since you told me that you wouldn't allow any collateral damage, we'll have to catch him en route to his first trial."

"I had a feeling you'd say that. Just one more problem to deal with."

"No one ever said this job was easy. Once we return stateside, we'll have our work cut out for us. Did Gabriel dig up some information on *la petite putain*?"

"Yeah. She's FBI."

"Fantastic. We'll both have the feds breathing down our necks when we return. That will make things infinitely harder. But who doesn't mind a little challenge?"

"It's not a game."

"Maybe not to you. I'm not completely attached to this body, after all. I can disappear and leave my life behind. You, on the other hand, are foolish enough to have dreams and an identity you have to keep. I don't envy you there."

"So you say."

Belial gave me an unfriendly look, clenching his jaw as if he wanted to argue. "Just get your stuff together so we can leave sometime this century."

He walked out, slamming the door. A petty part of my soul enjoyed the sound.

I tossed my stuff into my suitcase and sent a text to Jordan and Gabriel to let them know we were heading to the airport. Gabriel responded, but Jordan didn't. I suppressed yet another urge to call her. *Give her time, Michael.*

When everything was packed up, I woke Juliana. She blinked sleepily at me from beneath her long lashes, mumbling, "Where're we going?"

I smiled. "Home."

Eleven hours later, I stood on the ratty brown welcome mat to my wife's apartment—our apartment—with the keys that I had finally remembered in my hand. I took a deep breath and opened the door, not entirely sure of what I would see on the other side.

Jordan stood in the kitchen wearing one of my shirts and looking beautiful despite the fact that I knew how upset she had to be feeling. She glanced up at me when I walked in and a faint smile touched her lips.

"Hey."

"Hey," I said, pushing the door shut. I didn't waste any time crossing the hardwood floor and pulling her into me. It wasn't like our usual hugs. She wrapped both arms around the back of my shoulders and pressed her face into my chest, as if she wanted me to swallow her up and make her disappear. That alone told me how much pain she was in.

I held her for a long time, saying nothing even though I had about a million things I wanted to tell her. Eventually, she let go and I brushed the hair out of her eyes, trying to figure out where to start.

"You wanna talk about it yet?"

She shook her head. "No, I just…"

She sighed and there was an echo of something in her voice that I couldn't place. She leaned her forehead against mine, laying her hands on my cheeks.

"I need you. Now. Please."

I nodded. "Okay. I'm here."

~ 203 ~

I slipped my fingers between hers and led her to the bedroom. For now, we didn't need words. They had their place in our lives and it wasn't here. But for the first time, I wished she had said something because the way she touched me felt like she was afraid of losing me, as if we would never be here again. It scared the living hell out of me. She poured every ounce of herself into me with each kiss, and somehow, the dynamic between us changed. I could feel her sliding away; sand through my fingers. God help us.

After it was over, we lay in bed for a long while. She propped her head on my left shoulder and I threaded my fingers through her soft black hair, smoothing it away from her face. The silence carried on until I couldn't stand it, so I took a deep breath and spoke.

"Do you remember what I said before you died last year?"

She snorted. "Which time?"

"The first time."

Her brow furrowed. "Yeah, why?"

I shifted my head so I could look into her eyes while I talked. "I asked 'What if I need you?' when you told me that there were people on this Earth who needed me. I meant that, you know. If you had decided not to die in my place, I would've gladly remained a poltergeist instead of returning to heaven like my brothers."

Surprise flooded her features. "You're serious."

"Yeah," I whispered. "Because even back then, when I had only known you a few days, I knew that you were worth an eternity of displacement. As long as I could be beside you, it wouldn't have bothered me. I know that sounds crazy, but it's true. I thought I fell in love with you when we kissed for the first time, but I was wrong. You've always had this ability to draw me to you and that's something that will never change. I would turn my back on the world for you."

Jordan closed her eyes. "Please don't say that, Michael."

"It's the truth. Your mother told me that everyone is allowed to have a weakness, and my weakness is that I'm selfish. Irredeemably so. I'm sorry."

She opened her eyes and tears fell as she touched my cheek. "Stupid jackass."

I smiled. "Love you too."

She let out a weak, shaky laugh and kissed me. I felt a small piece of her return to normal and it gave me enough peace to fall asleep with the taste of her lips on mine.

It was dark and raining when I woke up. Automatically, I reached in front of me, but Jordan's side of the bed was empty. I opened my eyes. The clock read one a.m. I'd been asleep for around five hours, which was largely due to jet lag. I yawned and tilted my head towards the bathroom, checking to see if she was in there, but she wasn't. The bedroom door was open, but I couldn't see into the kitchen from this side of the mattress.

"Jor?" I called in a hoarse, sleepy voice. No answer. She must've gone out. Maybe down the street for a late night snack. All this traveling meant we were low on food.

I took a shower and got dressed before heading into the kitchen to get a snack. Right after downing half a carton of orange juice, I found a note on the counter in Jordan's handwriting.

"Michael,
I love you more than I could ever try to explain. Never forget that. And I'm so sorry for whatever happens in the future. I hope you can forgive me someday, but I will understand if you don't. Take care of yourself, mi amor.

Jordan"

My entire body went cold at once. Her cell phone sat next to the note. She never left her cell phone, no matter where she went. Something was terribly, terribly wrong here.

I forced myself to stop panicking and closed my eyes, stretching my energy out as far as it would go. After our souls were tied together, I could sense her within a certain range, but as I pushed my energy to its absolute limits, I couldn't feel her presence anywhere. She wasn't at my apartment, or the restaurant, or any of the local bars or clubs.

Where the hell had she gone?

CHAPTER TWENTY-ONE

JORDAN

I had never known this much vomit could come out of one person.

Someone knocked on the bathroom door. "Are you okay in there?" A concerned female voice. The lone flight attendant.

I spat a mouthful of saliva and stomach acid into the toilet before replying. "I-I'm fine. Just...air-sickness, that's all."

I hovered over the toilet bowl for another handful of seconds, but the nausea seemed to have passed for now. I flushed it twice just to be as clean as possible and rinsed my mouth out in the ivory sink. For years, I'd had anxiety problems related to hospitals and doctors, but this problem was new. I had never gotten so nervous or upset that it made me throw up. Then again, my near future was about to be full of things I hadn't done before.

I opened the door and the flight attendant, an older woman, white, late fifties, cast a concerned look over me from head to toe. "Are you sure you're alright, darling?"

I nodded. She gave me a kind pat on the arm and continued towards the front of the plane to speak with the pilot. Nice lady. I hadn't expected such hospitality on Belial's private jet.

The differences between his and Gabriel's jet were interesting, to say the least. First off, Gabriel's color scheme had been white leather seats and a burgundy carpet while Belial's was all black and grey. Daunting. Then again, that was just his style.

Secondly, while Gabriel's plane boarded at major airports, this one had been on a small airstrip practically in the middle of nowhere. Just as well. Belial probably needed to sneak out of the city at odd times and in places where there weren't many security cameras.

I plopped down in my seat and placed a hand over my stomach, hoping its emptiness would get rid of the sick feeling, but it didn't. After all, it was psychological. I had never done something so wrong that every inch of me felt ill. First time for everything.

To distract myself, I checked my watch. It had only been four hours since take off. I had an hour and a half before we'd land. Michael would probably be just waking up by now. I closed my eyes. *Calm down, Amador.* I had to stop thinking about him or I'd never be able to eat again.

The jet was of course Belial's idea. He had contacted me in my dreams again with instructions, just like he promised. I took out a load of cash and caught a cab to the airstrip he'd named and then boarded the jet bound for Lexington. If we hadn't been in a time crunch, I would have ridden a bus because it would have made it far harder for any of the archangels to find a trail to start searching for me.

Still, there was one advantage of a plane instead of a bus. I had a tail. The FBI tagged Michael as a suspicious character so by proxy, they had to monitor all of my movements as well. If I'd ridden a Greyhound, they could easily have had someone follow me. The plane left them with no idea where I'd be heading since we were flying under the radar. We suspected I would only be under direct surveillance until the rogue angel was sentenced and safely imprisoned. Afterwards, everything else would be monitoring calls and checking for suspicious activity in my bank account.

The rogue angel had been confirmed leaving São Paulo at four o'clock p.m. yesterday, which gave us a window of opportunity. His flight would be around fifteen hours so I'd definitely beat him to Lexington. After he got on the ground, the authorities would escort him to prison while he awaited his trial for the murder of Danny Bowen. In the meantime, Belial was going to give me the rundown on the operation and do his best to prepare me for it. After all, waitresses weren't exactly knowledgeable about breaking people out of the backs of police cars. Not even ones from New York.

The hardest part of the flight was not falling asleep. Michael, Gabriel, or Raphael could track me if I fell asleep within range of their energy. Consciously, they wouldn't be able to feel me, but when asleep, their powers can reach farther. That was how I had been able to contact Belial from an entire country away. It meant I would have to work on my mental shields to keep them from detecting me before we caught up with the rogue angel. Still, I didn't know where that left me if I successfully got the rogue angel to help me. He would have to go back to prison, or die by the archangels' hands to pay for his crimes. Would they forgive me? Or did my actions make me too untrustworthy to work with them anymore?

Another wave of nausea rolled through me and I closed my eyes, breathing slowly. I needed to focus on something else or I'd get sick all over again. I reached into the backpack under the seat and pulled out the first book I laid my hands on. Didn't matter what it was as long as it kept my mind busy.

At last, we landed in Lexington. I gathered my things, keeping careful watch as I shuffled off the jet. I stepped into the cold air outside, shivering and buttoning up my leather jacket as I glanced about the airstrip. It was half past one in the morning so the entire place was empty except for my ride—a dark blue SUV. I walked towards it, reminding myself to remain calm.

When I came up to the driver's side, the tinted window rolled down and I found myself looking at a brunette teenager.

"You Jordan?" she asked, cracking bubblegum between her teeth.

"Yeah."

She jerked a thumb behind her. "Hop in."

Trying not to frown, I brushed my energy across her body and confirmed that she was one of the Fallen. I opened the door and climbed in, tossing my suitcase on the other seat.

"Aren't you kind of young to be a demon?"

She adjusted her rearview mirror before heading towards the end of the strip to pull onto the road, her voice strangely energetic considering the time of night. "Aren't you observant?"

She had a point. "Sorry. I'm just not used to this sort of thing."

"No one ever is." The SUV pulled onto the street.

I had expected to pull up to a cheap motel, but the girl drove us to a Waffle House instead. Strange choice for breakfast, but I wasn't one to complain. My stomach wouldn't be stable enough for food any time soon.

She hopped out of the driver's seat and I did as well, lifting an eyebrow at her.

"Didn't know demons had a taste for cheap truck-stop breakfast."

She flashed me a grin. "Grab your stuff, Seer, and follow me."

Confused, I retrieved my suitcase and followed her inside the already packed restaurant. When we entered, she walked right past the waitress and nodded to the chef, who waved her back towards the manager's office. She opened the door and I walked in after her, biting my lip to keep from asking the obvious question hanging over my head. I'd already sounded like an idiot enough today.

The windowless office looked normal with a desk, a bookshelf, and a ficus pushed against the right corner. To my surprise, she walked over to the plant and tugged upward on its trunk. A floor panel in the left corner of the room opened, revealing a narrow flight of stairs.

Without a single word, the demon started descending and I followed her.

She led me into a fully furnished basement that looked like it had belonged in a rustic lake house somewhere. The walls had wooden paneling that complimented the plush tan carpet. A kitchenette with a fridge, sink, dishwasher, and stove sat against the left wall, and several feet along that same wall was a flat screen television and towering bookcase. The far wall had a dresser and nightstand. A king-sized bed was pushed against the wall to my right and beside it were two doors separated by about three feet.

Belial stood in front of the bed as we walked over. I had prepared something scathing to say, but then I noticed that the T.V. was on some sort of Nicktoons kids' show. When Belial stepped towards us, I could see a small dark-haired girl with coffee skin seated on the bed, enraptured by the cartoon. Yet another question sprung into my mind, accompanied by a strong sense of disapproval.

Belial smiled at the expression on my face. "I take it you didn't have a pleasant trip."

"No S-H-I-T," I said through my teeth.

The demon chuckled, turning his attention to my teenaged escort. "Well done, Mary. Here you are, as promised."

He reached into the pocket of his black slacks and withdrew a sizeable stack of bills. It looked to be over five thousand dollars. Maybe I should work for him.

Mary flipped the bills through her fingers as if mentally counting them and then popped her gum one last time. "Pleasure doing business with you, Bels."

She winked at him and sauntered off. I moved closer to Belial, keeping my voice down.

"Who's the kid?"

"My daughter."

I stared at him. "Um, not to be cold, but why is she here? It's incredibly dangerous."

"The danger of the situation is exactly why she is at my side. If the rogue angel does have an accomplice out there, she'll be safe with us."

"Don't you have millions of minions at your disposal? There's got to be someone more qualified for this than an archdemon and a Seer."

"Careful. I may seem like nothing but a murderous traitor to you, but I am more than capable of both protecting and caring for a child. Not that I'd want to, mind you."

I smacked him in the arm. "Don't say that in front of her."

Belial rolled his eyes. "She speaks little English. I'm safe."

Just then, the girl appeared at his right side, tugging on his pants leg. Portuguese and Spanish shared a few similarities so I was able to make out that she was asking him for a snack. He replied in some sort of positive manner and she smiled, and then noticed me for the first time. She asked me who I was and I answered using the only bit of Portuguese I knew: introduction.

"*Meu nome é Jordan. Muito prazer. O que é seu nome?*"

"Juliana."

"Ah, *muita bonita.*"

"*Obrigada.*" The child nodded, then ambled towards the refrigerator for a snack. It was nearly impossible to tell she had any of her father's traits. She was adorable.

When I faced Belial again, he was smirking at me, which made my smile vanish.

"What?"

"The maternal look isn't bad on you, Seer," he said, and then reached for me.

Automatically, I stepped back only to realize he was trying to take my suitcase. Blushing, I let go and he took it, shaking his head at me but not bothering to mock my reaction.

"Why is there only one bed?" I asked. "Because I tell you right now, I'll sleep on the floor before I sleep anywhere near you."

"So hostile," the demon said with a sniff. "We're already metaphorically in bed together. I don't see much of a difference."

"You wouldn't."

He chuckled, gesturing towards the first closed door on my right. "That is the guest room, where you and the child will be sleeping. Besides, you won't be getting much rest as we have to prepare for the breakout."

A streak of nervousness ran through my body—a cold, uncomfortable sensation. "Right. Sounds like fun."

He grinned. The feral expression made me shiver. "Tons."

Belial faced Juliana, catching her attention with a snap of his fingers. He told her something that sounded along the lines of "Be a good girl while Jordan and I are in the other room" and crooked a finger at me as he opened the door to the guest room.

Inside, I found another large space with a queen-sized bed, a nightstand, television set, and dresser, but this room also had a round oak table and three chairs.

Belial tossed my suitcase on the mattress and shut the door, which made me jump yet again. My nerves were shot. I needed to get past this or we'd both get killed.

"First things first," he said, sitting at the table and waiting for me to follow. "You will have to obey my orders to the letter if we want this to work. Is that understood?"

I glared at him as I sat down. "As long as they're at least pretending to be in my best interest, yes."

"Fair enough. What we're trying to accomplish here is simple. I've pulled similar jobs, but the difference here is that you're inexperienced for such highly sophisticated operations."

I lifted an eyebrow. "Why do I feel like I'm in a movie trailer for a heist film?"

He rolled his eyes. "My point is that this will be unlike anything you've ever done before, so it is imperative that you think and react as quickly as possible, and most importantly, without your usual morality."

"You're asking me to be *more* immoral? Wow. That's…" I sighed. "Fine, keep going."

"The rogue angel will be in one of two types of vehicles: an armored car with FBI agents or U.S. Marshals as guards, or a police car. There will most likely be between four and six officers escorting them on motorcycles or other cop cars. Our task is to isolate them, confuse them, and then strike."

He held up one long finger. "First, I've organized a riot in another part of the city. This will occupy all the officers who are not on this escort and therefore, the party will have little to no back up if things go sideways. Second, we're going to block their route so that they are forced to take one that is more beneficial to us. Third, we trap and confuse them. Once they're neutralized, we'll go in for the rogue angel."

"Will we have back up?"

"Not really. I wasn't able to round up many followers in this area since we are in the middle of Kentucky Fried Nowhere. I know you're familiar with basic firearms, but in this case, we're going to have the big guns so you'll need practice."

I bristled. "I'm not going to kill innocent officers who are just doing their jobs."

"If we do this right, killing won't be necessary. You'll be laying down cover fire since we both know you don't like getting your hands dirty."

"They're dirty enough," I mumbled, self-consciously rubbing my palm against the smooth leather of my jacket. The cool cloth helped me calm down, but I knew it wouldn't for long. I missed the familiar fabric of my grey duster, but I'd left it at home for a reason. I didn't deserve to wear it any longer.

Belial opened his mouth to say something else, but I cut him off.

"Where will we be headed after it's done?"

"A motel. After that, we have to stay mobile since we'll have the feds and your archangels on our trail."

"Fine. But I also have something to say."

He cocked his head to the side. "And that would be?"

I gave him my coldest stare. "I know you're going to betray me somehow. It may not be tonight or tomorrow or the day after that, but I'm not stupid. You have your own agenda and it's entirely possible that you're going to try and manipulate me into releasing the Leviathan. But I promise you that if you're foolish enough to do it, I'm going to kill you. It won't be like the last two times we've fought. I'm going to stab you in the fucking heart. Is that clear?"

Belial leaned in close until his face was inches from mine and his nicotine-laced breath brushed my cheek.

"I'm looking forward to it."

CHAPTER TWENTY-TWO

MICHAEL

The first thing I did after reading Jordan's note was turn her phone back on and check the last outgoing call. There was just one in the last twenty-four hours — to Lauren at seven-thirty. I dialed her number and waited with bated breath for her to pick up.

A sleepy voice greeted me. "Hello?"

"Hey, Lauren. It's Michael," I said, doing my best to hide the worry in my voice. "Sorry to wake you. This is silly, but Jordan left her phone at the apartment and I don't know where she went. Did she tell you?"

"No, she just said she wouldn't be able to pick up Lily from school this week because she'd be busy. Is everything okay?"

I tried to quell the guilt that rose in my gut. Lauren was Jordan's best friend, and even she didn't know what was going on. I wanted to tell her the truth, but I couldn't. I knew nothing at this point so there was no reason to make the girl worry.

"Yeah, it's fine. Just a little mix up, that's all. I'll talk to you later."

I was about to hang up when she stopped me. "Michael."

"Yeah?"

She sighed. "Look, you don't have to tell me what's going on, but I know something's wrong. There was something in her voice when she called me. She sounded…miserable. The last time I heard her sound like that was when you two separated last year. Just make sure you take care of her, okay?"

"I will. I promise. Bye, Lauren."

"Bye."

I hung up and the panic tripled inside me. *Think, Michael. Where could she have gone and why? You've been married to the woman for almost a year — you had damn well better know her habits.*

I opened her laptop, logging in and checking her bank account. We'd only been married a short time so it would be a while before we would get a joint one, but I knew her password and brought up her recent purchases. My face paled. She had taken five hundred dollars out of an ATM at the same time she called Lauren. I checked the address of the ATM and scribbled it on a nearby notepad for safekeeping, then called Gabriel.

"This is so unlike her," my brother said. "She always tells one of us where she's going. Do you think she's relapsing?"

"No. She hasn't had a drink in months and she hasn't shown any signs of needing one. Tell me exactly what she said after you and Raph showed her the page."

"We discussed the events on the map and that she'd have to stay guarded until the 31st passed by just to be safe. She suggested trying to contact the rogue angel before he served his first sentence in prison, but I told her we were under orders to kill him on sight."

I froze. "Wait. She suggested that?"

"Yes. Why?"

"What if she's gone off to try and talk to him herself? Without either of us to get in the way?"

"That's impossible. She doesn't have the influence to get a conference with him. Besides, isn't he en route to Lexington as we speak? She'd have no way to organize something like that without...help..."

He stopped talking as if he'd realized something. When he spoke again, his voice was as hard and cold as ice. "Call Belial. Now. Try every number you know for him. I'll do the same. If he doesn't pick up, we are definitely in trouble."

"Got it."

I hung up and called Belial's cell phone, praying for the first time in my life that I would hear that dry, supercilious voice of his. An automated voice answered instead and told me the number had been disconnected.

"Damn it, Jordan." I pressed my hands against the kitchen counter until my knuckles blanched. She couldn't do something like this to us — to me. She loved me. I knew that. How could she betray my trust only hours after we'd been together?

I called every other number we had on file for Belial's human alias, James Brennan. All of them reported him as 'indisposed.' I tried to sense him as well, but he was nowhere in the city, just like Jordan. We had boarded the same plane in Brazil and after we got back to Albany, he said he would call when he got confirmation of the rogue angel leaving São Paulo. He hadn't led me to think he would act on his own because of our agreement. Still, all the signs pointed to one terrible thought that I didn't want to face. My wife was working with the enemy behind my back. Just like Zora. Just like I had always feared.

Jordan's phone rang. Her ringtone for Gabriel was "Well Respected Man" by the Kinks. Under normal circumstances, I would have laughed. Instead, I just answered it.

"Yeah?"

"Any luck?" Gabriel asked.

"No. You?"

"No. What did her bank account show?"

"Five hundred dollars taken out. Her checkbook's gone too. I got the location of the ATM, but it isn't near any major airports or Greyhound stations so we're basically back to square one."

I rubbed my sinuses, pushing past my anger to analyze the facts. "Okay, let's think about this. She knows the FBI has me under surveillance so she wouldn't go to an airport, and she wouldn't book anything online because they'd be able to trace it. That leaves a bus or a car, right?"

"Possibly, but you also have to consider that Belial is just as wealthy as I am so he could have chartered a jet for her. Especially since he's an expert in illegal transportation."

"Then that would be the way to go since they're pressed for time. It takes about five and a half hours to get to Lexington from Albany so she's in the air right now. How long before your jet's ready?"

"I can have it at the airstrip in an hour. In the meantime, follow up on all the basics. Check the areas around that ATM and see if anyone spotted her getting a cab or doing anything else before she left the city. We'll assume she took a jet out until proven otherwise. I'll call you when I'm at the airport. Be careful, brother."

"You too."

I hung up and grabbed my jacket from the closet, running out the door and into the rain.

Jordan was always good at being inconspicuous. In fact, it was a skill. She had spent the two years after accidentally killing Andrew Bethsaida blending into the crowd so no one would notice her seemingly strange behavior when she talked to ghosts. Her average height and moderate attractiveness worked in her favor in that regard.

Most of the shops near the ATM she used were closed because it was nearly two in the morning, but I got lucky with a 24-hour gas station down the street. She had bought some water and a protein bar before hopping into a cab headed away from the main highway out of Albany.

If she took a jet, she would need an airstrip instead of an airport because the airport would have around-the-clock security. Most airstrips did too, but Belial bought people like they were nothing and so it would be easy to get them to look the other way while he snuck her out of town.

I stood outside the gas station just beneath the ledge so the rain wouldn't drip onto my head as I searched for nearby airstrips on my phone. There was bound to be someone still there, even at this hour, especially if they were of the crooked persuasion. A little aggressive interrogation would get me the information I needed. Once it was confirmed, Gabriel and I could head to Lexington and stop this thing before it got out of hand.

There was only one airstrip within a decent range of the city. Better start there. I shoved my phone back in my pocket and stepped out into the cold rain, shivering as it doused my hair and the back of my neck. The streets weren't crowded, but there were still people out and about—mostly teenagers, insomniacs, and the homeless. I walked to the corner to hail a cab and got lucky when one pulled up a couple of minutes later.

I climbed in and told him the address. He shifted gears and headed into the street, weaving through the light traffic towards my destination. I smoothed my wet hair back and closed my eyes, already shifting through my mind to remain focused on my next task. My thoughts halted when I felt the car come to a stop, but not at a light like I'd thought. I opened my eyes to see that we had pulled into a parking garage.

Immediately, I switched to warrior-mode. I'd heard of guys who stole cabs and kidnapped or mugged people after they got in. If he was one of them, he was in for an extremely unpleasant surprise.

"Hey, what the hell is going on?" I snapped, slamming my fist against the smudged glass, hard enough that the entire pane shivered.

The locks on the cab clicked.

Oh, this guy was about to get the shit beaten out of him.

The panel slid back, revealing a white man in his late forties with a receding hairline and a disturbingly pleasant smile on his face.

"Mr. O'Brien, we need to talk."

I glared. "How d'you know my name?"

The smile on his thin lips didn't falter. "It's my job."

He raised one hand and flashed me a badge. FBI. I sighed, not bothering to stifle the irritation in my tone. "You guys must have one hell of a budget to disguise yourselves as cabbies."

"We do what we can. May I ask where you're heading, Mr. O'Brien?"

"You just did."

He chuckled. "Sorry. Let me rephrase that. Why are you going to an airstrip?"

"To catch a plane," I deadpanned. "Don't you need probable cause to abduct a citizen of the United States?"

"Oh, we've got that. Your wife's in Lexington. She landed about half an hour ago."

I kept my face blank. "Why does that matter?"

"We're not stupid. Edmond Saraf's set to land there for his trial at seven o'clock in the morning. Are you going to tell me it's just a coincidence that your wife and Mr. James Brennan are in the same town?"

"Look, what do you want from me? Clearly, you already have the information. Why are you wasting my time?"

"We lost sight of Ms. Amador shortly after she landed and we didn't have the resources to track her down. We're guessing that you do."

"Why's that?"

"I've read your files, Mr. O'Brien. We don't know why your name keeps coming up in bizarre instances, although we're certain there's a reason for it. Right now, we need results. We want to avoid an incident that would make your life infinitely harder."

"Are you offering me a deal or an ultimatum?"

"A little of both, really. Find your wife and Mr. Brennan and bring them both back to Albany. If you do, we'll drop the investigation on your end. Mr. Solberg is still a person of interest, but you and Jordan will be left alone. If you don't, then the Bureau has no choice but to tag you both as potential threats. You will be detained and questioned and it will reflect on your permanent records. Is that clear?"

"Crystal," I said through my teeth. "Can I go now?"

He paused. "Want a ride home?"

"No, thanks. I'll walk."

He shrugged. "Suit yourself."

The lock on my door clicked a second time and I got out. The agent turned the car around and drove back into the rain, leaving me dripping wet and pissed off in the inky darkness. I grabbed my phone and hit the speed-dial. Gabriel answered on the first ring.

"Fire up the jet. We're on the clock now."

"How bad?"

"You remember Budapest, right?"

"Sadly, yes. I never did get my Porsche back. I'll meet you there in two shakes."

I hung up and left the garage, taking the storm with me as I went.

CHAPTER TWENTY-THREE

JORDAN

At first, my job felt easy.

To be honest, I had expected to be in the belly of the beast when the ruckus started, but Belial had plans for me, in more ways than one. I didn't expect to be crouching on top of a closed-down auto-repair shop with an assault rifle clutched in my gloved hands, its muzzle pointing down at the street. Waiting. I hated waiting.

Sunlight had crept across the sky, but it hadn't chased the night away quite yet. I found my eyes wandering upward often, watching the navy blanket as it loosened its hold over the horizon, giving way to gold. It made me think about how the world kept spinning anyway, even when my life had gotten as bad as it could get. It was the same with the early risers down the street from here. None of them knew what would be happening in just a few minutes. Lucky sons of bitches.

The link in my ear beeped, jostling me out of my solemn thoughts. "Truck's in full view. ETA two minutes."

"Got it," I said, hoping he couldn't hear the slight waver in my voice. I craned my neck to the right to scan the adjacent street. Lexington hadn't quite stretched its legs for the day. There were plenty of cars, but nothing rivaling the Albany traffic I saw every morning. The sidewalks were largely empty except for joggers and people headed to work.

I checked my watch. 7:15 a.m. I strained my ears and could hear the distant whoop of police sirens. "How many cop cars?"

"Four. Two up front, two behind."

"Roger that." I tried not to think about the officers escorting the rogue angel and FBI agents to the courthouse, but my mind still wandered. Had they been the type of officers who had never been in a firefight? Never drawn their guns? Never killed a suspect? Who were these men before we reached into their lives and upended them?

"They've crossed the checkpoint. Hitting the charges."

I heard a click over the receiver and then flinched as I spotted a huge plume of flames erupt one block away, courtesy of an empty fire truck Belial had stolen an hour earlier. Tires screeched and metal crunched—telltale signs that we had successfully created a roadblock.

"Taking the shot. Get ready."

I braced myself, returning my gaze to the street below. Gunshots bit through the crisp morning air, followed by screams of civilians and another round of screeching tires. He'd taken out the wheels of the police cars from his perch, forcing the armored vehicle to continue towards the courthouse on its own.

My pulse raced as I focused on the end of the street, waiting for the truck to come around the corner. My stomach lurched with nausea and anxiety, but I swallowed hard and ignored the painful twisting in my gut. At last, a large black truck swerved around the corner into view. I set it in my sights, let it drive past me, and then squeezed the trigger.

Bullets tore into the side of the truck, causing the driver to try and maneuver farther away from my building, but it was far too late by then. The back tires punctured, slamming the vehicle to an immediate halt.

I stood, touching the link in my ear. "Truck's down."

"Good. Pop smoke."

I set the M16 aside and retrieved the grenade launcher at my feet, aiming underneath the carriage of the truck. I fired. The canister hit the street, engulfing the entire truck and half the street with tear gas. *Go time.*

I pulled on my gas mask and slung the assault rifle around my shoulders before climbing down the ladder on the side of the building. The driver scrambled out of the truck, shouting orders to his companion — nothing but muffled sounds through my mask. As soon as my boots hit the ground, I opened fire, aiming in their general direction to force them to take cover on the opposite side of the truck.

I walked straight into the cloud of tear gas, sliding the gun to the small of my back. I could hear the scrape of their boots against the asphalt and let it beckon me closer until they were in full view — crouching near the tires waiting for me to show my face.

The first agent didn't see me until I was right in front of him. I slammed my forearm into his wrists, sending the gun spinning away into the gas, and blocked as he tried to punch me in the face. I jammed my knee into his stomach, but hit the Kevlar vest instead of actual flesh. He recovered and kicked my legs out from under me, forcing me to go into a back roll. I came up on my feet just as he drew his backup gun from his boot. I dove to the side as he opened fire, missing me by mere inches.

I took cover behind a dumpster in the alley beside us, cursing my mistake. I should have gone for his head, not the body armor. Belial was keeping the police busy, but if I didn't get rid of these agents soon, we'd be overwhelmed. I peeked around the edge of the dumpster to see that the gas had started to clear, giving me a better view of the FBI agent. Six-foot-two, lanky, goatee, probably early thirties. His partner, a stocky Hispanic guy, stood by the front of the truck, calling for reinforcements. Just one chance. Better not blow it.

I reached into my pocket and withdrew a flash grenade, pulling the pin and throwing it over my shoulder. I squeezed my eyes shut as I heard it hit the street, exploding. Pained cries reached my ears. I opened my eyes again to the agents stumbling around with their hands over their faces.

I darted around the dumpster and lowered my head, throwing myself at the first agent as hard as I could. The force knocked him into the side of the truck. He slumped over, out cold. I turned to attack the other agent only to take two bullets to the chest.

I hit the pavement with a cry of agony as pain spread through my chest in tiny electric shocks. I couldn't breathe for a handful of seconds. The world spun in front of my eyes as I gasped for air, writhing on the ground. No, I couldn't fail. Those people needed me. *Get up, Amador. Dammit, get up!*

The FBI agent stood over me with red eyes and tears streaming down his face, but his expression was cold and professional. I could see his lips moving, but I couldn't hear much through the ringing in my ears. It looked like he was telling to put my hands up. As if I could really move after getting two right in the vest.

I managed to raise both hands to shoulder level and his posture shifted, as if he felt more confident with me on the ground. *Perfect.*

I locked both legs around one of his ankles and jerked them towards me as hard as I could, knocking him off his feet. He didn't fall all the way, only hitting his knees, but it was enough. I pounced on his back, smashing his head on the ground. He went limp underneath me. I hovered over him, panting hard, half-amazed and half-horrified by what I'd done. A weak giggle flooded through me as I realized I sounded like Darth Vader with this stupid gas mask on. Yep. Hysteria had finally set in.

I touched the link in my ear. "The agents are neutralized. Going for the rogue angel. Where are you?"

"I'll be there in a moment. Don't disappoint me, Seer."

I wiped the sweat from my brow and reached for my utility belt, finding the small plastic explosive to blow open the back of the truck. I pressed the sticky bomb against the lock and took cover in the alley, listening to the beep of the ten-second count down.

A small explosion ripped through the air, scattering metal pieces of the truck's doors all over the ground. Instantly, the sound of gunfire filled the street. As predicted, they had left one more man inside the truck with the rogue angel to make sure he didn't try to escape—except this guy was a U.S. Marshal. In my hysterical state, I prayed it wasn't Raylan Givens.

I peeked around the corner of the dumpster, spotting the Marshal standing near the edge of the truck, scanning the street for any sign of me. As quietly as possible, I slid the assault rifle around to my hands, taking deep breaths so that my heart rate slowed just like Belial had shown me earlier. One shot. Just one.

I pulled the trigger. To my great honor and great horror, the bullet hit the side of his firearm, knocking it right out of his hands. I leapt up and raced in front of him, the M16 aimed at his head.

"Don't move!"

The Marshal, a tall brown-haired man, glared at me without saying anything. I motioned for him to get down. "Off. Now."

He stepped off the truck, granting me a view of the inside. The rogue angel sat motionless on the right side with his hands and feet in cuffs. He wouldn't even look at me. Why? Had he seen this coming? Did he know this was going to happen because of the Book of Time?

"This isn't going to work," the Deputy said in an unnervingly calm voice with just a hint of a Southern twang in it. "You've got nowhere to go but down."

I met his gaze and spoke honestly. "I know."

I jammed the butt of my gun into his forehead. He crumpled to the ground, unconscious. I stepped over him and yanked off the gas mask before climbing onto the truck.

"Stand up."

The redhead unfolded his gangly frame and stood. His face betrayed nothing—a blank slate, almost like a soldier.

"Did you know this was going to happen?"

He didn't answer. I shook my head. "Answer me, or I swear to God, I'll shoot you."

Finally, his lips parted. "Thou shalt not take the Lord thy God's name in vain."

Anger flared through me. "Really? You're gonna quote the Bible at me after murdering seven people?"

"*Qui finem vitae extremum inter munera ponat naturae.*"

I knew that quote. "'It is as natural to die as to be born.' Dying's not the same as being killed. Maybe one day you'll realize that. Now move."

I walked backwards, keeping the gun trained on the rogue angel, until I reached the edge of the truck. He followed me, still staring like he could see the soul beneath my flesh, and he didn't care for what he saw. Couldn't blame him.

I had reached a somewhat tricky place. For a normal person, getting off the truck with a hostage would be a piece of cake, but not with the rogue angel. In the milliseconds it took to hit the ground, he could go for the gun. I could make him get down first, but that would still leave me vulnerable when I jumped off. But there wasn't enough time to weigh my options. I could still hear sirens, screams, and gunshots in the distance. Belial was getting closer.

I took a deep breath and jumped down. My boots hit the ground and then the whole world tilted. For a second, I didn't know what happened. Then I felt his large hands rip the gun off the strap and toss it onto the sidewalk. Next, he reached for my neck. Time slowed down. His fingers inched for my throat. And then I remembered Belial's words.

"Angels are creatures of habit. He'll probably go for your throat again. Not strangulation. Thinking like a soldier, it would be easier to snap your neck instead of waiting for you to suffocate."

He shifted one hand to my chin and the other to the base of my skull. "This maneuver is very hard to block, especially since he's much stronger than you. If I become incapacitated or separated from you, you'll have to fend for yourself. When he reaches for you, it leaves his upper body vulnerable. Aim the heel of your hand at his Adam's apple and hit hard. The force will stop him long enough for you to get away or continue attacking."

"Got it."

He dropped his left hand, but kept the one underneath my chin, forcing me to meet his inhuman gaze. "I'm not stupid. I can feel your hesitation, your fear. One thing I have always liked about you is your ability to handle pressure. Most humans panic in life-threatening situations. You don't. So do not hesitate or he will kill you and this alliance will have been for nothing."

Just as the rogue angel's fingertips closed around my chin, I shoved the heel of my hand into his windpipe. His head snapped back and he gagged, his eyes going wide. I slammed my knee into his side and rolled us over, coming up with a syringe from my last hidden pocket. I plunged the needle into his neck, pumping the sedative into his system. He lay there gasping, then his eyes closed.

"Excellent timing."

I turned to see Belial behind me in a black SUV, his perfectly groomed head sticking out the driver's side window.

I glared at him. "You could have helped."

He climbed out and then grabbed the rogue angel's limp shoulders while I took hold of his feet, hefting the unconscious man between us. "You didn't need it. Now let's get moving. We don't have long to lose them."

We tossed Edmond in the back seat and cuffed his wrists to the overhead handle just to be safe. I got in the front seat and Belial hit the gas, driving around the armored truck. I dug the slugs from the bullets out of my vest, staring at them in my palm. If they'd been headshots, I wouldn't be here. *Christ.*

"You handled yourself well," Belial said.

I threw the slugs out the window. "Don't patronize me. Just drive."

He chuckled, making a right turn onto yet another empty street full of foreclosed businesses. Then he slammed on the brakes, nearly sending me flying through the windshield. I almost asked him what the hell he'd done that for when I noticed a blue pickup truck parked at a slant in the road about twenty feet away, blocking both lanes. But it wasn't just the truck.

Michael and Gabriel were standing in front of it.

My mouth went dry and my pulse skyrocketed. I wished I had been imagining them there because of my adrenaline rush, but I knew it was really them.

I kept my eyes on the pair and tilted my face towards Belial, my voice low. "What'll happen if we try to ram them?"

"They'll puncture the tires."

"So we have to get out?"

"Yes. We have to get out."

"Great," I whispered, opening the car door. Belial did the same. I swallowed hard and forced myself to walk towards the two archangels. The closer I got, the more I could feel both of their auras surging around them like a stifling fog. They were furious. Absolutely furious with me. It hurt more than any of the other injuries I had sustained so far.

"Gentlemen," Belial said in his best snake-oil salesman voice. "Fancy meeting you here. I'm guessing a little birdie told you about our impromptu vacation?"

They both ignored the comment. Gabriel spoke first. "You have one chance. Just one. Before anything gets more complicated."

"Pray tell, what chance is that?" the demon asked.

"The deal is that you both surrender the rogue angel and return to Albany. No charges, no arrests, and no further problems."

"Sounds pleasant enough. What's the counter-offer?"

Gabriel's blue eyes iced over. "Jail. Death. Take your pick, demon."

"Well, considering the fact that I've experienced both, I'd have to say I'm not a fan of either option. However, while I appreciate your little display, I'm afraid we have to decline."

Michael finally looked at me and the anger in his gaze hit me like a slap in the face. "So, what? Does he speak for you now?"

"No," I said in a quiet voice. "But my answer is the same."

Michael closed his eyes, a pained expression flickering across his handsome face. "Don't do this, Jordan. Just come home with me. With us. We can still fix this."

"I want to," I whispered. "Believe me, I want to, but I can't. I'm so sorry, Michael."

He sighed—a long, exhausted sound. "So am I. Gabriel?"

I heard the rustling of cloth and then Gabriel disappeared from view. It took me a second to realize he'd tackled Belial. The two immediately locked themselves into a vicious battle, rolling into the street behind me as each one fought for control. I didn't dare turn to watch them. I only had eyes for the man in front of me, my husband, the angel charged with stopping the woman he loved.

His voice came out soft. "I don't want to fight you."

"Neither do I."

"Then why are you doing this?"

I shook my head. "You wouldn't understand."

"How couldn't I? I'm your husband. I'm your best friend."

"You're an archangel."

He frowned. "What does that have to do with anything?"

"You're trained to accept the fact that there will be collateral damage and lives you can't save. You know the costs. You know the statistics. You can see the big picture because you know the exact date and time of the Rapture…but I don't. I'm human. I'm going to die someday. I don't have the luxury of knowing that everything will eventually be paradise. All I have is the time I'm given right now and the life in front of me. The life that I control. It's all I've got, Michael. And I have to make it count. Just like I have to do whatever it takes to stop the Leviathan from arising and killing those people."

"And what if the rogue angel decides not to help you?" he snapped, making me flinch. "What if it's impossible to change the future? What then? You'll have ruined your life, ruined our marriage, for nothing."

"I know. But that's a sacrifice I have to make, even if it's more than I can possibly bear. I have to believe that I can stop this because it's all on my shoulders. You can't understand that because there's always another way for you."

"We, ignorant of ourselves, beg often our own harms, which the wise powers deny us for our good; so we find profit by losing our prayers."

Shakespeare. Damn him, he knew exactly how to hit me where it hurt. "I don't have a choice."

He gripped my shoulders, pulling me close, leaning down to my height as his green eyes searched my brown ones. "Yes, you do. You always do. Jordan, I love you and I would forgive you for anything…except this. Don't do it. Don't make me hurt you. Please."

Tears burned at the back of my eyes, but I refused to let them fall. If this was the last time we were together before we became enemies, he wouldn't see my weakness, only my strength.

"I'm sorry."

Michael stared at me and then his hands dropped to his sides. He took a deep breath and I stepped back, waiting. He set his jaw and everything that had been my husband disappeared. The warrior inside him took over.

"Very well. I'll give you a sporting chance."

I threw myself at him. I used every single fighting move I knew. I held nothing back because I knew he could take it. He parried every blow, blocked every punch, and dodged every kick. I fought until my arms trembled, my breath was ragged, and my fists were numb. Through it all, he wore the same passive expression and waited for me to tire. Then he struck.

He used tae-kwon-do, at first, but I soon realized that his fighting style was more than just that. Michael had been alive for centuries and so he knew techniques I'd never even heard of or seen in action. He had a counter attack for every punch I threw, a way to break all of my blocking, and a speed that practically rivaled the Flash. Mercifully, he never aimed for my face but my arms, my ribs, my stomach, and my legs all took the punishment instead. He knocked me down at least four times. I stopped counting after that. By then, I had to use every last bit of my strength just to stand up.

The last time I fell, I stayed on the ground, staring at the holes in my gloves that exposed my bloody knuckles and watching my sweat pool beneath me on the pavement. I couldn't last any longer. My entire body had broken into tremors from head to toe and my head was pounding. Pain swarmed my senses, consuming me completely. Despair set in. I couldn't beat him. Not like this.

His long shadow fell across my face. He knelt beside me, his voice calm and distant, as if he felt nothing. Maybe he didn't. "Yield."

I laid my forehead on the ground, struggling to breathe through the stabbing pain in my ribs. Part of me wanted to give in. Just let him take me home and wait for the inevitable. Wait for everything to turn to shit and for me to somehow wake the Leviathan. At least I'd be with my family before it happened.

I cut my eyes across the street to see Belial on his knees, his Kevlar vest torn in several places, blood dripping down his arms. Gabriel stood before him, holding a short sword beneath the demon's chin as he ordered him to surrender. Belial met my gaze and gave a small nod.

I fumbled for the dagger sheathed at the small of my back. Michael glanced at it.

"That's not going to hurt me."

"I know." I sliced a quick line across my wrist. His eyes widened in horror. A tiny piece of my husband returned as he reached for me. The blood dripped onto my palm and I pressed my hand against his chest over his heart, smearing a dark red imprint.

"With blood, I bind you to this spot. Walk no more until the spell is broken."

A red light in the shape of my hand glowed on his chest and then on the ground as I laid my hand on the road to finish the spell. He screamed in pain and fell on his hands and knees as the power trapped him in that spot. I heard Gabriel call out to us and turned to see him start towards me, but then Belial stood up and used his left hand to snap his fingers. Gabriel stopped dead as a red light burst around him in a circle, traced in the demon's blood. Belial stepped outside of it with a satisfied smirk, waving at the angel.

"Sorry, Gabe. Looks like you'll be parking it for a while."

Enraged, the archangel reached for the demon but hissed as his hand hit the edge of the barrier, scalding his flesh. Belial walked over and offered to help me up but I refused, standing on my own.

Michael struggled against the spell enough to look into my eyes and my heart shattered in that instance. I felt the full force of my betrayal and everything inside me wanted the world to end just so I wouldn't have to face what I'd done.

I turned away, my voice hoarse. "Get me out of here."

Belial looped my right arm across his shoulder and helped me back to the SUV. Once I was safely strapped in, we drove away, leaving two broken angels and the last of my humanity in our wake.

BOOK FIVE: AWAKENED

"It is the business of the very few to be independent; it is a privilege of the strong. And whoever attempts it, even with the best right, but without being obliged to do so, proves that he is probably not only strong, but also daring beyond measure. He enters into a labyrinth, he multiplies a thousandfold the dangers which life in itself already brings with it; not the least of which is that no one can see how and where he loses his way, becomes isolated, and is torn piecemeal by some minotaur of conscience.
-Friedrich Nietzsche, "Beyond Good and Evil"

CHAPTER TWENTY-FOUR

JORDAN

The cut on my wrist itched after the blood finally clotted. I wanted to scratch it, but I knew that would only make things worse. Besides, the discomfort gave me an excuse to stay distracted. A few years ago, I'd had a similar problem. The night after I'd accidentally killed Andrew, I had been staring at a butcher knife and wondering how long it would take me to die if I slit my wrists.

The bathroom doorknob turned and I reached for my dagger on instinct. Belial walked in and I relaxed. Not long ago, the sight of the demon made my stomach clench and fear creep up my spine. Now, I only felt a vast emptiness whenever I saw him.

He shut the door with one hand and then placed a First Aid kit on the counter. He popped it open and took a few items out. "How's your wrist?"

"I'll survive."

"Yes, I suspect you will. I'm surprised, you know. I thought you might chicken out at the last minute, but you executed the blood spell perfectly. I'm rather proud of—"

"Don't," I snarled. "If you finish that sentence, I'll slit your throat."

He cast a sidelong glance at me and then smirked. "You tease."

I knew he was trying to get a rise out of me for his own amusement. I knew that I didn't have a drop of energy left in me. I knew that getting angry was pointless. But I still picked up the dagger and tried to stab him. He caught my wrist and pinned me against the bathroom door. The dagger clattered harmlessly onto the tile floor. My aching body sagged, only held up by his gloved hands on my wrists.

Belial arched an eyebrow, not hiding the haughtiness in his tone. "Feel better?"

"Listen to me, you sorry son of a bitch. I may be working with you right now, but that doesn't mean I hate you any less. So cut the shit or I swear, I'll wait until you fall asleep and find out if you really are immortal."

He clucked his tongue. "My, my. Your temper's awfully short. Upset because you've betrayed your husband and your friend just like you said you would?"

I thrashed against his iron grip, but he didn't budge an inch. "Fuck you, Belial."

He leaned in closer and then slid his knee between my legs, forcing a small sound out of my throat that made me ashamed of myself. "Careful. Don't offer it if you don't mean it."

"Let go of me."

"Or what? You'll kill me? Let us be honest, Jordan. You need me. You have no one else in this world but me right now. So don't take your anger out on the last person who has bothered to support you."

I glowered at him, swallowing my fury because I knew he was right. I was hurt. Mentally, physically, emotionally, all to the point where I just wanted to scream and hit something until it bled. It didn't help that he was pushing my buttons, though.

"Fine. Then why did you antagonize me?"

"You needed to vent. You may not realize it yet, but this little stunt did release some tension for you."

He paused, examining my surprised expression. "Besides, I like having excuses to press up against you. Especially when you're covered in blood. It's rather fetching."

The glare returned. "Great. Now let go."

The demon released me. I went over to the sink and rinsed the blood off, wincing as more leaked out after it all washed away. I poured rubbing alcohol over the wound, gritting my teeth as it stung. Belial waited for me to finish and took hold of my arm, keeping it steady while he prepared the gauze. He wrapped my wrist with surprising gentleness, but then again, he had probably done this a lot.

"How are your ribs?" he asked.

"Sore, but not broken."

"Pity. I had been looking forward to seeing you without a shirt on again."

I rolled my eyes, choosing not to rise to the bait. "How long before I get my energy back?"

"Probably a day. Blood spells take a lot out of both Seers and demons. I can't believe you've never tried one before."

"Sorry. The whole 'not evil' thing prevented me from learning about them."

He gave me an annoyed look. "Blood spells aren't all evil, you know. I suspect your father figure knew a few of them."

"Andrew? What makes you say that?"

Belial shrugged. "He was a practicing Seer for almost thirty years. Someone that experienced would have known about them."

He finished tying the bandage and glanced over me from head to toe. "There. That should hold you together for now. We need to get on the road."

"Where are we headed?"

"It's better if you don't know until we get your mental shields in place. You're still a young Seer so I'm going to teach you to construct ones that will prevent the angels from locating you."

"What about Juliana?"

"She's too young. They won't be able to sense her since her energy is barely readable. The child can probably see spirits, but she can't do anything else that a normal Seer can, and won't be able to until she's much older."

"Alright, let's go."

He held up his hands. "You need to change first. You've got blood everywhere and that will upset Juliana when she sees you."

I glanced at his bloody right arm, exposed since he'd rolled his sleeves up. "You're one to talk."

He ignored me and left the bathroom, then returned with a navy blouse and blue jeans. I let them unfold in my hands, horrified that they looked like they would fit me perfectly.

"Should I even ask how you knew my size?"

A slick grin touched his lips. "Don't flatter yourself. I've been on this Earth for centuries. It's not hard to figure out your measurements."

He left. I tossed the clothes on the sink and undressed. Unfortunately, I couldn't resist looking at my reflection. The sight was grisly. Bruises dotted my ribs, my forearms, and both knees, all of them purplish blotches against my brown skin. I looked like hell. Made sense. I seemed to be on my way there already.

After I got dressed, I checked my watch. Two hours since we fought the angels. By now, they had probably broken free from the blood spells. Belial told me they were only temporary. Demons rarely used them because it meant having to get in close quarters with an angel, and that almost always resulted in death. Still, I wondered if he'd been right about Andrew knowing about these spells. I hadn't even heard of them until this morning before the incident.

I walked out of the bathroom. Belial stood in front of the single bed in the cheap motel room he'd rented, shoving his old, soiled clothes into a duffel bag. We had driven straight out of Lexington after retrieving the rogue angel, who was currently in the trunk of our stolen car, still unconscious. The sedative would wear off in a few hours and that was when the interrogation would start. I wasn't looking forward to it after seeing the methods of intimidation Belial had used on the late Mr. Wallace.

We left the motel and drove several miles to meet Juliana with our new ride at the next rendezvous point. I hated the idea of bringing a child along with us — a pair of kidnapping felons — but Belial had a point. She would be safer with us than anyone else. Still, the real problem would be keeping her away from the rogue angel. She was too small to understand much, but just old enough to be at the age to ask a lot of questions. I suspected I would be the one dealing with them. Belial would probably just blow her off.

Our alternative mode of transportation turned out to be an RV, complete with a driver. On the outside, it looked rundown but the inside was almost as opulent as Belial's private jet. We stashed the unconscious rogue angel in the bedroom with plenty of restraints and locked the door before bringing Juliana on board.

The living room area had a pull-out couch and she curled up with an interactive children's book in no time at all. We hit the road right afterward, trying to put as much distance between ourselves and the angels as possible. The road ahead would be hard to navigate, but I'd chosen this path and now I had to walk it, step by treacherous step.

CHAPTER TWENTY-FIVE

JORDAN

"Jordan?"

I sat a small container of chocolate milk on the nightstand and continued rifling through the McDonald's Happy Meal box. Juliana swung her small, socked feet as she watched me, her brown eyes bright with interest. I'd heard that in Brazil, Mickey D's was actually a legitimate restaurant instead of a fast food joint. She'd never had the stuff before. Crazy world we live in.

"Yes?" I answered.

"How come we're driving so much?" Juliana asked, still in Portuguese. Thankfully, since she was small, she didn't talk too fast and I could understand the general gist of what she was saying. Belial had provided me with a huge Brazilian-Portuguese textbook and I'd crammed as much basic grammar as I could on the five-hour ride here. Earlier, I tested the child's knowledge of English and it was minimal. She knew introductions, a few questions, numbers one through twenty, half of the alphabet, and some slang phrases she heard on TV, but that was it. I wasn't surprised. Her mother was a professor, but Juliana wouldn't be fluent in the language for years. That is, if I got her out of this mess alive.

I handed her the kids' sized cheeseburger to hold and grabbed a fistful of napkins. "We're on a road trip."

I tucked a napkin in her collar and smoothed it out before helping her unwrap the food. Part of me had wanted to get her a healthier meal, but we were on the run from the law so I couldn't risk going into a grocery store. Cameras. The driver had nabbed the meal shortly before we arrived at the motel.

Juliana bit down into the burger only a second after I managed to get another napkin on her lap. It caught a glob of ketchup, much to my relief. I dumped the little baggie of fries on the plastic wrapper for her to pick through.

"Stay right here and finish this, okay? I'm going to go in the other room with Bel—er, James—for a while." I winced, hoping she wouldn't notice the mix-up with his name.

Juliana nodded, taking another bite of her food. I turned on the television for her and found the Disney channel. Her attention immediately went to the smiling children and bright colors. I rubbed the top of her head and squatted in front of her.

"And don't answer the door unless it's me or James. If anything bad happens, get the phone and dial 9-1-1. Understand?"

"Mmkay."

I stood, slid my cell phone in my pocket, and headed out, double-checking that my key card was safely in my wallet. I made sure that the door was indeed locked before walking down the narrow hallway to a room at the end. I knocked twice and waited.

A moment later, Belial opened it. "Took you long enough."

"Shut up," I grumbled, shoving past him to enter the room. "I'm babysitting *your* kid for free. You're not allowed to get snippy."

He shut the door. "And I'm paying for her meals and the rooms, so we're even. Now then, shall we get started?"

I exhaled, wishing my reservations would evaporate into the air. "Yeah."

I turned around. The unconscious rogue angel sat in a chair in the middle of the room with a black tarp underneath him, still handcuffed, but no longer wearing his prison garb. Belial had put him in a green flannel shirt, black tank top, and faded grey jeans. It clashed with his bright orange hair and nearly translucent skin. His head hung inches above his chest. He looked so…human.

Belial walked over to the bed and opened a black leather suitcase. I caught a flash of silver and felt my blood run cold as I saw an array of different knives neatly tucked in a velvet casing. He found a thin stick of smelling salt and snapped it beneath the rogue angel's nose.

Edmond's head jerked upward and he coughed several times. His brown eyes wandered around the room, then settled on us—first Belial, then me. His expression melted into a blank, unreadable slate just like when I'd gotten him out of the back of the armored truck.

"Morning, sunshine," Belial said. "Sleep well?"

Edmond didn't reply. "The strong silent type, hmm? Most angels are like that. After all, even lowly Scribes like you are trained not to succumb to torture or persuasion. If it were any other demon, you might be safe."

Belial bent his tall frame so that their eyes were level and lowered his voice. "But I'm not your average, run-of-the-mill demon. I'm an archdemon. I spent centuries in Hell finding every way in existence to torture a soul. So if you cooperate now, this will be quick and painless. But if you don't…we'll find out just how tough your Daddy made you."

Again, the angel said nothing. Belial shrugged and rose to full height. "Jordan, if you will?"

I stepped forward, my arms crossed over my chest. "Edmond, I need your help. I need to know everything you know about the page you ripped out of the Book. I want to stop the Leviathan from awakening. I know it looks bad that I'm working with a demon, but this is the only way I could talk to you. The angels are under orders to kill you on sight. Please help me. We have the same goal. I don't want to hurt you, but I will if you don't tell me what I need to know."

His eyes searched mine for what seemed like ages. At first, I couldn't quite describe what it felt like with those mahogany orbs boring into my skull. Then I realized it wasn't hatred. It was conviction. He believed he was righteous. I couldn't convince him of otherwise. Damn it.

"Very well," the demon said with a sigh. "Let's get started. Jordan, my pet, would you hand me that belt on the bed?"

I took a deep breath and picked it up. Belial grabbed Edmond's lower jaw, shoving his fingers between his teeth so that he was forced to open his mouth. He tied the belt around the angel's head and pulled it tight so he couldn't spit it out or make a noise loud enough to alert our neighbors. Then again, in a sketchy place like this, I doubted that the neighbors would care if they heard a scream for help. Plus, with our energy signatures suppressed—a trick Belial taught me on the way here—there was no hope of reinforcements. Not that the angels would be much nicer to him at this point.

I leaned against the far wall, wrapping my arms around my stomach as Belial chose the first knife—a slender one with a blade about four inches long. He rolled up the sleeves of his black turtleneck and tested the tip with one gloved finger.

"I always start with this little number. I've had the point sharpened almost to that of a katana. Most people think torture is all about pain. Not at all. It's about patience."

He pushed up the right sleeve on Edmond's arm. "You're an angel. Angels are incapable of death by human instruments. But pain…no, your Father has a sense of humor so he left that intact. It's always been one of the reasons I liked the Old Bastard."

He sliced a neat line along Edmond's forearm. Blood welled outward, spilling onto the arm of the chair. I breathed deep and told myself to calm down even though every inch of me felt sick. Edmond didn't even flinch. Belial placed the blade back in its proper place and then reached into his duffel bag. He retrieved a brown glass bottle with a white label. My eyes caught the black letters on the front as he unscrewed the cap. Iodine.

He poured a liberal amount of it on the fresh cut. Edmond stiffened, making a garbled noise of pain against his gag. I dug my fingers into my sides, looking away. Nausea rolled up my torso in a wave. I squeezed my eyes shut, clinging to any rational thought in my head. We had to do this to save those people. We had to.

Belial withdrew the iodine. "That loosen your tongue any, angel?"

Edmond glared at the demon, his chest rising and falling with uneven breaths, but made no indication of giving in.

Belial screwed the cap back on the iodine and set it aside. "Excellent resolve, my boy. You're quite the trooper."

The process continued. I lost track of time how long it went on for because I had huddled against the wall trying not to hear the angel's muffled groans of pain. He just wouldn't cave in, not even after Belial used about half the instruments in his suitcase. The tarp beneath the chair became slick with blood and other fluids. Finally, I couldn't take it any longer.

I caught Belial's shoulder and he paused, tossing a frosty look in my direction. "Can you…leave for a while? I want to talk to him alone."

He arched a thin eyebrow. "Good cop?"

I offered him a weak smile. "Something like that."

He sighed. "I despise that routine, but I suppose it's worth a shot. I'll go check on the child. Walk with me."

I followed him to the door. He kept his voice low, staring at me with that piercing gaze.

"You're not going to do anything stupid like untie him, right?"

I let out a hollow laugh. "After I just stood by and let you torture him? No. He'd snap my neck. Just trust me. Maybe I can get through to him."

"Are you sure that's all this is about?" he asked.

"What else would it be about?"

He exhaled, a hot burst of air that brushed my neck and made me shiver. "I feel your revulsion. I can practically smell it on you. You've got a weak stomach."

I glared. "Sorry, I'm not into torturing people like you are."

"You sure? You seem to enjoy what you're doing to me," he said, and the bitterness in his tone made me hesitate.

"What the hell are you talking about?"

He shook his head. "Nothing. Just hurry up."

He walked out, leaving me in a stupor. Where had that come from? I brushed my cluttered thoughts aside and closed the door. He wouldn't give me long. Better get this over with.

I walked over to Edmond and he flinched as I reached behind his head. I undid the belt and pulled it out of his mouth, letting it drop onto the tarp. He gave me a curious look, but didn't say anything as I sat down on the edge of the bed.

"Look, I can't...apologize to you. I mean, it would be pointless. I just let a demon torture you for half an hour. I should be burned at the stake, if we're being honest. But this isn't about me. This is about you."

I met his gaze, allowing him to see my unwavering resolve. "I know that I can't possibly understand what it's like to be an angel. I'd never assume I could. You've seen things I couldn't even fathom. You know about the actual universe, not just this little blue planet. So I'm sure I seem like a petty, insecure insect in the grand scheme of things. I think that's why it wasn't too hard for you to kill the other Seers. If you think about it, humans aren't even the smartest beings on the earth. I know I can vouch for that."

I licked my lips, choosing my words carefully. "But I also know that you still came to see me at the restaurant and you didn't try to kill me then. You could have. Michael was nowhere to be found and you could've slipped away in the chaos it would have caused...but you didn't."

Edmond winced. That one little physical reaction solidified the suspicion I already had in my mind. There was more to him than just his mission. There had to be.

I kept going. "Which means that some part of you knew it didn't feel right to kill those people, or to kill me. You apologized to me, for Pete's sake. Look me in the eye and tell me you don't care."

He held my gaze and then looked away. "Edmond, please. Help me. We can stop the Leviathan from awakening. You wouldn't have taken on this mission if you didn't think you could change the future. I believe you. And I understand what you've sacrificed now. I..."

My voice wavered. I swallowed to talk past the lump in my throat. "I gave up my marriage for this. I gave up my friendship with Gabriel for this. I wouldn't do that if it wasn't for a good cause so please say you'll help me. Please."

"Do you truly believe that?" he asked in a weather-beaten voice. "That you can change the future?"

"Yes."

He studied me before answering. "The Book told me this would happen. I knew you would come for me. I hoped somehow the others would stop you."

"Why?"

"I had never met Michael before our confrontation in São Paulo. I had only read about him and heard rumors. The way he spoke of you…the anger in his heart was extraordinary. He could not forgive himself for failing to protect you from me. For the first time, I understood the depths to which he loved you. So I hoped you would not ally yourself with the demon to capture me because now you will not be able to undo what has been done to your relationship. I know that it should be of no consequence to me, but Michael is still my brother whether he recognizes me as such or not. I have caused him great pain and I admit I regret it."

"But if we're able to stop this from happening, you'll be forgiven. You won't be dishonored any longer."

He smiled for the first time. It made him seem so young. "You are kind…and naïve."

I opened my mouth to argue, but he continued. "However, I appreciate your honesty. We are…more alike than I wanted to admit. Both of us have lost our families in pursuit of protecting the innocent and both of us have gotten our hands dirty in their name."

"So you'll help me?"

He nodded. Relief flooded through me. "Thank you."

"Do not thank me until we have stopped the Leviathan."

I scooted forward, rubbing my damp palms on my knees. "How much do you know about the events leading up to the 31st? It said that there will be a visit to the Garden of Eden. What happens there?"

"On the 30th, someone retrieves a piece of fruit from the Tree of Knowledge. It is later taken and given to the Leviathan to awaken it."

"Does it say who?"

"No. Merely a Seer."

"What about the actual event? How much do you know about it?"

"It is much like a large gathering. There are hundreds of angels there as well as two demons."

"Wait, two demons? Does it say who?"

He shook his head. I raked the hair out of my face in a quick, frustrated motion. "Shit."

"However, there was one thing of note. The page said that *she* will command control of the Leviathan. The demon is a woman."

I froze. "Are you sure?"

"Yes."

Panic rushed through my veins like ice water. "Only an archdemon could control something that powerful, right?"

"Yes."

"Mulciber," I whispered. "She's the only one. Damn it."

A curious look crept onto his features. "I have only read about her, this demon who built Pandemonium. Is she truly so wicked?"

"More than you can imagine. If she's involved, we're in deeper than I thought."

"If that is true, then shouldn't you inform the archangels of what they will be up against?"

"I…" I sighed. "I don't know. Everything's so complicated now. I was hoping learning the truth would make things easier, but it didn't."

"*Vi veri universum vivus vici.*"

A small smile touched my lips. "'By the power of truth, I, while living, have conquered the universe.' Aleister Crowley. You really are a Scribe."

He nodded to me, a tiny but polite gesture. I stood. "My…associate will be back soon. I know it's beyond distasteful, but could you stand to work with us until the 31st?"

His voice went subarctic. "I will have nothing to do with that creature."

"But for you and the child, I will cooperate," he continued, softening his tone. "You have my word as an angel."

"Thanks. I'm so sorry for what I've done to you."

He shook his head. "Again, I am owed no thanks. You did what you believed was necessary. So did I."

"I'll be right back."

I walked out of the room and yelped in surprise as I found Belial leaning against the opposite wall, his blue eyes cool and calculating. I shut the door, clearing my throat and pretending he hadn't noticed that he scared me even though I knew he did.

"How long have you been standing there?"

"Is this the part where I say 'long enough'?" he asked. The sarcasm was so thick I could have chewed on it and blown a bubble.

"Did you hear what he said or not?"

"No. I assumed you would fill me in since we're partners." My hands balled into fists. "We're not partners."

He smirked. "Your stubbornness is both your best and worst quality. Nevertheless, we have more pressing matters to worry about. What did he tell you?"

"That the Book said this would happen—us kidnapping him, the whole thing. But that's the least of our worries. He said that Mulciber's involved."

"He's sure?"

"Sounded pretty damn certain. Where has she been all this time?"

"In Hell," he said, running a hand through his hair. He'd pulled it into a ponytail while torturing Edmond but now it was unrestrained, framing his slender face. "My master was none too pleased with her work these past couple years, so she has been in what I would call a boot camp. I was not under the impression she'd be able to leave any time soon."

It occurred to me that he could be lying. Belial always had a hidden agenda, but this time, I wasn't seeing how it would benefit him to share his plan with her. They had been partners when they tried to create a false angel back in New Jersey last year, but it sounded like they had a falling out after that. I had assumed Belial would be the one to betray me and somehow force me to raise the Leviathan, but now things were different. Now, I wasn't sure where he stood. I needed to find out, and quickly.

"Can you verify that she's still in Hell?"

"I can make a few calls and have one of my minions check. Normally, I can sense whenever there's an archdemon on Earth, but she's always been good at flying under the radar. I should have an answer within two days. In the meantime, what are we going to do with Howdy Doody?"

I rolled my eyes. "I'm so mad I even get that reference. Edmond said he'd be willing to cooperate. Though understandably, not with you."

"What a pity. And here I was looking for a new best friend."

"Can it. How's Juliana?"

"Fine. Still watching television. She seems to be quite fond of that Bieber girl."

I smothered a giggle behind my hand. "That's a guy."

He stared. "You're joking."

"Afraid not. Now let's go untie the angel and get the hell out of dodge."

I opened the door and went to Edmond's chair, carefully undoing the restraints one by one. Belial stood on the other side of the bed with his arms crossed, watching with an impassive eye. Even with my energy suppressed, I sensed waves of annoyance pouring off him like steam. I had tried not to notice that he'd enjoyed torturing the rogue angel, but it was impossible. They were mortal enemies. Hell, the reason Belial agreed to help me was so he could torture and kill an angel. I could put up with him because even though he was an arrogant bastard, he was useful. Edmond certainly wouldn't have the same sentiment, and I didn't blame him one bit.

I undid the blood-drenched handcuffs last and helped Edmond out of the chair. He leaned all his weight on me, but since he was only about sixty pounds heavier than me, I could handle it. I led him to the bathroom and got him a First Aid kit, but he declined. He still had enough energy to heal himself, which was more than I could say, so I left him to shower on his own.

"Wait," I said, just before closing the door. He glanced at me questioningly.

"What's your real name? I've been calling you by your alias all this time."

He watched me with surprise and then spoke softly. "Avriel."

I offered him a faint smile. "Nice to meet you."

A sound similar to a laugh escaped him. "And you as well."

I shut the door, somehow feeling a little less terrible than before. Funny how angels could facilitate that feeling.

"There's one last thing left to discuss," Belial said, interrupting my thoughts.

"What?"

"If he's going to work with us, what will we tell Juliana? After all, he killed her babysitter and threatened her at knifepoint. Last time I checked, four year olds aren't great with reliving traumatic events."

"I know. We'll...handle it. Somehow. Poor baby's been through enough and she's not even a full-blown Seer yet. I'm starting to think the world would benefit from you getting a vasectomy."

He snorted. "Funny. I'll keep an eye on him while you're gone."

I couldn't stifle my anger. "She's your kid, y'know. She might want some comfort from her father."

"I'm a donor of genetic material, nothing more. Don't project your latent Daddy issues on me, Seer."

It took an ugly amount of will power not to punch him. I squared my shoulders and faced him, my voice quiet. "Just so you know, when this is all over...I'm going to enjoy kicking the shit out of you."

A devious smile curled across his lips. "Promises, promises. You're quite the tease, my pet."

I slammed the door behind me when I left, having no other way to end the argument. Smug son of a bitch. Why did demons have to be immortal? I'd give anything to be able to shut him up once and for all. The thought practically kept me warm at night. Then again, what would my life be like without him? Who would step into his narrow Armani shoes as my flirtatious tormentor? Would I miss him? It almost made me want to laugh.

Juliana was sitting on the edge of the bed when I came in. Her eyes lit up and she pointed at the screen, telling me how cool this American show was, or something similar. She was talking way too fast for me to catch up with my crash-course in the language.

"That's great, but we're just going to mute this for a second, okay?"

She pouted. "Why?"

I sat next to her, choosing my words. "I wanted to talk to you about something important."

A slight frown puckered her round cheeks so I placed a comforting hand on her head, smoothing dark curls away from her forehead. "James told me about the night he met you."

Her face fell. "Oh. I was really scared."

A painful spot opened up in my chest at her words. "I know. It must be hard. I know you miss your parents. I know what that's like. I didn't grow up with my mom and dad."

"That must've made you sad."

"Yes, it did. But it helped me learn a few things."

"Like what?"

I paused. "Like some people can become your family even if they aren't your blood."

She gave me a confused look and I tried to find another way to explain it in her language. Too bad that Bieber kid didn't have any songs about this. "Sometimes people can still be your family even if they're not related to you. Like James."

She glanced downward, twirling a finger in her shirt, a shy gesture. "Really? I don't think he likes me much."

Smart kid, I thought. "He does. He's just not good at showing how he feels. He needs time to warm up to you. Do you understand?"

"I guess so."

"Hey, look at me."

She lifted her face. I smiled. "Your parents love you. You'll see them again soon, I promise. But in the meantime, James and I will take care of you. But there's also someone who will be with us. He might seem a little scary to you, but he's a good guy. Whatever happens, I want you to remember that I'm always going to be here for you no matter what, okay?"

"Okay." She lifted up on her knees and hugged me. I wrapped my arms around her and the aching hole inside my chest expanded. Part of me knew this girl was the daughter of the man who had killed my ex-lover and wanted to destroy everything I loved. I should have kept my distance. But somehow, I knew it was already too late. We were both orphans. Birds of a screwed-up feather.

God help us.

CHAPTER TWENTY-SIX

MICHAEL

They were heading south. I was sure of it now.

Shortly after breaking free of the blood spells, Gabriel and I had hit the road looking for any sign of them. Unfortunately, with the FBI and the U.S. Marshals on our tail, we were forced to keep our heads down and use our instincts and resources to pick up a trail. There weren't any angels in the immediate Lexington area so I made a call to someone I knew for help—a hacker named Jocelyn. I gave her all the facts we had so far and told her to have something concrete by the time we made it to Chattanooga, Tennessee.

An emergency call tipped us off to the stolen SUV they had used to flee the scene of the crime. It had been dumped in a small man-made lake about fifteen miles outside of Lexington. No sign of Jordan, Belial, or the rogue angel, naturally. The demon would keep them mobile until they figured out their final destination, which I had to figure out just as quickly.

The map beneath my fingers was wrinkled and faded, but I knew the landscape well enough not to need every city printed in bold. With the feds looking for them, it would be easiest to travel by car rather than by plane or train. The authorities couldn't block off every single road in the nation just to catch one international serial killer and two felons. As much as I loathed the idea, I would have to think like a demon if I wanted to catch one.

He would have his minions run any errands they needed—food, supplies, transportation, the works. All I needed was to find an area they had passed by and I could lean on one for information. Demons were nearly impossible to break, being born from Hell and all, but Hell was nothing compared to me. I would invent new ways to tear them apart. Despair had ripped my world into pieces before me, but anger rebuilt it brick by brick.

"Michael."

I didn't turn when Gabriel called from behind me. His heavy feet made the hardwood floors creak as he walked across the dining room to where I stood, scouring the map for clues. He sat a mug of coffee by my hand on the table. I didn't touch it.

"Any luck?"

"No," I said. "What did Jocelyn say?"

He sipped his coffee, making a face as if it tasted bitter. "She ran the algorithm through all the available networks. Nothing yet, but I'm sure something will turn up. What are your thoughts?"

"We know someone's going to visit the Garden in four days. It'd take them a couple of days to even get to its location. Still, that's where things get confusing. If they want to prevent the Leviathan from waking, all they would need to do is just avoid it. The Book isn't telling us something. Why would they visit the Garden if it would facilitate the Leviathan's awakening?"

Gabriel rubbed his eyes. I could tell he was tired in more ways than one, hence the coffee. "Good question. Something has to happen. Perhaps someone bribes them into it or threatens a loved one."

I shook my head. "Lauren's covered. I've had angels watching over her and Lily since we left Albany. Same thing with Jordan's father. I even had someone keep an eye on her wretched Aunt Carmen. The only people left are you and me."

"I suppose that's a blessing. Jordan's small social circle means less babysitting for the other angels," my brother mused, but I didn't smile at the joke. He sat his coffee down and folded his arms across his chest.

"I know this isn't the right time to pry, but...what happened back there?"

"Back where?"

"The street. I expected you to subdue Jordan, but not like that. Why did you fight her? You could have just knocked her out."

"I don't know what you're talking about."

"Bullshit." I looked up and found he was glaring at me. Had I ever heard him curse before? Couldn't recall. It sounded wrong. Gabriel was always so calm and polite.

"What?"

"You fought your own wife. Look me in the eye and tell me that's not fifty different kinds of wrong. You've never been the kind for cruelty, brother. So what happened?"

I closed my eyes. I wanted to shut down like I had in the street. Just turn my feelings off and worry about the consequences of my actions later. But he deserved the truth. After all, he was damn near the only friend I had left now that Jordan was working with the enemy.

"I wanted to see how far she would go. I had been in denial about her working with Belial. I had to see it for myself."

"See what?"

"That she really would betray me. Betray us. It was the only way I could go through with stopping her."

He sighed. "I know what she did was unforgivable, even by our standards. But you can't pretend like it's all on her. This is all of our doing."

Offense rode high in my throat. "How so?"

"We agreed to the arrangement of Belial helping us. That was a contract between the four of us. If you want to blame her, fine. But don't pretend like you're just an innocent cuckold in this situation."

"Careful," I said, my voice low and practically vibrating with anger. "I am many things, but a cuckold is not one of them."

"Even so, you're not acting like my brother any more. I haven't seen you like this since the Second World War. I want to catch them and stop this just as badly as you do, but not if it costs me my soul."

I rounded on him. "What do you want from me, Gabriel? Of course I was angry. Why does that matter? We have a job to do and I'm not going to sit around with hurt feelings while the world goes to hell."

He rose to his full height, his sky blue eyes scorching holes through my skull. "I'm not trying to pick a fight, Michael. I am merely saying that you've been emotionally compromised. Perhaps you should take a moment to deal with this before things get out of hand."

I let out a scornful laugh. "Deal with what? My wife running off with a demon just like I was afraid she'd do? Being less than a week away from having to fight one of the most powerful creatures in God's creation? Sorry, but I'd rather piss glass."

He opened his mouth to argue, but then I heard Jocelyn's voice calling from her office. We shared a brief glare and then went into the room.

"What is it?" I asked.

"A maid in a Motel 8 in north Georgia made a call to the local PD when she noticed the burnt remains of what appeared to be prison clothing in the trash. The demon's been cleaning up his tracks, but it looks like the fire didn't destroy the entire garment. The color and size of the remains matches the last thing the rogue angel was seen wearing," she said, tapping her mouse to get a print-out of the information her computer had gathered.

"He was in a hurry," Gabriel said. "Normally, it would be easier to wait for the garment to burn completely and then toss it somewhere, like down a sewer drain. He's getting sloppy. Then again, it could be purposeful misdirection."

"True. He wants us chasing our tails for as long as possible. Still, I'll have someone in the area keep an eye out."

Jocelyn cast a worried look between the two of us as she twirled a lock of blonde hair between her fingers. "Look, I know you're both on edge, but do you mind if I tell you what I think?"

"Not at all," Gabriel said.

"I think your best bet is to head straight for the Garden. Belial's good at flying under the radar. I mean, my program's been working at full tilt since you called me and this is the only lead I've found. I think you're better off going there instead of trying to pick up on their trail."

"They're not gonna get that far," I growled, snatching the page from the printer. "We'll find them and this mess will finally be over."

"What happens when you find them, if you don't mind me asking?"

"The rogue angel will be returned to Heaven for judgment. Belial will be sent back to Hell. Jordan..." I stopped, unable to finish the sentence because I had no idea where she stood now.

"Jordan what?" Gabriel asked in a gentle voice.

"We'll figure out what to do with her later. But that's the plan and we're sticking to it."

"Jocelyn has a point and you know it, Michael. Maybe we should redirect our attention to the Garden instead of trying to find them."

"They've got a four-year-old girl with them, Gabriel. Do you really want her anywhere near a serial killer and a demon?"

"Don't use her like that."

"Like what?"

"As a smoke screen. You want to find them to get Jordan away from Belial. That's what this is all about. You're afraid she's going to be unfaithful to you."

"She's already proven to be unfaithful," I spat. "Using a blood spell on me was proof that loyalty means nothing to her."

"Michael, listen to yourself! This is Jordan we're talking about. Your *wife*. How can you turn your back on her when she needs you most?"

"She doesn't need me anymore!" I shouted. He went silent, giving me enough time to realize what I'd just admitted out loud.

Before either of us could say anything, my phone buzzed inside my pocket. I closed my eyes for an instant and dug it out, answering without even looking because I had needed the interruption.

"Yeah?"

"It's me."

My blood ran cold.

"Jordan?"

Gabriel went still, staring at me as if he'd overheard wrong. I stood there in total disbelief, not sure what to say. She stayed silent for a handful of seconds and then spoke again.

"Are…you still there?"

"Yes. Why are you…how did you…what's going on?"

"I have information. I thought it would be the right thing to do to tell you."

Several furious, sarcastic comments rose to mind, but I didn't want her to hang up so I stuffed them down in my gullet. "What information?"

"Edmond's real name, for instance. It's Avriel. And he said that the demon who will help raise the Leviathan will be Mulciber, not Belial. If we want to stop this thing, we need to find out where she is and stop her. Belial's got some contacts who should be able to find out if she's in Hell or not."

Anger bubbled up my throat and spilled out of my mouth before I could stop it. "Really? Well, make sure to thank him for me."

She sighed—a resigned sound, not at all like the Jordan I knew. A small part of me felt less angry upon hearing it. "I get it. I deserve that. But that wasn't the only reason I called. After Avriel tells us everything he knows, what's gonna happen to him? Can there be any leniency on him for helping us?"

"He killed seven people, Jordan. The law is the law, even if he did it in an attempt to save others. He has to be returned to Heaven for judgment."

"I know that, I just…" She exhaled. "…had to hear the truth for myself. I guess because I'm not far behind him."

Her words made my throat tighten. I had purposely kept myself from thinking about what would happen to Jordan if this mess ever resolved itself. As far as I knew, she hadn't made a contract with Belial. She was just using him as a means to an end, which meant she wouldn't be sentenced to Purgatory like Zora. Still, she had broken our trust and that couldn't be ignored. "Why? Did you agree to be Belial's servant?"

At last, the first spark of indignation flew through the phone. "No. How could you even ask me that?"

"Just had to be sure."

"Michael, I did this to at least try and create some sort of temporary truce. If you're just going to throw it back in my face, then we're done here."

"No, we're not. You have to surrender Avriel to us."

"I know that, but why now? He's the only one with a full, reliable account of the next week before the 31st. Besides, it wouldn't hurt to have one more soldier if we can't stop the Leviathan."

"Since when have you been so willing to forgive people who've tried to kill you? A couple of days ago, you were just as ready to get rid of him as I was. What happened?"

"I realized that everything isn't as black and white as I thought it was, okay? Sometimes, good people can do bad things and bad people can do good things. Sometimes there's a grey area."

"Is that where we are right now? The grey area? Because I honestly don't know where we stand any more, Jordan. This is your last chance to pick a side. Give us Avriel."

"I can't do that. Not yet. Not until it's November 1st and those one thousand people are safe."

I hardened my tone. "Fine. But I'd hoped you were better than this."

"Join the club."

The phone clicked dead in my ear. I shoved the phone back into my pocket and addressed my brother. "Get your stuff together and head for the Garden. I'll keep tracking them in the meantime."

"Michael, be reasonable. You can't make an informed decision like this—"

"Are you going to follow orders or not?"

He fell silent. When he spoke again, his voice was clipped. "Very well. I'll be in touch, *Commander*."

The way he sneered my title almost made me flinch. He swept past me and into the living room to get his stuff. Jocelyn wisely said nothing as I returned to the dining room to collect my thoughts.

The second my foot hit the doorway, an intense pain ripped through the back of my skull. I squeezed my eyes shut, resisting the urge to cry out. Someone had summoned me from above, someone powerful. Someone pissed.

~ 250 ~

I stumbled over to the nearest chair and meditated, allowing my soul temporary ascension to the astral plane between Earth and Heaven. When I opened my eyes, I stood on a pure white hilltop facing Jordan's adoptive father, Andrew Bethsaida.

I massaged the bridge of my nose as the last bit of pain drained out of my head and focused on the man in front of me. "Andrew, this isn't a good time."

"Just tell me if the rumors are true," he said in a quiet voice. I observed him, unsure of his intentions. One hand in the pocket of his grey duster—which had been suspiciously absent from Jordan the last time I saw her—the other at his side. His posture was as straight as a yardstick, at attention, like a soldier. The look on his face was nearly unreadable.

"What rumors?"

"About Jordan working with Belial and kidnapping the rogue angel. About you and Gabriel hunting her."

I dropped my hand. "Yes. It's true."

He punched me in the jaw. I hit the ground, too shocked to catch myself. I had forgotten it was possible to feel pain in this particular state.

"What the hell is the matter with you?" Andrew demanded as I stood, rubbing the spot on my chin where his knuckles had landed.

"I told you the day you married her that you had a responsibility to take care of her. I told you that I'd kick your ass if you let anything happen to her."

"Let?" I snapped. "I didn't let anything happen. She did this on her own. I tried to protect her. I tried to help her, but she pushed me away. What more do you want?"

"Don't you give me that. You're acting just as stupid as she is right now so don't play innocent with me, kid."

My ego swelled, making me stand up straighter even though we were about the same height so he didn't back down. "I'm not your son, Andrew. You have no right to treat me like a child."

"My ass, I don't. You're acting like a damned teenager, so I'm gonna treat you like one."

"What are you talking about?"

"Jordan didn't need a warrior to come tearing through the streets looking for her. She needed her husband. She's lost her way. Tell me you see that."

"Of course I do. I gave her a chance to make the right decision and she didn't. I can't control her. I did everything I was supposed to."

"So that's it, then? You're letting yourself off the hook just because your brilliant tactic didn't work the first time? Is that the best you got?"

"Look, I don't have to take this from you right now." I turned my back on him, heading towards the bottom of the hill to leave, but he caught my attention.

"I can't save her again."

I froze. For the first time, I could hear something other than fury in his tone. He was upset alright, but not just with me. I had forgotten that he wasn't an angel. He couldn't travel back to Earth like I could. He was human. Once someone crossed over, they couldn't come back unless it was ordained by God or the Son, like Jordan had been.

I turned. He was facing the gorge, his azure eyes watching the millions of wispy grey souls wandering through to the other side for Judgment. Anguish left his features ragged. He looked…exhausted. My indignation and arrogance retreated as I realized what was really going on here.

"I would give anything to trade places with you if I could," he murmured, balling his large, scarred hands into fists. "Because you don't know what it's like. Cat's beside herself right now. Her little girl's heading to a dark place and neither one of us can stop it. You're all we've got, son. You can't walk away from Jordan. Not now."

"I've done all I can, Andrew."

He glanced at me, not hiding the fierceness in his gaze. "Do more. Whatever it takes. Jordan has lost her family twice already. First her mother, and then me. Don't let there be a third time."

I opened my mouth to argue, but he kept going. "I know you're angry. Makes sense. You feel betrayed. You feel unwanted. But if there's one thing I've learned about you, it's that you don't give up. Cat told me you would've sacrificed your angelic life for Jordan. That kind of love doesn't just disappear. Anyone with eyes can tell you still love that girl and she still loves you."

"It was never about that. I know she still loves me. If she didn't, she would have killed me or let Belial kill me when we were bound by the blood spells. But it's not enough. I can't trust her."

"I'm not asking you to trust her. I'm asking you to save her."

Something tightened in my chest. "What if I can't?"

"Life's full of 'what ifs.' You'll end up wasting yours if you keep asking yourself that. Now get your ass in gear and stop acting like a soldier. Act like a husband. You know your wife. Go find her and set things right, or I'll drag you back here and kick you up and down the paved gold streets upstairs."

I almost laughed. He had always been good with words. I never questioned why Catalina loved him. He had an old soul. "You're a real son of a bitch, y'know that?"

Andrew's infamous smirk returned to his lips. "And proud of it. Now go save my girl."

I was surprised that my jaw still ached a bit when I returned to my body on Earth. I'd heard about Andrew's legendary left hook, but the fact that the pain still lingered meant that was definitely one hell of a punch. Still, his frank words had given me an idea, so I stood up and went back into Jocelyn's office.

"Mind doing me one more favor?"

"Sure. What's up?"

"Can you add certain items to your program that'll pop if purchased at the same time?"

She gave me a confused look, chewed on a pen cap, and then nodded. "Yeah, why?"

"Add Shea Butter hair product, Johnson's baby oil, Africa's Best Super Grow hair conditioner, and Sea Breeze astringent."

"Uh…okay. Any particular reason why?"

"Because I know my wife. Even if they're flying below the radar, she'll need that stuff or according to her, her hair will turn into a rat's nest. If we can track those purchases, it'll at least narrow down the search a bit."

"Pretty clever idea. How'd you think of that?"

I rubbed the sore side of my face. "I had help. Let me know if something shows up."

"Where are you going?"

"Gotta trace the call she made. Don't wait up."

"I wouldn't dream of it."

CHAPTER TWENTY-SEVEN

JORDAN

My hair was a mess.

In the grand scheme of things, it didn't matter, but it was yet another thing to add to the list of stuff wrong with my life. I'd packed a suitcase when I first left Albany, but in my hurry, I hadn't thought about hair-care products. My hair was shoulder-length and black, but it was only sleek like my mother's when I treated it. Otherwise, it got thick and curly, probably because of the genes I got from my Dad's side of the family. The humidity had been what messed up my hair most of all. I had no clue how girls dealt with it around here.

I had been in the bathroom for close to half an hour trying to comb out the tangles to no avail. Washing it wouldn't do me any good. The hotel shampoo was shit. After several garbled curses, I brushed it all into a ponytail and called it a night. One of Belial's minions would return tomorrow with supplies, so I would just add some things to the list. At least it gave me something to think about instead of upcoming events.

I shut off the light, opened the bathroom door, and then stopped when I heard a soft sound. I walked around the corner to see Juliana curled up in a ball on the mattress, crying.

"Julie," I whispered, sitting beside her on the bed and rubbing her back in soothing circles. "What's wrong?"

She wouldn't look at me, instead keeping her face buried between her knees. I could barely make out the words in Portuguese, but they sounded like "miss" and "mom." The poor thing was pining for her mother.

I slid closer and gently picked her up, placing her in my lap sideways. I laid my chin on the crown of her head and rocked her in my arms, whispering that everything would be okay and that she would see her mother again soon. I hated lying to her. I really did. Truth be told, I had no idea what had happened to her parents and I couldn't ask the rogue angel, who had fallen asleep exhausted from the amount of energy he'd used to heal himself. Besides, I'd gotten the feeling he hadn't done it. If Mulciber knew about the rogue angel, Juliana, and the Leviathan, then she could have had someone take them to use as bargaining chips later on.

Juliana gradually calmed down after I started to hum. The first thing that popped into my head was "Am I Blue?" because of its slow rhythm. I tried not to think about the lyrics too much because they made me miss Michael. We had spent many a Saturday sprawled on his bed, sheet music spread across the comforter, making up lyrics together. I'd prop my head on his back and listen to him hum the tunes, helping him finish lines and choruses. Perfect harmony, once upon a time.

"Do you think Mamãe is okay?" Juliana asked after a while.

I wiped her cheeks clean with a tissue from the nightstand. "Yes. Want to know how I know?"

She nodded. I shifted her so that she could see my face. "Well, my mother told me once that a family's hearts are tied together by an invisible thread. Especially mothers and daughters. It's a special link we have. All you have to do is close your eyes, put your hand over your heart, and think about her. As long as your heart's still there, so is hers. Go on, try it."

She pressed her small hand against her chest and closed her eyes. "Do you feel it?"

"Yeah. Can Mamãe feel it too?"

"Mm-hmm. So whenever you feel lonely, I want you to listen to your heartbeat and remember that she's right here with you, always. Okay?"

Juliana sniffled, giving me a little smile. "Okay."

"Good. Now, I want you to try and go to sleep. We have to be up early."

"Will you stay with me?"

I kissed her forehead. "Of course. Close your eyes."

She rested her head on my chest and I stroked her hair, humming away until her breathing slowed. Once she fell asleep, I lowered her to the mattress and tugged the covers up to her shoulders. I needed to sleep too, but I felt restless so I pulled on my tennis shoes and left the room.

We were on the second floor of yet another nameless motel somewhere in the South. I'd seen signs for Georgia interstates at some point. I walked down the hallway to reach the balcony outside.

To my surprise, someone was already leaning against the railing. Belial's tall frame still looked rather intimidating even in a black tank top and faded blue jeans. It was the first time I could recall seeing him in anything other than a suit or dress pants—though I could tell those were two hundred dollar jeans. He'd also taken his hair out of the braid for now, and the edges were damp as if he'd just gotten out of a shower. He didn't turn to face me when I came within earshot; instead lighting a cigarette and continuing to stare out into the night sky.

"Do you mind?" I asked.

"No," he said. "It's free air, after all."

I snorted, hopping up on the railing to sit. "Not with all those carcinogens you're blowing."

"Every man has a vice."

"Well, if I remember correctly, you like pain. Lung cancer's definitely painful."

"How morbid of you. I suppose you'd be pleased if I were done in by cancer. Does that happy thought keep you warm at night?"

"Please. That's too peaceful a death for you. I'd like something better, like flesh-eating bacteria or maybe a raging rhinoceros."

He coughed out a laugh, surprised by my comment. "I'm flattered you've put that much thought into my death. Perhaps I should have you arrange the funeral."

"I'd have you cremated for the sake of irony. You were reborn in fire so it's only fitting that you'd be buried in it, so to speak."

He blew a stream of smoke. "How poetic. Perhaps you should have been a writer instead of a waitress."

"My life's bad enough without being a starving artist, thanks."

Silence settled between us. I listened to the wind blow through the trees and the distant barking of a dog across the street. I was so used to the urban surroundings of Albany that it felt weird not to hear tires screeching, horns blowing, and ambulance sirens screaming every few minutes. Out here, there was just a blanket of natural sounds — frogs, crickets, cicadas, and the occasional owl. Interesting.

"What's it like?" I asked.

"What's what like?"

"Being an archdemon. I mean, do you get direct face-time with Old Scratch?"

"Why do you want to know?"

I shrugged. "Just making conversation."

"Since when have you ever wanted to converse with me on your free time?"

I gave him a dirty look. "I can't sleep. I can't go get a drink or I'll backslide. I need a distraction, okay?"

He smirked. "If you need a distraction, I can think of a couple things we could do right now…"

"One more comment like that and I'm leaving."

He shook his head, exhaling smoke out of his nostrils. It made him look like some sort of dragon in human form. "Killjoy."

Belial sucked in another mouthful and then spoke in a less humorous tone. "It's just a job, like anything else. Some of my orders are direct, but for the most part, I'm a free agent. Your angels have one mission and that is to serve and protect. Mine is the opposite. My only mission is to corrupt. As long as my activities fit within that creed, I may do as I wish."

"So you've been on Earth since the beginning?"

He nodded. "For the most part. Hell is similar to Heaven in that it is independent from what you consider to be time. It's impossible to describe, before you ask. You have a very limited understanding of these concepts, being human and all."

"And what about the other archdemons?"

"They have preferences. Moloch, Beelzebub, and Mammon stay in Hell. They hate humanity and would rather work with other demons planning things. They're not field men. Mulciber and I prefer things up top because there's more to control. Besides, demons are strangely predictable whereas humans can surprise you sometimes."

"Seriously?"

"Indeed. Granted, most people are predictable, but every so often, you get a couple of exceptions."

"Like Zora?"

He seemed to examine me momentarily and I felt a sudden spike in his energy. He wasn't angry that I'd mentioned her name, but he definitely felt something. "Why so interested in my former servant? Reconsidering my offer?"

I sighed. "Forget I said anything."

I started to slide off the railing, but then he appeared in front of me, both hands on either side of my thighs, not touching me, yet close enough that my heart rate tripled. A blush curled across my cheeks when I realized that someone behind us would think he was doing something naughty because our bodies were almost aligned due to the height difference.

He removed the cigarette stub from his lips and tossed it aside, blowing one last lungful past my right cheek. I cleared my throat and adopted an indifferent look so he wouldn't know he'd unnerved me.

"I think we need to establish some boundaries. You seem to have trouble understanding personal space."

"Always with the jokes," he said. "Sometimes I find it charming, but other times, it just pisses me off."

I frowned. "What are you getting at, Belial?"

"How long shall we continue playing this game? Another year? Two? Three? A decade?"

"Look, I don't know what you're talking about—"

"Yes, you do," he snapped, and I could hear the venom in his tone like a splash of boiling water against my skin. His energy flared around him, raising goosebumps on my bare arms. Part of me knew he wouldn't hurt me just for getting on his nerves, but I wasn't entirely sure where this conversation was heading.

"It's no secret that you hate me," he continued. "I'm perfectly fine with it. I'm not too fond of you, either. But what I can't abide is being manipulated. That's my forté, if you don't mind."

"How the hell am I manipulating you?"

He let out a dry chuckle. "You've been doing it from the beginning. It began when you came to The Morsel to ask for my help. If it had been just the angels, I would have told them to piss off. But I didn't. You knew that. You also knew you'd be safe working with me because of my desire to have you for myself, and you went along with it, despite having no intention of becoming my servant."

"Then what's the problem? If you already know I don't want to become your servant, why are you so mad at me?"

"Because you pull stuff like this. One minute, you hate me and try to kill me. The next, you laugh with me as if we're friends or lovers. I think it's only fair to ask what you truly want from me instead of pretending like there is nothing between us."

"That's because there isn't anything between us. At least not on my end."

"Is that so? Then why is your heart beating so fast?"

"Because I'm scared of you."

"Scared of what? That I'll kill you? You know I won't, so that's a lie. Tell me the truth, Jordan. I deserve that much after what I've had to put up with from you."

"Deserve? You deserve to burn in hell for all eternity. How can you possibly think I'd want you after you stabbed me in the chest and murdered my ex-boyfriend in cold blood?"

"You're right. You should want nothing to do with me after what I've done to you, and yet here we are. All alone in the dark at a motel, miles away from the husband you claim to love."

His words made me so livid that I dug my fingers into the rusted metal railing to keep from slugging him. "I love Michael. I will always love Michael. There's nothing you can say that will change my mind."

"How could you not? He's perfect, after all. Handsome, charming, funny, noble, and of course, good in bed. Let me guess. He's the type that likes it missionary style, because he likes looking down at that sweet little face of yours."

"Y'know what?" I said slowly. "Why don't you go into your hotel room, open up the refrigerator, and look on the bottom shelf. There's a bottle of old fuck you in there."

I shoved him away and jumped down, stalking through the hallway to return to my room. It took a tremendous amount of will power not to slam the door because it would wake up Juliana. There were so many things welling up inside me that I practically threw myself in the shower. I turned it on full blast, stood underneath the scalding water, and told myself Belial was wrong. He was trying to play mind games. That was all he did. It was all him, not me.

The heat of the water on my skin unraveled a memory through my mind, one that caused the raw wound in my chest to ache. Our six-month anniversary.

"This is the girliest idea you've ever had…and yet somehow the best."

Michael chuckled, and the sound tickled up my spine through the hot skin of his chest. I crossed my ankles and propped them on the rim of the tub, watching the water drip off my calves, dispersing the layer of bubbles below. I took a sip of champagne, appreciating the way the candlelight glinted off the glass. Michael shifted behind me as he reached for one of the strawberries in the bowl perched on one side of the tub. He held it out for me and I started to bite down, but he moved it at the last minute, laughing at the sound of my teeth clicking.

He took a bite of the fruit and then let me have the rest. "Yeah, it's pretty girly, but I figured you could use some time to relax. No ghosts, no job, no friends, just us. Gotta stop and smell the roses every once in a while."

"True. Though I would've been fine with ordering a pizza."

He poked me in the side. "You don't have a romantic bone in your body, do you?"

"Not yet, I don't," I said with no small amount of slyness.

He choked halfway through another sip of champagne, alternating between laughing and coughing. I felt immensely proud of myself for making him lose his composure.

"I'm writing that one down," he said when he caught his breath. "Just so you know."

"Glad I could amuse you. So what is gonna happen when we hit our five year anniversary? Keep this up and it'll be hard to top them after a while."

"Well, if you're a good girl, one day I'll take you flying with me."

I glanced at him over my shoulder, shocked. "Seriously?"

He brushed a lock of hair away from my forehead. "Yeah. Granted, it's ten times harder to do with all these satellites and that damn Google Earth, but I'm sure we could figure it out."

"I...can't even make a joke right now. That would be amazing, Michael," I said, sliding my body so I could sit in his lap sideways. I touched the side of his face and he kissed my palm, losing some of the humor.

"Don't sound so surprised. I'd do anything to make you happy, you know that."

"Me too." I leaned forward enough to kiss him.

He cradled my cheek, trailing his fingertips over the nape of my neck.

"Besides, I think you find my wings to be a bit of a turn-on."

I giggled, smacking him in the arm. "They're not. I just think they're beautiful."

He grinned. "Uh-huh. So if I take you in that bedroom right now and reveal them, that wouldn't be a big deal, right?"

I lifted my eyebrows, adding a sultry purr to my voice. "Why wait?"

He wrapped his arms around my waist, pulling me closer, muttering, "Tease" before allowing me to sink into his embrace.

I leaned against the cold tiles, weakened by the memory. Would he even want me back after what I'd done? A year ago, my soul had been damned and somehow, I felt the same way now as I did back then. Not worth saving. But it was more than that. In some sick, twisted way, the demon was right. If I hated him so much, why was he such a large part of my life? Was my anger just a mask to hide behind?

I pressed my forehead to the wall, biting my bottom lip. No. I did hate Belial. I hated him for what he had taken from me and what he wanted to take from me still. I wanted him to suffer. I wanted to wipe that insufferable smirk off his face once and for all and prove that I was better than him. That he couldn't control me. That he could never, ever own me.

All at once, I realized my heart was racing again. No, couldn't be. Probably just heat exhaustion. How long had I been in this shower?

I climbed out, drying off and telling myself I didn't have time for an existential crisis. God willing, I'd be able to do that after this mess was over. For now, I needed sleep.

I crawled into bed next to Juliana, and thankfully she didn't wake up. I stared at the ceiling until the darkness spun around and blurred my vision. Sleep dragged me down into its clutches, only releasing me once sometime around three a.m. I rolled over onto my side and cuddled the thin pillow against my cheek. I could have sworn I felt someone's long fingers smooth the hair away from my face, but when I opened my eyes there was no one there. I closed them again and slept on.

CHAPTER TWENTY-EIGHT

JORDAN

Four obnoxiously loud knocks woke me. I groaned, rolling my head over to look at the clock. It was so early that even Juliana hadn't gotten up yet. She burrowed underneath the comforter, becoming nothing more than a lump on the mattress, just as I got up to answer the door.

Belial stood on the other side with a cold expression that reflected my own. "Rise and shine, Seer. We should keep moving. Do you need any supplies? Our driver is currently at a supermarket."

"Yeah, hold on." I got a slip of paper off the nightstand and handed it to him. "Make sure he gets exactly what's on this list or I'll have to walk around looking like Don King."

The first sign of amusement appeared in his voice as he let his gaze sweep over the haphazard state of my crowning glory. "For once, you're not exaggerating. Though to be fair, I think you'd look good with curls."

It might have been because I just woke up, but I swore that sounded like sincerity. I eyed him. "You're messing with me, aren't you?"

"I would never." He then whipped out his phone, snapped a photo of me, and returned it to his pocket along with the paper all before I could even move.

Ignoring the death glare I'd aimed at him, he handed me a sack full of food from Burger King. "Eat quickly. We've got a lot of ground to cover."

"How's Avriel?"

"Better. He should be able to tell us more information on the road."

"Have you heard back from your contact yet?"

"No, but I should be getting a call soon."

"Alright. We'll be ready in about fifteen minutes."

As I shut the door, I noticed his gaze slip down to my bare legs. Even after a fight, he was still the same guy—a complete and total lech, and an unapologetic one at that. The wonders never ceased.

"Juliana, wake up," I called, flipping on the bathroom light as I walked in. As predicted, my hair had formed a curly black cloud around my head. Belial would definitely enjoy that photo until the day

I died. I brushed it back into a ponytail and checked my wounds. My limbs were still a bit stiff due to the bruising, but I could feel that my energy had returned so I could heal them on my own.

Juliana hadn't replied so I walked towards the bed only to find her in the exact same spot — an L-shaped mound beneath the white comforter.

"C'mon, time to get up, hon."

She whined at me, something along the lines of "I don't wanna" in Portuguese. I considered this for a second and then dug my fingers in the middle of the lump, finding her stomach. She squirmed and giggled as I tickled her without mercy for about a minute. I couldn't resist smiling when I peeled back the covers to reveal her cute face and frizzy hair. She went after me and we both fell back on the bed laughing like idiots.

Once we had calmed down, we split the breakfast her father had bought and got ready to go. I tried to make sure she had as much fun as she could before we left because I knew it wouldn't be easy when she saw Avriel again.

I flipped on the television while Juliana was using the bathroom, gnawing my bottom lip as I channel-surfed. I'd gotten a rotten feeling in my gut. It occurred to me that with the FBI sniffing around Michael, Gabriel, and me, there was a good chance we'd be in the news. A couple minutes later, I found a report on the attack we'd organized on the armored truck.

"...police believe two people are responsible for the breakout. Their names have not been released at this time, but reportedly, the authorities are looking for a young black woman and dark-haired white male in his late twenties. Their last known whereabouts are in Athens-Clarke County, where a hotel staff member recovered what is believed to be suspect Edmond Saraf's prison uniform."

The broadcast switched from the reporter to a photo of Avriel — sullen as always in his orange jumpsuit. I swallowed hard, praying they wouldn't show a picture of me next. If Lauren or Lewis caught wind of this, they'd panic. I didn't need that right now. I was in deep enough.

"If you have any information regarding this man, please call the number below. Back to you, Jim."

The bathroom door opened and I quickly shut off the T.V. as Juliana walked over. I covered the worried look on my face with a smile and asked her if she'd washed her hands. She turned right back around and I followed, helping her turn on the faucet. It was one thing to know I was a wanted criminal now, but an entirely different thing to see the evidence firsthand. Somehow, the situation had been surreal up until this point. I wished I could get back to that big, numb place inside me where I kept plugging along by being in denial. Then again, nothing lasted forever.

I checked the hallway, pulled my baseball cap down low over my face, and exited the hotel room with Juliana in tow. Belial and Avriel weren't outside. Maybe they were already in the RV. We went to the top of the staircase, but then stopped dead. Downstairs, two parking spots away from the RV, sat a cop car. The policeman was chatting with someone and drinking coffee, paying me no mind. Better keep it that way.

I tugged Juliana along with me, telling her to watch her step as we descended the short staircase, but keeping the cop in my peripheral vision. I told myself to calm down. They hadn't released a sketch of me, but my pulse still pounded through my skull like drum beats.

We got to the door of the RV and much to my dismay it was still locked. The driver was nowhere to be found. Same for Belial and Avriel. Great.

I whipped out the temporary cell phone Belial had bought me and dialed his number, praying for him to hurry and pick up.

"May I help you?" he answered on the fifth ring, sounding annoyed.

"Get your sarcastic ass down here. We've got a problem."

"Pray tell, what problem?"

"Excuse me, ma'am?"

I froze as I heard a male voice behind me. I turned slowly to find the cop standing there. My mouth went dry.

"Yes, sir?"

"Just wanted to take a second of your time to ask you if you've seen this man." He held up a photo of Avriel.

I cleared my throat, holding up a finger to let him know I needed a second to finish talking on my phone. "James, do you have any of your Burger King food left? I have a sudden craving for bacon."

"What the hell are you talking about?" Belial demanded.

"I dunno why, but I can't get enough *pig* these days," I said through clenched teeth.

There was a pause over the line. "How many?"

"One."

"Chat him up, preferably away from our transportation. I'll take care of it."

"Thanks." I hung up and addressed the ever-patient policeman, getting a good look at him this time. White, mustached, six-feet-tall, blond, late thirties, in pretty good shape all things considered. Definitely trouble.

I pretended to examine the photograph. "No, sir, I don't recognize that man. Why? Is there a problem?"

He sighed, tucking the picture in his pocket. "I'll say. A couple folks busted this guy out of an armored truck. Feds want us checking for out-of-towners hoping to catch a break. I swear, the way they described it on the news...the whole thing sounded like a scene from *Inception*."

Aha. Conversation starter. I scooped up Juliana because she was getting fidgety and walked away from the RV, putting on my most charming smile. "Really? Sounds crazy. I loved that movie."

He grinned at me, revealing dimples in his cheeks. He scratched his mustache, following me around the other side of the vehicle. "Me too. My wife rented it a month ago."

"I'm a big Nolan fan, actually. Have you seen the Batman movies?"

"Yeah, they're awesome. My kid's obsessed — he's got the bed sheets, the shoes, the Halloween costume, you name it."

He glanced at Juliana, who had shyly tucked her face into my neck. "What about this one?"

"Not yet. It's a little too scary for her. She's only four. I get the feeling the Joker would give her all kinds of nightmares," I said with a fake laugh.

"That's a pretty good point. Hell, he gave *me* some nightmares."

Out of the corner of my eye, I saw Belial and Avriel appear on the second floor. Belial had given the angel a pair of Aviator sunglasses and a skullcap to hide his bright red hair. All I had to do was keep this guy talking until they slipped inside the RV and we'd be home free.

"It's so sad that Heath Ledger didn't get to see the end result, though," I said, trying my best to keep my eyes from straying behind the cop's head. "He was so talented."

"Yeah. Hadn't seen him in a bunch of stuff myself, but my wife loved him back in the nineties."

"Right, he was in that remake of a Shakespeare play. *10 Things I Hate About You.*"

"That's the one. Boy, you got a good memory for this stuff. How old are you?"

"Twenty-three. It's sort of a hobby."

At last, Belial and Avriel disappeared around the other side of the RV. Just then, Juliana happened to look up and waved, shouting, "Hey, James!"

My blood froze. The cop turned and looked, not seeing them, and then raised his eyebrows at me. "I miss something?"

"No, it's just my husband. He's around front unlocking the RV."

"Oh, got it. Let me check with the mister real quick before I let you get out of here."

Shit. He jogged around the back of the RV and I followed, trying to figure out if I could knock him out, but Juliana would freak if I did. I held my breath as I rounded the corner to see Belial standing there. Avriel was already inside the RV. Thank God.

"Seen this man?" the cop asked.

The demon shook his head. "No, sorry. We'll keep an eye out for him, though."

"Thanks. Y'all have a safe trip." The cop smiled and waved, heading towards his car. I let out the breath I hadn't realized I'd been holding. We went inside and shut the door.

"Bacon? That was the best you could come up with?" Belial asked.

"Sue me. I had to improvise."

I put Juliana down and she hugged Belial, who suppressed an annoyed look and accepted the embrace. It was both funny and sad at the same time. Her big brown eyes spotted Avriel leaning on the counter in the miniature kitchen. She tugged at Belial's pants leg, pointing.

"Who's that?"

I knelt in front of her, taking a deep breath. "Remember what we talked about the other night? About our new friend?"

She nodded. "Well, that's him. His name's Avriel. He's gonna come with us on our road trip for a little while."

The uneasy look on her face didn't change. I wondered if some part of her could sense that he was an angel, but I doubted it. It was probably the skullcap and the glasses, both of which made him look pretty sinister. I didn't want him to take them off because then she'd recognize him, but chances were that she'd have to see his face sooner or later.

I glanced at the angel. "Take off the disguise."

Belial gave me a look. "You sure that's a good idea?"

"No, but she's gonna find out one way or another."

Avriel pulled off the cap and glasses. Juliana grabbed Belial's hand and buried her face in his leg. "That's him! That's the scary man!"

Belial sighed, stroking the top of her head, though he spoke to me in English. "I told you."

"Stop being a jackass and take her in the back room for a while. She needs to calm down."

"Why me?"

"Because you speak fluent Portuguese and I don't," I snapped. "She needs comfort right now. Nut up and do it."

He frowned at me, but picked the child up and carried her into the bedroom, shutting the door behind them.

A moment later, the front door to the RV opened and our driver appeared with a set of keys in one hand and a bag of groceries in the other. He glanced between Avriel and me, arching an eyebrow.

"Who died?"

"Long story."

"Ah. Here's your stuff." He handed me the bag and relief spread through me as I recognized my hair-care products.

"Where's the boss?" he asked.

"In the bedroom. Let's get the hell out of here before the cop comes back."

"Will do."

He took a seat, fired up the RV, and pulled out of the parking lot. I took a seat on the white leather couch and Avriel sat on the one across from me, his dark eyes still focused on me. His gaze was heavy, so I kept myself distracted by tossing off the baseball hat and undoing my ponytail.

"There are some things I've been meaning to ask you," I said, unzipping my suitcase to find my comb and brush.

"Such as?"

"Juliana's parents went missing the same night you came for her. Did you have anything to do with that?"

He shook his head. I winced. "I had a feeling you'd say no. I think Mulciber caught wind of our situation somehow and got a hold

~ 267 ~

of them. She probably figured that if she could get to them first, she could ransom them in exchange for Juliana."

He folded his large hands. "But how? It was difficult enough for Belial and Michael to track me down."

"Well, we're dealing with demons here. They have no problem with selling each other out at the drop of a hat. One of Belial's henchmen could've been a mole."

"And you don't think Belial and Mulciber are working together?"

"No. Belial's ego wouldn't allow for her to butt in. I understand that they had a falling out after their last failed mission. Besides, he's sort of Satan's favorite and if he pulls off awakening the Leviathan on his own, that'll cement him as *Numero Uno*."

"So you are aware that he's going to betray you…but you still use him anyway."

I winced a second time. "I guess you could say that. He's the means to an end. Nothing more."

"You are taking quite a risk."

"That's the biggest understatement in the universe. Still, he has resources that I need. Especially since the angels have pretty much divorced me."

"I'm sorry."

"Don't be. I brought this on myself."

"As did I."

"If you don't mind me asking…why didn't you ask for Michael's help? Or maybe one of the other angels below him?"

Avriel wrung his hands. "I am…not exactly a very social person. Since the beginning of time, my job was to translate the Book, so I never developed the ability to speak to others naturally. When I discovered the event, I tried many times to work up the courage to speak with Michael, but when I heard he was married to you, I knew he wouldn't understand. Someone would have to make the hard choice and I didn't want our Commander to be forced to do something so sinful. I took it upon myself to complete the task. However, now I see that Michael was right. I should have had enough faith to bring this problem to his attention instead of causing undue tragedy to you and your family." His gaze had switched to the floor and shame filled his features.

I paused, lowering the comb. "I know that you will have to face judgment for your crimes, but I truly believe that you'll be forgiven. I bet my life on it."

"How? What makes you so sure?"

I tugged the collar of my shirt aside, revealing the scar over my heart. "This. Avriel, if they were willing to forgive my selfish, sarcastic, antisocial ass, you'll be fine. Trust me."

A faint smile touched his lips. "In spite of everything you've been through, you still have faith in them. I hope they know that."

"I have to. It's not like I can believe in myself these days."

He tilted his head. "You are very self-deprecating."

I snorted, parting my hair with the comb. "Bad habit. Michael used to flick me in the forehead when he caught me doing it. Used to have bruises the size of a grapefruit."

I poured a bit of astringent on a cotton ball and began cleaning my scalp, amused as Avriel watched me with a fascinated look. He was definitely a Scribe. I doubted there was a lot of literature in Heaven about how black girls took care of their hair. Normally, I'd just wash my hair and oil my scalp, but I needed answers from Avriel now. I could worry about it later.

"There was one more thing I wanted to ask. In the event that we can't prevent the Leviathan from rising…would you know how to stop it?"

His expression sobered. "That…is a very complicated matter. I have not come across any literature that states it is capable of being destroyed. That is why it was sent to sleep. No one short of the Father can kill it."

"What about sending it back to sleep?"

"Theoretically, it is possible. In the early days, the angels fought the Leviathan and weakened it enough that one was able to lock its jaws. Thus, it can only be contained by an angel."

"What about the key? What was it made of?"

"It was not a key in the literal sense. In reality, it was a holy weapon. Any item blessed with Heaven's touch could act as a key."

I thought about it. "So Michael or Gabriel's swords could do the trick, right?"

"Yes. But it's no easy task. The Leviathan's mouth is a gateway to Hell. All manner of creatures would be pouring out of it. The angel who originally locked its jaws nearly died. Any angel who tried would run the risk of being dragged down to Hell if he or she got too close."

"Geez. I can see why you were so desperate to stop it from coming back."

He nodded. "It is one of the foulest creatures on Earth. It does not only kill and release demons. These demons drag innocent souls back with them to Hell. We are not simply trying to stop those one thousand people from dying. We are trying to prevent their souls from burning for all eternity."

I shivered, rubbing my arms. "No pressure."

He hesitated before speaking again. "May I confess something?"

"Of course."

"Now, having spoken to you, I realize I was mistaken. Not about my mission, but rather about the strength of a Seer. This whole time, I have feared that a Seer would be too weak to resist a demon's temptation. Perhaps if I had more faith in humanity, things could have turned out differently."

I offered him a sympathetic look. "I can't really blame you too much, though. An eternity of reading about our failures and insecurities would warp anyone's opinion of us."

"True, but I hope I can redeem myself. You have placed your trust in the angels. It is only fair that one of us returns the favor."

A short silence descended and we smiled at each other because somehow or other, we had found common ground. That was a miracle in itself.

"Are you guys done having a Kodak moment? I wanna turn on the radio."

I glared at the back of the driver's head. "Shut up and drive."

"Whatever you say, lady."

We drove until late night before taking refuge at another back-roads motel in the middle of nowhere. We'd reached Florida. Part of me felt sad this wasn't a real road trip. I would have loved to stretch out on the beach for a while. Still, the Spanish moss hanging off the trees was almost as interesting. I'd never seen it before. It made them all look like old men huddled over the sides of the roads, watching over them like sentries.

Over the course of the ride, Juliana had slowly gotten more acquainted with Avriel. It helped that he was five-foot-six, gangly, and had a gentle voice. We explained to her that he hadn't meant to hurt her and that he had been sick the night they met. She still didn't seem to trust him, but at the very least, she stopped crying around him. It wasn't until an hour before we reached our destination that she felt comfortable to ask him questions — who he was, where he came from, what he did for a living, etc. Avriel had a little fun with his made-up backstory and it endeared her to him.

Avriel and I were watching television in our room as Juliana slept, when we ran out of ice so I volunteered to grab some from down the hall. Unlike the last hotel, this place at least had an actual amenity. Wireless Internet too. Thank God for that.

Ice clunked into my pail, filling the hall with the sound. The unnerving quiet still bugged me a little, but I was getting used to it now. Halfway back the room, I stopped as I heard a baritone voice floating through the air. Belial. But what was he doing out of his room?

Suspicious, I crept to the end of the hall and peeked around the corner. He stood near the far wall with one hand over his ear, the other holding a cell phone. The rooms must have had bad reception.

"What do you mean she almost escaped? Where the hell are you keeping them?"

A cold feeling filled my gut. I knew Belial had other horrible things going on in his life, but this was the first time I heard it firsthand.

"Look, it shouldn't be too damned hard to keep track of two middle-aged Brazilians. It's nothing more than a babysitting job. Three days and this entire debacle will be over. You can handle it for that long, can't you? If not, you'll answer to me and my knives. Is that clear? Good."

Anger flooded through me in a wave. I crossed my arms and didn't move when he came around the corner. He stopped dead in his tracks as he spotted me.

I forced a smile onto my lips, my voice sickly sweet. "May I have a word with you?"

He slid both hands in his pockets, his face nonchalant, but his eyes didn't stray from mine. "Not in the hall. I'd rather not draw attention."

He led me to his room and opened the door. I put the bucket of ice down on the nightstand and counted to ten before facing him.

"Were you ever going to tell me that you kidnapped Juliana's parents?"

"That was not my intention, no."

"So this whole arrangement with you getting custody of Juliana was your doing?"

He continued staring down at me with a cool, calm exterior. "It was the most practical way to be able to track her movements and make sure she didn't come to harm."

I allowed a dry laugh to escape. "Harm, huh? So traumatizing a four-year-old by forcing her to go on the run with two felons and a serial killer isn't harmful?"

"Her parents would have complicated matters. I simply removed them from the equation. They have not been hurt. If Mulciber got a hold of them, would she be able to say the same?"

I shook my head. "Every time I think I have you figured out, you somehow manage to make me hate you even more. How much lower can you sink, Belial? Please tell me. I'm genuinely interested at this point."

An unpleasant smirk tugged at the edge of his lips. I felt the air between us thinning because we were both getting so angry. "You forget your place, girl. I told you once that I could kill you and suffer the consequences just fine. That has not changed."

"Really? Then why don't I believe you? You seem like you're tired of taking shit from me anyway. Go ahead. Kill me. I dare you."

"Don't tempt me, human," he snarled.

"So a human can tempt a demon? I didn't know that. Maybe I've finally gotten you all figured out, Bels," I sneered, moving closer, invading his personal space like he had done to me so many times.

"All your insults are just part of your mask. Maybe deep down, you're hurting and you want me to make it stop. You're nothing but a wounded little boy inside, aren't you?"

He closed his eyes, balling his hands into fists. "Utter one more word and I will rip out your throat."

"You said you wanted me to tell you the truth. Are you not man enough to face it?"

He opened his eyes then. "The truth, you say? Very well. But before you continue, you should know it's a two-way street. Would you like to know what Terrell's final words were before I killed him?"

I froze. The world swam in front of my vision for a handful of seconds. It was like he'd sucked the oxygen out of my lungs in one quick breath.

He stepped forward and I backed up, speechless as he kept going. "He didn't beg for his life. He didn't try to bargain with me. He just accepted it. When he realized that he was going to die, he simply said, 'Do what you gotta do.' Impressive man, really, and yet he was utterly taken with you. You were so cruel for leaving him the way you did, sweet Jordan. Even when he died, he wished he could say goodbye to you."

"Shut up," I whispered as my entire body break out in tremors. My back hit the wall beside the bed and he placed his hands on it, trapping me, his piercing gaze scorching a hole through my skull.

"So you were right. How could I not lust for you when I have never met another human who could torture a soul as effectively as I could?"

"Enough!" I yelled. "Just leave me alone!"

I slammed my hand against his chest, right below his neck, on the circle of flesh left bare from the tank top. I expected his skin to burn, to blacken, like it had when I stabbed him with Gabriel's feather over a year ago.

Nothing happened.

The blood rushed out of my face as I stared in horror at my hand on his skin, chocolate on ivory, and he didn't burn. I dropped it and then stared at my palm, swallowing hard to speak around the lump in my throat.

"I don't understand."

Belial leaned towards me and I flinched, terrified by the placidness in his expression. "Don't understand what, my pet?"

"M-Michael said after we got married, demons wouldn't be able to touch me. He said it would burn your skin."

He gave me a slight nod. "True. Other demons will be burned if they touch you."

Belial took hold of my chin, forcing me to meet his harrowing gaze. He leaned in even closer, allowing his hot breath to roll over my cheeks as he spoke.

"Do you remember when I kissed you?"

"Like you'd let me forget."

He smirked. "True. It was genuine, of course. I really did want you to become my servant and I had hoped you would give in, but you didn't. So I implemented a contingency plan. I put a mark on you that negates the contract you made with Michael upon marrying him."

"How?"

"When I kissed you, you ingested my blood and I ingested yours. That is the first part of the process. If I were to…" He licked his bottom lip, dropping his eyes to my neck and lower.

"…take you, that would be the second step. After you verbally pledged yourself to me, you would be my servant. After you didn't give in, I simply let you believe I couldn't touch you in order to lure you into a false sense of security. I knew I wouldn't be able to steal you from Michael, but I figured I could at least level the playing field."

My wrath came rushing back. "Playing field? This is a game to you? My life, my marriage, is a game?"

His smirk widened. "The best kind."

I punched him in the face. He reeled, touching his chin in surprise, but I wasn't done. Blind rage enveloped my entire body and I kept hitting him, bruising my knuckles as they collided with his chest and abdomen. He toppled over backwards onto the bed and I kept coming for him, aiming for that smug mouth of his. I hit him twice more before he caught my arms.

"Let go of me, you bastard! Let go so I can kill you and end this!" I snarled, thrashing in his iron grip to no avail.

He arched an eyebrow. "Kill me? Aren't we presumptuous?"

"Shut up! I hate you! God, I hate you so *much*." I heard my voice crack on the last word and knew he had finally gotten to me.

Something flickered through his eyes then. "Would you really do it, Jordan? Could you kill me in cold blood?"

"In a heartbeat," I said, hating the hot tears making tracks down my cheeks.

Belial shuddered underneath me and then the world flipped. He pinned me below him, bending down to whisper in that chilling voice of his. "How would you do it? A gun? A knife? Another worthless holy feather? How much would you enjoy seeing the life drain out of my body?"

"It would be the happiest moment of my life," I spat, struggling beneath his large hands.

"How would you feel after you murdered me? Would you mourn me? Would you regret my death?"

"Not even for a second."

He let out a long breath. "Perfect."

His lips covered mine in a searing hot kiss and his knee slid between my thighs, adding sweet pressure along the front of my body. His energy surged around me and flared goosebumps across my skin like wildfire. I couldn't move, couldn't breathe, couldn't focus on anything other than how much I hated him in that one moment. No matter how hard I tried, no matter how hard I fought I couldn't beat him. I just couldn't.

Then something else happened. The longer he held me there, the more I could feel the hatred melding into a solid heat between us. A feverish sensation flooded through my senses and I stopped trying to move my face so that he couldn't kiss me anymore. My limbs relaxed one by one until I felt completely detached, as if he had siphoned the life out of me.

As soon as he felt me go limp, Belial used his knees to nudge my legs apart and stretched out on top of me. I shivered as he slid his tongue inside my mouth and rocked his hips into mine. He wanted me so bad. I knew it deep down inside, in my bones somewhere. He wasn't like Michael, who had respected and treasured me as his wife. Belial wanted to consume me, to swallow every inch of me and leave nothing but an empty husk; to break me into tiny fragments and hold me in the palm of his hand. He wanted to own me.

A corner of my mind returned as he broke from my lips and kissed my throat, sliding his hot tongue over my pulse as if he were thinking about eating me.

I fought the drunken lethargy in my veins, shaking my head. "No…get off of me…I won't betray my husband…"

"You're wrong," he murmured in my ear. "It's not betrayal. You are giving in to your true nature. I did more than place a mark on you when I first kissed you. I planted a seed of doubt that grew into what is between us now. Deep down in your heart, you are afraid you will do something so terrible that the good angel will leave you. If you give in to me, you will have nothing left to fear. Face it, Jordan. You think you don't deserve Michael. That is why your energy has blended with mine so willingly. That is why your body aches for my touch. We are sin and darkness. One and the same. Accept it."

In that moment, I realized Belial had been telling the truth. Part of me—a selfish, cowardly, reckless part—really did want him. He offered the basest of human instincts—to indulge in something wicked because it felt good and was easier than doing the right thing. How else had we reached this point? I had been in denial for so long, but now I could see it. God help me.

He watched my expression switch from anger to horrified acceptance and whispered my name, inching towards my lips again.

He stopped less than a millimeter away from kissing me and then lifted his head. His brow bunched deeply in a frown. "Do you feel that?"

"What?"

"Where are Juliana and Avriel?"

"In their room down the hall. Why?"

"I feel the presence of hellhounds…and an archdemon."

"Oh, God, no."

CHAPTER TWENTY-NINE

JORDAN

He scrambled off me and we raced out of the hotel room. I fumbled for my hotel key, but Belial just kicked the door in as if it was made of balsawood. Neither of them were in the room. The window was smashed and glass littered the floor. The mattress was nothing more than ripped-up chunks of foam and cloth. The sheets lay beside it, shredded with claw marks.

"Come on!" Belial shouted, climbing through the window. "They're in the parking lot!"

I followed him. On the sidewalk, I nearly tripped over the body of a dead hellhound, its head lying at a weird angle as its neck had been broken. There was a faint trail of blood leading away from the dead beast towards the RV. I could tell Avriel hadn't the time to call for help. He had tried to get Juliana to somewhere more secure.

There were few cars in the parking lot when we arrived, but witnesses were the least of our worries. Eight hellhounds had backed Avriel up against the side of the RV. I couldn't see Juliana yet and the knowledge that she might be hurt or dead made me want to scream.

"Avriel!" I yelled over the fearsome growls of the hellhounds. "Where's Juliana?"

He grabbed one enormous beast by the throat and threw it against another that had been trying to bite his left heel. "Here, behind me. She's okay."

After I spoke, three of the hellhounds turned their heads and snarled at Belial and me, their ears flattening against their skulls as they crawled towards us. I readied my energy shards, preparing to throw them, but Belial pushed me behind him.

"You dare turn your fangs on me?" he said in a deadly whisper. The growling died down. A cautious look entered their red eyes, as if they understood him.

"What is the meaning of this?"

The hellhound up front barked at the others — a loud, spine-tingling sound — then they leapt for him.

Belial shoved me out of the way and the four of them rolled backwards on the pavement in a heap. He ripped out the throat of the closest one and flung its body across the lot. The other two grabbed an arm and a leg in their jaws and worried them, trying to rip his limbs out of their sockets.

"Strike!" I sent a shard through the spine of the one closest to me. It shrieked and let go of the demon as blood spurted from the wound, turning on me instead. It pounced. I threw myself to the side. It smashed into an SUV behind me, scattering glass. It shook its head, standing on shaky paws, and I launched three more energy shards at it. They plunged through its matted black fur and it collapsed, dead.

I turned to Belial, who was still fighting off another one. "Forget about me. Help Avriel!"

I ran towards the mob of creatures, throwing up my forearms. "In the name of the Father, I reject!"

My shield rose and I shoved my way through the beasts until I reached Avriel. Juliana had curled up underneath the RV by a tire, safely out of reach from the hounds, but she wouldn't stay that way for long. Avriel, Belial, and I killed the remaining four but as soon as we did, several bloodcurdling howls cut through the night. Dark, hunched shapes crept around the cars in the lot, pouring out of the shadows like a wave of inky death. There were at least two-dozen of them now. Shit.

Belial swept his gaze over the approaching monstrosities. "You need to get out of here. Even I can't kill all of them at once. Get the child. The angel and I can give you a head start."

I knelt and stuck my head under the RV. "Juliana?"

"Lose something?"

My blood ran cold as a pompous female voice spoke from above me. I stood up to find a dark-haired woman on top of the RV with Juliana in her arms. Her brown eyes had pupils just like Belial's — thin slits instead of round ones.

"Mulciber."

The demon smiled and spoke through a thick Welsh accent. "Nice to see you again, Jordan."

"Yes, it is. Why don't you come down here so I can give you a hug before I rip your arms off and beat you to death with them?"

She clucked her tongue. "Now, now, don't be rude. I am holding all the cards at the moment, so you'd better curb that sharp tongue of yours."

"Mulciber," Belial said, his energy flaring around him like invisible flames. "Since when have you had the balls to attack me?"

Her sickening smile stretched. "Sorry, Beli. I'm a bit tired of being Number Two. Besides, the Master has grown impatient with your plan of attack. He told me that if I pull this off, I'm back in his good graces, so to speak. You shouldn't have let the human turn you soft. Otherwise, you wouldn't be in this predicament."

He balled his hands into fists. "You think a few measly hellhounds will keep you safe from me? If you don't put my daughter down and leave, there will be nowhere on this planet that you can hide from me."

"Oh, I have no intention of hiding, darling. I'm here to make a deal."

I spoke up this time. "What deal?"

"Go to the Garden and get the fruit from the Tree of Knowledge. Bring it to the Leviathan's sleeping place and awaken it. Then and only then will I give you back your trinket," she said, squeezing Juliana, who let out a tiny squeak of pain.

I launched myself forward, trying to climb the side of the RV, but Belial held me back. "Let go of her, you psychotic piece of shit! Take me instead. You don't need her."

"Oh, but I do. See, nothing motivates you more than threatening someone you care about. If I took you, I could spend all day torturing you and you'd never break because you don't care about your own safety. It's only those you love. After all, human sentiment is one of the most powerful weapons in the universe."

Tears burned in my eyes as the truth of her words hit me. The fear on Juliana's face made my heart ache, made me feel as if the demon were holding it in her hand and digging her claws in until it was nothing but a clump of wet red ribbons. Belial's arm tightened around my front, holding me against him because he knew that if he let go, I'd climb up there and eviscerate her with my bare hands.

"So this is where we say our goodbyes. Belial will know how to contact me once you've gotten the fruit. I'll meet you with this little bundle of joy in tow. Fair enough?"

I opened my mouth to reply, but Avriel beat me to the punch. "I am afraid not."

He crouched for a split second and then leapt into the air, landing on top of the RV right in front of Mulciber. He landed one magnificent punch to the side of her face. She dropped Juliana, reeling backward. He grabbed her head between his hands, preparing to break her neck, when the blade of a machete ran through his chest.

"Avriel!" I screamed.

He fell to his knees in front of her, his breath stilted and shallow.

Mulciber wiped the blood from the corner of her mouth and glared at him. "Insolent whelp."

She kicked him off the RV and he fell, hitting the pavement beside us. Mulciber grabbed Juliana before she could jump off and snapped her fingers at the hounds surrounding us. "Keep them busy!"

Belial let me go to scoop up the machete that had fallen along with Avriel and whirled on our attackers. The hounds threw themselves at us from all sides. My shield barely held, but I fought back, slashing at them with shard after shard. Before long, it faltered, and then disappeared entirely.

The beasts slashed at me with their razor sharp claws, covering my arms and legs in scratches and blood, both mine and theirs. We managed to kill nearly the entire horde before the last few stragglers gave up and slunk off into the night. Their job was done. Mulciber was gone and so was Juliana.

I dropped to my knees beside Avriel, pulling his head into my lap. I patted his cheek, trying to rouse him. "Avriel, open your eyes. Come on, damn you!"

His eyelids flickered and then slid back. Blood trickled from his mouth and down his chin. His skin was deathly pale and the few freckles dotted along his nose stood out like ink blots. I ripped open the tear in his shirt, unable to suppress a small sob at the sight of the huge gash Mulciber's machete had left. She'd pierced a lung and possibly severed his spine.

"Stay with me, okay?" I whispered, holding my hand over the wound and concentrating my energy on the spot. "I can heal this, I know I can."

He gave me a grim smile. "Her…weapon is born of Hell. You cannot heal a mortal wound inflicted by a demon's blade."

"Don't say that. You're supposed to help me stop the Leviathan. You can't die. It's not your time."

"No one has a time, Jordan. All the world's a stage…and all the men and women merely players…"

He closed his eyes, struggling to finish the line, so I did it for him. "They have their exits and their entrances, and one man in his time plays many parts."

"Smart man, that Shakespeare," Avriel murmured. "I thought my part was to save the world, but instead, it was to believe in something greater than myself."

"What?"

He met my gaze. "You."

His eyes closed. They didn't open a third time. Belial's hand touched my shoulder. My legs numbly pushed me upward from the ground. As we drove off into the night, I knew that part of me would forever remain in that lot.

Even though it felt wrong, we had no choice but to leave Avriel's body at the scene of the murder. The hounds' corpses evaporated into ash that the wind would eventually blow away, but the ruckus we'd made hadn't gone unnoticed. We had to ditch town.

Our driver was nowhere to be found. Not surprising. Belial suspected he was the one who had revealed our whereabouts to Mulciber, which meant the guy would definitely have a target painted on the back of his head now. Hell would be nothing compared to what Belial would do to him for selling us out.

We couldn't track Juliana or Mulciber because Juliana's energy was undetectable and Mulciber was shielding herself. Belial had gotten lucky when he sensed her proximity. If he'd talked me into sleeping with him, we wouldn't have found out about the hounds until it was far too late. It was the only consolation prize I could grasp in my mind.

Six hours later, I was sitting on the edge of a tub in yet another rundown hotel in the middle of nowhere. My energy was all but spent, so my arms and legs were heavily bandaged. A dull pain had settled beneath my skin. I barely felt the scratches and the scabs. I was just tired. So damned tired. Tired of fighting, tired of losing, and tired of whatever side I considered myself to be on at the moment.

I heard a knock at the door, but didn't answer. The knob turned. Belial walked in. He didn't speak, just knelt in front of me and peeled off the bandages adorning my right forearm. After he rested his hand over the cuts, a cool tingling sensation crept through the limb. The dried blood disappeared first and then the skin healed, becoming smooth once more.

Once he finished there, he moved on to my bicep and continued the process on the other parts of my body.

"I suppose this is the part where I tell you Avriel's death was not your fault," the demon said in a detached sort of tone.

"Don't. I mean it. Just don't."

He let the silence stretch on for a bit. "Do you think yourself to be strong when you bottle up your emotions?"

I glared at him. "I don't know — do you?"

He snorted. "That's different. I'm a demon. I don't have emotions. You're human. It's perfectly natural to feel a sense of loss when you can't save someone you like."

"He was a murderer. He tried to kill me twice."

"And you still liked him anyway. You can't lie to me, Jordan. It's not a crime to realize that the world isn't as black and white as you think."

"Look, what do you want from me?"

"If you need to grieve, then grieve. That is the only way you'll be able to move on. You'll be of no use to me if you're repressing your sadness. It will come out one way or another, and if you wait until it's too late, you'll get yourself killed."

"Yes, because that'd be such a tragedy, wouldn't it? The only reason you'd be upset if I died is because it means you'd be cheated your prize."

"Is that what you think?"

"I don't have any evidence to the contrary. I'm just a trophy to you. Even if you made me your servant, you'd get tired of me in a month. Maybe even less. You'd move on to someone more worthwhile, more interesting."

"How can you be so sure of that?"

"Everyone bails. It's the way of the world."

He searched my gaze. "Would you like to know why I kept the scar you gave me?"

I shrugged. "Symmetry. I realized that scars are what have brought us together. We never heal them; they just stay with us until our bodies turn to dust. I thought mine ran more deeply than yours, but I was wrong. Your problem is not simply repression. You do not love yourself and so you pour your heart and soul into others because you believe they are more worthy. That is why you are so afraid of giving yourself completely to me or Michael. You think we won't like what we find."

"Belial —"

"You will never reach your full potential until you make peace with who you are, Jordan. Good and evil. Black and white. Sin and savior. You are both. Accept it."

I bowed my head, trying to hide my face. "I can't."

"You can and you will. Someday."

His words pushed me over the edge. I had tried to stuff all of my emotions in a little box to deal with later, but truthfully, I was on the verge of breaking down every second since Mulciber took Juliana. I felt her fear like it was my own since once upon a time, I too had been a child ripped away from her mother. I had been left with a cold, heartless woman who beat me at the slightest provocation, who told me every day that I was a worthless orphan. Juliana didn't deserve to go through that—demon's daughter or not. I failed her, just like I failed Michael and Gabriel.

I didn't remember moving, but somehow, I was in Belial's arms and my face was buried in his chest. He smelled like expensive cologne and Lucky Strike cigarettes. Nothing like Michael.

We stayed pressed together on the floor of the bathroom for a while. I never sobbed, never made a sound, but my cheeks were hot and sticky with tears. He was right. Avriel was no savior, but he shouldn't have died like that.

I expected Belial to be stiff and uncomfortable as he held me, but strangely, he wasn't. His hands lay on my upper back, nowhere near my backside. His chin rested on the crown of my head and his every breath was slow and measured, further calming me. It was like he had turned into a completely different person within the span of a couple minutes. It was both fascinating and frightening.

Finally, the demon spoke up. "I hate to rush things, but we are pressed for time."

I took a deep breath and lifted my face. "Sorry."

"Nonsense," he said, wiping my eyes. "But if you tell anyone I was this close to you and didn't make a pass, I'll drop you in a vat of liquid nitrogen and mail you back to your husband as an ice sculpture."

A choked laugh escaped me. "If it makes you feel any better, you can try."

He frowned. "It's no fun if I have your permission."

I rolled my eyes. "Pervert."

"I take that as a compliment." He helped me stand up, but didn't let go just yet.

"There is one last thing I need you to do that you're not going to like."

"What?"

"Call your husband."

CHAPTER THIRTY

MICHAEL

The second time I was summoned, it didn't hurt as it had when Andrew called for me. The sensation was hard to describe—almost as if someone were ringing a doorbell in my mind. I could feel it hum through my bones like some sort of sound wave. I was in the parking lot of a tiny diner in the middle of God-knew-where Florida. Good thing I hadn't been driving.

I climbed into my borrowed car, locked the doors, and exhaled, slipping into a meditative state. My soul exited Earth, rising to the astral plane where the one who summoned me awaited my arrival.

Uriel appeared in the form he had taken back when he was still serving on Earth—a tall African man with a salt-and-pepper goatee. His brown eyes were always striking and serious these days, but a long time ago, when he had Zora with him, they were warm. He was still a great friend, though, so I offered my hand as soon as I saw him.

"Good to see you again, brother."

He shook my hand once. "And you as well."

"What's going on?"

"I was told to contact you when a certain soul crossed over."

He nodded towards the bottom of the hill where I saw two angels escorting the rogue angel. My entire body tensed. It must have worried Uriel because he laid a large hand on my shoulder.

"Relax. He came willingly."

"Then what's with the muscle?"

A thin smile touched his lips. "For his protection."

I grimaced. He had a point. The urge to wrap my hands around the Scribe's throat was rather intense, even without my earthly form tempting me. I took a deep breath and let it out slowly as they reached the top of the hill.

"Ithuriel, Zephon, good to see you," I said, nodding to them. We were all technically related, but these two were nigh inseparable and always had been. They had even adopted the form of tall, olive-skinned twins with dark curly hair. The only distinguishing feature between them was their voices—Ithuriel's was a few pitches higher than Zephon's.

"Same to you, Commander," they chorused, and I nearly smiled.

I turned my gaze on the rogue angel, who kept his eyes on the ground. "I was told your name is Avriel, right?"

He cleared his throat and looked up at me. "Yes."

"Well, Avriel, what happened? Did Belial do this?"

He shook his head. "No. We were ambushed. Mulciber showed up and abducted Juliana. She is using the child to bribe Jordan into awakening the Leviathan."

"Shit," I said. "Is Mulciber working with Belial?"

"No. She betrayed him too. She claimed that if she were able to awaken the Leviathan, she would be restored to her former honor."

I ran a hand through my hair, letting my thoughts pour over this new information. In order for Mulciber to be able to kill Avriel, she would have needed help. Probably hellhounds. Lots of them. That would create an incident so Jordan and Belial would most likely leave the scene as soon as possible. That also meant Avriel's body was with the authorities by now and the FBI would have even more reason to be hunting them. More good news for all of us. I needed to find them before it got even worse, if that was even possible.

"Where did this happen?"

"I remember seeing signs for Englewood, Florida. Mulciber showed up at around two o'clock in the morning."

"Is there anything else I should know?"

"Yes. Earlier, we were all debating whether the future can be changed. The page in *Et Liber Tempor* did not speak of my death. I believe that by intervening, I changed my own fate. I think it is still possible to stop the Leviathan, or at least save those one thousand people."

I eyed him. "You're sure?"

"I would bet my soul on it. And if it's any consolation, Commander...I am truly sorry for the grief I have caused the people I killed as well as you and your wife. I underestimated you both."

Part of me wanted to laugh, as ridiculous as it sounded. There was no apology for this man — one of my brothers — trying to strangle my wife to death. Still, even though his efforts were misguided, he did it in service to the world. The warrior in me appreciated the sacrifice, though the husband in me wanted to yank his limbs off one by one and light them on fire.

After a strained silence, I gave him a brief nod of acknowledgment. Then I glanced at the angels on either side of him. "Escort him to Judgment. When you return upstairs, I want my best infantry on alert just in case things go south. Make sure they're ready for immediate deployment."

"Yes, sir."

They headed back down the hill. I watched them go, my mind miles away until Uriel spoke up next to me.

"He seemed to be a very conflicted soul when I first heard about him. Now? I sense peace there. What do you think changed?"

"Faith. He has more faith in himself and in the rest of us."

"Too little, too late. I doubt Father will be lenient on him considering the enormity of his crimes."

"True. But that's not the point, is it?"

I turned to him, offering my hand once more. "I've got to get back. Hold down the fort, old man."

He gave me another faint smile as he shook it. "Always."

Less than thirty seconds after I returned to my body, my cell phone rang. Good timing. I fished it out of my pocket along with my keys and fired up the car before answering.

"Yeah?"

"Guess who."

Four and a half hours later, I found myself in a scummy motel hallway, my stride slow and heavy like an inmate on death row. Nervous was not the right word. I didn't get nervous. But I could feel my joints lock up as if I were the damned Tin Man. When I reached the room, I had to take a deep breath and shove all of my anxiety into a little box in my mind. I'd deal with it later, when the world wasn't about to end.

I lifted my fist to knock on the door, but it opened just as I did. Belial stood there wearing his most insufferable smile. "Welcome back, pretty boy."

I glared. "Kind of the pot calling the kettle black. Your shoes cost more than this room. You do the math."

He pushed the door open wider so I could come in, his voice scornful. "I fail to see your point. I clearly have my priorities straight."

I came around the corner to see Jordan seated on one of the beds. As soon as I spotted her, my stomach wound itself up into a knot. There were dark smudges underneath her eyes, as if she hadn't slept in days, and they were red-rimmed. She didn't look into my eyes at first;

instead her gaze tracked upward from my shoes all the way to my face. Her expression reflected the guarded one I wore.

"Michael," she said in a soft voice.

"Jordan," I echoed.

"My, the affection in this room is just stifling," Belial said.

She shot him a dirty look. "Don't start."

"Oh, come now," he continued, sitting on the other bed and lighting a cigarette. "Are we really going to walk on eggshells for this entire little pow-wow? There's enough hatred and sexual tension in this room to fuel an entire season of *True Blood*."

She sighed in exasperation, and I decided to intervene. "What's this all about, Jordan? Why did you call me here?"

"It's Juliana. We have to get her back."

I crossed my arms over my chest, leaning against the wall and fixing her with a distrustful stare. "So why are you asking for my help? Get your buddy here to do it."

"Don't do that. He can't even get me anywhere near the Garden."

"So you're going to go through with it? Get the fruit and raise the Leviathan just like you've been fighting not to do this entire time?"

"No. I called you because I thought we could collaborate. I get the fruit, bring it to Mulciber in exchange for Juliana, and then we take her down. No Leviathan, no deaths, no Apocalypse."

"That's still cutting it too close."

"What's the alternative, Michael?"

"Demon bodies have trackers implanted in them, right? Contact the Puppeteer and get the coordinates to where she is."

"That was the first thing I thought of. Archdemons don't have trackers. It's a mark of royalty. We also can't make a fake fruit. She'll be able to sense the difference. If you have a better plan, please, feel free to tell me."

"Are you really willing to risk those people for the life of one child? *His* child?" I said, pointing at Belial.

"I thought you of all people would understand that, Michael."

"Why?"

"Were you lying when you told me you'd turn your back on the world for me?"

I shook my head. "That was before you did this. Things are different now."

"How is it any different?" she demanded. "It is my job as a Seer to protect the innocent. Juliana may have been fathered by a demon, but that doesn't mean she's not worth saving."

"Yes, but the angels are the ones who will have to pick up your slack!" I yelled. "If you're wrong and if Mulciber gets a hold of that fruit, it's my army and my soldiers who will die. Can you look me in the eye and tell me you can live with that on your conscience?"

She stood up then. "So that's it? You don't believe in me anymore? After all we've been through, you don't believe I can do this?"

My throat tightened as her words hit my skin like boiling acid. "I have always believed in you, Jordan. Even when no one else did. But what you're asking me to do requires trust and faith and right now, I have neither of them in you."

"Fine. Then I'm sorry you wasted your time coming here."

She brushed past me, heading for the door. Belial stood up and slid his arm around her torso, stopping her. I moved without thinking, grabbing his forearm.

"Get. Your hands. Off. My wife," I snarled over her head, spitting each word in his face.

He chuckled, but not like the comment was funny. There was an echo in that laugh that reminded me of the way a tiger growled when cornered. "You're cute when you're angry. But I would advise you to let go before this little spat turns into a cock fight."

"Michael," Jordan said in warning, pressing her hand against my stomach to make me back up. I let go of Belial and he released Jordan.

He straightened the cuff of his shirt, sending a measured look between the two of us. "The point of this exercise was not to cause an argument. You need to find a solution to this issue and you are not leaving this room until you do."

"What do you care?" I demanded. "You want the Leviathan to rise just as badly as Mulciber does. What's your angle this time, demon?"

"This was my operation. Not hers. If Mulciber succeeds, my perfectly sculpted ass is on the line. I will stop her at any costs in order to secure my position. There are other ways of serving my master that don't require the presence of the Leviathan."

"Good answer, but I still think you're full of shit."

He smirked and blew out a mouthful of smoke. "Of course. But that's not your major concern right now. You have a problem. Fix it. I'll stand watch while you work it out."

He went to the door, opened it, and then glanced back at us. "Unless you're considering that threesome idea I had earlier."

"Shut up, Belial," Jordan and I chorused. He shut the door behind him, laughing all the way.

Jordan sat on the bed on the far side of the room, rubbing her sinuses. "Was he that annoying before he became a demon or did it happen later on?"

"No. The popular theory is that going to Hell amplified his worst qualities," I said, returning to my place leaning against the wall. A painful silence descended. However, the longer it went on, the more anger dissipated from within me. I could think semi-rational thoughts by the time she spoke up again.

"I haven't been able to check up on Lauren and Lily. How are they?"

"Fine. Worried about you, but they're safe. I've had people keeping an eye on them. Your Dad and Ms. Lebeau too. Hell, even your aunt."

She snorted. "Don't suppose you can tell the angels watching her to rough her up a little?"

"The thought crossed my mind," I admitted. "But Gabriel told me to be the bigger man."

"Where is he?"

"I told him to head for the Garden just to be safe. That was before you called."

"I see." Another short pause. "I take it you saw Avriel when he...passed."

I fought the urge to frown. "Yeah. He was different from the last time I saw him. I'm betting you had something to do with that."

She looked at me. "What makes you say that?"

"You're not good at a lot of things, but you do have this weird ability to change people's minds. Make them see things from a different perspective, even if by accident."

"Hmm. Never knew that." She ran a hand through her hair, which was smooth and silky. Made sense. The reason I had been only four hours away was because my idea to track her hair products had worked. Well, that and Jocelyn's search program.

"I'm guessing Andrew and my mother aren't happy about all of this."

"Not in the least. Andrew punched me in the face."

She gaped. "Seriously?"

"Seriously."

"I didn't know he was allowed to do that."

"Me neither. The guy has a serious left hook."

"Why'd he hit you?"

I licked my lips as I chose my words carefully. "To motivate me to find you."

She winced, averting her gaze. "You weren't looking for me?"

"I was, but apparently not hard enough."

"You can let me have it, y'know," she said, her tone softening. "I know I've put you through hell and worse."

"Now isn't the right time. As much as I hate to say it, Belial is right. We need a plan."

She leaned her head against her hand, obscuring part of her face. "Michael, we have to save Juliana. I don't care what it takes. We can't let them win. Not this time. For God's sake, she's just a little girl."

I pushed off from the wall and knelt in front of her so that our faces were level. I hesitated at first and then lifted her chin. "You know what this is really about, don't you?"

"What?"

"How old is Juliana? Four, right?"

"Yeah, why?"

"How old were you when they turned you over to Aunt Carmen?"

She closed her eyes. "Michael, don't—"

"It's true and you know it," I said, my voice firm but not hostile. "You see yourself in her and it's clouding your judgment. She's not you."

"Well, she's on a pretty damn similar path," Jordan snapped, glowering at me. "Are you telling me you wouldn't give anything to stop her from turning into me someday?"

"Part of me would."

"And the other part?"

"Jordan, you're a lot of things, but if the worst thing to happen to Juliana is that she turns into you, then it's not the end of the world."

She bowed her head, hiding one side of her face behind a curtain of hair. "Don't say that. If you knew who I really was, you'd never love me."

"You're such an idiot," I murmured. "I don't love you in spite of your faults. I love you because of them."

She shook her head. "You shouldn't. You really shouldn't."

"There are a lot of things I shouldn't do. I shouldn't drink alcohol. I shouldn't eat junk food. I shouldn't give bad tips."

I brushed the hair behind her ear, making her look at me. "And I shouldn't throw you down on this bed and rip all your clothes off. But I still want to anyway."

"Even though you're mad at me?"

I arched an eyebrow. "Are you kidding me? That's *why* I want to so bad."

She made a hoarse sound similar to a laugh. "You're such a guy."

"I choose to take that as a compliment. But I meant what I said. If you can honestly tell me that you think you can separate yourself from Juliana enough to listen to my plan, then I'll help you."

"I'll do my best. I promise."

"Alright."

She leaned her forehead against mine. The scent of her skin, of cocoa butter, made me shut my eyes. I feared I'd never be this close to her again.

"Thank you."

"You're welcome," I whispered. I wanted to kiss her, but I knew I shouldn't. She didn't understand. In my head, I felt angry, betrayed, and resentful, but my body wanted nothing more than to lay her out on this stupid cheap bed and try my best to break the headboard. Shallow, carnal, and completely true.

The evidence arose when I noticed my other hand had somehow found its way to her thigh and was rubbing it like I did whenever I was trying to comfort her. I'd done it on reflex. Did she even know she did stuff like this to me?

Still, she didn't say anything when the wandering hand disappeared underneath the hem of her shirt, resting on the soft skin of her hip. Damn it. Why did it feel like years since we'd had sex?

"We should probably call Belial back in," she said in a vacant tone, which clued me in to the fact that she realized we were getting into dangerous territory, but didn't have enough sense to tell me to stop touching her.

"Mm-hmm."

"Michael…I have to tell you something…"

"It can wait." Somehow, my lips were now on her throat and both hands were beneath her shirt and I had no idea when that had happened. She sank back on the bed and I followed her, taking a bite at the spot between her neck and shoulder as my fingers worked at the clasp of her bra. I nearly groaned as she pulled the hem of my shirt up, palming my abs in that familiar way she always did.

"Ahem."

I had to suppress a growl of annoyance when I heard the arrogant male voice of my demonic counterpart behind me.

"Am I interrupting something?"

Jordan and I answered simultaneously. "Yes."

"Good. I assume you've made up since you're rounding second base," he said with no small amount of sarcasm. I noticed his eyes were fixed on what was visible of my wife's cleavage. I stood up and she pulled her shirt down, which made me feel better and worse at the same time.

"We came to an agreement."

He lifted an eyebrow. "Did you, now? Didn't think you had enough time for that."

Jordan buried her face in one hand with an audible slap. "We're never gonna live this down, are we?"

"Not likely."

"I hate you."

"I know. Now let's get going, lovebirds."

CHAPTER THIRTY-ONE

MICHAEL

Belial left the room first. Jordan and I stood there in truly awkward silence. She absently rubbed the spot where I'd bitten her as if it hurt, and I felt a bit guilty when I noticed. She kept her eyes on the floor as she spoke. "Should we talk about what just happened?"

"Yeah," I admitted. "But not now."

The words "I'm sorry" clung to the back of my throat like phlegm. I just couldn't say them. Partly because I was still angry and partly because I didn't really mean it. I knew the limits of my personality and at my worst, I was an arrogant, self-centered bastard who wanted to mark my territory. She probably knew that. But she wasn't healing the hickey either. Interesting.

"I assume we're taking your car," she said, changing the subject. "Belial's driver gave us the last one and we're pretty sure he was the mole who turned us in."

"An untrustworthy demon," I said as I opened the door for her. "Who woulda thunk it?"

She glared as she passed me. "I'd tell you to bite me, but it looks like it's too late for that."

That stung. Then again, I had walked right into it. I followed her out and we headed down the hallway towards the parking lot. Just as we reached the corner, I heard the unmistakable squawk of a megaphone so I grabbed the hem of her shirt, yanking her back. I pressed us both against the wall, peeking around the corner. What I saw made the blood rush out of my face.

"James Brennan...we have a warrant for your arrest. Put your hands up and get on your knees or we will open fire."

There were two police cars blocking off the lot from the main road and I spotted two more parked in spaces. Four officers stood behind the cars by the exit, their guns drawn with the other four closing in from the rear. Belial stood in the middle, the center of attention as always, his arms at his sides. We were only two floors up so I could see the unnervingly calm expression on his face. I watched as his eyes tracked the policemen. He was sizing them up, a butcher whetting his knife. Things were about to get ugly.

"How the hell did they find us?" Jordan hissed. "I thought he was covering our tracks."

"Maybe people down here actually watch the news," I said, examining the road leading out of the lot. I couldn't see from here if there were more of them on the way or if they had blocked the intersection off to prevent an escape route. Damn it.

"What are we gonna do?"

I faced her. "What can we do? The guy's got to have a lawyer who can get him out of this mess."

"But in less than forty-eight hours? We have three days to get to the Garden and he's our only way of contacting Mulciber."

"What do you want me to do, Jordan? They're packing way more heat than the two of us can handle."

"Yeah, but guess what the alternative is? We let Belial take them on. He's no longer bound by demonic law, Michael. How do you think that's gonna turn out?"

I gritted my teeth, hating that she was right. Without the contract to tame him, Belial would smear the police all over the asphalt, and he'd do it with a smile. The demon always had a sore spot when it came to human authorities, mostly because he found the concept preposterous. He was a Prince of Hell. To him, they were insects.

"Brennan, this is your last warning. Put your hands up and get on your knees or we will use deadly force."

Belial flashed them a toothy grin and I heard his joyful yet nefarious voice echo across the lot. "Promise?"

He reached to the small of his back and withdrew a knife about half the length of his forearm. He examined the way the light bounced off the brilliant silver and then spread his arms wide, as if welcoming them.

"Have at me."

Belial took one step forward. The cops opened fire. Gunshots ripped through the air, but of course the demon had disappeared from view, running so fast that he looked like a white streak from here. I cursed under my breath and grabbed Jordan's arm, tugging her to the opposite end of the hallway.

"What the hell are you doing? The bloodbath is *that* way!" she shouted.

I hauled her down the flight of stairs and onto the sidewalk. There were a few emergency vehicles closing off the road. I spotted someone coming towards us to tell us to go around. I scanned the line of parked cars on the opposite side of the street until I found what I needed.

I let go of Jordan as we came up to the side of a large black pickup truck. All the people were crowded near the sectioned off road so there were no witnesses when I punched out the window and unlocked the doors. I'd done a lot of things, but stealing a car hadn't been one of them recently. Luckily, Jordan grew up in New Jersey with a rough crowd and picked up a few helpful things.

"Still remember how to hotwire a truck?"

Jordan unbuttoned her sleeves and rolled them up, still frowning. "Yeah. Whenever you want to enlighten me on what's going on, I'm all ears."

"Just do it, and quickly," I snapped, walking around to the bed of the truck. I jumped up into it one fluid movement, examining the contents. Three shovels, a rake, four bags of fertilizer, a few empty buckets, a box of nails, and a huge bag of silt. Offhand, this stuff looked pretty useless, but I knelt and checked out the 25 pound bag of silt.

"Jordan, you still carrying that .38?"

"Yeah, but I'm pretty sure that's not gonna scare off the cops with the Glocks."

"It doesn't need to. How much do you bench press?"

"What does that have to do with anything?"

"How much?"

"I can take 75 pounds if I'm being macho about it. Why?"

The truck rumbled to life beneath my sneakers and she climbed out, dusting off her hands. I withdrew my pocketknife and sliced open the top of the silt bag before hopping down.

"Get in the back. When I signal you, you're gonna toss the bag in the air. That should give us some cover for when we go get the demon. Right before I ram them, I want one warning shot to get their attention. It should be a quick grab. If Belial refuses to get in, shoot him and throw his ass in."

"My pleasure." She jumped in the back and I climbed into the truck, revving the engine. This plan was stupid, reckless, and probably would result in adding several more crimes to my already long list of indiscretions. I closed my eyes for a second and thought of Juliana. I thought about her chubby brown cheeks, her wily hair, and the dimples that only showed up when she laughed. If I wanted to save her, I'd have to save her piece-of-shit father first. Go figure.

I hit the gas, hard. The tires screeched and the enormous vehicle pitched forward, gaining momentum. Several cars honked at me as I swerved around them, driving over the median, and two EMTs dove out of the way as the truck smashed through the wooden barriers they'd set up. I shoved the pedal down on the gas as far as it would go and then shouted to Jordan through the open panel in the rear window.

"Now!"

Jordan raised her gun and shot once in the air just before the truck smashed through the two cop cars blocking off the parking lot. I spotted Belial near the hotel's main entrance, his white dress shirt drenched in blood, one officer dangling perilously in his grip. His eyes widened as he saw me slam on the brakes. Jordan tossed the bag of silt, quickly shrouding the area in a thick, stifling mist.

"Get in!" I heard her shout just before I rolled up the windows. She flattened herself against the bed as the police opened fire again.

Belial dropped the cop and strode over to the passenger's side, getting in. I turned on the windshield wipers and swerved around, keeping my head down. Bullets whizzed past, punching holes in the seat cushion between us and puncturing the glass on either side of us. I managed to maneuver the truck back through the way we came. We peeled out into the road and I headed for the nearest highway at breakneck speed.

"What the hell were you thinking?" I spat at Belial.

He coughed a couple times, brushing the remains of the silt off his hair and face. "I was defending myself."

"You could have run. You could have distracted them with hellhounds. You could have just let them take you and then get one of your fancy lawyers to get you out."

"And you could have left me there," he said with a smug grin. "What's the matter, Mikey? Did you miss me too much?"

"No," I growled. "I just wanted to murder you myself."

"How intriguing. I can't wait."

Further arguing was interrupted as police sirens filled the air. We'd wrecked two of their units, but there was another pair coming in hot with their red-and-blue lights blazing. The truck was great for brute strength attacks, but with all this weight, there was a good chance they'd catch up with us.

"Jordan!" I yelled through the window. "Got anything else back there that can stall them?"

"Do I look like I have a utility belt?"

"Stop arguing with me and look, woman!"

She tossed several things aside and then came up with cardboard box full of nails. "Not sure if this'll work, but I can try. Can you make a sharp turn soon?"

"Yeah, hold on!"

I shot across two lanes and made a left turn that almost flipped the truck, but through the grace of God, we just burned some rubber instead.

Jordan tossed the nails out, making a wide path behind us. One of the cop cars' tires punctured and it spun out, smashing into a fire hydrant nearby. The other rolled straight over the nails and kept coming.

"You have energy shards. Why don't you just take them out?" Belial asked as his hair whipped over his face from the wind.

"Cop cars have cameras, genius. Do you really want evidence that demons and angels exist right now?"

"If the Leviathan rises, that'll be a moot point, I'd say."

"Not an option. Think of something else if you're so damn smart."

"Tell your wife to give me the gun and I'll shoot out the tires."

"Yeah, after you just massacred several people, I'm sure you'll only shoot out the tires," I said, making sure he heard the sarcasm over the sound of the sirens.

I raised my voice again so Jordan could hear me. "Can you hit the tires?"

"Not with you swerving around like this," she said, clinging to the edge of the bed with one hand, her pistol in the other.

I scanned the upcoming road, searching for something else to get rid of our last pigtail. "What if I give you a bigger target?"

"Like what?"

"That." I pointed to the enormous gorilla balloon hovering in front of a car dealership.

"Seriously?"

"You got five seconds. Don't miss."

She shook her head at me and then braced her knees against the edge of the bed, propping her elbows on the roof of the truck to steady her. I counted down and she timed it perfectly, shooting three times. The gorilla deflated and fell forward right behind us, covering the front end of the cop car. It veered off the road and hit a tree, completely totaled.

Jordan climbed in through the window and sat down in the middle, tucking the gun in the small of her back. With her safe inside, I was able to do what I did best—disappear.

JORDAN

There were four bullet wounds for me to deal with: one in Belial's right shoulder, one in his left shoulder, and the other two were in his biceps. Apparently, the police had been instructed to take him in alive so they went for non-lethal shots.

At this point in my life, large amounts of blood no longer bothered me. What did bother me was the fact that Michael had left to cover our tracks and update Gabriel, which left me and the demon alone. Bad idea. In Belial's mind, no Michael, no excuse to behave himself.

I had a pair of forceps in my hand as I stood over him, carefully trying to grip the bullet in his left shoulder. I kept a fully-stocked medical kit in my panic pack, as I liked to call it. Painkillers were an integral part of said emergency pack, but Belial had refused to take them at first since he liked pain quite a lot. Eventually, I'd stuffed a couple in his mouth. He'd been so impressed by my ruthlessness that he didn't spit them out. Go figure.

My problem wasn't just that the third bullet was lodged in a rather tricky place. It was that the painkillers made him a bit loopy, so he wouldn't stop touching me. With him sitting on the bed, my legs were what he focused on the most, running his long fingers up and down the back of my thighs. He knew I was ticklish there because Terrell had known that, and I tried my best not to think about it. I slapped his hands away several times until it became too much of a bother so I let him amuse himself. Besides, there were only two more slugs to pry out and then he could heal. I'd just have to deal with the temporary discomfort.

"Have you ever thought about becoming a nurse?" he asked, trailing his fingertip over the inside of my right thigh.

I kept my voice level and patient even though he was annoying me. "No. Medical school's expensive as hell."

"Yes, but that was when you were younger. Now you've got the angels on your side, so to speak. I'm sure they wouldn't mind footing the bill."

"It's not just the money. It's bad enough having the souls of the dead depending on me. I don't need the living adding to that too," I said, concentrating as I inched the bullet closer to the opening of the wound.

"Of course. The ever-so-noble-and-conscientious Jordan. Still, I think it'd be a good fit on you. You have a soft touch. A rather fetching, womanly—Ow!"

I yanked the slug out, satisfied when he got cut off mid-speech. I dropped the bullet in the trashcan beside the bed and pressed a large wad of gauze to the wound as fresh blood trickled out. "Keep pressure on this."

He obliged without a fuss. Odd. I shifted over to his right shoulder, tucking a wayward lock of silt-streaked hair behind my ear. I had occupied one of his hands, but the other one continued tracing absent patterns on the back of my jeans.

"I'm sensing some hostility here."

"Really. What gives you that idea?" I made a point to dig the forceps in a bit so that he cringed. It made me feel better.

"Let me guess. You're sore about the policemen I hurt."

"No shit," I said, no longer caring about being gentle with the wound. "You put our lives at risk just because you were having a temper tantrum. If I didn't need you to contact Mulciber, I'd have let Michael jump rope with your small intestines."

"It wasn't a temper tantrum. Some people drink to relieve tension. I just use violence as my outlet."

For a moment, I caught myself contemplating simply jabbing my finger in the bullet hole. No. That'd definitely make me a sadist. "You should really stop talking if you want me to get this out of you. I'm very tempted to leave it in."

"Is this the part where I say, 'that's what she said'? Ow!"

He glowered at me. I ignored him, focusing on removing the slug instead of twisting it this time. There seemed to be a particular type of pain he liked, but this wasn't it. Ha.

"Your hubby wasn't too thrilled about having to spring me," Belial said, sounding more coherent as he sneered when he said "hubby." Then again, his body processed medicine faster than the average human's.

"Naturally. But he still did it, so cut him some slack."

Belial snorted. "It is my eternal duty not to do so. That's a battle you'll just have to lose, Seer."

His words piqued my curiosity and some of my anger slid away. "Eternal? You two didn't like each other even before the Fall?"

He paused, seeming to consider my words. "Not necessarily. We were friends, actually."

~ 301 ~

"Really?"

He smirked. "You may hate me, but I was quite popular back then. I believe John Milton mentioned something about 'a fairer person lost not Heav'n.' It wasn't an exaggeration, you know."

I rolled my eyes. "Uh-huh. Hold still, I've almost got it."

"I sometimes wonder what would have happened if I hadn't rebelled. Maybe he and I would be as chummy as he is with Gabriel."

Again, genuine surprise rolled through me. "So you do think about stuff like that?"

He fixed me with his gaze. "You seem surprised."

"Of course I am. It never occurred to me that you could have regrets like a normal person. You're so...*you*."

He chuckled. "Why thank you."

The bullet finally came free and I tossed it in the wastebasket. When I straightened up, Belial let the gauze fall and wrapped his arms around my waist, tugging me so close I had to prop my hands on his collarbone to keep from falling into his lap. I prayed Michael wouldn't walk in to see this little stunt.

"Let go. Just because you're hopped up on painkillers doesn't mean my personal space rule is void," I said, though I could hear my voice waver.

"Relax," he murmured. "I need sexual energy to heal myself. It will only take a moment."

He closed his eyes and breathed deeply, as if inhaling the tension stretched between us. I kept still, trying not to feel the heat from his bare skin. I felt part of the long burn scar across his chest underneath my palm and it felt rough in contrast to the rest of him. The burn was relatively new, but there were plenty of other, older scars on his body. He had been right when he said we were both covered in them.

The wounds on his biceps healed first, returning his arms to their sinewy perfection, and then the ones in his shoulders eventually closed up. He exhaled a blast of hot air against my throat. I waited for him to let go, but instead he leaned his forehead against my breastbone.

"How poetic that you're healing the very wounds you've inflicted upon me," he said, his voice muffled by the fabric of my button up shirt.

I couldn't reply because his tone was unlike anything I'd ever heard before. He sounded so...human. There was an undercurrent of pain that I wasn't sure could truly be faked, even by a master manipulator like him. It scared me and thrilled me at the same time.

I shivered as he slipped his hands beneath my shirt, sliding his fingers over my hips, his fingertips finding the edges of the scars on my back. I licked my lips, forcing myself to raise my voice enough for him to hear.

"Belial...are you in love with me?"

He nudged the collar of my shirt aside, kissing the scar over my heart. "Don't ask rhetorical questions, my pet."

I heard the door close and then leapt out of his grasp. Michael came around the corner, already frowning in suspicion as he spotted me standing next to the fully healed demon.

"I take it we're done here."

"In more ways than one," Belial said, but he was staring at me when he spoke. I looked away, rubbing my arms, as he stood up.

"I'll clean up and then we can get going."

Michael frowned deeper as Belial disappeared into the bathroom, slamming the door behind him. "I'm guessing I missed something."

I shook my head. "Nothing important. So where are we headed? Where's the Garden?"

"I'd rather not say while he's around. We're gonna have to fly under the radar, literally. Gabriel set us up to get smuggled across the Atlantic. We've got to go now. The pick up's on the coast and we're still a couple miles out."

"And I'm assuming Belial's coming with us."

"He'll land with us, but he's not going any further. It's forbidden, and for good reason. Demons cannot ever know where the Garden is. I'm sure he'd do his best to try to destroy it, or worse."

"What's worse than destroying it?"

"Leading other people to it. If normal people found out it was real, that we were real, it would mean total chaos. Society would break down overnight. There'd be witch-hunts. Wars. Genocide."

"Why haven't the demons tried to expose you if that would be the end result?"

"We're still in a symbiotic relationship. They profit from us in some ways, so there would be no reason to kill their benefactors. Besides, there are some rules in place that demons can't break, just like the contract we made with him."

"Wait. Wouldn't Satan know where the Garden is? He's been there before."

Michael shook his head. "Not necessarily. Think about how much time has passed. Back when Eden was first created, the geography of the earth was completely different. He'd have no idea where it is now. The Garden is also now underground, so it wouldn't matter even if he told Belial the last location he knew about."

I sank onto the bed, pushing my hair out of my eyes. "Speaking of which, what happened back there? Why did Belial go Rambo on those cops? It couldn't have just been for 'stress relief.'"

Michael stared. "You're surprised that he likes killing people?"

"No, of course not, but..." I paused, trying to figure out what I meant. "It seemed like he was getting better. Not good, mind you, just better. I haven't seen him behave like that since the war in Jersey last year."

"It's bloodlust. It's not something you would ever be able to understand. That quality is inherent in every demon, especially archdemons. Belial is good at hiding his vicious nature when he wants to, but it's always there. He's incapable of changing."

I winced, and hoped Michael didn't see me do it. He had been only seconds too late to hear my question to Belial and part of me wanted to tell him what had happened, but I knew it would only enrage him.

The very thought of Belial being in love with me was beyond ludicrous. He had no heart and his soul was as black as a crow's wing. But there were times when he looked at me, times when he smiled at me, times when he acted like a person and not the murderous scum I hated over the years. Was it possible that somewhere amongst the filth inside him, there was a semblance of something good? He'd told me I was sin and savior. Did he have a bit of both in him too?

"I don't like that look," Michael said. His expression had shifted from a frown to something much more somber.

"What look?"

"You're hiding something."

"I'm not—"

He shook his head once, a quick jerk. "Don't insult me. I was married to you for a year. I know that look."

My throat tightened. "Was? Are you saying it's off now?"

He looked away. "No. But that's a conversation for another time."

"And when is that? After the world's come to an end?"

He turned those unwavering sea-green eyes on me. "You were my world."

The bathroom door opened and Belial came out, drying his damp sable locks with a white towel. He glanced between the two of us, seeming confused.

"Who died?"

Michael ignored the question. "You all healed up?"

"Yeah."

"Good."

I didn't see Michael move—I only heard the crash of Belial's body against the mirror on the far wall. It took me a second to realize Michael had punched him so hard and so fast that my human eyes couldn't track the movement. My mouth fell open as he lunged for the demon, grabbing fistfuls of his bloodstained shirt and slamming him into the wall with enough force that it left a dent.

Belial punched him twice in the solar plexus and the archangel's grip loosened, allowing the demon time to kick him. Michael fell backwards and hit the nightstand by the bed, forcing me to hop onto the mattress to avoid getting grazed. He growled, picked up the broken piece of furniture, and hurled it at him.

Belial ducked and it smashed to pieces against the wall. Michael used the extra seconds it took him to move out of the way for a vicious roundhouse kick that caught a glancing blow across Belial's temple. He stumbled, but caught himself and then there was suddenly a switchblade in his hand. The sight of it snapped me out of my shocked state.

I leapt down from the bed and withdrew my .38, clicking the hammer. "The next one of you to land a punch gets shot in the kneecap."

Both men froze, breathing hard, then stared at me.

"You wouldn't dare," Belial said with a sneer.

I pointed the muzzle at him. "Try me."

"I didn't even start the fight."

"No, but you could have stopped it. Now you had both better calm the hell down or I swear I'll shoot you and head for the Garden by myself."

"You saw what he did," Michael said, his voice settled in a tone so dark it made my skin crawl. There was something feral in his eyes. He had slipped into warrior mode—a cold, calculating soldier that wanted nothing but justice. "He can't be trusted. He needs to learn his place."

Belial snorted. "My place? It's right where it's always been. In your wife's bed."

Michael took another menacing step forward. I switched targets. "Don't."

"Why are you defending him?" he snarled.

"I'm not, you idiot! We don't have time for this. Yes, Belial should be punished for endangering us and hurting innocent people, but we can't do it right now. After this mess is all over, you can rip each other to shreds. I won't stop you. But until then, suck it up and stop letting him get to you."

Michael glared at me for another second or two, seeming to realize I was right, and then met the demon's gaze. "When this is well and truly over, I will enjoy sending you back to Hell."

"And I will enjoy making you eat those words," Belial replied, his smile laced with malice.

Once I was sure they wouldn't try anything funny, I shook my head and put my gun back where it belonged. "I swear, sometimes I think you two are perfect for each other. You're both macho arrogant hotheads."

Belial made a rude noise in the back of his throat as he wiped fresh blood from his lip. "And what does it say about you that you're attracted to both of us?"

I opened the hotel door and glanced at them over my shoulder. "That I should become a lesbian."

CHAPTER THIRTY-TWO

JORDAN

"You don't have to do this, you know."

"Yes, I do."

Michael gave me a long, intrusive stare, then sighed. "Fine. Five minutes."

"Okay."

"I mean it. Any longer and they'll be able to trace it."

"Got it."

He stepped back and I slid the rusty, dingy door to the phone booth shut. There were barely any of these contraptions left in the States, but we'd gotten lucky outside of a gas station. I hadn't used one in years. Never needed to until now.

My fingers trembled as I pushed the change into the slot and dialed the number. *Five minutes, Amador. Keep it short.*

The phone rang four times before someone picked up and my stomach plummeted into my feet. "Hello?"

"Hey, Lauren."

Silence. Then, a pained whisper. "Jordan?"

"Yeah."

I heard movement, then the sound of a door slamming. She'd probably gone into her bedroom, away from Lily. "What the hell is going on? I saw your picture in the news, for Christ's sake! The cops have been by here twice asking if I have any information on your whereabouts. Do you know what I've been through these past couple days? How could you do something like this?"

The lump in my throat made it hard to reply. "I know. I know, and I'm so sorry."

"You had damn well better be!" she yelled. "How many years have I been your friend? How many times have I stood by your side when you needed me? How could you lie to me like this?"

She broke away from the phone, cursing in Korean. I waited until she stopped before speaking. "It's complicated. More than you'll ever know."

"I won't ever know anything unless you tell me. Kidnapping a serial killer? Busting a felon out of police custody? Who are you? Tell me the truth."

"I can't. I want to, but I can't."

"Then why did you bother calling? To make me even more upset than I already am? Because it's a phone call I could have lived without."

"I just…wanted to make sure you were safe. And tell you that I'm sorry for lying to you. You were right. I've been shielding you from the truth for years and it's not fair. But if I make it out of this mess alive, I'll tell you everything. I swear."

"Don't do that. Don't you dare say that to me. I don't want the next phone call I get to be from a goddamn morgue. I don't want some cop showing up at my place to tell me you're dead. If you care about me at all, you'll either tell me what's going on or leave me the hell alone."

"I…"

"You what?"

"I love you, Lauren. And I'm sorry. If this is the last time I ever speak to you, then tell Lily I love her and I'll miss her too."

A pause. Then, her voice, ice cold, said, "Goodbye, Jordan."

She hung up. I replaced the phone on the receiver. My throat was so tight I had to clear it several times before dialing the next number.

A gruff voice answered on the first ring. "Hello?"

"Lewis? It's me."

"Jordan? Where the hell are you? What's going on? You've been all over the local news for the past couple days."

"I can't explain, okay? I just…wanted to tell you I'm alive. I felt I owed you that much."

"Is it Lamont? Did he frame you for the murder charges?"

"No."

"Stop lying, girl. I may have only known you for a short time, but you ain't a killer. I know there's more to this situation than what you're sayin.' I been a liar for half my life and I can hear it in your voice."

"Lewis…"

"Look, I know I can't talk you out of whatever you're doing, but you've got to know that you can't keep heading down this path for long. You don't want to know where it ends."

"I don't have a choice."

"You always have a choice. And if you're as much like your mother as I think, when the time comes you'll make the right one."

A small disbelieving snort escaped me. "Why are you being so understanding? A normal father would be screaming at me to turn myself in."

"Normal fathers don't have daughters who are wanted for murder. Giving you that kind of advice would be pretty useless. Besides, you're stubborn. You wouldn't listen to me anyway."

A couple of days and he already knew me that well. Maybe I was predictable. Just then, Michael rapped his knuckles on the glass.

I took a deep breath. "I have to go now. I'm sorry. If I don't see you again, I want you to know I'm sort of glad that I met you. Even if it almost got me killed."

"Don't be sorry. Just come home in one piece, girl. Alright?"

"I'll try. Bye."

"Bye." I hung up and walked away from the last part of my normal life.

After an exhausting twenty-three hours of travel, I found myself seated behind my silent husband as we paddled in a papyrus reed boat called a tankwa over the muddy waters of Lake Tana—the largest lake in Ethiopia and the source of the Blue Nile. We'd been smuggled on a plane from Miami to Addis Ababa, then drove from Addis Ababa to the city of Bahir Dar, home to the lake. While the air between Michael and I was strained, the scenery almost made up for it.

The lake stretched for miles and the sun glanced off the water around us, making it shimmer. Flocks of great white Pelicans soared overhead, occasionally diving to catch fish. It was a hot, oppressive day, so there were a lot of animals gathered at the shores to cool off. Under normal circumstances, I'd be enjoying myself, maybe touring one of the twenty monasteries on the thirty-seven islands of the lake. One of them was even rumored to have housed the Ark of the Covenant. I absently wondered if Michael would be able to confirm or refute the legend.

Despite my enticing surroundings, I knew I couldn't stall any longer. I licked my dry lips and cleared my throat, addressing Michael. "So. How's this going to go down? What can I expect at the Garden?"

Michael's broad shoulders tensed a bit when I spoke. He'd been dreading this conversation, I could tell, but there were too many theories buzzing around my head as to why.

"We're gonna have to steal the fruit."

I stopped rowing. "I'm sorry, what?"

He kept his voice flat, eyes forward. "The Garden is guarded by the angel Uzziel. Do you really think it's going to end well for us if we tell him we're bargaining the fruit that could unleash the Leviathan for the life of a four-year-old girl, whose father is an archdemon?"

"No, but aren't you the Commander? Can't you order him to let us in?"

Michael shook his head. "Uzziel is not bound by heavenly authorities. His eternal task is to watch over the Garden until the Rapture. Since the order was ordained by God, there's nothing I can do about it. If Uzziel were to find us, I'd have to fight him to the death and I refuse to kill one of my brothers just for doing his job."

A worrying thought wormed its way into my brain. "Does that mean you're going to get in trouble for helping me?"

"It's likely."

My gaze softened on him. "I'm sorry."

"You've already said that."

"And I meant it that time too."

The birdcalls and splashing water around us didn't hide the sound of his sigh. "Forget it. It's the least of our worries. We're going to have to get in and out as quickly as possible."

"Well, you've been there before. Shouldn't be too hard, right?"

"Not for me, no."

I frowned. "Don't like the way that sounds. Elaborate."

"This is the Garden of Eden, Jordan. Do you know what that means?"

"I thought I did, but your tone is really starting to make me think twice."

"It's paradise. Literal, actual utopia. The longer you spend there, the more you'll start to lose your grip on reality. The Garden has an atmosphere that can alter your mind because it was meant to be perfect in every way. I'm going to have to lead you in and you can't leave my side for any reason or you'll lose yourself in it."

"I don't get it. Why didn't the Bible or *Paradise Lost* say anything about that?"

"Because neither is told from a first-person account of it. Adam and Eve were born in the Garden, so they were able to handle it. You weren't. Therefore, it'll be hard to resist."

My mouth felt dry. I suspected it had nothing to do with the heat of the sun. "Okay. I'll do my best to prepare myself, then."

Finally, we reached a shore. An African darter watched our tankwa glide up to the muddy beach, cocking its brown head to the side. Michael stepped out and the darter took off into the air, scattering a couple of slick black feathers in its wake. I couldn't resist tracking its flight into the sky, flapping its wings with long, slow strokes against the wind. Some part of me envied it.

Michael turned and held his hand out for me to grab so I could climb onto the shore. For some reason, seeing him standing there, waiting for me, ready to potentially throw his life away even after all I'd done, made something inside my chest constrict. I took his hand.

He helped me out, his brow furrowing at the pained look on my face.

"Jordan, are you—"

I let go, refusing to meet his gaze. "I'm fine. Here, help me lug this thing out of sight."

He didn't press the matter. Smart man.

We hauled the tankwa into a secluded spot by the nearby trees and began the long trek up the hill. I didn't know exactly where we were going, but I didn't need to, after all. Part of me always felt more at ease with Michael in control. Even though my life was hectic, I could always trust and depend on him. Even before we were romantically involved, he had the air of leadership perfected. Gabriel told me that while Michael hadn't been the nicest fellow a few centuries ago, he had been a fair and worthy leader regardless.

Before long, sweat beaded on my forehead. Tendrils of hair stuck to it, and I started to lose track of time until I looked at my watch. We had been hiking for close to half an hour. I opened my mouth to ask Michael how much farther we had to go, but then I got my answer. I could hear a faint roar in the distance. The air became much more humid. Every other gust of wind blew a fine veil of moisture against my overheated skin and then I knew where we were.

My boots crunched against the sparse grass and rocks as we reached the edge of the cliff that spilled down into the Blue Nile Falls. The sight nearly took my breath away. Lush green forests bordered both sides of the waterfall, the bottom of which was hidden due to the thick mist the falling water kicked up. I couldn't remember ever seeing anything so beautiful in my life.

"Let's go."

I snapped out of my thoughts, glancing at the angel by my side. "Huh?"

He gestured towards the falls. "The entrance is that way."

I stared at him. "If you're saying we have to jump into this river, you're on your own."

He rolled his eyes. "Of course not. But we do have to climb onto the cliff side."

I ventured a nervous peek over the side. "That sounds like a horrendously bad idea."

Michael shot me a sarcastic look. "Where have I heard that before?"

"Point taken. Lead the way. I'll follow. Probably."

He walked to the edge and lowered himself one careful movement at a time. I began to get more and more skittish as he descended a couple feet onto the craggy face of the waterfall.

"Wait, shouldn't we have some sort of support rope?"

"Jordan, I can fly. If you fall, I'll catch you. Now come on, we haven't got all day."

"Alright, keep your pants on, Indiana Jones," I said, mentally preparing myself for what I was about to do. What was it they always said in the movies? Don't look down? Right. Piece of cake.

The pounding of my heartbeat in my ears drowned out the sound of the waterfall only several feet away as I inched my way over the side of the cliff, testing each place I'd put my foot with my toe first. I made sure to follow Michael's movements exactly, keeping my breath slow and steady so I wouldn't panic. The rocks were damp to the touch but not slippery, though the thought didn't make me feel any better. It was a long way down. Some part of me giggled at the thought of dying right now, if only because I had survived so many brushes with death that biting it via cliff-diving would be just plain silly.

About halfway down the cliff, Michael reached into his pocket and withdrew a large silver feather. I knew it had come from his own wings as no other angel had that magnificent color — a mixture of pearl and aluminum. He held it up in front of a long seam and I felt a rolling wave of vibration emanate through the ground. Pebbles tumbled from above as the seam slowly split apart, revealing the entrance to a cave. It opened enough to the width of Michael's body — no more, no less. He swung himself once and jumped inside with the grace of a gymnast. Damn perfect angel.

I took a deep breath and maneuvered myself to the spot where he'd been, praying that I could emulate an ounce of his muscle control. I swung towards the cave and he held one hand out, steadying me as soon as my feet hit the earth. With the sun at my back, I could only see a couple of feet in front of us, leaving the rest in a gaping black abyss.

"Don't suppose you brought a flashlight?" I asked.

Before he could answer, the cave rumbled again and I whirled around to see the seam closing up by itself. We were instantly swallowed in darkness and I lost what little sanity I had left.

"Michael, what the hell was that?"

His large, strong hand wrapped around mine in the dark. "Calm down and look up."

I started to argue, but then I noticed a soft blue light glowing from above. I raised my gaze to the ceiling and found that it came from what looked like stalactites made of crystal. They formed a line through the inky space in front of us, leading the way. I thought Michael would let go now that I could see, but he tugged me along after him as if it were an unconscious habit. He'd remembered I wasn't too fond of tight spaces. Damn him.

The path he led us through dipped down after only a few steps, heading at an angle away from the surface. The air cooled considerably and I could no longer hear any signs of the river around us. For a while, there was just the crunch of our boots against the soil, Michael's warm fingers around mine, and the ethereal light within the cave.

Then, I could see a white light at the end of the tunnel. It looked like a speck at first, but before long we were coming up to whatever was at the other side. I squinted, letting Michael lead me out. I stumbled a bit and he caught me on reflex, leaving us in a momentary caustic silence as it pressed the front of my body along the line of his. Even here, he was still so warm. I missed the way it felt to lean against his chest.

I tore my gaze away from the conflicted expression on his face, sliding out of his arms and focusing on the sight before me. I had been wrong about the Blue Nile Falls. What lay in front of me was the most beautiful thing I'd ever seen.

The cave's exit hovered above a gushing waterfall that wasn't as large as the falls, but was still mighty and impressive. The water was crystal clear and flowed downward at least ten feet into a pool. The pool spilled out into a river that led across a grassy plain and surrounded the grounds like a moat. The gates of Eden were huge and made of gold, glimmering so brilliantly that it looked like it had just been polished only a moment ago. The gates connected to huge white stone walls that enclosed the compound. Enormous torches held by elegant sconces on the surrounding cave walls lit the entire area. The most curious thing of all was that the fire licking up from these torches was pure white. It gave the illusion of sunlight, which made sense. Down here, the plants and animals of the Garden would need sunlight to survive.

From here, I caught a glimpse of Eden itself — mostly huge treetops bursting with bright green leaves that spanned for acres. The cave had to be several miles wide and that was just the entrance. It was spectacular.

It took me a moment to remember that we had a job to do, but strangely Michael didn't rush me. Maybe he knew what an honor it was to be able to see this since only two other human beings had that privilege. As soon as I remembered we were about to steal from this place, shame consumed me. The mother and father of the entire human race had been born here. I was about to boost some fruit from the holiest place on the planet. Only in my life would something like this happen.

"Where's Uzziel?"

"He's not just the guard. He's also the caretaker so he doesn't stay at the gate all the time."

"Can he sense us?"

"You've learned how to shield yourself, right?"

"Yes."

"Then we're fine, unless he sees us. Speaking of which, we're obviously not going to use the gate. This river circles the entire garden. That's how we get in. Follow me and don't stray."

I nodded. He leapt in first, disappearing in the frothing pool. I waited until I saw his dark shape heading towards the outflow and jumped. The water was so cold it almost shocked the air out of my lungs, but I focused on the sight of Michael ahead of me and swam in long, strong strokes to catch up with him. Slowly but surely, we made it past the front gate with no sign of the angel guarding it and circled towards the right side of the grounds.

It wasn't hard to keep up with Michael since the river's current was strong, but I could feel my lungs burning with the need for air. I didn't know how much farther I would have to stay under and the thought made fear creep through my stomach. My head started to pound with pain and I fought the voice in the back of my head screaming that I was going to drown before we made it there. My

~ 314 ~

vision blurred and my chest started to shake, but I kept swimming until my arms went numb.

Then, miraculously, we made it beneath the wall and swam up to the surface. I sucked in a huge mouthful of air, wiping water out of my face so I could see. Michael pressed an index finger to his lips, miming for me to keep quiet while we headed for land. The part of the river we came out into was an oval pool. I spotted a couple of deer on the opposite side drinking. They raised their heads when they saw us, but to my surprise, they didn't run away.

Michael checked the area thoroughly before motioning for me to follow him onto land. The pool was framed by grass on all sides and the clearing was surrounded by shrubs that reminded me of the forests up north. Interesting. Maybe Eden was set up like a wildlife preserve where each set of animals had their own specially made environment. After all, it made the most sense.

I squeezed all the water I could out of my shirt and crouched behind the same shrub as Michael. He closed his eyes and I could tell he was listening for footsteps or the sound of a voice. I couldn't hear anything yet other than the faint lapping of the deer's tongues in the water.

"Coast seems clear," Michael said, looking at me. "How are you feeling?"

I shrugged. "Normal, I guess. Maybe a little cold."

"I noticed," he said, glancing at my chest, and I smacked him in the arm.

"You're in the Garden of Eden. Have some class."

He rolled his eyes. "Wear a bra with padding next time. Now come on."

Again, he took my hand and led me from behind the shrubbery into the woods. We made a quiet, careful path through the trees, keeping our eyes peeled for any signs of the angel. Still, I couldn't help getting distracted by the sheer beauty of the plant life. The treetops stretched higher than I could see and the leaves were a rich green I couldn't recall having seen before. Birds wheeled overhead, casting playful shadows across the ground as we crept through the underbrush. Flowers tickled my calf muscles and the sweet scent of nectar teased my nose. It took me a second to realize I had starting smiling from out of nowhere. Weird.

The forest gradually turned into jungle terrain. The air became humid and the sounds around us changed from chirps to rolling growls and monkey chatter. I could hear insects humming in clusters nearby and the hairs on the back of my neck stood at attention as I heard leaves cracking underfoot behind us. I had seen environments like this on National Geographic. However, it was one thing to watch crazy white people wander around predator-infested jungles and another to be doing it myself.

"Is it just me or are we being followed?" I asked, my voice hushed.

Michael didn't turn around, which worried me. "We are, but relax. The animals are the least of our worries."

I wanted to believe him, but the way the twigs snapped in our wake made me think our stalker was something large. I could hear husky breathing every few seconds. It chased away the temporary wonderment I'd felt earlier. I didn't like being followed, and being hunted even less.

Finally, I stopped and tugged on his arm so he had to look at me. "I'd feel a lot better if we got rid of it."

Michael gave me an even stare, his face neutral. "I wouldn't turn around if I were you."

"Wow. Now I *have* to look."

He sighed, but didn't stop me as I turned my head to peek over my shoulder. My throat closed up.

There was a Bengal tiger staring at me from about two feet away.

I heard a squeak escape my lips, then realized I hadn't formed an actual sentence. I swallowed, trying to remember my language skills. "Um…is there a polite way to tell a four-hundred-pound killing machine to back off?"

"I told you, it's not going to hurt us. The animals in Eden are under the effect of paradise as well. They view humans as something to be respected, not eaten. She's just curious."

A rather illogical thought entered my head. "…does that mean I can pet her?"

A dry laugh escaped the archangel. "Probably, but I wouldn't press your luck."

Now that we'd seen it, the tiger's behavior shifted fully into inquisitive. Its wide pink nose flared as it sucked in my scent, taking a step closer until it could sniff the toe of my boot. This felt too surreal for words. I kept waiting for it to open its massive jaws and swallow me whole, but after a few seconds, the tiger yawned and loped off into the jungle. Guess I wasn't as fascinating as I thought.

We resumed our hurried pace through the rain forest and once more I lost track of time. There were so many sights and sounds around me, draining the attention I should have been paying to the path we were making. At some point, I became lightheaded. It didn't feel the same as when I was nauseous or having a migraine. In fact, it was almost pleasant—like my brain was detaching from the worries that plagued me.

At last, the jungle foliage thinned. We were coming up to a clearing. The heat slackened, leaving the air cool and comfortable. The grass was low and felt as soft as moss as we stepped inside the secluded spot. There were two trees side by side in the clearing, both with trunks the size of SUVs. The thick branches stretched upward, seeming to go on forever.

The tree on the left had shiny dark-green leaves and a peculiar blood-red fruit hanging from it. The fruit grew in clusters like grapes yet they were about the size of strawberries. Too big to be cherries. I'd never seen it before.

The other tree had triangular leaves that were light green and vines woven about the trunk like snakes. The fruit that hung from the branches was about the size of a pear, but its skin was a beautiful color somewhere between gold and peach.

I stood between the two trees, inhaling the sweet scent of both, and finally understanding why Eve had been unable to resist. It was unlike anything I'd ever experienced. The aroma filled my lungs and sent a wonderful calm through me. What did I have to worry about? I was here, in the Garden, safe from harm, safe from anything that could possibly hurt me. I was home.

Michael's hand squeezed mine as he led me towards the tree with the golden fruit, pointing. "It's this one. Hurry, Uzziel can't be too far from here."

"Mmkay," I said, reaching up. I plucked a fruit from the tree. Dew droplets fell from the branch, kissing my cheeks. I smiled, nodding to the plant in silent thanks for its offering. The skin of the fruit was firm like that of a plum. My mouth watered. My tongue ached for a taste. Why couldn't I indulge? After all, this was my reward for my journey. I deserved it, didn't I?

I brought the fruit up to my mouth, but Michael stopped me. "Jordan, you can't eat that. Come on, let's go."

"Go where?"

He stepped close to me, cradling my face in his hands without saying anything. Then, he let out a soft curse.

"Jordan, do you remember why we came here?"

I wrinkled my nose, thinking. The thoughts in my head swirled around in a fog, untouchable, abstract, unimportant. "For the fruit. I just wanted to taste it, that's all."

"It's not to be eaten. We have to bargain it for Juliana," he said, and his voice sounded so pained that it confused me. That name. I knew it. But from where?

"Does she live here? Where is she? I'd like to meet her," I said, glancing at my surroundings expectantly.

Michael shut his eyes for a second. "We have to go. Now."

"Sure, what should we see? Do they have an oasis here? I'll bet it's lovely."

"No. We have to leave the Garden."

I frowned, stepping back. "Why? It's our home, Michael."

"This is not our home."

"Shouldn't it be? Look at it." I waved my free hand around. "Listen to the birds. Listen to the stream. It's perfect. There's nothing that can hurt us. We could stay here forever. We could be happy. Always."

Michael touched my shoulders, bringing me in close, and the sorrow in his eyes frightened me. "We can't stay. We can't."

I cupped his cheek. "Yes, we can. Isn't that what you've always wanted? It'll just be the two of us. No demons, no pain, no suffering, no labor. Just you and me and the rest of our life together."

He pressed his forehead against mine, his voice a hoarse whisper. "Baby, don't say that. Please, don't say that to me. I would give anything to let you have this kind of peace, but it's not real. You're not yourself. We have to go."

"But we're—"

"We're not home." His grip tightened on my arms. "Jordan, I need you to focus. I need you to remember why we're here."

I shook my head. "I don't understand."

"We're leaving. Come on."

He gripped my wrist, pulling me towards the jungle, but I dug my heels into the downy soft grass, not moving. "No."

"Jor—"

"No. I'm not going. This is where I belong. This is where we belong."

A flock of birds flew past us from the left side of the clearing. Michael's green eyes widened, darting back and forth as if trying to see through the forest. Something was coming.

He dragged me towards the tree with the golden fruit and shoved me against the trunk, pressing his hand over my mouth. "Don't move. Don't say anything."

I heard more movement from the other side of the clearing, so I tilted my head until I could see. An olive-skinned man in white linen emerged from the rain forest. He was at least seven feet tall and his hair was dark grey. A brown leather quiver full of arrows was strapped to his back along with a huge bow. His blue eyes swept across the clearing like he was searching for something. He examined the grass where we'd stood only moments ago and walked over to the other tree, placing one hand against the bark. After a minute or so, he walked towards the tree we hid behind.

Michael stooped down, keeping his hand over my lips, and picked up a flat stone near the roots of the tree. He took careful aim and hurled it into the woods with all his might just as the angel crept near to our side. There came a terrible animal cry in the distance and the angel's head whipped around in that direction. He hurried out of the clearing to check the disturbance, leaving us alone once again.

Michael sighed in relief, but he still wouldn't move away. He met my eyes instead. "You may never forgive me for this, but I hope you'll understand someday."

He reached up towards the tree, pulled a vine from it, and tore off the end. He took his hand off my mouth and tied the vine around my head so it served as a gag. I thrashed, trying to cry out for help, but he caught my hands and held me still. He tied my wrists and ankles and threw me over his shoulder, carrying me back into the jungle while I begged him to stop. He didn't listen. Why wouldn't he listen?

When we reached the riverside, he put me down and held my face between his hands. "Take a deep breath for me. We're almost out, okay? I promise, I won't let go."

He wrapped one arm around my waist and jumped into the river, holding me against him as he swam. The frigid water washed away my tears, but I could still feel the screaming agony of loss in my chest as I watched Eden slip away. I had lost my home. I had lost my paradise. I had lost everything.

When we reached the pool on the other side of the cave, Michael put me on his back and climbed the wall to reach the exit. It wasn't until we were inside the tunnel that the unbelievable wave of anguish receded from my body. When Michael saw me calming, he untied my hands and feet.

I threw myself into his arms. He hugged me with all his might, crushing me against his chest while I cried.

"I'm so s-sorry," I said through hiccupping sobs. "I said such horrible things to you in there."

"It's okay," he whispered, stroking my hair. "It wasn't your fault. You didn't mean it."

He pulled back, wiping my tears away. "Come on, before Uzziel sees us. Follow me."

He held my hand and led me through the dimly-lit tunnel to the outside world waiting for us. The seam opened up once more after he presented the feather and we climbed the face of the cliff. Michael got there first, hauling me over the edge and into his arms. He kissed my forehead.

"We made it, baby. We made it."

Before I could reply, I heard the chilling sound of someone slow-clapping behind us. My body went cold as a deep, dry voice spoke.

"Well, well. Congratulations, lovebirds."

We both turned around and found ourselves staring into the triumphant eyes of Belial.

CHAPTER THIRTY-THREE

JORDAN

"No," I whispered, my voice thick with disbelief. "Not possible. Can't be you."

Belial sent me a questioning look. "Why not?"

"We left you in Addis Ababa with eight angels guarding you. You can't be here. You can't be."

"Ah, yes. They were quite effective guards, you know—strong, smart, brave, and fiercely loyal. Your mistake was not in ordering them to keep an eye on me. Your mistake was underestimating what it means to be an archdemon. You could have hired eight hundred angels and I still would have found you."

"How?"

"Because, my pet, I am the best at what I do. Always."

The shock hadn't worn off yet, but I realized that Michael hadn't said anything. In fact, he hadn't even moved. He just stood there, his hands still resting on the back of my arms. Wet, tangled brown hair hung over his eyes so that I couldn't see them. He had gone so still when Belial spoke that I'd forgotten he was even there. Fear rushed through me in a suffocating burst of adrenaline as I realized the true gravity of what had happened. An archdemon found the location of the Garden of Eden. God have mercy on us all.

"Michael?" I said, gripping his forearms, hoping it would snap him out of whatever trance he had slipped into. He didn't move. Then, I felt it.

Michael's energy exploded out of his body. It was unlike anything I'd ever experienced. I choked on it—gasping for air as a shroud of searing hot anger broke free from inside the archangel and expanded like some great phoenix spreading its wings. His shoulders rose and fell as his chest heaved deep breaths. His fingers clamped down on my arms because I was the closest thing to him, because he was so furious that he couldn't control his own body.

"Michael, don't—"

"Demon," he said in a voice so low that it sent vibrations through my bones. "I am going to rip out your soul and cast it into the Lake of Fire myself."

He let go of me and began walking towards Belial. I shoved my hands against his shoulders, pushing with all my might, but he was a wall of solid muscle intent on murdering the demon standing behind me. My boots slid across the dirt, leaving a trail, and panic gripped me when I realized Michael had disappeared completely. Only the Commander remained, and he would have his vengeance.

"Look at me, dammit!" I yelled, hoping to get through to the rational part of his brain. "Don't do this! Think about Juliana. We still need him."

Michael's large hands closed over my arms and he threw me aside. I hit the ground hard, crying out. Michael grabbed Belial by the neck and threw him with a force so tremendous that the archdemon ploughed through four trees, snapping them in half like twigs. He hit the ground about twenty feet away, leaving a small impact crater.

Michael lifted his right hand towards the sky, palm flat, and a dark grey cloud immediately formed. Thunder roared overhead and lightning flashed, forcing me to cover my eyes as a blinding light filled the area. The bolt connected with his raised arm and his silver sword materialized in his hand. He hadn't been bluffing. He was about to kill Belial.

Before I could move, his wings sprouted from his back and he launched himself into the air, heading towards the demon. I scrambled to my feet and sprinted through the path Belial's body had made in the forest, praying I could beat Michael there. I spotted Belial sprawled at the base of a tree, covered in fallen leaves, branches, and dirt, bleeding from a cut on his scalp.

Michael landed in front of him, raised his sword, and brought it down to smite him.

"No!"

I threw myself in front of the demon, spreading my arms to make myself a bigger target. My eyes squeezed shut as I expected the sword to slice into me like the Spear of Longinus had done a year ago. I waited for the agony of life leaving my body, of blood seeping out of my skin.

Nothing happened.

Panting, I opened my eyes to see Michael's sword had stopped a mere inch from penetrating my breastbone. God bless him, he had the restraint not to skewer me.

"Move," Michael said in that same gravelly, damn near inhuman pitch.

I stayed where I knelt in front of Belial. "No. Killing him won't do anything. You know that. It's too late. Put the sword down."

"I won't tell you again, woman."

"If you kill him, we can't contact Mulciber and we can't save Juliana. If you kill him, it'll just send his soul back to Hell and he will still know where the Garden is anyway. Put the sword down."

"You still defend him. Even after all of this, you'd throw your life away for this worthless carrion. You disgust me."

It hurt to hear him say that, but I pushed past his words because I knew what was going on. All of these interactions led me to one conclusion.

"I don't care what you think about me, Commander," I said. "Now put the fucking sword down and give me back my husband, you son of a bitch."

His eyes were as hard as glass. No, this was not my lover. This was the other half of his soul, the one that could be as cold and ruthless as the demon lying behind me. They were divided right down the middle—two men sharing the same soul. Not a split personality, but definitely something similar. This was the first time I'd addressed him by name. I could tell he saw my demands would not change. He had a decision to make one way or the other.

At last, he lowered the sword, but his gaze didn't leave mine. "Very well. But know this, woman. I will suffer you no more. He may love you, but you have betrayed my trust for the last time. It will not happen again."

He closed his eyes and the sword and his wings vanished in a plume of silver vapor. Michael's body swayed and then he opened his eyes, frowning when he saw me.

"What just happened?"

I stood, wincing as my injured arm stung. Blood dripped down my forearm, thick under the oppressive heat. "You went after Belial."

He ran a shaky hand through his wet hair. "All I could see was red. I…I don't understand. This has never happened before."

He noticed my disheveled state and touched my elbow, examining the cut. "Did I do this to you?"

"You weren't yourself. I'm alright, I swear."

"I *hurt* you, Jordan. How are you alright with that?" he demanded.

"Because we have bigger fish to fry. We'll worry about it later. Besides, I'd rather not discuss it in present company."

With that, I turned, glaring at the demon. "You're welcome, by the way. You could have at least tried to defend yourself, you prick."

Belial stood, dusting himself off and grinning at me. "Why? I knew you would come to my defense. Isn't that your thing?"

It took me a few seconds to process what he'd just told me. "So you took that blow just because you knew I'd stop him? Are you getting off on me protecting you?"

"Getting off is such a crass term, my pet."

I punched him in the face. It felt extremely good. Unfortunately, it only made him chuckle and wipe his split lip in amusement.

"What about that?" I sneered. "That feel good?"

"Delicious," he purred, licking the blood from his fingers. I balled my hands into fists, considering aiming for his crotch this time, but I decided it wasn't worth it.

"Really? How about I give it a shot?" Michael snarled, stepping forward, but I raised my hand to stop him.

"Don't bother. We're running out of time as it is. Let's just go so we can get Juliana back and end this nightmare."

"Ah, ah, ah," Belial said, crooking a finger at me when I began walking away. "Let's see the goods first, dear Jordan."

I scowled, reached into the large pocket of my capris, and withdrew the fruit. His reptilian eyes lit up with interest, but I stuffed it back in my pants after only a couple seconds.

"There. Now let's go."

"As you wish, my pet."

I glared at him as he passed me. "I should have let him kill you."

Belial met my gaze and a slow smile grew across his lips. "But you didn't."

Damn him.

He picked up on the first ring.

"Hello?"

"Hey, Gabe."

A short silence. Then, he spoke and his voice was stiff. "Jordan. I take it you got the fruit."

"Yeah. Belial's sending word to Mulciber. According to him, it's some sort of grape vine trick that archdemons use. We'll be in the air shortly."

"Very well. Meet you there."

"Wait," I said, biting my bottom lip. I was taking a chance here. He could very well have hung up already and I wasn't about to call him back. Even I had my limit.

"Yes?"

"Look, I know we're not exactly *simpatico* with each other right now, but could you answer a question for me? Please?"

A few seconds of quiet. I could practically hear him fighting with himself in his head. In the end, he sighed. "Sure. What is it?"

I sat on the closed toilet, crossing my legs and folding one arm around my stomach. Michael was in the bedroom pacing. I didn't want him to hear this conversation so I'd taken a shower to give myself an excuse to escape. "It's going to be an unpleasant question. You're welcome to choose not to answer."

"Go on."

I took a deep breath. "Is it possible for a demon to revert back to his previous angelic state?"

"What would lead you to believe that could happen?" he asked, sounding both surprised and suspicious at the same time. Couldn't blame him.

I played with the end of my ponytail, relieved we weren't having this talk face-to-face because his expression was probably disapproving. "Promise you won't tell Michael what I'm about to tell you."

"Jordan—"

"Promise," I said with a firmer tone.

"Fine. I promise."

I forced the words out of my throat. "When we were still in Miami, I asked Belial if he was in love with me. He didn't say yes, of course…but he didn't say no either. And I know it's ridiculous to think he could be in love with me because that's impossible, but I've been noticing something about his behavior lately. He's still a bastard, he's still a killer, and he's still soulless piece of shit, but there have been a couple of times where he seemed like he was more than that. Like maybe part of him isn't completely evil."

"Can you give me an example?"

"After Avriel died, I…wasn't in good shape. He comforted me. And I'm not talking about a pat on the shoulder or a cheer-up speech. He hugged me. He told me I was going to have to accept that I am both good and evil if I want to reach my potential someday. Hell, he didn't even try to make a pass at me. I'm not saying this wasn't all just part of his master plan, but I wanted to know if something like that could be possible. Just for the sake of my own sanity, if nothing else."

"I have to be honest here," Gabriel said. "I've never heard of something like this happening before. But at the same time, you may have a point. It may not be possible for him to revert back into an angel, but it is likely that spending time around you has caused him to fall into his old angelic habits."

"Really?"

"Think about it. How does Belial choose to manipulate you? He lies. He tells you what you want to hear. So, in effect, he thinks he is playing a role to win you just like he did with Zora. However, perhaps he's not actually pretending. Part of him may genuinely care for you and that is the part he has tapped into as he tries to seduce you. I doubt he realizes it himself. He considers it to be nothing more than a character to play so he can get what he wants."

"I see. So do you think there may be some good in him?"

"I wouldn't know. But I suppose crazier things have happened."

"Tell me about it," I muttered, absently touching the spot on my elbow where there had been a scrape. Michael had healed it on the way back to the city. He hadn't said much after that since he was still shaken up about blacking out. I wanted to comfort him, but we were still at an impasse in our relationship. We weren't ready for reconciliation yet, not hardly.

"Now answer my question: why do you want to know?"

"I'm not considering his offer," I said. "I would never. I still want him dead and I hope it's my doing. But he did help me and I wanted to put something to rest in my head in case I don't make it out of this mess alive. If I have unfinished business when I die, I might stick around."

"Point taken. But I don't believe that is the whole truth."

"Gabe—"

"You're trying to justify whatever interest you have in him. Don't deny it. I can hear it in your voice. You may not love him, but he has found a way to bury himself beneath your skin and that scares you. I don't sympathize, but I do understand what is happening, probably better than Michael does because I've been on Earth longer. I know what temptation feels like. He doesn't. He's only had eyes for you since he met you and so he is incapable of comprehending that you can be attracted to someone else, especially someone who is his polar opposite. Does that sound about right?"

I sighed. "Why are you so damn perceptive?"

"Comes with the territory. God's Messenger and all that."

"You should be more disappointed in me."

"That would accomplish nothing. The important thing is that you have not given in to your desires. You still fight them. It's admirable. Millions of women have fallen for Belial. You're the only one who has remained strong. Don't hate yourself for being attracted to him. Find a way to conquer it. That is all you can do for now."

"I'll try my best. Thank you for listening. I'm sorry for hurting you. I really am. I love you, Gabriel, and I know I don't say it enough. You were there for me when I had nothing. I appreciate everything you've done for me through the years. I wish I could pay you back somehow."

He let out a soft breath, one that broke my heart. "Don't. I may not be happy with you, but I would never ask you to repay me. You've done enough, more than any Seer should have to do in their lifetime. And I love you as well, you sarcastic, cynical little curmudgeon."

I laughed, only because it was to hide the fact that he was making me cry. He always tried to cheer me up whenever things got heavy between us. "I have to go. Got that big day ahead of me."

"Yes, you do. Be careful, Jordan."

"I will. Bye."

"Goodbye."

CHAPTER THIRTY-FOUR

JORDAN

I had assumed that screwing up my marriage and getting people I loved killed had been my worst fears realized. I was wrong. Mulciber calling the shots on this little hostage exchange was much worse. Since I found out about the prophecy, I had been trying to figure out where the one thousand people in danger would come from but never came up with anything concrete. Unfortunately, it turned out to be on a boat.

We caught a nine-hour flight to Tromsø, Norway—a city north of the Arctic Circle. Mulciber instructed us to hitch a ride on the MS Midnatsol, the largest cruise liner running past the city. She would have already boarded with Juliana at a different port and then meet us on the ninth deck just before midnight on the 31st, when the gates of Hell were the closest to open. She wanted plenty of people around to ensure her own safety and that we didn't try to snatch the child out of her grasp in the confusion. She also demanded Belial's presence, mostly so she could rub her supposed victory in his face. After he found this out, he called her a "cock-juggling thunder-cunt." As much as I hated him, I agreed whole-heartedly.

I checked my watch for what had to be the billionth time. Less than fifteen minutes to midnight. My hands were shaking, and not just from the bitter cold surrounding us. The ship drifted quietly through the frigid waters and a tiny slice of the moon reflected off of the waves it made below. I was bundled up in a huge parka with black gloves over my hands and the fruit from the tree in my left pocket. It hung close to my thigh, a heavy weight, reminding me of its importance every time it bumped into me.

Every sound made me flinch, from the low rumbling cracks of ice chunks sliding off the occasional floe to the sound of Michael's boots on the wooden deck as he paced behind me. Belial had paid off the crew to get us this secluded spot on the ship so late at night. Every so often, I heard a distance voice from the other side, but no one would see or hear us tonight.

I forced myself to think about something else. Most prominently, what my life would be like if nothing in the past week had happened. I'd be lying on the couch watching TV and waiting for Michael's call. He had this annoying habit of sneaking and changing my ringtone to something different every other week. Last week, it had been "Big Bad Handsome Man" by Imelda May. Arrogant of him, but then again, that was part of his M.O. Lauren always made fun of me when she overheard whatever ridiculous new song he picked.

Not that he was any better, mind you. His ringtone for me was currently "Fascinating New Thing" by Semisonic. He was a sucker for smart teen comedies. On a more disturbing note, I'd caught a bit of my ringtone on Belial's personal cell for the temporary phone he got me—"I Can't Decide" by Scissor Sisters. Typical.

The cold feeling in my lungs sprouted through my veins as my thoughts drifted back to Lauren. She'd never forgive me for what I'd done. Lauren loved hard, but she hated being lied to. Her sorry ass ex-husband had ensured that she built a wall around her heart and if anyone dug their way out, they were out for good. I couldn't help wondering what she had told Lily, if she had lied to her if the child overheard the news or if she told her the truth. It was a situation I couldn't picture in my head, having to decide whether to tell your daughter if her Auntie Jordan was a murderer. She would have to be the strongest mother alive to choose either path. I admired her for that, even now.

"Keep pacing and you'll wear a hole in the boat," Belial's smooth voice interrupted my morose thoughts. He was leaning against the railing to my right, tracking Michael's tight circle a few feet away. I simply couldn't quantify how he could be so damn calm with hell literally about to break loose in several minutes. His "perfectly sculpted" ass would be on the line too, but I couldn't tell in the least if he cared. Belial always had a backup plan, after all.

Not surprisingly, Michael ignored him. Even in the moonlight, I could see the dark spots beneath his eyes. He too hadn't been sleeping well, and the jet lag from all our recent flights meant he was running on empty just like I was. I had urged him to try and rest, but he wouldn't listen. I couldn't blame him. With so much at stake, I hadn't slept either.

Belial sighed out a stream of smoke, the lit tip of the cigarette becoming a tiny orange beacon in the darkness the next time he inhaled. He caught me looking and smirked.

"What? No comments from the Peanut Gallery?"

I glared. "Got nothing to say to you."

"Really? Would you rather I fill the silence?"

"No. Keep your tongue behind your teeth where it belongs."

He licked his lips, the smirk widening into a grin as he flicked the used cig over the side of the ship. "You know *exactly* where my tongue belongs."

Anger flared through my upper body, warming me up in an instant. I took a deep breath, fighting the urge to punch him. "I cannot express how not in the mood I am right now."

"Not in the mood, you say? I don't recall that being a problem the other night."

I froze. He wouldn't dare bring that up. Not now.

Michael stopped pacing, tilting his head enough to cast a suspicious eye over the two of us. "What's he talking about?"

"Nothing," I said through my teeth. "He's just trying to push my buttons."

Belial laughed—a soft, intimate sound in the dark. "Which ones? The ticklish spot beneath your right ear or the one behind your left thigh? And I seem to recall an especially sensitive one between your—"

I launched myself at him before he could finish the sentence. "You son of a—"

Michael's arm looped around my stomach, holding me back just in time. My fist missed Belial's nose by mere inches. I opened my mouth to finish screaming obscenities at the smug bastard, but then a sultry female voice cut through the air, catching my attention.

"Am I interrupting?"

I stared past Belial's shoulder to see Mulciber walking towards us from the other end of the deck, half of her swathed in shadows. She wore a brown mink coat and black gloves. One hand was wrapped around Juliana's wrist. She led the child and as they got closer, I could see the little girl's red-rimmed eyes and wet cheeks. The wound in my heart reopened and bled at the sight.

"Juliana," I whispered before I could help myself. She spotted me and tried to run forward, but Mulciber jerked her backwards. I instinctively tried to move towards her, but Michael held me in place, his tall form rigid against my back like a pillar.

"I'm so happy to see you made it here in one piece," the female demon purred, keeping a secure four feet away from us.

"You must be awfully tired with that fruit burning a hole in your pocket."

She stretched out her hand, smiling. "Allow me to unburden you."

Michael kept me in his grip, seeming unsure of what I'd do on my own, and spoke. "The girl first, then you get your damned prize, demon."

She shook her head, scattering dark strands of hair across her face. "Sorry, but that's not how it works in the hostage world. It's time for Jordan to do her job."

"I'm not doing shit until you let her go," I snarled.

She sighed, a bored sound, but I knew it was just an act. Then, in a blur of movement, she reached down and broke Juliana's pinky finger. The four-year-old screamed, a high-pitched wail that echoed off the water, and I lost control of myself.

"You fucking bitch, *I'll kill you!*"

Michael wrapped both arms around me as I struggled with every inch of my strength to get to her, to rip out her eyes and throw them into the ocean, to tear out her ribs and spear her lungs with them, to set her on fire and bathe in the ashes. I hated her more than anything on this earth. I would see her burn. I would make her pay.

In my rage, I bellowed out the only coherent thought in my mind.

"Gabriel, take the goddamn shot!"

His voice echoed in my ear, three words, all firm with resolve. "You got it."

Mulciber's brown eyes widened for a millisecond before a gunshot ripped through the clearing. A cloud of blood exploded out of one side of her skull as the bullet tore through the bone and grey matter, splattering it on the shiny wooden floor. Juliana fell to the side, curling up into a ball by the railing, too hurt and scared to move. Mulciber's body twitched and slumped over, her eyes rolled back until only the whites showed.

Michael finally let me go. I raced towards the broken child, scooping her up in my arms and hugging her with all my might. I buried my face in her curly hair, sobbing and not caring that Belial would see my weakness.

"I'm sorry, I'm sorry, I'm sorry, I'm so fucking sorry," I whispered over and over again, rubbing her back to try and soothe her. Behind me, I caught snippets of Belial and Michael's conversation.

"You failed to mention the sniper rifle."

"It was on a need-to-know basis."

"What kind of ammo did you use?"

"Silver blessed from the Pope himself. So don't try anything funny if the mood strikes you."

Once I composed myself somewhat, I turned my head. "Guys, we need to get Juliana to a doctor as soon as possible."

The girl shifted in my arms, catching my attention. She spoke, and I was surprised that it was in perfect English. "That won't be necessary."

I drew back, trying to see her face. "What did you say?"

She opened her eyes and then I saw them. Her pupils.

They were slits.

Mulciber had just possessed Juliana.

Then, a second later, I felt a knife beneath my chin. She held a wicked curved blade that was almost larger than her entire forearm yet slender enough to fit in a child's coat pocket. I didn't move an inch, staying where I knelt next to her previous body.

I couldn't see Michael or Belial behind me, but I knew both of them hadn't moved either when they realized what was happening. Mulciber kept one hand on the back of my neck, forcing me to hold her in my arms because if I let go, she'd slit my throat.

"Now, then. I wasn't finished," she said in the Brazilian child's delicate voice. "Jordan is going to be lowered into a lifeboat. We will go out to the Leviathan's resting place and awaken it. Once this is done, you're all free to burn like the insects you are."

"Listen to me, you antediluvian, scum-sucking mammet," Michael said in a slow, low voice that carried the threat of death on its back. "You put that knife down and let her go or so help me God, I'll rip your pathetic soul out of that girl and decorate the lowest level of Hell with its entrails."

"Pretty words, Mikey, but harmless." She faced me, jerking her head upward. "Stand. And if one word of Latin exits any of your lips, I'm gonna carve my name into her jugular."

I stood up one painful inch at a time, keeping a death grip on her borrowed body. She was right. The angle of the knife meant I couldn't talk without it scraping my throat, making an exorcism impossible on my part or Michael's. Gabriel was perched on an ice floe several yards away, too far to perform one himself.

"Gabriel?" Michael spoke into the link he and I shared in our ears.

"No shot. She's too damned close. I'd hit Jordan."

Mulciber was near enough to hear his response with her clinging to me like a limpet. She giggled, a horrible sound coming out of Juliana's mouth. "Told you so. Now then, Belial, would you kindly lower the lifeboat for us?"

I still couldn't see him, but I could hear the utter contempt in his tone. "I'm not your whipping boy, bitch."

"I'd never accuse you of being such, but since you're in love with Little Miss B-Cups, I suggest you do what I tell you to do unless you'd like to watch her die...again."

Silence. Nothing but the lapping sounds of the waves against the side of the ship. Would he let her murder me? It all came down to this. Belial had killed me once. Was twice enough?

Then, he walked past us in a quick, angry stride to head for the end of the ship with the emergency lifeboats on them. We were on Deck Nine and the boats were attached to the side of Deck Six, meaning we'd have to go down the stairs.

Michael shoved Mulciber's former body into the ocean and cleaned up the mess the best he could. He stepped forward, as if to follow us, but Mulciber spoke again. "Ah, ah, ah, pretty boy. You're staying put. And this time, I mean it."

She looked at me. "Put him under a blood spell. I hear you're good at those."

My blood ran cold. "No."

She dug the blade in harder. Another millimeter and I'd bleed out. I glowered at the demon. "Go sit on a knife, you sack of vaginal discharge."

Mulciber started to press on my neck again, but Michael spoke before she could. "Jordan."

I turned a bit, enough to see him. Half of his face was cast in shadow, but I could still see the pain and the anger in it anyway. "Do it."

"Michael—"

He shook his head only once. "I can't watch you die. Not again. Just do it."

A lump formed, one so large I could barely swallow it as I stepped towards him. Tears stung in the back of my eyes as I raised my left wrist enough for Mulciber to cut it. Blood spilled outward, soaking my glove, hot and sticky.

I lifted my arm and pressed my hand to his chest, my voice trembling. "With blood, I bind you to this spot. Walk no more until the spell is broken."

Red light shot outward from the handprint on his chest and he buckled to his knees, his face contorted, but he didn't cry out. So much pain and it was all my fault. For a fleeting second, I thought about letting Mulciber kill me. Anything was better than facing the fact that Michael was in agony at my feet once again.

"Much better," Mulciber simpered. "Now get moving. And Gabriel, dearest, you had better keep your distance or I'll make you join him."

She motioned for me to walk and I followed Belial towards the other end of the ship. Now that we were risking being seen, Mulciber moved the knife down from my neck and held it between her body and mine, the tip digging in under my left breast. One quick plunge upward and I'd be dead on the spot.

"I don't get it," I said under my breath as we descended the stairwell. "Demons aren't supposed to be able to possess people without the mind breaking down."

"Demons cannot possess adults with ease, but children are different," Mulciber answered with the utmost smugness as I walked. "Their personalities and minds are soft and malleable. Your precious Juliana has already suffered massive amounts of trauma. Taking her over was a cakewalk."

"I hope you're enjoying this because it doesn't matter if the Leviathan rises or not. I will take my sweet time killing you."

"I look forward to it," the female demon replied.

At last, we reached Deck Six. The rowboats were massive and hard to maneuver, but Belial was no slump so he could handle it on his own. He said nothing as he worked, his face unnervingly blank. I almost wanted to hear him mock me or say something disparaging to the beast holding me hostage, but then a frightening truth hit. For the first time ever, Belial might have accepted the fact that we weren't going to win this battle. I wanted him to have a backup plan like he always did, an Ace up his sleeve, but this time, he met me with nothing but silence. We couldn't win. We just couldn't.

When everything was ready, I climbed inside, moving towards the front of the lifeboat, but she stopped me. "Oh, no. With you at the controls, you could throw us both overboard. Belial, darling, would you be so kind as to drive us out?"

The derision in his eyes was so intense I could practically taste it in my mouth like the burn of whiskey. His energy frothed around his body, so thick it reminded me of a swarming mass of bees. Still, he maneuvered himself over the side and continued lowering us into the water — which was twice as hard to do without help. We hit the surface of the ocean with a wild smack, and I noticed the knife nick my skin as a result as she had moved it back up to my neck. The air was ten times colder down here so I barely even felt it, nor did I feel the wound on my wrist. The only thing I could still feel was the wetness of the blood in my glove.

"Sit," Mulciber ordered. "And don't move an inch until we're there. Get moving, Beli."

He headed towards the front while I took a seat in the first row. A moment later, he fired up the engine and we pulled away from the ship, heading into the pitch black before us. The lifeboat's spotlight was our only guide. I didn't know how Belial and Mulciber knew the location of the Leviathan but I suspected their master had told them, the same as he told them about the fruit.

The MS Midnatsol disappeared from sight after a while and my hope vanished with it. The way I saw it, there was only one way out of this mess. I had tried to avoid it for so long. I wanted every available alternative. I wanted another option, something, anything, but every avenue had been exhausted. Belial showed no signs of having a plan and so it was left up to me. I had failed so many times, but I would not fail again.

"Stop. We're here."

We reached a huge, flat ice floe that stretched for hundreds of feet, safely hidden from the prying eyes of the ship or anyone else for that matter. Belial shut off the engine and climbed onto it, finding a craggy chunk to tie off the lifeboat on. Mulciber made me follow him further onto the ice, which looked midnight blue with the weak moonlight around us.

We walked for a bit until we reached a section of ice with what looked like some sort of insignia carved into it. I couldn't figure out what it was until I realize I was looking at a sculpture of a creature no one had laid eyes on for centuries. Its face was a strange mix between a lizard and some sort of squid. The snout was long and ribbed with two nostrils at the end and long, curling lines coming out of it like whiskers or tentacles. Its jaws were lined with needle-like teeth. It was repulsive.

"Let's get to it, Seer," Mulciber said. "Take out the fruit and place it in the center. I may be in a Seer's body, but the ceremony won't work if I do it."

I took a deep breath. "No."

She groaned—an almost immature sound. "Shall I come up with another threat or would you prefer that I break another finger on this child's hand?"

"Neither one is necessary," I said in a quiet voice.

"I'm not going to do it. We're alone out here. There's no one else for you to threaten except for the two of us."

While she was distracted, I grabbed her arm and pinned it with the tip to my chest so she couldn't threaten Juliana's body with it. She struggled, unable to wedge it from my grip because of her tiny hand, not even with her demon strength.

"So do what you've got to do. Kill me. Because I am not going to let you hurt another person."

"You insignificant worm!" she screamed. "I will cut out your lungs and use them as candy dishes if you don't awaken the Leviathan."

"Do your worst. I died once. Can't be that bad the second time around."

Enraged, her arm flexed to drive the knife inside me, but Belial appeared behind her, grabbing both of her arms. He slammed her down into the ice, cracking it, and shouted,

"Now! Exorcise her!"

I dropped to my knees, drawing a cross in the air and chanting the incantation frantically in Latin. "*In nomine Dei, proferres uirgo!*"

She roared, unable to move with Belial holding her down. I raised my voice until it echoed through the clearing, bouncing off the frozen corridors surrounding us. Juliana's body arched upward once, twice, writhing as Mulciber's black soul tore from it inch by inch. At last, a dark shape rose from the child's body and dissipated into mist, proving that she had been sent back to Hell where she belonged. Juliana shuddered a final time and went limp. I checked her pulse, relieved to find her alive.

Without thinking, I threw myself into Belial's arms. He held me close, saying nothing, because he didn't really need to. I could feel the tears pouring out of my eyes, carving heated ridges in my frigid cheeks.

"Thank you," I whispered. "Thank you for saving her."

~ 336 ~

His hand drifted down my side, stroking me in comfort. "You're welcome."

I started to draw back, but he wouldn't let go. His arm wandered to my left hand as if he were going to hold it, but then something else happened. I felt something round being pressed against my palm, the one still stained with blood, and then he laid it on the ice behind us. I opened my eyes only to find that he had slipped the fruit out of my coat pocket and placed it in the Leviathan's mouth with my fingers around it.

No.

Please God, *no.*

I tore away from him, scrambling for the fruit, but in an instant, it sank below the ice into the water below and disappeared in a rush of bubbles. My breath turned into panicked gulps of air as I knelt there in the dark, unable to believe what had just happened. Belial stood up. I stayed where I was, paralyzed.

"Why?" I whispered.

He met my gaze. There was something mournful in his eyes, and yet there wasn't. I couldn't find a word for the way he was looking at me. It just existed somehow. His lips parted and I almost didn't hear his reply because it came out so hushed.

"It's who I am."

CHAPTER THIRTY-FIVE

JORDAN

The ground beneath my feet rumbled like there was thunder trapped underneath it, but I couldn't tell if it was really happening or if I were hallucinating that my world was crumbling. The worst had finally happened. All of my fighting, all of my sacrifices, all of my pain, meant nothing now because I had failed. A hollow spot yawned and reached outward from inside me. Despair filled my veins and sucked me down into its clutches.

Faintly, I realized I might have been slipping into shock, but then Belial knelt and swept up Juliana, shoving her into my arms. "Take the child and go. It won't be long before the Leviathan emerges."

I raised my tearstained eyes, knowing that he could see both the sorrow and the hatred in them as I looked at him. "What do you care? It's the end. She and I are both about to die anyway."

His expression hardened. "Leave this place, Seer. It would be a shame for all of your hard work saving my daughter to go to waste."

I didn't want to believe him, but he was right. I had gone this far to protect one child. It would make no sense to let her die now. My legs shook but held as I stood up, raising my voice over the sound of the ice cracking around us.

"I hope it was worth it, Belial. If I live through this, I swear that I will spend every waking moment of my life finding a way to destroy you."

He stepped close, his eyes piercing, his voice heavy with emotions that I would never understand and never care to understand again. "I would have it no other way, my pet."

A kiss burned on my lips seconds before he shoved me away. I ran for the lifeboat, firing up the engine and speeding away just as the ice floe ripped apart. I never looked back, squinting through the inky darkness to catch sight of the Midnatsol.

When the cruise ship reappeared in my spotlight, I rode up beside it and touched the link in my ear. "Gabriel?"

He didn't answer. Then, I heard the unmistakable whoosh of wings and then the boat rocked to the side as he landed behind me, the sniper rifle slung over his broad back. His eyes immediately snapped to Juliana's motionless form on one of the seats.

"She's alive," I said.

"I know. I overheard. Everything." The last word came out accusatory and it hurt. He probably hadn't seen what happened and thus it made him suspicious. He was disappointed in me. I had never felt that from him before, not in person. Shame curled around me like a suffocating blanket, but I shoved it aside.

"Where's Michael?"

"On the deck, still trying to fight off the blood spell. Come."

He offered his hand. I picked up Juliana and he wrapped one arm around me, launching into the air. He flew us to the other side of the ship, landing a few feet away from where Michael was, still on his hands and knees, trying to break the spell.

I handed Juliana to Gabriel and then ran to him, lifting my hand just outside of the circle. "Untie the bonds of blood once made and walk the world again."

The eerie red imprint of my palm on his chest disappeared. He let out a gasp as the spell vanished, releasing him. I caught him before he could collapse and buried my face in the side of his neck. I couldn't look at him, not now, not after what I'd done.

"Jor," he wheezed, trying to catch his breath. "The Leviathan…?"

"I'm sorry," I mumbled. "I'm so sorry. I tried to stop it, but I wasn't strong enough."

He straightened, pulling away, and cupped my cheek in his hand. "We're still here. That's what counts."

He stood, shaky at first, and then found his footing. "Get Juliana to a doctor and then get the hell out of here."

I frowned. "I'm not leaving."

He sent me a harsh look. "Now is not the time to be unreasonable."

"I woke the damn thing up. I'm not going to let you clean up the mess alone."

"What are you going to do, Jordan? Use your vast arsenal of rapier wit on it?"

"There's got to be a way to stop it —"

"Yes, it's called a war."

"Excuse me," Gabriel interrupted. "But we haven't got all night with the Apocalypse brewing and whatnot. Jordan, get this child medical attention and you can continue arguing after we've saved these people."

I tore my gaze away from Michael, forcing myself to listen to reason. "Alright. Keep the link open so I know where you are. And be careful."

I gathered the little girl in my arms as Gabriel snorted. "A little late for that, I'm afraid."

"That's never stopped you before."

A ghost of a smile touched his lips. "Point taken. Now get moving, Amador."

I hurried away, my footsteps pounding almost as loud as my heartbeat. Once more, I found myself running to save someone I had put in harms' way.

Bad habits die hard.

MICHAEL

"What's the plan?" Gabriel asked, fixing his arctic stare on me rather than in the direction of the oncoming threat. So far, all I had heard was the ice cracking apart. I knew things wouldn't stay quiet for long. They never did.

"Sink the ship."

"What?"

"Fly down and punch a hole in the side, somewhere with the lowest risk of casualties. That'll force them to evacuate the passengers. They'll head back to the nearest town and at least they'll have a head start. Besides, less witnesses means less mess to clean up if we make it out of this thing alive. I'll gather the troops and strategize."

"What about Jordan?"

I hesitated. The two sides of my soul were pulling in opposite directions, and it scared me. Maybe the angelic part had been a soft still voice that I hadn't realized was getting louder over the past few weeks. Now that voice was like a bullhorn. He wanted to get rid of her because she was a distraction, my Achilles' heel, the permanent thorn in my side. I couldn't fight as well when I knew she was in trouble. But the husband in me knew it wouldn't be right to remove her from the equation just because she was human. What right did I have to stop her from trying to help? After all, this wasn't just on my head — it was on the both of us.

"We'll worry about that later," I said finally. "Go."

Gabriel gave me a curt nod and hopped over the side of the ship, his golden wings stretched to carry him on the wind. I shrugged out of my cumbersome parka and then closed my eyes, concentrating until my own wings sprouted from my back.

I leapt off of the deck and soared towards the place where I could feel an unstoppable power bubbling just beneath the surface of the water. I found a nearby ice floe and perched, scanning the spot where the creature would rise. Presumably, Belial had gone down below to assume command of the beast.

I remembered reading the report on the previous battle with the Leviathan. I had deployed my best angels to take care of the job because it would be tactically improbable for me to intervene. If I had gotten dragged into Hell, someone else would become the new Commander, but back then none of my soldiers were quite ready for that kind of responsibility. Now, things were different. If the unthinkable happened, someone could ensure the safety of Heaven. Someone more worthy than me.

I heard the sound of metal crunching in the distance and knew that Gabriel had followed orders. I closed my eyes and ascended to the astral plane. The cold night of the Arctic Circle disappeared. I opened my eyes to a field of white and thousands of angels armed to the teeth, waiting for my command. I stood on the crest of the hill, dragging my gaze across them.

"Soldiers," I said, slipping on my most authoritative voice. "Once again, I ask you to lend me your metal. Some of you may have heard rumors. Unfortunately, they are true. The Leviathan has been awakened and is threatening the safety of the people we are charged with protecting. Many of you have served with me before so you know what to expect, but some of you do not. The Leviathan is unlike any other creature in God's creation. It is the living embodiment of evil. It is not just a monster. Its mouth is the gate to Hell, meaning that anything from the world of the damned can come through at any time. Your task will be containment. Gabriel, Raphael, and I will concentrate on sealing its jaws while you make sure that none of the entities escaping the Hellmouth are able to claim an innocent life. I have faith in each of you. I know that the odds are stacked against us, but I have never seen a more formidable, honorable force in this universe or any other one. I want you to go down there and show that demon what the true power of Heaven is like. Do not give that piece of filth the satisfaction of killing even one of you. Understood?"

Thousands of voices spoke in unison. "Yes, Commander."

I lifted my hand. Seconds later, my sword came flying down. I gripped it and the silver armor flowed down my arm, over my chest, across my back, until I was completely covered. It solidified into metal that bore the markings of my most important battles in history — of demons and monsters falling before my blade. The pieces were lightweight and separated at my joints for maximum flexibility. The helmet left only the center of my face visible. I only wore the ensemble in the direst of times, but it felt like slipping into a comfortable pair of jeans and t-shirt. It felt right.

I allowed a smirk to rest upon my lips.

"Wreak havoc, my friends."

In a flash, I returned to my body on Earth, which had also been outfitted with my sword and armor, and looked up at the sky. Huge grey clouds had formed in my wake, lightning slashing the black with white, thunder crashing like great cymbals. Seconds later, angels poured out from the billowing mists of the clouds, some of them choosing to hover in the air to wait for the Leviathan to surface, others taking spots on the icebergs nearby.

Not long afterward, Gabriel and Raphael came to stand with me, one on either side, both decked out in their warrior garbs — gold and bronze, respectively.

"Do you think we can win this?" Raphael asked.

"Doesn't matter what I think," I said. "We don't have a choice."

Just then, the last bubbles in the water of the clearing stopped. All I could hear was my own breathing and the sound of thousands of wings flapping. The clouds slid aside, pouring moonlight across the placid sea. A low sound emanated through the clearing, the kind that made my bones hum inside my body. The average person would have thought it was a whale, but I knew better. It was the Call.

The Leviathan's head burst from the water first. It was about half the size of the Midnatsol — over sixty-five meters in length and about half the width. The top of its skull looked like a lizard; it had black and green scales rather than skin, and two enormous yellow eyes with pupils like slits. Its upper jaw was laced with gigantic razor-sharp teeth around the ridges of its gums, but that was just protection. The inside of its mouth was another matter entirely. Thick, slimy pink tentacles burgeoned from its throat like a second mouth with a sickening, pulsating black hole at the center. This was where Lucifer had hidden his greatest treasure — the only other entrance to Hell besides the Demons' Door. Old Scratch himself could no longer walk the earth, but that didn't mean his flunkies couldn't.

The Leviathan's neck was covered in poisonous spines that led down to its body, which was easily four hundred feet in length from chest to tail. Its four limbs were long and powerful, ending in webbed feet with deadly claws at the ends.

Belial stood on the creature's forehead, a dripping wet pale beacon in the night. His feet were firmly planted and he held an antenna in each gloved hand, feeding his thoughts directly into the Leviathan as they were now linked.

Fully risen, the Leviathan bellowed a hoarse, unearthly growl that I knew would echo for miles and send chills down the spines of all who heard it.

I gripped my sword as the familiar rush of adrenaline pumped through me. At long last. War.

"Well done, Commander," Belial called out mockingly. "You did not disappoint. Your armada is impressive. I look forward to slaughtering them all."

I smiled. "I told you I'd enjoy sending you back to Hell, demon. Today I get to keep my word."

I raised my sword, lifting my voice so my soldiers could hear the declaration. "Attack!"

My angels let out a fierce war cry and launched themselves at the Leviathan. The monster roared a second time and the hole inside its mouth opened wide. A ghastly brownish orange light filled the clearing. The nauseating stench of sulfur permeated the air. Seconds later, dozens of scavenger demons with leathery black wings soared from the Hellmouth, their tiny sharp teeth aiming for the throats of my men. They were in charge of the level of Hell on the outermost ring, the First Circle, reserved for the least sinful patrons — mindless bat-like beasts that fed on fear and desolation.

I turned to Gabriel and Raphael. "Our best bet is to concentrate all our efforts on knocking Belial off that thing, or killing him. Once the Leviathan no longer has a host, it'll be slower and less intelligent. That'll give us the edge we need to lock its jaws. Belial will want to focus on me, so I'll serve as the bait while you two find any vulnerabilities that you can."

They both nodded. I threw myself off the side of the ice floe, slashing at the odd demon that tried to attack as I made a beeline for the Leviathan's face. The angels around me followed orders to the letter, chasing any demons that tried to escape the clearing. We were at least a mile out from the ship where the people were being evacuated, but I knew the next wave of creatures would be harder to stop than the scavengers so time was a factor, especially with the Leviathan swimming towards them.

Belial saw me coming and aimed the Leviathan's head at me, trying to bite me in half as I flew past. The foul stench of the creature overwhelmed my nostrils and made my eyes tear, but I focused on where he was standing and tried to find an opening. He ducked when I swept overhead, swinging at him from behind. Damn it. He was too fast, even with all the confusion around him. I couldn't get too close because he could move its mouth around to me in an instant, and if one of those tentacles caught my ankles I'd be sucked into Hell.

Gabriel and Raphael moved in perfect synchronization, swiping at him, but it proved futile as well. He always saw them coming. Even if all three of us attacked, we wouldn't be able to reach him, not even with energy attacks. I needed a Plan B, and quickly.

The link in my ear beeped, distracting me. "How's it going out there?"

"Not good," I answered Jordan with a grimace, slashing a scavenger demon in half. It disappeared in a puff of ash.

"Are you clear?" I asked.

"No. I told you, I'm staying."

I gritted my teeth. "Damn it, Jordan! For once in your life, listen to me and get the hell out of here!"

"If you want me gone, you'd better send someone to drag me out. I'm not leaving. Juliana's safe and half of the passengers are already on lifeboats. Besides, I think I might have a plan."

I paused, trying to figure out if I should listen to her or not. So far, we were at a disadvantage and my soldiers had their hands full with the first bunch of monsters. It would only get worse from here. We didn't have time for worse.

"What plan?"

"Meet me on Deck Nine and I'll explain."

I cursed under my breath, hailing Gabriel. "Keep trying. I'll be right back."

"Ten-four," he answered.

I turned in the air and flew towards the slowly sinking Midnatsol, staying high so that no one would spot me. When I reached the ninth deck, my wife was waiting for me.

I landed, narrowing my eyes at her with impatience. "Make it quick."

"The fruit is what woke the Leviathan, right? What if we removed it?"

"What the hell do you mean remove it?"

She took a deep breath. "What if I got inside its stomach and took the fruit out? Would that weaken it enough for you to send it back under?"

I stared at her. "Have you lost your mind?"

"Answer the question, Michael."

I fought not to shoot a string of obscenities in her direction. "Theoretically, it would undo the awakening and the Leviathan would

~ 345 ~

fall back into its dormant state. We'd still have to lock its jaws, but that wouldn't be as difficult."

"Good. Then let's do it."

"No. Absolutely not. That's the worst plan I've ever heard in my life."

"And you've got a better one? How long have you guys been fighting that thing? It's only going to get worse the more time we spend arguing."

"Do you understand what you're asking me to do? You don't know what it's like inside that thing. You could suffocate, you could get dissolved by stomach acid, or you could get lost. There are a million things that could go wrong. I trusted you once. Don't ask me to do it again."

I turned my back on her, ready to fly into the fray, but her voice stopped me. "I have to do this, Michael. It's my mess and I told you that I would do everything it takes to stop these people from dying."

I cast a hard look in her direction. "What makes you think you can?"

"The Book was wrong. It said that Mulciber would be controlling the Leviathan. She isn't. She's in Hell."

I froze. For the first time, I could see her point. "Wait. But that means—"

She stepped forward, imploring me. "We changed the future, Michael. Nothing is certain any more. We can fix this. I can fix this."

I opened my mouth to respond, but she kept going. "And I'm not asking you to trust me. I'm telling you that I have to face the consequences of my actions."

"But why does it always have to be you?" I asked, unable to keep my frustration at bay. "Why can't you let me do this for you?"

She smiled, surprising me. "Because your soldiers and the people in this world need you more than I do. If I die, it's just a girl dying. If you die, it could throw the entire world into chaos. That's who you are. It's who you'll always be."

An unspeakable amount of pain swarmed through me at her words. She was right. There were always lives at stake, always lives I had to save, lives that depended on my every action. She didn't have that weight on her shoulders. She was only human.

I tried to regain composure. "If I could get you in there, can you promise me that you'll come out alive and not doing anything reckless like try to kill Belial on your own?"

A determined look crossed her features. "I can promise one of the two."

I sighed. This woman would be the death of me. "That'll have to do, then. But first, you need supplies. Find a waterproof flashlight, a strong diving knife, and an oxygen tank. I'll talk to Gabriel."

She nodded, hurrying away. I touched the link in my ear. "You get all that, Gabe?"

"Yes, but I wish I hadn't," he replied in a tight voice over the sound of battle. "Are you seriously considering her cockamamie plan?"

"I heard that," Jordan chimed in with a less-than-amused voice.

I almost smiled. "It's not my first choice. How's it going on your end?"

"Badly. There are too many of these things and I can tell the next wave is on its way. We're going to need reinforcements."

"Go round them up. Raphael and I can cover you in the meantime."

"Will do."

A thought occurred to me. "Wait!"

"Yes?"

"I think I've got a less suicidal idea. Would you mind doing me a quick favor?"

"And that would be?"

"Bring Avriel with you."

A momentary shocked silence followed. "But isn't he scheduled for Judgment?"

"Tell them I authorized the order and it's just a temporary postponement of his trial. Hurry."

"Whatever you say, Commander." The link shut off. I began to pace back and forth, my mind racing to come up with a comprehensive strategy. Preferably one that didn't involve my wife getting digested by a hellbeast.

Just as Jordan returned with the supplies, I heard my link crackle again and then Gabriel's winded voice. "I'm on my way."

I raised my gaze to see Gabriel and another angel flying towards us. I couldn't help lifting an eyebrow when they landed. Souls couldn't exist on earth without bodies for more than a few minutes, hence why he needed to share one with another angel. The body they'd found for Avriel was actually a short, blonde female angel.

Gabriel caught the weird looks Jordan and I gave him and shrugged. "It was short notice. Now then, what's this idea of yours?"

I turned to Avriel. "In your extensive studies about this event, did you happen to read any literature about the Leviathan?"

She—he—nodded. "Yes, sir."

"What about the biology of the Leviathan?"

"Yes, sir."

A spot of hope at last. "Tell me everything you know."

"Well, while the Hellmouth is a portal to the underworld, the Leviathan itself is flesh and blood like any other creature. It has many supernatural qualities, but like anything else, it has organs—a brain, lungs, intestines, and so on. The esophagus leads down into three separate stomachs and the food digests slowly. The Leviathan shares more qualities with a reptile rather than a fish. In fact, it has often been said to be an amalgamation of several types of species."

"If we were to get someone inside the first stomach, could they find the fruit and take it out?"

Avriel frowned. "Theoretically? I suppose so. But I wouldn't recommend it. The first stomach may not give you too much trouble, but the other two would be the problem. You could cut your way into the first stomach and get the fruit, but as soon as its body learns that there is a foreign object inside it, the antibodies will attack and attempt to pull you into the second stomach for digestion. You would have mere minutes to get out. Otherwise, death is imminent."

"Sounds like my kind of party alright," Jordan said. "Where would I enter the stomach?"

"The scales on the Leviathan's belly are thinner than the ones on its back, much like an alligator's. However, any incision will re-seal within seconds. You'll need to find the exact spot where you entered and cut your way from inside the stomach. Cutting the same place twice gives you a better chance of getting out."

"Is there any way that Belial would be able to sense Jordan's presence and make the Leviathan throw her back up?" I asked.

Avriel shook his head. "Its stomach is much like a horse's. It can't regurgitate anything, which is also why she can't climb out of its throat. A huge membrane closes behind the esophagus."

Jordan glanced at me. "It's worth a shot."

Everyone's eyes settled on me. I let the new information swirl around in my head for a few seconds. Was this still a bad plan? Hell yes. Was it better than the alternative? Maybe. Did I have time to debate with myself? No.

"Alright," I said softly. "Jordan, you're with me. Gabe, Raph, cover us. I'm going to submerge and find a weak spot. Where would that be, Avriel?"

"The first stomach is about thirty five to forty feet from the front of its chest. Make the hole as deep as you can so it will penetrate the inner walls. And Jordan, please remember that you will have less than five minutes to get out of there."

Jordan nodded. "Thank you. I'll do my best."

She slid the flashlight into the innermost pocket of her parka, donned the diving gear, and climbed into my arms.

I glanced at Avriel one last time. "I appreciate the help. You can continue fighting down here for now in case we need you again. Make sure not to be a nuisance to your host."

"Yes, sir."

I leapt into the air, holding Jordan close and weaving past the fighting angels and snarling demons surrounding the Leviathan. It was on the move now, swimming slowly but surely towards civilization, and the next wave of monsters was dropping out of the Hellmouth now—hellhounds.

In Hell, they were five times the size of the ones on Earth, had two heads, and could swim better than sharks. I watched as the soldiers dove after them, shooting bubbles and the spray of water upward as they attacked. The corpses floated up to the top, turning the water even darker with blood and entrails. The hellhounds snapped at the heels of the angels flying overhead, dragging them down into the briny depths to drown. I set my jaw, telling myself that they could handle themselves, but I already knew there would be many casualties.

Gabriel and Raphael took the lead, making sure to keep Belial distracted while I flew to the side, searching for the right spot to dive. This was it. The moment of truth. No turning back now.

Jordan's hand brushed the back of my neck, the spot where my helmet met the chassis, so I'd look at her. She smiled, a gentle one, like the world wasn't crumbling around her and she wasn't walking into the literal belly of the beast. "It's okay. I know what I'm doing."

"Why don't I believe you?" I whispered.

She let out a tiny, hoarse laugh. "Because you're not an idiot. Wish me luck?"

I shook my head. "Wish you victory. Go get 'im, baby."

She touched the side of my face and kissed me. The chaos around me melted so that I could only feel the soft touch of her lips. It chased away the last bits of resentment and fear inside me. I knew that no matter what was going to happen, she would give it her all and she wouldn't give up. That was her strength, her center, what made me love her. Jordan never gave up on anything—not her friends, not her faith, and not me.

She broke away first, letting two last words drop from her lips. "*Te amo.*"

I returned them to her without hesitation. "*Te amo.*"

And then we dove into the darkness together.

CHAPTER THIRTY-SIX

JORDAN

There were no words for how cold the water was when Michael plunged down into it after I pulled on my oxygen mask. I nearly passed out, in fact. Distantly, I remembered reading somewhere how long it would take the average person to die in subfreezing temperatures and knew that I had probably less than two minutes before I would succumb, even though I was wearing at least four layers of clothing.

Michael swam in strong strokes towards the underbelly of the titanic creature, leaving me to cling to his shoulders as he moved. His angelic body could handle these temperatures, but I could already feel my vision starting to blacken around the edges.

Once we were underneath it, I pulled out the waterproof flashlight to help him see where we were. He scanned the area, dodging behind the Leviathan's massive clawed feet, until we reached the area Avriel had told us about. The scales here were long, flat, and appeared to be a dirty cream color.

Michael tapped my arm, signaling me to let go, so I swam alongside him as he unsheathed his sword from his waist. He shoved it into the flesh between two giant scales and began sawing at the seam. Black blood rushed outward. He kept slicing until the hole was large enough for me to fit through. I wondered if the creature could even feel it due to its immense size.

I took a deep breath, swimming upward. I grabbed the slippery ridges of the hole and forced them apart, grabbing at its insides. I felt Michael's hands at my waist, pushing me up through the sticky membrane. I could see nothing but a disgusting pink film as I burrowed into the Leviathan's innards, blindly reaching for anything to grip. My feet hit the edge of the hole and I grabbed the knife in my pocket, cutting through the last bit of skin before me.

At last, I burst free into a humid, murky, place and fell onto my knees, panting because my claustrophobia had started to kick in. I kept my eyes closed until my heart rate slowed and raised my head to figure out where I was.

A thick green fog hung in the air. The lining of the Leviathan's stomach was a filthy brown color. My boots sunk into it like mud, forcing me to learn how to balance on the squishy surface. I lifted the flashlight, keeping the knife in my other hand, and tried to get a bead on my surroundings. The "ceiling" of the stomach was about twenty feet above my head, capped off with a disgusting puckered hole. I could tell it was the membrane that Avriel had mentioned that cut off access to the throat.

Digestive fluid dripped from the curved walls around me. I stood on what appeared to be the "shore" of its stomach. I spotted a lake of stomach acid a few feet away. Bare bones and skeletons glistened on the surface—a hideous sight. The state of their decay led me to believe these were its original victims from when it was still active all those centuries ago. It might have had some sort of hibernation survival method. Yippee-skippy.

I checked my watch. I had about four and a half minutes left. Time to get to work.

I swept the flashlight back and forth, scouring the contents of the stomach not covered with green goo. I found nothing in the piles of half-eaten shellfish and miscellaneous trash and cursed my lack of luck. The fruit must have fallen in the drink, so to speak. Perfect.

I walked to the edge of the lake, searching for something to test the potency of the stomach acid. I found half of a fish and tossed it in. Nothing happened. It didn't instantly dissolve or catch on fire. Not yet, anyway. The stomach acid wasn't too deep, either—it came up to my thighs.

I heaved a sigh and waded into the abysmal muck, trying not to focus on the sucking noise my body made as it entered the thick substance around me. I breathed deep and began to feel around the bottom, plucking out any object that felt round. Another minute ticked by and I hadn't found anything yet, much to my irritation.

"Come on, where are you, you son of a bitch?" I muttered around my mouthpiece, tossing aside yet another skeleton of God-knew-what. Just then, my boot hit something solid and I bent, reaching for it. My fingers met something soft, but definitely round. I yanked upward, elated to find the fruit. There were a few holes in it and it was a great deal softer, but the fruit was still in one piece. Hallelujah.

I turned to head back to where I'd come from only to hear a bizarre sound echoing through the stomach. A growl, but not like the kind caused by hunger. Something else.

The hairs on the back of my neck stood up. I couldn't shake the dreadful feeling that something was behind me. I cocked my head to the side and that was when I saw them. The antibodies. Except they were not giant white blood cells.

They were hellhounds.

Well, of course.

Avriel, if I make it through this, I am gonna kick your ass, I thought, stuffing the fruit in my pocket and fumbling for my knife. The hellhounds here in the stomach weren't like the ones I'd faced before, which had shaggy fur, red eyes, and claws. These ones had short, slick black fur, two heads, and white eyes with no pupils. None of them flinched when my flashlight hit their faces. I realized they must have been blind, going off sound and smell alone. That at least gave me a slight advantage.

Holding my breath so they couldn't hear me, I stooped and picked up an emaciated dorsal fin that appeared to have belonged to a killer whale. Then I flung it as hard as I could behind them.

It hit the far wall of the stomach with a loud splatter. They whirled, lunging for it. I made a break for the other side, cursing the sticky stomach acid that slowed me down. I got about halfway there before the hounds realized they'd been tricked and jumped in after me. Their sleek bodies cut through the slime like a knife through butter. I'd never make it to the edge in time.

The first hound lunged for me. I threw myself backwards, holding up the knife. It plunged into the hound's chest, but the weight of the creature shoved me into the acid. I shoved its corpse away and got my feet beneath me, flailing through the mire. When I resurfaced, the stomach acid clung to my skin like mucus and I could feel a faint stinging sensation. I cleaned off as much as I could before as the other two hellhounds started closing in. I climbed onto the side of what used to be part of a whale, brandishing the knife at them as they paddled closer. I checked my watch again. Only a minute left. Shit!

The hound on the left lurched for me. I ducked. It sailed past my head and hit the opposite wall with a yelp, knocking itself out. The last one grabbed my ankle with one of its mouths, trying to drag me into the acid with it, but I stabbed the other head repeatedly, forcing it to let go. I heard growls in the distance towards the other end of the stomach where the tract led to the second one. Reinforcements were on the way.

I heard a crackling sound in my ear, realizing that I hadn't taken the mic out. The water and muck had damaged it, but I could still hear bits of words.

"Jor…find…fruit…?"

I lowered the oxygen mask, nearly gagging in the noxious air when I tried to talk. It took me a couple of tries to get a full sentence out.

"Yeah," I yelled back, wading as fast as I could to get to the spot where I'd climbed in. "If you can hear me, I'm almost out. Just hold on."

There was a faint crevice in the lining of the stomach indicating where I'd gotten in. I fell to my knees and hacked at it as hard as I could. The hounds behind me barked as they got closer.

My knife snapped in half. I screamed in frustration, shoving the broken blade in my pocket and digging with my hands instead, tearing at the thick skin until it gave out beneath me and ice cold water gushed in. Just as the nearest hound leapt for me, I shoved myself down into the hole and pulled myself out the other side. I swam into the sea, checking to see if the hound had followed me through, but the scales had already sealed up. I was free.

I swam up through the icy water until I broke the surface, tearing off my breathing apparatus and screaming for my husband. "Michael!"

Behind me, the Leviathan let out a terrible sound of agony. Our plan had worked. Its limbs slowed and it stopped swimming forward, its head shaking back and forth weakly, nearly sending Belial flying from his perch on its forehead.

Michael came soaring towards me and plucked me out of the sea, unable to stop a smile from overtaking his face.

"You're definitely a sight for sore—"

He was cut off as the Leviathan's arm smashed into us, knocking me out of his grip and sending him spinning out of control. I shrieked as I plummeted towards the water, my oxygen tank torn away, trying to brace myself, but then the huge hand came around again and caught me. It lifted me up to the top of its head where Belial stood, seething.

"You just don't know when to give up, do you?" he snarled, losing that infinite cool he always seemed to have.

My arms were pinned to my sides. I couldn't move an inch. Nothing to attack the bastard with except for sarcasm. "Sorry, Bels. It's who I am."

"Give me back the fruit and I will let you live."

"Get bent."

The Leviathan squeezed all the air out of my lungs. My vision spun in front of my eyes and my ribs began to crumple inside me, almost to the point of cracking. I tried to ignore the pain, giving him nothing but a contemptuous stare. When he saw that I wouldn't break, he let out a growl of frustration.

"Stubborn girl."

The Leviathan dropped me at his feet. I gasped in a lungful of air, shaking all over with relief that I could breathe again.

Belial let go of the creature's antennas, instead grabbing me by the throat and pulling me up against him. I struggled to no avail. His other arm crushed me into the front of his body and trapped my arms by my hips.

"It always comes down to this, doesn't it?" he murmured with a smirk. "You and me, and the end of the world. I think it's destiny, to be honest. An eternity spent playing this game until someday, one of us wins. What do you think, sweet Jordan? Am I the victor, or are you? Or are we both going to lose?"

"The only thing that's destined to be is me killing you," I said in a low voice. "It may not be today or tomorrow or the day after that, but I will make you pay and you will never hurt anyone ever again."

He leaned towards my lips, chuckling. "How could I refuse such a woman?"

He stopped a millimeter away from kissing me, speaking louder. "I wouldn't do that if I were you, archangel."

I tilted my head to see over his shoulder. Michael stood behind him, the tip of his sword resting at the base of Belial's spine. The archangel's chest was heaving and I could tell every inch of him wanted to run the demon through with his blade.

"Why not?" Michael said, his voice at a growling pitch in his rage.

"Because you'll have to kill us both. Do you have the restraint to stab only me in your current state? I'm guessing not. So I'd back off if I were you."

"Your Leviathan is dying, Belial. All I have to do is wait it out and you'll be finished."

The demon sighed, a rush of hot air against my cheeks. "And all I have to do is snap her precious little neck. Here is what is going to happen. Jordan will give the fruit back to the Leviathan and I will let her live. Sound fair to you?"

Michael's grip tightened on the sword. He wanted to do it so badly. Part of me wanted to let him. My death would be a minor loss compared to sending this bastard back to Hell where he belonged. But I could see in Michael's eyes that he knew Belial would do it. Even after all of his double crossing, Belial wanted victory more than he wanted me.

Slowly, the archangel lowered his weapon. Belial's smile widened, his eyes joyous as they burned into mine in the silvery moonlight. "You see? I always get what I want."

I slipped my hand into my pocket. "Not anymore."

I grabbed the broken end of the knife and stabbed him in the chest with it. He jerked against me, shock blooming across his pale face. Blood flowed over us both, dripping down between our bodies like an intimate secret. He swayed as the wound took its toll, not enough to kill him, but enough to slow him down so that Michael could make the final blow. I expected him to say something insulting, but instead, he laid his cold lips against my cheek and whispered three words.

"That's my girl."

He fell to his knees, clutching the wound. Michael walked around to face him, staring down at the archdemon with vengeance in his eyes. He lifted the sword's tip to Belial's chest.

"*Vaya con dios*, you son of a bitch."

He ran Belial through with his sword, twisting it just to make sure he hit the space where the demon's heart should have been.

The Leviathan let out a deafening wail. It had gone too long without the fruit. Its body started to sink into the ocean, nearly knocking me off my feet as its head fell forward.

Michael grabbed my wrist and launched us into the air. The demon's body tumbled off of the Leviathan and sank into the water below.

With me in tow, Michael flew around to the side of the dying monster's head. He shoved his sword into the mark shaped like a gate underneath its jawbone. It glowed a lovely golden hue. The Leviathan's mighty jaws closed and the writhing tentacles sucked back inside them before it vanished into the depths of the ocean, hopefully never to be seen again.

Good riddance.

CHAPTER THIRTY-SEVEN

JORDAN

The aftermath of the Leviathan's rising was as disastrous as the path left by a hurricane. Hundreds of people reported the supernatural sounds they'd heard after leaving the ship, but thankfully, Michael's angels had prevented any of the passengers from getting killed. Unfortunately, many of them lost their lives in the process.

Avriel returned to Heaven for Judgment. It would be a while before I heard his sentencing or if he'd be pardoned since he ended up helping us after all. I almost wished I could defend him myself, but it wasn't like I was someone Heaven was happy with at the moment.

Belial's body was never recovered. With the Leviathan defeated, the demons who had abducted Juliana's parents let them go. I personally handed her back to her mother, who cried and thanked me so graciously that it was painful. I didn't want the thanks. The girl had been put through so much and this wouldn't be the end for her, either. Someday, she would grow up and these terrible choices would rest on her shoulders as well. I couldn't tell her parents the truth, but I left them with my number and made them promise to keep in touch. I couldn't help her now, but God-willing, I could help her when she needed guidance in the future. The path of a Seer was long, painful, and cruel. I wouldn't let her walk it alone.

It was a long flight back to Albany, especially since I knew what awaited me there. Michael and I argued before we left Tromso. I was going to turn myself in while he wanted me to head to a non-extradition country until the heat was off of our unfortunate case. We couldn't resurrect Avriel's body, so there was no way to prove I didn't kill him. Even if we could, there was still the nasty business of breaking Belial out of police custody and kidnapping a federal suspect. The cops probably hadn't been able to identify me with my gas mask on, but my face was unhidden when we busted the demon out. Either way, I was up shit creek.

I wasn't thrilled about the idea of prison. It scared me half to death knowing I'd be without freedom, without choice, without the few people left that I cared about. However, after three years filled with murders, the deaths of loved ones, and the threat of the end of the world, I figured I could survive. After all, with me put away, my friends had nothing to worry about. The demons would know I was neutralized. Other Seers would arise to take my place. The world wouldn't be threatened due to my actions. I made the choices. Now, I would have to live with the consequences.

These thoughts circulated in my head as I sat in an interrogation room of the Albany Police Department, my hands cuffed behind my back, staring at my reflection in the mirror. It had almost been hilarious watching the look on the officers' faces when I told them who I was. Then again, maybe shock had set in and I was just numb now. Not sure.

At last, the door opened. A short white man in his late thirties with a receding hairline and a black suit walked in. He was smiling. It was unusual.

"Mrs. O'Brien?"

I flinched. Still didn't sound right to me. "Sir?"

"Please, call me Agent Clark," he insisted, taking the seat across from me.

"Agent Clark, then. How can I help you?"

"I'm impressed, you know. Most people with your sort of charges don't waltz right into the arms of the authorities. You've avoided capture for, what? Seven days? That's no mean feat, I've got to say."

I stared at him, confused by his cheerfulness. Maybe he was playing good cop. "Um, thank you?"

"You're welcome. Before we proceed any further, I need to ask you why you decided to turn yourself in."

"I've made mistakes. I've hurt people. There's a price to pay for that, and I'm going to pay it because it's the right thing to do."

"That's very noble of you," he said, and it sounded oddly genuine. "I don't see that a lot in my line of work, trust me."

"Doesn't surprise me."

"You don't seem like the type who is easily surprised. I didn't think I was either, until this afternoon."

I arched an eyebrow. "What happened this afternoon?"

"Someone called me. You might know him. About six feet tall, black, nice smile, big ears, pretty wife?"

I paused. "Why the hell did Will Smith call you?"

He laughed. "Good guess, but no. It was the President."

My mouth went dry. "The President of the United States called you?"

"Yeah. And you'll never guess what he had to say."

I licked my dry lips, completely out of my depth. "What?"

"That he read about your case and thought you should be acquitted of all charges."

My jaw dropped. "You're shitting me, right?"

"I'd love to be shitting you, but you're focusing on the wrong issue here, Mrs. O'Brien. Please take a look at this sheet for me and tell me what you see."

He slid a piece of paper forward. I leaned in, scanning it. It was a list of phone calls to the Oval Office, hundreds of them, with only one highlighted in yellow. I let my eyes drift across to the digits and felt the blood rush out of my face. I knew those digits.

It was Gabriel's phone number.

"Agent Clark, I don't understand—" I began, but he held up his hand.

"I'm sure this may come as a shock to you. Maybe you don't know your friend Mr. Solberg as well as you think. That phone call lasted only two minutes. It took him two minutes to call in a favor to the President of the United States. That kind of power isn't something that just any old body has. This man has connections that go beyond anything I've ever seen before. He knew that if he made this call, his position would come under a fire so heavy that it will take years to recover. As you can understand, we've frozen all his assets and he's going to be under a serious investigation for quite some time."

Agent Clark folded his hands, setting his brown eyes on me. "However, after an extensive Q and A with the Big Guy, he has not changed his position on you. I can't believe I'm saying this, but you're free to go."

I didn't move from my spot. This new information just buzzed around my head like a dozen drunken flies. Gabriel had so much power that he could talk to the freaking President. What in God's name happened during that phone call? What the hell did Gabriel do to get him to pardon me?

"I…" Words failed me. I had to swallow hard twice just to finish the sentence.

"…honestly don't know what to say."

"Yeah, I wouldn't either, if I were you." The smile was gone and there was a serious look in its place. "Mrs. O'Brien, I hope you understand the gravity of your situation. You may be cleared of the charges, but from this day forward, there is nothing that you can do which won't be under a microscope. My suggestion? Learn from this.

Build a new life. Take care of your loved ones. And I hope for your sake that we never meet again because if we do…I'm going to nail your ass to the wall. Do we understand each other?"

"Perfectly."

Then, like magic, the chipper smile returned. "Now, if you don't have any other questions for me, I suggest you head home. It's nice out. I'd walk instead of taking the bus."

He stood, walked around my chair, and undid my handcuffs. Numbly, I got up and walked out of the door, thoroughly confused and yet somehow vindicated.

He was sitting in my kitchen by the time I got home, calmly sipping coffee and eating the last piece of banana bread. I walked in front of him, opening my mouth to talk, but there were so many things I wanted to ask him that the only thing to come out was:

"What the *shit*, Gabriel?"

He chewed, swallowed, and merely arched an eyebrow at me. "Pardon?"

"You called the President? The *fucking* Commander in Chief?" I screeched.

He let out a dry chuckle. "You know, most people would be thanking me right now."

"Most people don't get pardons from the bloody leader of the free world!" I shot back, unable to control myself any longer. "What did you do? Threaten his family? Offer him a free pass into Heaven?"

Gabriel shook his head. "Don't be so dramatic. It was the simplest of matters."

I waved a hand at him. "Feel free to explain at any time."

He wiped his mouth with a napkin, crossing one leg and regarding me with a frustratingly patient look. "I knew him long before he was in office. Ages before, in fact. I actually saved his life once when he was a young man. We've kept in touch over the years and I thought nothing of it until your husband ordered me to intervene."

I palmed my forehead. Of course he did. "Why am I not surprised?"

"He loves you, Jordan. Even though he is angry with you, Michael has never wanted to see you suffer, especially since you were only trying to do the right thing."

"But doesn't he care what this will do to you?" I said, slumping against the counter in defeat. "To your company? You've done unimaginable amounts of good for other people and now it's going to all be jeopardized because of me."

"I admit, it's not something I wanted to happen either, but I told you once that I loved you and this is the proof."

The archangel stood up, dusting off the front of his suit pants. "However, that brings me to my next point."

He took a deep breath, softening his tone. "As my company and my integrity have been compromised, I have been ordered to leave your side for the immediate future."

I closed my eyes. And there it was. The catch. I had felt in my gut that something was wrong. This was the price of my freedom— losing the man I had considered to be my older brother for the last four years.

I heard movement as Gabriel's impossibly large hands rested on my shoulders. I couldn't look at him, not now, or I'd cry. "Jordan. Look at me."

I shook my head. He sighed. "Please, promise me that you will not blame yourself. The Leviathan incident has changed everything we know. I bear no grudge towards you for what you've done. Know that. It is the truth."

"It's okay," I murmured in a hoarse voice. "I understand. I do."

He leaned his forehead against mine. "I have loved you since the day I laid eyes on you and I always will. I may not be around anymore, but I promise I will look out for you from afar. This is not goodbye, Jordan Amador. I swear it."

"I know."

A warm droplet hit my cheek and it was impossible to tell if it was his tear or mine. He inhaled deeply and then straightened up, collecting himself.

"Besides," he said with a small, unsteady laugh. "I've brought you a present so you can't be sad any longer."

I forced myself to open my eyes then. Gabriel picked up a rectangular gift wrapped in golden tissue paper that had been sitting on the counter behind me. I tore it off, finding a large leather-bound journal with no name on the front. Inside, the pages were worn and faded. The untidy scrawl was familiar.

"Once he found out I'd been reassigned, Andrew told me to find this for you. It's his journal from his days as a Seer. It became lost after he died, but I made some calls and managed to unearth it. I think it might answer some questions you have."

"Gabriel, it's…" I had to pause to swallow the lump in my throat. "Perfect. Thank you."

"There we go. There's my smile." He brushed a lock of hair behind my ear. I shut my eyes again and threw my arms around his neck. He picked me up, hugging me tight, as if he did it the right way, I'd never miss him even though I knew I would. I couldn't recall how long the hug lasted because I didn't want it to end, but eventually, he lowered me to the floor.

"Be strong, my sister, my heart," he whispered before kissing my forehead one last time. Then he wiped the tears from my cheeks and walked away without looking back.

Hours after Gabriel left, I was still sitting at the kitchen table, staring at my phone. Technically, I was a free woman. I wanted to call Lauren. I wanted to call her so badly, but every time I reached for the phone, I lost my nerve. She hated me now. I'd done something unforgivable to one of the only people who bothered to love me. How did I even start that conversation? How could I possibly apologize for that? *"Hey, Lauren, sorry I forgot to tell you that I'm on the FBI's Most Wanted list!"* Yeah, that would end well.

My brain settled into this miserable thought pattern so deeply that I didn't even jump when I heard a key in the lock. I glanced over at the door. I tensed, surprised to see Michael walk in. He had been running errands all day long to make sure that the Leviathan incident didn't leave any loose ends that needed tying. It was his job to handle most of them now that Gabriel was out of the frying pan and into the fire. Michael was still a person of interest to the bureau, but he didn't have a target painted on his back any longer now that I was pardoned.

"Hey," I said, unable to keep from sounding hesitant.

"Hey." He closed the door and locked it just like always, his voice also a bit hollow.

He walked over to the table and settled his hands on the back of a chair instead of taking a seat, which only made me more unsettled.

"I take it you talked to Gabriel."

"Yeah."

He winced. "I wish I could change what happened. I know how much you care about him and vice versa."

"Why did you ask him to do that for me?"

Michael frowned. "Would you have let me go to jail for a crime I didn't commit?"

"But that's the thing, Michael. I did commit a crime, even if I did it to save people. You can't just go around changing the system. It has consequences. Gabriel will have to basically start over now and that's not fair to him. He's worked so hard building that company."

"Gabriel is stronger than you think. He'll bounce back from this. He always does. Besides, he's on this earth for eternity. You've only got one lifetime and I won't let you spend the rest of it behind bars."

"Look, I'm not saying that I'm not grateful for what the two of you have done. If I had a year, I couldn't express the depth of my gratitude. But I'm just saying that I don't know if you understand the gravity of this decision. It's going to change everything."

"Everything has already changed, Jordan. Everything." The last word came out hushed. He glanced away, trying to hide a flicker of pain across his face. Something was wrong. Deeply, deeply wrong. Not just Gabriel's situation, either. A cold spot filled my stomach and stretched outward.

He sighed before he began again. "Jor, I—"

"No, wait. Let me say something first."

I stood up, leaning against the counter with my arms crossed beneath my chest. "This is not going to be easy for you to hear, but I'm supposed to be doing the right thing, so here it goes."

I met his gaze. "I let Belial kiss me a few days ago."

His jaw clenched. I kept going, even though it hurt like hell to see that furious look on his face. "I've been fighting my hardest not to become like him yet somehow, that's exactly what happened. I've let this incident twist me into the worst version of myself. I've lied and stolen and indulged in awful things. This horrible event has made me see the truth. I'm not in love with Belial. I know that."

I swallowed hard. "But part of me did like him, even though I know he is evil and he will never change. I think it's because when I'm around him, I don't have to watch what I say or care about how I treat him. Being around him seems to make me revert back to how I was before I met you. It's like a reflex, I guess. I'm not saying it's okay. I'm not saying you should understand that or accept it or forgive me for it. I'm just telling you the truth. I also want you to know that it doesn't matter because I refuse to let my attraction to him ruin my life—or our life—again. I know who I am now. I know what kind of choices I'm supposed to make. So I can tell you in all honesty that something like this will not happen again because I won't let it. You deserve better. It might not mean much to you now, but I will become a better person. A stronger person. A more worthy person. I'm asking you if there's a second chance for us in the future. I know it's not fair, but I have to find that out before we go any further."

He didn't respond right away, and that alone tore the hole in my heart wider. I forced the question out of my throat.

"Michael, do you still love me?"

A pained exhale escaped him. He touched my shoulders, tugging me closer, leaning down to my height so I could meet his gaze. "Jordan, I want you to listen to me carefully. I love you. I will always love you. I will love you until the stars turn cold and fall into the ocean and the mountains crumble and the universe unravels into the abyss. Nothing will ever change that: not you, or me, or some piece-of-shit demon. *Nothing.* And I am willing to give you a second chance and start over."

He shut his eyes, steadying himself. "But I also need some time to myself. Time to forgive you. If I stayed here with you, now, I would just be angry and resentful and I wouldn't treat you the way you deserve. There are some things inside me that I have to sort out before I can be the kind of husband I need to be for you. I need you to be patient and to have faith in me. Can you do that?"

I nodded, even though I wanted to say no, that he was wrong, that time apart wasn't the right thing to do because it'd be easier for him to never come back if he wasn't near me. I could feel him slipping through my fingers like sand, but I couldn't find the words to tell him to stay. He needed to forgive me. I had done terrible things. He deserved the right to be angry. He did.

The only thing I could squeeze out was a question. "How much time do you need?"

"A few weeks, a month at the most."

"Promise?"

"I promise."

He lifted my chin with his hand and kissed me, gently, as the tears rolled down my cheeks. My fingers gripped his shirt and trembled with the thought of letting him go, of letting him walk out that door without me. *Tell him the truth. Tell him to stay. Tell him he's wrong. Please, God, don't let him leave.*

He broke from my lips and bumped his forehead against mine. "I'll call you, okay?"

"Okay."

He walked to the door, stopped, and turned to look at me. His sea-green eyes were all that I could see as he spoke the same two words I had been hearing for ages.

"*Te amo.*"

"*Te amo.*"

The door shut behind him.

And I was alone once more.

EPILOGUE

Realistically, I shouldn't have called him, but it wasn't like my judgment was any good these days. Maybe it would get better over time. And maybe I'd win the lottery and end world hunger.

"Yeah?"

"Is that how you always answer the phone?"

A pause. "What? You want me to recite a sonnet instead?"

I rolled my eyes. "No, but you could be more polite."

"I've lived in Detroit for thirty years. Polite's not in my vocabulary, girl. And why are you callin'? You out of trouble or did you get yourself into more of it?"

"I'm out. For good, so far."

"Should I ask how?"

"No. Mostly because you wouldn't believe me if I told you."

"Well, they stopped showing your name on the news, so it's got to be legit. I'm guessing it was that blond guy you were with at the riverside. Heard his name before. He's definitely somebody."

I fought a cryptic smile, mostly because he wouldn't be able to see it anyway. "You have no idea."

"Don't take this the wrong way, but what's up? Doesn't seem like you to call for a chat. Need something?"

"No, I, uh, just wanted to make sure you got to your flight alright."

"I'll be on board in a little while." He paused again. "You sure you're alright?"

"What makes you think I'm not?"

"The whole 'accused of murder' thing, for starters," Lewis said with heavy sarcasm. "And there's the fact that you sound like you want to jump off the Empire State Building."

My throat tightened. How could he possibly hear that in my voice? I hadn't known him that long. Maybe he really did have paternal instincts deep down. I bit my bottom lip, trying to figure out how to throw him off the scent.

"I'm fine."

"Bullshit. You could have just texted to ask if I was at the airport. If you need to talk, then talk. What's wrong?"

I rubbed my forehead, attempting to shove my insecurities back inside my skull, but I knew it was pointless. He'd caught me red-handed. "It's nothing life-threatening, I promise. It's just...I did some pretty bad things and now I'm alone for the first time in years. It's starting to get to me."

"Alone? Where the hell's your husband?" Offense made his voice reach a higher pitch. It was almost funny.

"He's taking some time off. Needs to clear his head."

"You don't take time off in a marriage. Even I know that. What happened? Was it another girl?"

"No, of course not."

"Another guy?"

"Sort of."

"You sleep with 'im?"

"No. But I wasn't Wife of the Year either."

"He say when he'd be coming back?"

"Yeah."

"You believe him?"

I winced. "I want to."

"Mm. Been in that boat before, trust me. Your mom and I split up for a couple months about two years into our marriage."

"Why?"

"She was a headstrong woman and I didn't like apologizing. Can't remember what that particular fight was about, but it was a big one."

"How did you fix it?"

"Wasn't really us if you ask me. It was fate. One day I went for a walk and stopped to get a snack at a vendor. After I got out of line, she was there. Madrid's not a small place. That wasn't a coincidence. Your mother, she believed in signs. She believed we couldn't give up just yet since someone had gone through a lot of trouble to put us in the same place at the same time. So I decided to nut up and said I was sorry and we made up."

"So you think the universe will make everything right, huh?"

"Sneer if you want, girl. I'm just telling you what I know. There's no way your husband went through all that trouble of giving me that speech just to ditch you for good. I've only met the guy twice, but even I can tell he's got it bad for you. He'll come around."

"What am I supposed to do in the meantime? Both of my best friends are no longer speaking to me, I got fired for being a felon, and every time I leave the house, I get stared at like a freak of nature. I don't know what to do with myself any more. I just…"

I stopped, breathing deep to calm down. "I'm lost. I'm just lost."

"Welcome to the real world, Jordan. Everything hurts and then you die."

A bitter chuckle escaped me. "Thanks."

"I mean it. I can't tell you how to get through this. All I can tell you is that you've made it this far and it'd be stupid to quit now. Your story ain't finished, girl. It's just hit a rough spot. You'll pull through. It's in your blood."

I heard a soft ringing sound and then the distant echo of the airport staff calling the flight's passengers over to start lining up.

"Listen, I gotta go," Lewis said. "But I'll call you when I land and you'd better pick up, y'hear?"

"Yeah. I will."

"Alright. Keep your head up."

"Thanks."

"Told you not to thank me."

"Well, you did say I was stubborn."

He laughed. "Yeah, I did. Bye."

"Bye."

I hung up and shoved the phone in my pocket, leaning my head against the lamppost behind me. The liquor store sign still glowed an impassioned, tempting red but I no longer had the urge to go inside. I would hold for now.

I pocketed the phone and walked back to my apartment next door. My old cell phone had literally dozens of voicemails on it from everyone I knew asking about why I had been a suspect in a murder investigation. Colton had called three or four times, but I didn't call back. At work, three no-call, no-shows meant instant termination, and as much as I hated getting fired, I knew it was the right thing to do. I had only shown him and my coworkers half of who I was. It wasn't fair to stick around and keep lying to them, especially if my presence would bring bad press to the restaurant. I would miss the Sweet Spot, but it would live on without me. So would Lauren and Lily.

When I got home, I collapsed in front of my laptop and screwed around for a while before losing interest. My eyes eventually wandered to Andrew's journal, still sitting where I'd left it the night before.

I cracked it open for a read and twisted my mother's rosary around my fingers as I read. As of late, it seemed to be turning into a habit of mine. Thankfully, my mother had been about the same size and body type as me so the cross hit me at my bellybutton rather than dragging too low. The teeth marks were a surprisingly nice reminder of happier times gone past. So far, I was starting to build a pretty little pile of items with memories in them—first, Andrew's duster, then my mother's diary, then Andrew's letters, then her rosary, and now Andrew's journal.

Andrew wrote in a very peculiar fashion—dropping subjects randomly kind of like Rorschach from the *Watchmen* graphic novel by Alan Moore. Still, it was easy to hear his gruff but lovable voice in the pages. It made me feel less lonely and I needed that while I waited for Michael to come back. I was taking it one day at a time. It wasn't going well, but I tried to have faith in him like I promised. Tried my hardest.

About thirty pages in, it occurred to me how rare it was that I had something from a Seer on paper. Wouldn't hurt to save a copy in case shit hit the fan again. I opened a new Word document and began transcribing it page by page. My lips mouthed the words as my fingers flew across the keyboard, and soon I was consumed in Andrew's diction once again. His world and my world turned out not to be too different. Maybe someday, I would pass this down to Juliana and she could learn from it as well. After all, it was my responsibility to look after those who had no one else to fight for them. Well, Andrew said it best.

This job, it ain't all it's cracked up to be. I see things that would make a normal person's brain turn into jelly and pour out his ears. It's pain and horror and ugliness. It's a lot of hotel rooms, a lot of dive bars, and a lot of nightmares. It's scars and empty bottles of Jack Daniels, and one night stands when things get too bad. But I do it anyway. Why? Probably because I'm too ruttin' stupid to do anything else. Probably because I can shoot the wings off a fly from a hundred yards while being chased by a wildebeest at night. Probably because I can kick the ass of any demon stupid enough to cross my path.

But I'll tell you one thing. Even though this shit will wear you down and make you doubt everything you've come to know about the world, you still gotta do it. Do the work. Get up in the morning. Pour yourself some coffee. Hell, slip a little Bailey's in there if you're feeling frisky. Strap on your boots. Sharpen your knives. Clean your guns (that shit is important, trust me). Open that door and do your damn job. Do it because they can't. Do it because you can. Do it because you're supposed to and because someone in this world deserves to wake up with their family alive and happy thanks to something you did. Demons, they want you to believe that nothing we do will change the future, but they're as wrong as they are butt-ass ugly. What you do—what we do — matters. At the end of the day, that should be your reward. Never forget that, kid.

       Ever.
       -The Man Who Sees
       Couldn't have said it better myself.

FIN

Acknowledgments

To my mother, who proves every day that you don't have to be a snarky, demon-killing Seer to kick ass and fight monsters. You taught me how to be strong, intelligent, and grateful for the things I've been given. You are a gift and I am proud to call you my mother.

To my father, who has helped make my craziest dreams feel like they might be within my reach. You've never had a doubt about my writing, even when I did, and that is something I will never forget as long as I live, and I cannot thank you enough for it.

To Sharon, who tirelessly combed through these hundreds of pages helping me unearth the gems I never would have seen otherwise. You are a shining example of everything beautiful and powerful about being a woman, and I am so grateful to call you my new sister.

To Bryan, who helped poke and prod the squishy guts of my supernatural world to help me make it better, and who has always supported me in your own demented sort of way. I couldn't have done it without you, bro.

To Andy Rattinger, who literally helped me dig myself out of an enormous Kyoko-sized grave with several parts of this novel. I am in your debt still. Who knows where I'd be without your guidance. You always know when to gentle ruffle my hair and when to bonk me on the noggin for being a neurotic cynic. You are the sensei that I don't deserve, but somehow managed to snag anyhow. Never stop being awesome, old man.

To Jill, who marched through the endless field of words of my novel fearlessly. You are every author's dream of an editor. Thank you so much.

To Christopher T. Coureas, Linda Wilkins, Kathleen Wright of the FBI, thank you so much for your assistance with the bits of research I needed for Jordan's tussle with the U.S. government. I know I stretched the blanket of Willing Suspension of Disbelief over what you taught me, but I sincerely thank you for your sound advice.

To Cris Lira, who helped me gather facts about the fascinating, beautiful world of São Paolo and Jandira. You were one of my favorite college professors and I still have a huge fondness for Brazilian Portuguese as a result. *Muito obrigada.*

To my family, who has stood with me through perilous times all these years. You are irreplaceable.

To my friends, who are still riding the rollercoaster that is our friendship. Thanks for sticking with me through the thunder, hail, and lightning. I wouldn't have gotten to where I am without you. This book is as much a piece of you as it is of me.

To Gunjan Kumar, who continues to blow my mind with the endless amounts of imagination that you put into my book cover. I adore your work. You are a goddess. Thank you for your tireless labor because this cover is gorgeous.

To the KBoards community, who saved a young, depressed indie author from drowning. You are my life raft, my Wilson, and my patch of dry land in the dark ocean that is self-publishing.

To my fans, I only hope that I continue to entertain you and that you don't try to put a car bomb underneath my Saturn Ion for the ending of this novel. You are my air.

To any new readers...(*Joey Tribbiani voice*) How YOU doin'? I hope you had a good time. And I hope you don't hold semi-dated *Friends* references against me because I love you. I hope you feel compelled to stay with the series. *Join me.* Together, we can rule the galaxy. Or at least sit up late on Twitter eating Nutella and geeking out about nerdy stuff.

Author's Note

Alright, fellas, no offense, but clear the dance floor. It's Ladies Night.

Lllllllllllllllladies. I have no problem admitting that this book is dedicated to you. I'm not pandering, either. I'm just being honest. I couldn't have become the author and person I am without the awesome women in my life, and so I couldn't help but take a second to chat with you wonderful darlings.

She Who Fights Monsters isn't just a clever title inspired by a great Nietzsche quote. Every woman everywhere fights monsters every day. Could be her personal demons, could be her significant other, could be her family, could be her coworkers, could be society itself. We are all ass-kicking, sword-swinging, lasso-twirling, batarang-throwing queens. And I love writing about us, even in a setting that is largely a boys' club.

Truth be told, I could have based this series on the life story of Michael the archangel, but I didn't because I love being a girl. I love writing about girls. I love the challenges presented alongside a female protagonist, because there are many of them. Make her "too sexy" and people call her a slut. Make her "too smart" and she's a know-it-all. Make her "too stupid" and she's an airhead. Make her "too assertive" and she's a bitch. Make her have a love interest and she's "too dependent." Make her too much like yourself and she's a "Mary-Sue." Make her have personal demons and she's an "Emo." There are all kinds of thorns out there to prick your finger on when you write a series with a female main character, and it goes double for one in the urban fantasy/paranormal romance genres. It doesn't matter if I'm not a bestseller. People are scrutinizing every word, some of them just waiting for the chance to spring out of the bushes and declare me a hack.

But you know what? Who cares? If real women are lovely and imperfect, then why shouldn't I be? Why shouldn't Jordan Amador be?

So you may not be the woman stabbing an archdemon in the chest with a diving knife, but you and Jordan are not so different at the end of the day. We all have our crosses to bear, our battles to fight and lose and sometimes win, and we have to find out who we are along the way. If we're lucky, we find someone to walk the path alongside us. Some of us need that. Some of us don't. But I think what any lady reading this book should take away from it at the end of the day is that you are enough. The world out there expects us to work just as hard as our male counterparts for less and look "attractive" while doing it. To hell with that. Do you. More than that—do you *well*. The next time you fall and scrape your knees, get up and don't yell at yourself. Wonderful creatures that men are, a lot of them don't realize half the battles we fight are in our own heads. Every single woman has an abusive psychopath who shouts negative things at her constantly, helping us—and sometimes even forcing us—to make terrible decisions. We internalize it and try to hide it, but it's something I wish more women discussed among each other. Give yourself a break. It's too cliché for me to tell you to love yourself—because, hell, even I don't do that—so my personal request is for you to take it easy and remember that you aren't superhuman, but you are a monster-slayer, madam.

And I salute you.

-Kyoko M.

Read on for a special preview of

The Holy Dark

The final novel in the *Black Parade* series by Kyoko M.
Coming in spring 2015.

CHAPTER ONE

JORDAN

Honest to God, I hadn't meant to start a bar fight.

"So. You're the famous Jordan Amador." The demon sitting in front of me looked like someone filled a pig bladder with rotten cottage cheese. He overflowed the bar stool with his gelatinous stomach, just barely contained by a white dress shirt and an oversized leather jacket. Acid-washed jeans clung to his stumpy legs and his boots were at least twice the size of mine. His beady black eyes started at my ankles and dragged upward, past my dark jeans, across my black turtleneck, and over the grey duster around me that was two sizes too big.

He finally met my gaze and snorted. "I was expecting something different. Certainly not a black girl."

I shrugged. "What can I say? My mother was a religious woman."

"Clearly," the demon said, tucking a fat cigar in one corner of his mouth. He stood up and walked over to the pool table beside him where he and five of his lackeys had gathered. Each of them was over six feet tall and were all muscle where he was all fat.

"I could start to examine the literary significance of your name, or I could ask what the hell you're doing in my bar," he said after knocking one of the balls into the left corner pocket.

"Just here to ask a question, that's all. I don't want trouble."

Again, he snorted, but this time smoke shot from his nostrils, which made him look like an albino dragon. "My ass you don't. This place is for fallen angels only, sweetheart. And we know your reputation."

I held up my hands in supplication. "Honest Abe. Just one question and I'm out of your hair forever."

My gaze lifted to the bald spot at the top of his head surrounded by peroxide blonde locks around the rim. "What's left of it, anyway."

He glared at me. I smiled, batting my eyelashes. He tapped his fingers against the pool cue and then shrugged one shoulder.

"Fine. What's your question?"

"Know anybody by the name of Matthias Gruber?"

He didn't even blink. "No."

"Ah. I see. Sorry to have wasted your time."

I turned around, walking back through the bar. I kept a quick, confident stride as I went, ignoring the whispers of the fallen angels in my wake. A couple called out to me, asking if I'd let them have a taste, but I didn't spare them a glance. Instead, I headed to the ladies' room. Thankfully, it was empty so I whipped out my phone and dialed the first number in my Recent Call list.

"Hey. He's here. Yeah, I'm sure it's him. They're lousy liars when they're drunk. Uh-huh. Okay, see you in five."

I hung up and let out a slow breath. Only a couple things left to do.

I gathered my shoulder-length black hair into a high ponytail. I looped the loose curls around into a messy bun and made sure they wouldn't tumble free if I shook my head too hard. I took the leather gloves in the pocket of my duster out and pulled them on. Then, I walked out of the bathroom and back to the front entrance.

The coat-check girl gave me a second unfriendly look as I returned with my ticket stub to retrieve my things — three vials of holy water, a black rosary with the beads made of onyx and the cross made of wood, a Smith & Wesson .9mm Glock complete with a full magazine of blessed bullets and a silencer, and a worn out page of the Bible.

I held out my hands for the items and she dropped them on the counter with an unapologetic, "Oops."

"Thanks," I said with a roll of my eyes. I put the Glock back in the hip holster at my side and tucked the rest of the items in the pockets of my duster.

The brunette demon crossed her arms under her hilariously oversized fake breasts and sent me a vicious sneer. "The door is that way, Seer. Don't let it hit you on the way out."

I smiled back. "God bless you."

She let out an ugly hiss between her pearly white teeth. I blew her a kiss and walked out the door. The parking lot was packed outside because it was half-past midnight. Demons thrived in darkness so I wasn't surprised. In fact, I'd been counting on it.

There was a large white four-door pickup truck idling in the rear of the lot. Its driver had the window down so she could blow smoke out every so often and watch it spiral up into the cloudy night sky. She was black like me, but in her mid-forties; her hair, peppered with grey streaks, elegantly permed and pulled back into a neat short ponytail. Even though we were here to work, she still wore dark red lipstick and mascara just because she liked looking good.

I opened the passenger's door and climbed in. She glanced at me with a smirk as I put my seatbelt on. "Took you long enough."

"They patted me down, remember? It kind of takes a while, especially after I kicked the bouncer in the nuts for groping me."

She glanced at my shirt, hiding 34 B-cups, and that was being generous. "Where?"

I smacked her in the shoulder. She laughed, making her own 38 C-cups jiggle and turning me green with envy. "Shut up and drive, Myra."

She took one last drag on her cig and tossed it out the window, adopting a feral grin.

"*Avec plaisir.*"

She revved up the engine, threw the truck into gear, and then drove straight towards the building in front of us at breakneck speed.

The impact rocketed the two of us forward in our seats. The seatbelts did their job, keeping us from flying headfirst out the windshield as the guard rail smashed straight through the wood and plaster holding the rear wall together. Dust and rubble kicked up everywhere, engulfing the vehicle. I let out the terse lungful of air I'd been holding and unbuckled the belt before leaping out.

I drew the Glock and pointed it at anything that moved within my line of vision. The demons clustered around the wreckage in anger and confusion, but they stayed back when they saw the gun. The fat demon I'd interrogated stumbled from around the overturned pool table, his cigar forgotten somewhere, fury blazing in his eyes.

"What the hell did you do that for?"

"I told you I was looking for Matthias Gruber. You have something I need."

"I don't know what you're talking about."

"Bullshit," Myra spoke up, cocking back the shotgun she held. She kept it steady on him, her voice clear and hard as glass.

"You can either hand it over or we'll tell your mates why we're here."

He spat at her feet contemptuously. "Rip 'em apart, boys."

His five hulking bodyguards darted forward — two heading for me, three heading for Myra. They were liquid fast, almost too fast for me to see, but unfortunately for them, our bullets were faster.

I plugged the dark-haired guy first, two in the chest. The bullets hissed as soon as they hit him and steam issued from the wounds. He fell to his knees, screaming and clawing at the wounds as they burned him alive.

I swung the barrel towards the blond. He grabbed it just as I fired and the bullet tore straight through his palm. He didn't even flinch—instead, he wrenched it out of my grip and grabbed me around the throat. He slammed me into the hood of the car, squeezing so hard that white specks popped up all over my vision.

I grappled for the holy water in my pocket and smashed the vial into the side of his head. His skin bubbled red with a second-degree burn, but he wouldn't let go, digging his calloused fingers in harder. He was trying to outlast me, ignoring his own injuries because it would only take another minute before I'd suffocate.

With my last bit of strength, I grabbed the torn Bible page and pressed it to his chest, gurgling the words, "*In nomine Patris, et ego repellam te!*"

The paper glowed brilliant white and then his entire body burst into flames. He dropped me and screamed, clawing at his clothing, but it was more than that. His very skin was reacting to the purity of the holy item and decomposing from the inside. The other demons scattered as he rolled past them, thrashing violently until the fire took its toll. As soon as he died, the fire vanished, leaving a charred corpse.

I rubbed my sore throat and picked up the page, then the gun. The tussle had distracted my attention from Myra, but thankfully, she had fared much better. Her shotgun had left three victims on the ground and she only had a bloody cheek to show for it. She was ex-military so I wasn't surprised, merely jealous because I only knew basic martial arts and self-defense. Plus, I was only a hundred and twenty pounds soaking wet.

"We can do this all night, Matthias," I rasped. "Give us what we came for or this is going to get even nastier."

"Blow me, Seer."

I narrowed my eyes at him. "Fine. Have it your way."

I raised my voice to the throng of demons watching us. "Attention, bar patrons. The man standing in your midst who so kindly provided you with drinks and probably sacrificial virgins is on the Top Ten Wanted List of every angel in the known world. He is in possession of a piece of silver that we and the angels have been searching for. In fact, it is right there around his neck."

Many of them glanced over to confirm it. The necklace was a thin chain holding a gold coin slightly larger than a quarter. "That ain't silver, lady."

"Because he painted it gold so no one would figure it out. So if you all don't want a first class ride back down to the Pit, please proceed to tear his head off and hand over the coin."

"Bullshit, Seer," one of them said.

I holstered the Glock and reached into my pocket, this time withdrawing a lighter. I lit it and held it just underneath the Bible page, lifting my voice so they could all hear. "Afraid not, friend. This is a page from the personal Bible of Pope Benedict XVI. If I light it, it sends out a wave of energy so pure that it'll burn your rotten souls right out of your bodies. Test me and I'll toast the lot of you."

Furtive glances darted between the demons, some whispering to each other for confirmation. It was understandable. Not many common demons like these knew the sorts of stuff Myra and I did. And we'd been counting on it.

"You saw what it did to your buddy. Do you really think I'm bluffing, assholes?"

Matthias swallowed hard as he noticed the unfriendly looks he began to receive. He raised his huge hands, backing away from the crowd. "Don't listen to her. If you guys rush her all at once, she can't stop you all."

By the looks of things, they believed us and not him. Myra spoke up then. "Well, now you have two options, Mr. Gruber. We can take you alive or let them take you dead. What's it gonna be, buddy?"

"There's forty of them. You can't get out of here alive."

"Wanna bet your life on it?"

He cursed under his breath, stumbling over to the truck. "Fine, fine! Get me out of here!"

"Get in the back, fat ass."

He climbed into the truck as the other demons advanced, some licking their lips and flexing their hands eagerly as they cornered us.

"Jordan?" Myra said.

"Got it."

I nodded to Myra and she got in the truck first, firing up the engine. I stepped back until I could reach the rear passenger side, opening the door.

"Oh, and one more thing."

I lifted the lighter to the paper, grinning. "*Vaya con dios*, bitches."

~ 380 ~

The page exploded a blinding white light through the room. The demons didn't even have enough time to duck for cover. It blew them straight off their feet, evaporating their bodies into ash. The burning paper fluttered to the ground.

I got in the truck. Myra pulled out of the gigantic hole we'd punched in the back of the building and drove off into the cool October night.

"So what are you gonna do with me?" Matthias grunted, eying the Glock I kept aimed at his enormous midsection.

"You gonna burn me too? Aren't servants of God supposed to have moral codes?"

"Usually, but you really ticked me off by lying," I said, and it was the truth. Being tasked with helping souls with unfinished business cross over to the other side meant trying to do good whenever possible. Still, it was a rather loose creed to hold.

"So hand over the coin and we'll see where it takes you."

He sent me a hateful look. "Do you have any idea what it took to get this thing? It cost more than a three-level house in Beverly Hills. You really think I'm just gonna hand it over to some skinny broad with a gun?"

"You got in the truck, didn't you?"

He shook his head, letting out an ugly chuckle. "Sorry, sweetheart. You'll have to pry it from my cold, dead—"

I shot him in the kneecap. He screamed, clutching the large bloody hole and rocking back and forth in his seat. The silencer did its job—turning what would've been an excruciating gunshot to a loud 'pop.' It still made my ears ring and so I could hear the muted sound of Myra scolding me.

"I just had this truck cleaned, Jordan!" she shrieked, glaring at me over her shoulder.

"What? I had to prove a point," I said, wiggling a finger in my ear. Okay, realistically, yes, that had been a dumb thing to do in the back of a truck, but I had to let him know I was being serious. Although the accompanying headache and having to pay for getting the truck cleaned would be a bitch.

"You psycho!" Matthias snarled, reaching for me, but I held the gun up higher. He restrained himself, nursing the wound with his left hand instead.

"Now that I have your attention, are you going to give me the coin or do I have to give you a second limp?"

"You think I can't endure a little pain? I was born in Hell. You're nothing but a barely evolved monkey playing with fire."

I aimed at his other knee, starting to pull the trigger, but he swore again and ripped off the necklace. "Here. I hope you choke on it, bitch." He tossed it in my lap.

"And they say demons don't have good manners," I said, picking up the coin. It was the right size—about 58 millimeters in diameter—and the emblem of Augustus on the front side matched the others I'd seen. I rubbed my thumb across its surface and gold flakes came off, revealing the worn silver beneath it.

After a second, I frowned. No, this was too easy. Why would he just have it around his neck? Why not put it in a safe or bury it somewhere like other demons had done?

"Before we let you go, I have some questions as to how you got this thing—"

Matthias kicked open the rear door with his inhuman strength and dove out of the speeding vehicle. Myra slammed on the brakes. I pitched forward, smacking my head against the back of the seat.

"Shit!" I yelled. "Reverse, go, go!"

She backed up the truck to turn around when we both heard the ominous horn of an eighteen-wheeler. I could only watch in horror as it rammed into Matthias, sending him flying. He hit the pavement several feet away, his head lying at an awkward angle, his busted legs splayed in opposite directions. I knew beyond a shadow of a doubt that he was dead.

"Son of a bitch," Myra panted, sending a shocked look at me. "What the hell was that?"

"I don't know, but we'd better not stick around to find out. Punch it."

I climbed into the front seat and she hit the gas, speeding off into the dark before the unfortunate truck driver could capture our license plate number. Forty-six dead demons in one night. We were definitely setting a new record.

My cell phone rang inside my pocket. I jumped, scared shitless thanks to the adrenaline. However, the area code confused me. It was from Albany, New York. No one had called from there in months.

"Hello?"

"I'm looking for Jordan Amador."

"Speaking."

"This is in regards to Lauren Yi, who had you listed as an emergency contact. I'm sorry, but there's been an incident."

My blood ran cold. It must have shown on my face because Myra gave me a concerned look.

"What? What is it?"

"Drive me to the airport. Right now."

To be continued in *The Holy Dark*, coming soon to Amazon in 2015!

Bacon, Francis. "Of Death." 1612.

Milton, John. *Paradise Regained*. 1671.

Reuss, Theodore. *Das Erotische in Goethes Faust und die Tantriks*. Publication date unknown.

Shakespeare, William. "Antony and Cleopatra." 1623.

Cover designed by Gunjan Kumar. Background image courtesy of Katie Litchfield. Silhouette courtesy of Bonny Truong.

Edited by Jillian Leigh.

Interested in the *Black Parade* series? Go to http://www.shewhowritesmonsters.com for previews on the next book, contests, giveaways, and all kinds of goodies. You can follow Kyoko M. on Twitter as @misskyokom or on Tumblr at http://minaminokyoko.tumblr.com. Or, if you're lazy, simply like the Facebook page to get all those updates conveniently placed on your timeline: https://www.facebook.com/pages/She-Who-Writes-Monsters/161227150647087.